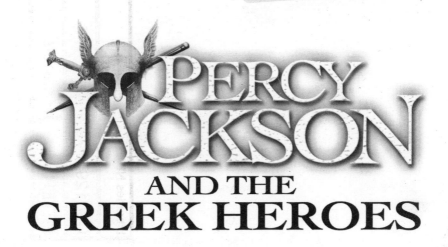

PERCY JACKSON

AND THE
GREEK HEROES

RICK
RIORDAN

PUFFIN

PUFFIN BOOKS

UK | USA | Canada | Ireland | Australia
India | New Zealand | South Africa

Puffin Books is part of the Penguin Random House group of companies
whose addresses can be found at global.penguinrandomhouse.com.

puffinbooks.com

First published in the USA by Disney • Hyperion,
an imprint of Disney Book Group, and published
simultaneously in Great Britain by Puffin Books 2015
001

Text copyright © Rick Riordan, 2015

Set in Centaur MT
Printed in Great Britain by Clays Ltd, St Ives plc

A CIP catalogue record for this book is available from the British Library

HARDBACK ISBN: 978–0–141–35542–9

INTERNATIONAL PAPERBACK ISBN: 978–0–141–36051–5

www.greenpenguin.co.uk

MIX
Paper from
responsible sources
FSC® C018179

Penguin Random House is committed to a
sustainable future for our business, our readers
and our planet. This book is made from Forest
Stewardship Council® certified paper.

For Becky, who has always been my hero
— R.R.

TABLE of CONTENTS

INTRODUCTION

Look, I'm only in this for the pizza.

The publisher was like, 'Oh, you did such a great job writing about the Greek gods last year! We want you to write another book about the Ancient Greek heroes! It'll be so cool!'

And I was like, 'Guys, I'm dyslexic. It's hard enough for me to *read* books.'

Then they promised me a year's supply of free pepperoni pizza, plus all the blue jelly beans I could eat.

I sold out.

I guess it's cool. If you're looking to fight monsters yourself, these stories might help you avoid some common mistakes – like staring Medusa in the face, or buying a used mattress from any dude named Crusty.

But the best reason to read about the old Greek heroes is to make yourself feel better. No matter how much you think your life sucks, these guys and gals had it worse. They totally got the short end of the Celestial stick.

By the way, if you don't know me, my name is Percy Jackson. I'm a modern-day demigod – the son of Poseidon. I've had some bad experiences in my time, but the heroes I'm going to tell you about were the original old-school hard-luck cases. They boldly screwed up where no one had screwed up before.

Let's pick twelve of them. That should be plenty. By the time you finish reading about how miserable their lives were – what with the poisonings, the betrayals, the mutilations, the murders, the psychopathic family members and the flesh-eating barnyard animals – you should feel better about your own existence. If that doesn't work, then I don't know what will.

So get your flaming spear. Put on your lion-skin cape. Polish your shield and make sure you've got arrows in your quiver. We're going back about four thousand years to decapitate monsters, save some kingdoms, shoot a few gods in the butt, raid the Underworld and steal loot from evil people.

Then, for dessert, we'll die painful tragic deaths.

Ready? Sweet. Let's do this.

PERSEUS WANTS
A HUG

I HAD TO START WITH THIS GUY.

After all, he's my namesake. We've got different godly fathers, but my mom liked Perseus's story for one simple reason: he *lives*. Perseus doesn't get hacked to pieces. He doesn't get damned to eternal punishment. As far as heroes go, this dude gets a happy ending.

Which is not to say that his life didn't suck. And he *did* murder a lot of people, but what are you gonna do?

Perseus's bad luck started before he was even born.

First, you gotta understand that, back in the day, Greece wasn't one country. It was divided into a gazillion different little kingdoms. Nobody went around saying 'Hi, I'm Greek!' People would ask you which city-state you were from: Athens, Thebes, Sparta, Zeusville or whatever. The Greek mainland was a huge piece of real estate. Every city had its own king.

Sprinkled around the Mediterranean Sea were hundreds of islands, and each one of them was a separate kingdom, too.

Imagine if life were like that today. Maybe you live in Manhattan. Your local king would have his own army, his own taxes, his own rules. If you broke the law in Manhattan, you could run away to Hackensack, New Jersey. The king of Hackensack could grant you asylum, and Manhattan couldn't do anything about it (unless, of course, the two kings became allies, in which case you were toast).

Cities would be attacking each other all the time. The king of Brooklyn might decide to go to war with Staten Island. Or the Bronx and Greenwich, Connecticut, might form a military alliance and invade Harlem. You can see how that would make life interesting.

Anyway, one city on the Greek mainland was called Argos. It wasn't the biggest or most powerful city, but it was a respectable size. Folks who lived there called themselves the Argives, probably because 'Argosites' would've made them sound like some kind of bacteria. The king was named Acrisius. He was a nasty piece of work. If he were your king, you would totally want to run away to Hackensack.

Acrisius had a beautiful daughter named Danaë, but that wasn't good enough for him. Back then it was all about sons. You had to have a boy child to carry on the family name, inherit the kingdom when you died, blah, blah, blah. Why couldn't a girl take over the kingdom? I dunno. It's stupid, but that's how it was.

Acrisius kept yelling at his wife, 'Have sons! I want sons!' but that didn't help. When his wife died (probably from stress), the king started getting really nervous. If he died without male offspring, his younger brother, Proteus, would take over the kingdom, and the two of them hated each other.

In desperation, Acrisius took a trip to the Oracle of Delphi to get his fortune read.

Now, going to the Oracle is usually what we call a *bad idea*. You had to take a long trip to the city of Delphi and visit this dark cave at the edge of town, where a veiled lady sat on a three-legged stool, inhaling volcanic vapour all day and seeing visions. You would leave an expensive offering with the priests at the door. Then you could ask the Oracle one question. Most likely she'd answer you with some rambling riddle. Then you'd leave confused, terrified and poorer.

But, like I said, Acrisius was desperate. He asked, 'O Oracle, what's the deal with my not having any sons? Who's supposed to take the throne and carry on the family name?'

This time, the Oracle did not speak in riddles.

'That's easy,' she said in a raspy voice. 'You will never have sons. One day your daughter Danaë *will* have a son. That boy will kill you and become the next king of Argos. Thank you for your offering. Have a nice day.'

Stunned and angry, Acrisius returned home.

When he got to the palace, his daughter came to see him. 'Father, what's wrong? What did the Oracle say?'

He stared at Danaë – his beautiful girl with her long, dark hair and lovely brown eyes. Many men had asked to marry her. Now all Acrisius could think about was the prophecy. He could never allow Danaë to marry. She could never have a son. She wasn't his daughter any more. She was his death sentence.

'The Oracle said that *you* are the problem,' he snarled. 'You will betray me! You will see me murdered!'

'*What?*' Danaë recoiled in shock. 'Never, Father!'

'Guards!' Acrisius yelled. 'Take this vile creature away!'

Danaë couldn't understand what she'd done. She always tried to be kind and considerate. She loved her dad, even though he was scary and angry and liked to hunt peasants in the woods with a spear and a pack of rabid dogs.

Danaë always made the appropriate sacrifices to the gods. She said her prayers, ate her vegetables and did all her homework. Why was her dad suddenly convinced she was a traitor?

She got no answers. The guards took her away and locked her in the king's maximum-security underground cell – a broom-closet-sized room with a toilet, a stone slab for a bed and twelve-inch-thick bronze walls. One heavily grated air shaft in the ceiling allowed Danaë to breathe and get a little light, but on hot days the bronze cell heated up like a boiling kettle. The triple-locked door had no window, just a small slot at the bottom for a food tray. King Acrisius kept the only key, because he didn't trust the guards. Each day, Danaë got two dry biscuits and a glass of water. No yard time. No visitors. No Internet privileges. Nothing.

Maybe you're wondering: if Acrisius was so worried about her having children, why didn't he just kill her?

Well, my evil-thinking friend, the gods took family murders very seriously (which is weird, since the gods basically *invented* family murders). If you killed your own child, Hades would make sure you got a special punishment in the Underworld. The Furies would come after you. The Fates would snip your lifeline. Some major bad karma would mess up your day. However, if your child just 'accidentally' expired in an underground bronze cell . . . that wasn't strictly *murder*. That was more like *Oops, how did that happen?*

For months, Danaë languished in her underground cell. There wasn't much to do except make little dough dolls out of biscuits and water, or talk to Mr Toilet, so she spent most of her time praying to the gods for help.

Maybe she got their attention because she was so nice, or because she had always made offerings at the temples. Or maybe it was because Danaë was knockout gorgeous.

One day, Zeus, the lord of the sky, heard Danaë calling his name. (Gods are like that. When you say their names, they perk right up. I bet they spend a lot of time Googling themselves, too.)

Zeus peered down from the heavens with his super-keen X-ray vision. He saw the beautiful princess trapped in her bronze cell, lamenting her cruel fate.

'Dude, that is *wrong*,' Zeus said to himself. 'What kind of father imprisons his own daughter so she can't fall in love or have kids?'

(Actually, that was exactly the sort of thing Zeus might do, but whatever.)

'She's kind of hot, too,' Zeus muttered. 'I think I'll pay that lady a visit.'

Zeus was always doing stuff like this. He'd fall in love with some mortal girl on first sight, drop into her life like a romantic hydrogen bomb, mess up her entire existence and then head back to Mount Olympus, leaving his girlfriend to raise a kid all by herself. But really . . . I'm sure his intentions were honourable. (*Cough.* Yeah, right. *Cough.*)

With Danaë, Zeus's only challenge was figuring out how to get into that maximum-security bronze cell.

He was a god, of course. He had skills. He could simply blast the doors open, but that might scare the poor girl. Plus, then he'd have to kill a bunch of guards, and that would be messy. Causing explosions and leaving a trail of mangled corpses didn't set the right mood for a first date.

He decided it would be easier to turn into something small and sneak in through the air vent. That would give him plenty of privacy with the girl of his dreams.

But what should he turn into? An ant would work. Zeus had done that once before with a different girl. But he wanted to make a good first impression, and ants don't have much of a 'wow' factor.

He decided to turn himself into something totally different – a shower of gold! He dissolved into a swirling cloud of twenty-four-carat glitter and sped down from Mount Olympus. He poured through the air shaft, filling Danaë's cell with warm, dazzling light that took her breath away.

FEAR NOT, said a voice from the glitter. *I AM ZEUS, LORD OF THE SKY. YOU LOOK FINE, GIRL. DO YOU WANT TO HANG OUT?*

Danaë had never had a boyfriend. Especially not a god boyfriend who could turn into glitter. Pretty soon – like in five or six minutes – she was madly in love.

Weeks passed. Danaë stayed so quiet in her cell that the guards outside grew incredibly bored. Then one day, about nine months after the glitter incident, a guard was pushing a food tray through the slot in the door as usual when he heard a strange sound: a baby crying inside the cell.

He ran to get King Acrisius – because this was the kind of thing the boss would want to know about. When the king got there, he unlocked the door, stormed into the cell and found Danaë cradling a newborn baby in a blanket.

'What . . .' Acrisius scanned the cell. No one else was there. No one could've possibly got in, because Acrisius had the only key, and no one could have fitted through Mr Toilet. 'How . . . Who . . .'

'My lord,' Danaë said with a resentful gleam in her eyes, 'I have been visited by the god Zeus. This is our son. I have named him Perseus.'

Acrisius tried not to choke on his own tongue. The word *Perseus* meant *avenger* or *destroyer*, depending on how you interpreted it. The king did *not* want the kid growing up to hang out with Iron Man and the Hulk and, from the way Danaë was glaring at him, the king had a pretty good idea who she wanted destroyed.

The king's worst fear about the prophecy was coming true – which was kind of stupid, because if he hadn't been such a butt-brain and locked up his daughter, it never would've happened. But that's the way prophecies work. You try to avoid the trap, and in doing so you end up building the trap yourself and stepping right into it.

Acrisius wanted to murder Danaë and the little boy. That was the safest bet. But there was that whole *taboo* thing about killing your family. Annoying detail! Also if Danaë was telling the truth and Perseus was the son of Zeus . . . well, angering the lord of the universe wasn't going to help Acrisius's life expectancy.

Acrisius decided to try something else. He ordered his

guards to find a large wooden box with a hinged lid. He had some airholes drilled in the top, just to show he was a nice guy, then he stuffed Danaë and her infant son inside, nailed the lid shut and had the box tossed into the sea.

He figured he wasn't killing them directly. Maybe they would perish from thirst and hunger. Maybe a nice storm would smash them to pieces and drown them. Whatever happened, it wouldn't be his fault!

The king went back to the palace and slept well for the first time in years. Nothing like condemning your daughter and grandson to a slow, horrible death to really ease your mind. If you're an airhole like Acrisius, that is.

Meanwhile, inside the wooden box, Danaë prayed to Zeus. 'Hi, um, it's me, Danaë. I don't mean to bother you, but my dad kicked me out. I'm in a box. In the middle of the sea. And Perseus is with me. So . . . yeah. If you could call me back or text me or something, that would be great.'

Zeus did better than that. He sent cool gentle rain that trickled through the airholes and provided Danaë and the baby with fresh water to drink. He persuaded his brother, the sea god Poseidon, to calm the waves and change the currents so the box would have a smooth journey. Poseidon even caused little sardines to leap onto the box and wriggle through the airholes so Danaë could enjoy fresh sushi. (My dad, Poseidon, is awesome that way.)

So, instead of drowning or dying of thirst, Danaë and Perseus survived just fine. After a few days, the S.S. *Wooden Box* approached the shore of an island called Seriphos, about a hundred miles east of Argos.

Danaë and the baby still might have died, because that box lid was nailed shut tight. Fortunately, a fisherman named Dictys happened to be sitting on the beach, mending his nets after a hard day of pulling in the fish.

Dictys saw this huge wooden box bobbing on the tide and thought, Whoa, that's weird.

He waded into the water with his nets and hooks, and dragged the box to the beach.

'I wonder what's inside?' he said to himself. 'Could be wine, or olives . . . or gold!'

'Help!' said a woman's voice from inside the box.

'Waaaaah!' cried another, tiny voice from inside the box.

'Or people,' Dictys said. 'It could be full of people!'

He got out his handy fishing knife and carefully prised off the top of the box. Inside sat Danaë and baby Perseus – both of them grubby and tired and smelling like day-old sushi, but very much alive.

Dictys helped them out and gave them some bread and water. (Oh boy, Danaë thought, more bread and water!) The fisherman asked Danaë what had happened to her.

She decided to go light on the details. After all, she didn't know where she was, or if the local king was a friend of her dad's. For all she knew, she'd landed in Hackensack. She just told Dictys that her father had kicked her out because she'd fallen in love and had a child without his permission.

'Who's the boy's father?' Dictys wondered.

'Oh . . . um, Zeus.'

The fisherman's eyes widened. He believed her immediately. Despite Danaë's grubby appearance, he could tell she was beautiful enough to attract a god. And, from the way she talked and her general composure, he guessed she was a princess. Dictys wanted to help her and the little baby, but he had a lot of conflicting emotions.

'I could take you to see my brother,' he said reluctantly. 'His name is Polydectes. He's the king of this island.'

'Would he welcome us?' Danaë asked. 'Would he give us asylum?'

'I'm sure he would.' Dictys tried not to sound nervous, but his brother was a notorious ladies' man. He would probably welcome Danaë a little *too* warmly.

Danaë frowned. 'If your brother is the king, why are you only a fisherman? I mean, no offence. Fishermen are cool.'

'I prefer not to spend too much time at the palace,' Dictys said. 'Family issues.'

Danaë knew all about family issues. She was uneasy about seeking help from King Polydectes, but she didn't see another option, unless she wanted to stay on the beach and make a hut out of her box.

'Should I get cleaned up first?' she asked Dictys.

'No,' said the fisherman. 'With my brother, you should look as unattractive as possible. In fact, maybe rub some more sand on your face. Put some seaweed in your hair.'

Dictys led Danaë and the baby to the main town on Seriphos. Looming above all the other buildings was the king's palace – a mass of white marble columns and sandstone walls, with banners flying from the turrets and a bunch of thuggish-looking guards at the gate. Danaë started to wonder if living in a box on the beach wasn't such a bad idea, but she followed her fisherman friend into the throne room.

King Polydectes sat on a solid bronze throne that must have offered little in the way of lower-back support. Behind him, the walls were festooned with war trophies: weapons, shields, banners and a few stuffed heads of his enemies. You know, the usual decor to brighten up an audience chamber.

'Well, well!' said Polydectes. 'What have you brought me, brother? It looks like you finally caught something worthwhile in your fishing nets!'

'Um . . .' Dictys tried to think of a way to say *Please be nice to her and don't kill me.*

'You are dismissed,' the king said.

The guards hustled the poor fisherman away.

Polydectes leaned towards Danaë. His grin didn't make him look any friendlier, since he had some nasty crooked teeth.

He wasn't fooled by Danaë's ragged clothes, the sand on her face, the seaweed and tiny sardines in her hair or the bundle of rags she was holding. (Why *was* she holding that bundle? Was it her carry-on bag?) Polydectes could see how beautiful the girl was. Those eyes were gorgeous. That face – perfection! Give her a bath and some proper clothes, and she could pass for a princess.

'Do not be afraid, my dear,' he said. 'How I can help you?'

Danaë decided to play the victim, thinking the king would respond to that. She fell to her knees and wept. 'My lord, I am Danaë, princess of Argos. My father, King Acrisius, cast me out. I beg you for protection!'

Polydectes's heart wasn't exactly moved. But his mental gears definitely started turning. Argos – nice city. He'd heard about Acrisius, the old king with no sons. Oh, this was too good! If Polydectes married Danaë, he would become the ruler of *both* cities. He would finally have two throne rooms with enough wall space to display all those stuffed heads he kept in storage!

'Princess Danaë, of course I grant you sanctuary!' he said, loud enough for all his attendants to hear. 'I swear upon the gods, you will be safe with me!'

He rose from his throne and descended the steps of his dais. He meant to take Danaë in his arms to show what a kind, loving dude he was. As soon as he got within five feet of her, the princess's bundle of rags started screaming.

Polydectes jumped back. The screaming stopped.

'What sorcery is this?' Polydectes demanded. 'You have a bundle of screaming rags?'

'It's a baby, my lord.' Danaë tried not to smirk at the king's horrified expression. 'This is my son, Perseus, whose father is Zeus. I hope your promise of protection extends to my poor tiny child as well.'

Polydectes developed a tic in his right eye. He hated babies – wrinkly, pudgy creatures that cried and pooped. He was sorry he hadn't noticed the kid earlier, but he'd been distracted by Danaë's beauty.

He couldn't take back his promise now. All of his attendants had heard him say it. Besides, if the baby was a child of Zeus, that complicated matters. You couldn't chuck demigod babies in the bin without angering the gods – most of the time, anyway.

'Of course,' the king managed. 'What a cute little . . . thing.

He will have my protection, too. I'll tell you what . . .'

The king edged closer, but Perseus started screaming again. The kid had an evil-king radar.

'Ha, ha,' Polydectes said weakly. 'The boy has a strong set of lungs. He can be raised in the Temple of Athena, far away at the other end of the city – I mean, conveniently located in the *best part* of the city. The priests there will take excellent care of him. In the meantime, you and I, dear princess, can become better acquainted.'

Polydectes was used to getting his way. He figured it would take fifteen, maybe sixteen minutes tops to get Danaë to marry him.

Instead, the next seventeen years were the most frustrating time in Polydectes's life. Try as he might to become *better acquainted* with Danaë, the princess and her son thwarted Polydectes at every turn. The king gave Danaë her own suite of rooms at the palace. He gave her fancy clothes, beautiful jewellery, maidservants and an all-you-can-eat coupon book for the royal buffet. But Danaë wasn't fooled. She knew she was just as much a prisoner here as she had been in that bronze cell. She wasn't allowed to leave the palace. Aside from her servants, the only visitors she would have were her son and his nursemaids from the Temple of Athena.

Danaë loved those visits from Perseus. While he was a baby, he would scream every time the king got close to Danaë. Since the king couldn't stand the sound, he would leave quickly and go take some aspirin. When Perseus wasn't around, Danaë found other ways to rebuff the king's flirting. Whenever he came to her door, she would make retching noises and apologize for being sick. She would hide in the palace laundry room. She would weep uncontrollably while her maidservants looked on until the king felt embarrassed and ran away.

For years the king tried to win her affection. For years she resisted.

Their mutual stubbornness was kind of impressive, actually.

Once Perseus got older, things got easier for Danaë and harder for Polydectes.

After all, Perseus was a demigod. The dude had mad talent. By the time he was seven, he could wrestle a grown man to the floor. By the time he was ten, he could shoot an arrow across the length of the island and wield a sword better than any soldier in the king's army. Growing up in the Temple of Athena, he learned about warfare and wisdom: how to pick your fights, how to honour the gods – all good stuff to know if you want to live through puberty.

He was a good son, which meant he continued to visit his mom as often as possible. He didn't scream any more when Polydectes came around, but if the king tried to flirt with Danaë, Perseus would stand nearby, glaring, his arms crossed and several deadly weapons hanging from his belt, until the king retreated.

You'd think Polydectes would have given up, right? There were plenty of other women to bother. But you know how it is. Once you're told you can't have something, you want it even more. By the time Perseus turned seventeen, Polydectes was out of his mind with irritation. He wanted to marry Danaë before she was too old to have more kids! He wanted to see his own children become the kings of Argos and Seriphos. Which added up to one thing: Perseus had to go.

But how to get rid of a demigod without directly murdering him?

Especially since Perseus, at seventeen, was the strongest and best fighter on the island.

What Polydectes needed was a good trap . . . a way to make Perseus walk right into his own destruction without any of the blame splashing back onto Polydectes.

Over the years, the king had seen a lot of heroes gallivanting around: slaying monsters, rescuing villages and cute puppies, winning the hearts of princes and princesses and getting major endorsement deals. Polydectes had no use for such nonsense, but he'd noticed that most heroes had a fatal flaw – some weakness that (with any luck) would get them killed.

What was Perseus's fatal flaw?

The boy was a prince of Argos, a son of Zeus, yet he'd grown up as a castaway in a foreign kingdom, with no money and only his mother for family. This made him a little touchy about his reputation. He was anxious to prove himself. He would take on any challenge. If Polydectes could use that against him . . .

The king began to smile. Oh, yes. He had just the challenge in mind.

Later that week, Polydectes announced that he was collecting wedding presents for the princess of a neighbouring island. Her name was Hippodemeia. Her dad, King Oenomaus, was an old friend of Polydectes, but none of that was really important.

It was just an excuse to collect presents.

Polydectes gathered all the rich and famous of Seriphos for a party at the palace to see what kind of loot they would cough up. Everybody wanted to impress the king, so they competed with one another to give the coolest presents.

One family contributed a silver vase studded with rubies. Another gifted a golden chariot and a team of pure-white horses. Another offered a thousand-drachma gift certificate for iTunes. Nothing but the best for the old what's-her-name who was getting married to whoever!

As the gifts piled up, Polydectes complimented everybody and made all the rich and famous people feel special (like they didn't already). Finally he spotted Perseus over by the hors d'oeuvres table, hanging out with his mom and trying to go unnoticed.

Perseus didn't want to be at this stupid party. Watching a bunch of snooty nobles suck up to the king wasn't his idea of fun. But he had a duty to look out for his mom in case Polydectes got flirty, so here he was, drinking lukewarm punch and eating mini-weenies on toothpicks.

'Well, Perseus!' the king called across the room. 'What have you brought as a present for my ally's daughter's wedding? You are the mightiest warrior in Seriphos. Everyone says so! Surely you have brought the most impressive gift.'

That was really low. Everyone knew Perseus was poor. The other guests snickered and turned up their noses, glad to see the young upstart put in his place. They didn't like it when handsome, strong, talented demigods from out of town topped them at anything.

Perseus's face turned bright red.

Next to him, Danaë whispered, 'Don't say anything, my son. He's just trying to make you angry. It's some sort of trap.'

Perseus wouldn't listen. He hated being made fun of. He was the son of Zeus, but the king and his nobles treated him like a worthless bum. He was tired of Polydectes and the way he kept Danaë prisoner in the palace.

Perseus stepped to the middle of the room. The nobles parted around him. He called to the king, 'I may not be the richest one here, but I keep my promises. What would you like, Polydectes? Name any wedding gift for what's-her-name. Name it, and I will bring it.'

The crowd tittered nervously. (Yes, I looked it up. *Tittered* is totally a real word.) Polydectes just smiled. He'd been waiting for this.

'A fine promise,' said the king. 'But promises are easy. Would you swear a binding oath . . . say, on the River Styx?'

(FYI: Don't swear on the River Styx. It's the most serious oath you can make. If you don't keep your word, you're basically inviting Hades, his Furies and all the daimons of the Underworld to drag you down to eternal punishment with no chance of parole.)

Perseus glanced at his mother. Danaë shook her head. Perseus knew that making an oath to an evil guy like Polydectes was unwise. The priests who'd raised him at Athena's temple would *not* approve. Then Perseus looked around at the crowd sneering and smirking at him.

'I promise on the River Styx!' he shouted. 'What do you want, Polydectes?'

The king reclined on his uncomfortable bronze throne. He gazed at the stuffed heads decorating his walls.

'Bring me . . .'

Cue the dramatic organ music.

'. . . the head of Medusa.'

Cue the gasping crowd.

Even *saying* the name *Medusa* was considered bad luck. Hunting her down and cutting off her head? That wasn't something you'd wish on your worst enemy.

Medusa was the freakiest monster known to the Greeks. Once she'd been a beautiful woman, but after she had a romantic get-together with Poseidon in Athena's temple (possibly the same temple where Perseus was raised), Athena had turned the poor girl into a hideous creature.

You think your morning face is bad? Medusa was so ugly that one glance at her would turn you to stone. No one had ever seen her and lived, but according to rumours she had gold bat wings, brass talons for fingers and hair made out of living poisonous snakes.

She lived somewhere far to the east with her two sisters, who had also been transformed into bat-winged monsters — maybe because they had dared to stay with their sister. Together, the three of them were known as the Gorgons, which sounds like an awesome name for a backup band. *Now appearing: Johnny Graecus and the Gorgons!* Okay, maybe not.

Many heroes had ventured off to find Medusa and kill her, because . . . well, I'm not sure why, actually. She wasn't bothering anyone as far as I know. Maybe just because it was a hard quest. Or maybe there was a prize for killing the ugliest monster. Whatever the case, no hero who went after her had ever returned.

For a moment, the throne room was absolutely still. The

crowd looked horrified. Danaë looked horrified. Perseus was so horrified, he couldn't feel his own toes.

Polydectes smiled like Christmas had come early. 'You did say "Name it and I'll bring it", correct? Well' – the king spread his arms – 'bring it.'

The tension broke. The crowd howled with laughter. Looking at Perseus, a seventeen-year-old nobody, and imagining him cutting off the head of Medusa – it was just too ridiculous.

Somebody yelled, 'Bring me a Gorgon T-shirt while you're at it!'

'Bring me a snow cone!' someone else shouted.

Perseus fled in shame. His mom called after him, but he just kept running.

On the throne, Polydectes basked in applause. He ordered party music and a round of lukewarm punch for everyone. He was in the mood to celebrate.

At the very least, if Perseus chickened out, he'd be too embarrassed to ever come back. Maybe the gods would kill him for breaking his oath. And if the kid was actually stupid enough to find Medusa . . . well, Perseus would end up as a colossal demigod paperweight.

The king's problems were over!

After fleeing the palace, Perseus ran to the cliffs overlooking the sea. He stood at the edge and tried not to cry. The night sky was covered in clouds, as if even Zeus was ashamed to look at him.

'Dad,' Perseus said, 'I've never asked you for anything. I've never complained. I have always made the right sacrifices and tried to be a good son to my mom. Now I've messed up. I opened my big mouth and made an impossible promise. I'm not asking you to solve my problem for me, but please, I'd really appreciate some guidance. How do I get myself out of this?'

At his shoulder, a voice said, 'What a nice prayer.'

Perseus jumped, barely avoiding a fall off the cliff.

Standing next to him was a twentyish-looking guy with an impish smile, curly brown hair and a strange cap with a brim only in the front. The man's clothes were odd, too – brown leggings, a close-fitting brown shirt and laced black shoes like a combination of boots and sandals. On the left breast of his shirt was sewn a pocket, and cleverly stitched above that were letters that didn't look Greek: UPS.

Perseus figured the guy must be a god, because no mortal would dress that dorky. 'Are you . . . my father Zeus?'

The newcomer chuckled. 'Buddy, I'm not old enough to be your dad. Seriously, do I look a day over one thousand? I'm Hermes, the god of messengers and travellers! Zeus sent me to help you out.'

'That was fast.'

'I pride myself on quick service.'

'What are those symbols on your shirt?'

'Oh.' Hermes looked down. 'What century is it? Sorry, I get confused sometimes.' He snapped his fingers. His clothes changed to something more normal – a wide-brimmed hat like travellers wear to keep off the sun, a white tunic cinched at the waist and a wool robe across his shoulders. 'Now, where was I? Right! Zeus heard your prayer and sent me with some cool magic items to aid you on your quest!'

Hermes snapped his fingers again. He proudly held up a leather bag the size of a backpack.

'It's a sack,' Perseus noted.

'I know! After you cut off the head of Medusa, you can put it in here!'

'Wow. Thanks.'

'Also . . .' Hermes reached into the sack and pulled out a simple bronze helmet: just a skullcap, like the king's foot soldiers wore. 'This little baby will turn you invisible.'

'Seriously?' Perseus took the cap and looked inside. 'Why is it inscribed *Made in Bangladesh*?'

'Oh, don't mind that,' Hermes said. 'It's an unauthorized reproduction of Hades's helmet of darkness. But it works great. I promise.'

Perseus put on his cheap Bangladeshi knock-off helmet. Suddenly he couldn't see his own body. 'That's cool.'

'Right? Okay, take off the helmet, 'cause I got something else for you. I had these made special.'

From his leather sack of fabulous prizes, Hermes pulled a pair of sandals. Tiny dove wings sprouted from the heels. As the god dangled the shoes from their laces, they flapped around, straining for freedom, like birds on leashes.

'I use a pair of these myself,' Hermes said. 'Put them on, and you can fly! Much faster than walking or swimming to Medusa and, since you'll be invisible, you won't have to log a flight plan or anything!'

Perseus's heart beat as fast as the dove wings. Ever since he was little, he'd wanted to fly. He tried on the sandals and instantly shot into the sky.

'YEAH!' he whooped with joy. 'THIS IS AWESOME!'

'Okay, kid!' Hermes yelled at the tiny dot zipping in and out of the clouds. 'You can come down now!'

Perseus landed, and Hermes explained what would happen next. 'First, you gotta find these three old ladies called the Grey Sisters.'

'Why are they called that?'

'Because they're grey. Also, they're ugly and immortal. And if they get the chance they'll cut you up and barbecue you.'

'So why do I want to find them?'

'They know the location of Medusa's secret lair. Even I don't have that information. Plus, they have a couple of extra items that will help you with your quest.'

'What items?'

Hermes frowned. From his pocket, he pulled a piece of paper and read it. 'I dunno. They're not listed on the manifest. But I got this info from Athena, and she usually knows what she's talking about. Just start flying due east. After two days, you'll see the island of the Grey Sisters. Can't miss it. It's . . . uh, grey.'

'Thank you, Hermes!' Perseus was so grateful he tried to give Hermes a hug.

The god pulled away. 'Okay, kid, let's not get excited. Good luck, and try not to run into any mountains, yeah?'

Hermes disappeared in a cloud of smoke. Perseus launched himself into the air, flying east as fast as his ankle-mounted dove wings would carry him.

The island of the Grey Sisters was definitely grey.

A big grey mountain rose from a grey forest, blanketed in ash-coloured fog. Slate cliffs dropped into a churning grey sea.

This must be the place, Perseus thought, because he was smart like that.

He put on his invisibility cap and descended towards a line of smoke rising from the trees – like someone had a campfire going.

In a dreary clearing next to a scum-green lake, three old ladies sat around the fire. They were dressed in grey rags. Their hair looked like dirty straw. On a spit over the fire was a big hunk of sizzling meat, and Perseus really did not want to know where that meat had come from.

As he got closer, he heard the women arguing.

'Give me the eye!' one yelled.

'Give me the tooth and I'll think about it!' the second one said.

'It's my turn!' wailed the third. 'You took the eye when I was in the middle of the last season of *The Walking Dead*. You can't do that!'

Perseus edged closer. The old ladies' faces were withered and sagging like melted masks. Their eye sockets were empty – except for the middle sister, Ugly No. 2, who had one green eye.

The sister on the right, Ugly No. 1, was enjoying a chunk of mystery meat, ripping off pieces with her single mossy incisor. The other two sisters seemed to have no teeth at all. They slurped unhappily from cups of Dannon non-fat Greek yogurt.

Ugly No. 1 popped another piece of meat in her mouth and chewed it with relish. (I mean, with pleasure. She didn't actually have any relish.)

'Fine,' she said. 'I'm done eating anyway. I'll trade you for the eye.'

'That's not fair!' said Ugly No. 3. 'It's my turn! I don't have anything!'

'Shut up and eat your yogurt,' said Ugly No. 1. She yanked the tooth out of her mouth.

Ugly No. 2 put her hand over her eye and forced a sneeze. The eyeball popped out into her palm, and Perseus tried not to puke.

'Ready?' asked Ugly No. 1. 'We'll toss them on the count of three, and no funny business!'

Perseus realized this was his chance to do something sneaky and very disgusting. He crept forward.

'One . . .' said Ugly No. 1. 'Two . . .'

As the grey lady yelled 'Three!' Perseus stepped up. All his training at the temple of Athena and his hours playing *Call of Duty* must have really improved his hand–eye coordination, because he snatched the eye and the tooth right out of the air.

The grey ladies kept their hands out, ready to catch their traded body upgrades.

'What happened?' asked Ugly No. 1. 'You didn't throw.'

'I threw the eyeball!' Ugly No. 2 said. 'You didn't throw the tooth!'

'I did so!' shrieked Ugly No. 1. 'Someone else must have taken it.'

'Well, don't look at me!' said Ugly No. 3.

'I can't!' screamed Ugly No. 1. 'I don't have an eye!'

'I have it,' Perseus interjected.

The Grey Sisters fell silent.

'And your tooth,' he added.

All three ladies whipped knives out from under their rags and lunged towards the sound of his voice. Perseus stumbled back, barely avoiding becoming mystery meat on a spit.

Note to self, he thought. *Invisibility doesn't work on blind people.*

Uglies No. 1 and No. 2 knocked heads, fell down and started wrestling. Ugly No. 3 tripped into the cooking fire and rolled out shrieking, trying to smother her burning clothes.

Perseus circled the perimeter of the camp. 'If you want your eye and tooth back, you'd better behave yourselves.'

'They're our property!' wailed Ugly No. 1.

'They're our precious!' cried Ugly No. 3.

'Wrong story, you idiot!' snapped Ugly No. 2.

The three sisters got to their feet. They looked creepy in the firelight – shadows dancing across their hollow eye sockets, knife blades glinting red.

Perseus stepped on a twig. The sisters all turned towards him, hissing like cats.

Perseus tried to steady his nerves. 'Attack me again,' he warned, 'and I'll squish your eye right now.'

He gave the slimy orb a gentle squeeze. The Grey Sisters shrieked, clawing at their empty sockets.

'All right!' wailed Ugly No. 1. 'What do you want?'

'First, directions to the lair of Medusa.'

Ugly No. 3 made a sound like a rat being stepped on. 'We can't tell you that! We promised to guard the Gorgons' secret!'

'And to guard the weapons of the prophecy!' added Ugly No. 2.

'Right,' Perseus said. 'I'll also need those weapons of the prophecy.'

The sisters wailed some more and slapped one another upside the head.

'We can't give you the weapons!' said Ugly No. 3. 'The

Gorgons are counting on us! They'll hunt us down and kill us!'

'I thought you were immortal,' Perseus said.

'Well . . . true,' Ugly No. 1 conceded. 'But you don't know the Gorgons! They'll torture us and call us bad names and –'

'If you don't help me,' Perseus said, 'no tooth and no eye – ever again.'

He squeezed the eyeball a little harder.

'All right!' Ugly No. 1 relented. 'Give us the tooth and the eye, and we'll help you.'

'Help me first,' Perseus said, 'and I promise I'll release your eye and tooth immediately.'

(Which was an easy promise to make, because those things were disgusting.)

'The cave of the Gorgons lies to the east,' said Ugly No. 2. 'Another three days as the crow flies. When you reach the mainland, you will see a high cliff rising from the sea. The cave is right in the middle, five hundred feet up. A tiny ledge is the only approach. You will know the place. Just look for the statues.'

'The statues,' Perseus repeated.

'Yes!' said Ugly No. 3. 'Now, give us our property!'

'Not so fast,' Perseus said. 'What about those weapons you mentioned?'

Ugly No. 3 howled in frustration. She lunged at Perseus. He dodged easily, and she ran face first into a tree. 'Owww!'

'The weapons?' Perseus asked again, applying more pressure to the community eyeball.

'Fine!' Ugly No. 1 cried. 'A mile south of here is a huge

dead oak tree. The weapons are buried between the two largest roots. But don't tell Medusa we gave them to you!'

'I won't,' Perseus promised. 'I'll be too busy killing her.'

'The eye!' said Ugly No. 2. 'The tooth!'

'Yep.' Perseus threw them both into the scum-green lake. 'I promised I'd release them immediately, but I can't have you following me for revenge. You'd better start diving before some fish decides that eyeball looks tasty.'

The Grey Sisters screamed and hobbled blindly towards the water. They dived in like a pack of raggedy walruses.

Perseus wiped his hands on his shirt. Eyeball slime. Gross. He started up his sandals and flew south through the forest.

He found the dead oak tree with no problem. Perseus dug between the two biggest roots and unearthed something like a manhole cover wrapped in a leather blanket. He unwrapped the oiled leather and was immediately blinded by the shininess of a round bronze shield. Its surface was polished like a mirror. Even in the gloomy forest, it reflected enough light to cause a traffic accident.

Perseus peered into the hole he'd dug. There was something else down there – something long and narrow, also swathed in oiled leather. He pulled it out and unwrapped a sweet-looking sword: black leather scabbard, bronze and leather hilt. He unsheathed it and grinned. The blade was perfectly weighted. The edge looked razor sharp.

He swung it at a thick oak branch, just to be sure. The blade went through the branch, then through the trunk, cutting the whole tree in half like it was made of Play-Doh. If you'd seen a demonstration like that on the Demigod Shopping Network, you totally would've ordered the sword for $19.99 plus shipping and handling.

'Oh, yeah,' Perseus said. 'This'll work.'

'Be careful with that,' said a woman's voice.

Perseus spun and nearly decapitated the goddess Athena.

He recognized her right away. He'd grown up in her temple, with its many Athena statues, banners, coffee mugs and drink coasters. She wore a long white sleeveless dress. A tall war helmet crowned her long black hair. In her hands she held a spear and a rectangular shield, both glowing with magic, and her face was beautiful but a little scary, the way a warrior goddess *should* look. Her storm-grey eyes – unlike all the other grey stuff on this island – were bright and full of fierce energy.

'Athena!' Perseus knelt and lowered his head. 'Sorry about almost cutting your head off!'

'It's cool,' said the goddess. 'Rise, my hero.'

Perseus got up. His sandals' little dove wings fluttered nervously around his ankles. 'Are these . . . are these weapons for me?'

'I hope so,' Athena said. 'I put the sword and shield here, knowing that some day a great hero would come along – someone worthy of ending Medusa's curse. I hope you are that hero. I think Medusa has suffered long enough, don't you?'

'So, you mean . . . Wait, I'm confused. You're going to change her back into a human?'

'No. I'm going to let you chop her head off.'

'Oh. That's fair.'

'Yes, I thought so. Here's the deal: you will sneak into the Gorgons' cave during the day while they're asleep. That sword is sharp enough to cut through Medusa's neck, which is as thick as elephant hide.'

'And the shield?' Perseus's eyes lit up. 'Oh! I get it! I use it like a mirror! I look at Medusa's reflection rather than looking at her directly, so she can't turn me to stone.'

Athena smiled. 'Very good. You have learned some wisdom in my temple.'

'And also from playing *God of War*,' Perseus said. 'There's this one level –'

'Whatever,' the goddess said. 'Be careful, Perseus! Even after Medusa is dead, her face will still have the power to petrify mortals. Keep it safely in that leather sack, and don't show it to anyone unless you want to turn them into solid marble.'

Perseus nodded, mentally storing away that safety tip. 'What about Medusa's sisters, the other two Gorgons?'

'I wouldn't worry too much about them. They're sound sleepers. If you're lucky, you'll be out of there before they wake up. Besides, you couldn't kill them even if you tried. Unlike Medusa, the other two Gorgons are immortal.'

'Why is that?'

'Heck, I don't know. Just roll with it. The point is, if they wake up, get out of there. Fast.'

Perseus must have looked pretty terrified.

Athena raised her arms in blessing. 'You can do this, Perseus. Bring honour to me, and Hermes, and our father, Zeus. Your name will live forever! Just don't screw up.'

'Thank you, great goddess!' Perseus was so overwhelmed, he tried to give Athena a hug, but she backed away.

'Whoa, there, big boy. No touchy the goddess.'

'Sorry – I just –'

'You're welcome. Now, get going! Good hunting, Perseus!'
The goddess disappeared in a shimmer of light.

In the distance, Perseus heard the Grey Sisters screaming
something about murder, and he decided it was time to leave.

Medusa's lair was having a clearance sale on lawn statuary.

Just as the Grey Sisters had described, the cave sat halfway
up a steep cliff overlooking the sea. The mouth of the cavern
and the narrow trail leading up to it were decorated with life-
size marble warriors. Some had swords raised. Others cowered
behind their shields. One dude was crouched with his pants
around his ankles, which was a really a bad way to be frozen for
all time. All the would-be heroes had one thing in common: an
expression of absolute horror.

As the sun rose over the cliffs, shadows moved across
the statues, making them look alive. That didn't help
Perseus's nerves.

Since he was flying, he didn't have to worry about the
treacherous path. Since he was invisible, he didn't have to worry
about being seen.

Still . . . he was super tense. He looked at the dozens of
mortals who'd tried to do what he was about to do. Each of
them had been brave enough to come here. Each had been
determined to kill Medusa.

Now all of them were dead. Or *were* they dead? Maybe they
stayed *conscious* after they were turned to stone, which would
be even worse. Perseus imagined standing frozen forever, no
matter how much your nose itched, waiting until you cracked
and crumbled into pieces.

This time will be different, Perseus told himself. *These guys didn't have two gods helping them out.*

But he wasn't sure about that, either. What if he was only the latest in a long line of godly experiments? Maybe Hermes and Athena were sitting up on Mount Olympus, watching his progress, and if he failed they'd be like, *Well, that didn't work. Send in the next guy.*

He landed at the entrance of the cave. He crept inside, his shield raised, his sword unsheathed.

The interior was dark and crowded with even more marble heroes. Perseus navigated around a spear-wielding guy in full armour, an archer with a cracked stone bow and a hairy, pot-bellied guy wearing only a loincloth who was completely unarmed. Apparently the guy's plan had been to surprise Medusa by running in, yelling, waving his arms and being even more ugly than the Gorgons. It hadn't worked.

The further Perseus went into the cave, the darker it got. Frozen heroes stared at him from contorted faces. Stone blades poked him in uncomfortable spots.

At last he heard a chorus of soft hissing from the back of the room . . . the sound of hundreds of tiny snakes.

His mouth tasted like battery acid. He raised the polished surface of his shield and saw the reflection of a woman sleeping on a cot about fifty feet away. As she lay on her back with her arms folded over her face, she seemed almost human. She wore a simple white chiton, and her belly looked unusually swollen.

Wait . . .

Medusa was *pregnant*?

Suddenly Perseus remembered how Medusa had been cursed

in the first place. She'd been playing hanky-panky with Poseidon in Athena's temple. Did that mean . . . oh, gods. Ever since Medusa had been turned into a monster, she'd been pregnant with Poseidon's offspring, unable to give birth because . . . well, who knew why? Maybe that was part of the curse.

Perseus's courage faltered. Killing a monster was one thing. Killing a pregnant mother? Uh-uh. That was completely different.

Medusa turned in her sleep and faced him. Behind her, one of her gold wings unfolded against the cave wall. Her arms dropped, revealing sharp brass talons on her fingers. Her hair writhed – a nest of slithering green vipers. How could anyone sleep with all those little tongues flicking across her scalp?

And her face . . .

Perseus almost glanced over to make sure he was seeing it correctly in the reflection. Tusks like a wild boar's jutted from her mouth. Her lips curled in a permanent sneer. Her eyes bulged, making her look vaguely amphibian. But what really made her ugly was how her features were so misshapen and disproportionate. The nose, the eyes, the chin, the brow – taken all together, the face was so *wrong*, it didn't make sense.

You know those optical-illusion pictures that make you dizzy and nauseous if you stare at them too long? Medusa's face was like that, except a thousand times worse.

Perseus kept his eyes on the reflection in the shield. His hand was so sweaty he could barely hold his sword. The reptilian smell of Medusa's hair filled his nostrils and made him want to gag. Despite the fact that he was invisible, the vipers must have sensed something was wrong. As he got closer, they hissed and bared their tiny fangs.

Perseus couldn't see the other two Gorgons. Maybe they were sleeping in another part of the cave. Maybe they were out shopping for snake-friendly hair products.

He inched closer until he was standing right over Medusa, but he wasn't sure he could kill her.

She was still a pregnant whatever-she-was. Her ugliness just made him feel pity . . . not anger. He should be cutting off King Polydectes's head instead. But Perseus had made an oath. If he lost his nerve and backed out now, he doubted he'd ever get a second chance.

Then Medusa made up his mind for him.

She must have sensed his presence. Maybe her snake hairdo warned her. Maybe she smelled the scent of demigod. (I've been told we smell like buttered toast to monsters, but I can't vouch for that.)

Her bugged-out eyes snapped open. Her talons curled. She shrieked like an electrocuted jackal and lunged, ready to slash Perseus to ribbons.

Blindly, Perseus swung his sword.

Ka-flump.

Medusa fell backwards, collapsing across her cot.

Bump, bump, bump. Something warm and wet rolled to a stop next to Perseus's foot.

Eww . . .

It took all his nerve not to look, not to scream like a pre-schooler and run away. Little dying viper heads tugged at the laces of his sandals.

Very carefully, he sheathed his sword. He slung his shield over his shoulder and opened the leather sack. He knelt, keeping his eyes fixed on the cave ceiling, and grabbed the head of Medusa by its dead, snaky hair. He stuffed the head into the bag and made sure the drawstring was tightly tied.

For the first time in several minutes, Perseus exhaled.

He'd done it. He looked at the headless body of Medusa sprawled across the cot. On the floor, dark blood pooled, swirling and making strange patterns. Was blood supposed to do that?

Two forms began to grow from the pool – swelling and rising as Medusa's body withered away to nothing.

Perseus watched, transfixed, as a full-size stallion burst out of the liquid like it was charging through a doorway. The horse reared and whinnied, spreading eagle-like wings still flecked with blood.

Perseus didn't realize it, but he'd just witnessed the birth of Pegasus, the first winged horse.

Then the second shape burst out of the blood: a man in golden armour with a gold sword in his hand. Later he would be named Chrysaor, the golden warrior, and he must've inherited some of his mother's looks, because Perseus backed away from him really quick.

You're probably wondering: why were Medusa's kids a golden warrior and a winged horse? And how had they been stuck in Medusa's body all those years?

Heck, I dunno. I'm just telling you how it was. You want stuff to make sense, you're in the wrong universe.

I don't know if Chrysaor would've fought Perseus or thanked him or what, but before they could even exchange phone numbers Perseus backed into one of the marble statues. It toppled into another statue, which toppled into another, domino-style, and . . . well, you get the idea. The cave filled with the sound of shattering stone heroes.

'Oops,' Perseus said.

From the left side of the cavern, a female voice hissed: 'Medusa! What is wrong?'

From the right, the third Gorgon hissed back: 'Intruder! Murderer!'

Perseus still wore his invisibility hat, but he wasn't going to trust that to protect him. He kick-started his winged sandals and blasted out of the cave at full speed.

The two Gorgons screamed and launched after him. Their gold wings beat the air like crashing cymbals. The sound got louder, but Perseus didn't dare look back. He willed his sandals to give him more speed. The little dove wings began to burn against his ankles. Something scraped at the sole of his shoe, and he had a bad feeling it was a Gorgon's claw.

In a desperate move, he spiralled so the sunlight flashed off the shield on his back. The Gorgons shrieked, momentarily blinded, and Perseus sped upward into the clouds.

A few hours later, he was pretty sure he'd lost the Gorgons, but he didn't stop until his sandals began to smoke. At that point, FAA regulations say, you really have to land and do a safety check.

Perseus came to rest on a barren outcropping of rock in the middle of the sea. In all directions, he saw only water, but he could make out the last glow of sunset on the horizon.

'Well,' he said to himself, 'at least I know that direction is west. If I fly that way, I should eventually get home.'

Wrong. Dude must not have been paying attention while he was trying to get away from the Gorgons. Either that or he was using Apple Maps, because he was *totally* off course.

The next time he spotted land, it wasn't the island of Seriphos. It was a big swathe of mainland: burnt red hills and sandy desert stretching as far as he could see in the moonlight.

Perseus had studied some geography at the temple of Athena. He could only think of one place that looked like this. 'Africa? Is this seriously *Africa?*'

Yep. It was the coast of Africa, which meant Perseus had flown *way* too far south.

At that point he was so tired, hungry and thirsty he didn't care. He figured he would find a town, get directions and rest for a while. He flew along the coast until sunrise, when he spotted the towers of a city in the distance.

'Hooray,' he said to himself. 'Cities mean people! I like people!'

As he flew closer, he saw that something weird was going on. Several thousand people had gathered along the docks of the harbour. They were staring at the water as if they were waiting for something. Towards the back of the crowd, a silk pavilion was set up, where it looked like the king and queen of the city were observing whatever was going on.

At the entrance to the harbour, a single spire of jagged rock jutted up from the sea. On a tiny ledge about forty feet above the waves, chained to the rock, was a teenage girl.

This is not normal behaviour, Perseus thought. He took off his cap of invisibility so as not to startle the girl (like a dude with winged shoes flying towards you out of nowhere isn't startling) and flew down to see her.

The girl was strangely calm. She stared at him with beautiful dark eyes. Her hair was as black as ebony, her skin like polished copper. She wore only a plain green dress that showed off her lovely arms and neck.

Perseus hovered next to her in the air. 'Uh. Um . . .' He tried to remember how to form a complete sentence. He was pretty sure he'd been able to do that a few moments before.

'You shouldn't be here,' the girl told him. 'The sea monster will be here any second to kill me.'

'Sea monster?' Perseus snapped out of his daze. 'What's going on? Why are you chained to this rock?'

'Because my parents are super *lame*.'

'Okay . . . details?'

'My name is Andromeda. I'm the princess of that kingdom over there – Aethiopia.'

'You mean your parents are the king and the queen?' Perseus asked. 'And they *let* you be chained out here?'

Andromeda rolled her gorgeous eyes. 'It was their idea! Long story. My mom – Queen Kassiopeia – she's totally vain. About a year ago she started bragging that she was even more beautiful than Poseidon's Nereids.'

'Oh, snap.' Perseus had never met a Nereid, but he'd heard about them. They were Poseidon's troupe of underwater sea goddesses, and they were supposedly stunning. He also knew that the gods *hated* it when humans compared themselves to immortals.

'Yeah,' Andromeda agreed. 'So Poseidon got angry and sent this stupid sea monster to terrorize our city. It's been sinking ships, blowtorching the harbour, chomping up the fishermen and totally making it impossible to get a tan on the beach.

So this stupid local priest or whatever, he told my dad, King Cepheus, that the only way to make Poseidon happy was to chain *me* to this rock as a human sacrifice.'

'That's messed up,' Perseus said. 'It wasn't your fault.'

'I tried to explain that to the townspeople. It didn't go over so well.'

'You don't seem very frightened.'

Andromeda shrugged as best she could with her arms in chains. 'There's not much I can do about it. Besides, getting killed by a sea monster doesn't sound as bad as living with my jerk parents. If they think I'm going to scream and plead for my life, I'm not giving them the satisfaction. When that monster shows up, I plan on cussing at him so bad his little aquatic ears will bleed. I've been practising.'

Perseus thought for a moment. 'I'm sure your cuss words are formidable. But what if there's another way? What if I cut you free and save you?'

'That would be cool,' Andromeda said. 'But it doesn't solve the sea-monster problem. I mean, the townspeople were pretty horrible to me, but I don't want the sea monster to slaughter them. Besides, the monster would probably follow me wherever I lived.'

'Nah,' Perseus said. 'Because I'll kill him.'

Andromeda stared at him. 'No offence. You're cute. And I'm sure you're brave. But the sea monster is, like . . . Well, actually, there he is now.'

Next to the spire of rock, the water boiled. The sea monster reared his dump-truck-sized head. His face was covered in greenish-blue scales. Needle-sharp teeth lined his mouth. His neck arched out of the water until his yellow reptilian eyes were even with Andromeda's perch. Below sea level, the shadow of the thing's huge body looked like Nessie on steroids.

The monster hissed, spewing drool and flames. He'd apparently been eating whales for appetizers, because his breath was ultra rank.

On the shore, the townspeople screamed and yelled. Perseus couldn't tell if they were terrified or just excited.

After fighting Medusa, though, Perseus wasn't too impressed with this sea monster.

'Andromeda,' he said, 'close your eyes.'

'Okay.'

'Hey, buddy,' Perseus asked the monster, 'you wanna see what I got in the bag?'

The sea monster tilted his huge head. He wasn't used to mortals talking to him so calmly. Also, he loved surprises.

Perseus closed his eyes and pulled out the head of Medusa.

A crackling sound ran down the length of the monster's body, like a lake flash-freezing.

Perseus counted to three. He stuffed Medusa's head back in the bag and opened his eyes.

The monster had turned into the world's largest sand sculpture. As Perseus watched, it crumbled back into the ocean.

'Uh,' Andromeda said, 'can I look now?'

'Yeah.'

'Is it gross?'

'No, not really.'

Andromeda stared down at the huge patch of monster dust swirling in the waves. 'Wow. How did you do that?'

Perseus explained about the head of Medusa. Andromeda glanced at the bag hanging from his belt. 'Cool. So about these chains . . .'

Perseus cut her free. 'You want to get married or something?'

'Sounds awesome,' Andromeda said.

'Can I get a hug?'

'You can absolutely get a hug.'

That's when Perseus knew it was true love. They hugged and kissed. Then he grabbed her around the waist and they flew to the city.

They landed at the king and queen's pavilion. As you can imagine, a Greek warrior flying out of the sky after turning a monster to dust gets a lot of oohs and aahs. Andromeda explained what had happened and announced that she had decided to marry this handsome Greek prince.

'Unless there are any objections,' Perseus added.

King Cepheus looked at the son of Zeus with his buff muscles and his winged shoes, his blood-splattered armour and his extremely sharp-looking sword.

'No objections!' the king announced.

The queen gulped like she was trying to swallow a dry scone.

'Great!' Perseus said. 'I want you guys to give thanks to the gods for my victory, okay? And, you know, to apologize for being boneheads. On that rock spire where you chained your daughter, I want you to build three shrines. The one on the left should be to Hermes. The one on the right will be for Athena. And the one in the middle will be for Zeus. If Poseidon gets mad about his sea monster being killed, well . . . those shrines should convince him this city is under the other three gods' protection. Unless he wants a war with them, he'll back off. And while you're at it, sacrifice some cows for the gods.'

'Cows,' the king said.

'Yeah. Three should be good. Now, let's have a marriage feast!'

The crowd, which had been cheering for Andromeda's death a moment ago, now cheered for her marriage. The king and queen hastily arranged a party at the palace with lots of feasting and clogging and square-dancing or whatever else those crazy Aethiopians did when they busted loose. Queen Kassiopeia spent most of her time admiring her reflection in Perseus's shield. (Because some people never learn.)

Unfortunately, not everyone was happy about the marriage. This local rich dude named Phineas had been promised Andromeda's hand in marriage, back before the whole sea-monster problem. Now that the danger was past, Phineas got angry that his future bride had been given away to some Greek with a flashy sword and a head in a sack.

During the feast, Phineas gathered fifty of his toughest friends. They drank too much wine, talked some trash and decided they could totally take down this newcomer Perseus.

They charged into the dining hall, waving weapons and making noise.

'Give me back my wife, you scum!' Phineas threw a spear at Perseus, but since Phineas had been drinking the spear sailed over Perseus's head.

(Let that be a lesson to you, kids. Don't drink and throw spears.)

Perseus rose from the table. 'Who is this joker?'

'That's Phineas,' Andromeda grumbled.

'What kind of name is Phineas? Sounds like a cartoon character.'

'He's a local rich jerk,' Andromeda said. 'Thinks he owns me.'

'Would it be okay with you if he died, like, suddenly and violently?'

'I could live with my grief,' said the princess.

'You heard her, Phineas,' Perseus warned. 'You and your friends leave while you can.'

'Scummy Greek!' Phineas yelled. 'Let's get him!'

Another piece of advice: *Let's Get Him!* is a terrible thing to be carved on your tombstone as your last words.

Fifty Aethiopian warriors charged, and Perseus went to work.

Did I mention that he was the best warrior in Seriphos? Well, it turned out he was the best warrior pretty much anywhere. He lopped off one guy's head. He stabbed another guy in the chest. He sliced the arms and legs off several others and basically turned the feast into a bloodbath.

Phineas bravely stayed at the back of the crowd, chucking spears and missing. Finally Perseus got annoyed with that. He caught one of the spears and threw it back. It would have impaled Phineas, but at the last second, Phineas ducked behind a statue of Athena. The spear clanged off the goddess's stone shield.

'Oh, that's low!' Perseus yelled. 'Hiding behind my favourite goddess!'

He got even angrier. He killed more guys.

Ultimately Perseus backed Phineas and his remaining friends into a corner.

'Give up,' he said. 'I'm getting tired of this, and you got blood all over my wedding outfit.'

'We'll never surrender!' cried Phineas. His friends brandished their swords, though they didn't look quite as sure about it any more.

'Okay, whatever,' Perseus said. 'I warned you.' He shouted so everyone in the room could hear. 'Anyone who's a friend of mine, cover your eyes! I'm bringing out the head of Medusa!'

The smart people all covered their eyes.

'Oh, please!' Phineas said. 'He's just trying to fool us with his lies. That sea monster was probably just a clever illusion he conjured up to make himself look tough. He doesn't *really* have Medusa's head in his –'

Perseus brought out Medusa's head. Phineas and all his friends turned to stone.

Perseus put the head back in the sack and wiped his bloody sword on the nearest curtain. He looked at his new in-laws, the king and queen.

'Sorry about the mess,' he said.

'No problem,' the king squeaked.

The queen didn't respond. She was too busy checking out her reflection in her goblet.

'Andromeda,' said Perseus, 'you ready to get out of here?'

'Yeah.' The princess gave her parents one last contemptuous look. 'This kingdom blows.'

Together they flew off into the sunset, heading for Seriphos after carefully checking the best route on Apple Maps.

At this point, the Ancient Greek and Roman writers added a bunch of side adventures for Perseus. They claimed he visited

Italy and a dozen different islands, but I think they just wanted to get in on the Perseus tourism boom. Like: 'Perseus slept here!' And: 'Get your photo taken on the spot where Perseus killed the fearsome Warthog of Malta!' I don't buy all that.

One story even told how Perseus flew to the western edge of Africa, saw the Titan Atlas, who was holding up the sky, and turned Atlas to stone with Medusa's head. They claim that's where the Atlas Mountains in North Africa came from.

I don't buy that either, because 1) Medusa's head couldn't turn immortals to stone, 2) Atlas appears in a bunch of other stories later on, very much alive, and 3) I've met Atlas personally, and he was definitely *not* a statue. Hard-headed, yes, but not a statue.

Eventually, Perseus and Andromeda found their way back to the island of Seriphos. When they arrived, they got a shock even worse than a pack of Gorgons.

The whole city was decked out with banners and flowers. It looked like someone important was getting married, and Perseus had a sinking feeling it wasn't the king's old friend what's-her-name.

He and Andromeda swooped over the castle walls. They flew through a window straight into the throne room, where a crowd was assembled for the wedding ceremony.

King Polydectes stood on his dais, dressed in white and gold, a big smile on his face as two burly guards hauled Perseus's mother, Danaë, towards the throne. She struggled and screamed, but no one tried to help her except the king's brother, the fisherman Dictys, who had rescued Danaë and Perseus from the sea many years before. As Perseus watched, the fisherman tried to pull off one of the guards, but the guard cuffed the old man in the face and knocked him to the floor.

'STOP!' Perseus roared. He and Andromeda landed in the middle of the room. The crowd gasped and fell back.

King Polydectes blanched. He couldn't believe Perseus was back, alive, now. The kid couldn't wait another *five minutes*? Also, the king didn't like the look of Perseus's new sword, or the bloody leather sack tied to his belt. But, since they had an audience, the king put on his brave face.

'Well, look who it is,' Polydectes sneered. 'The ungrateful waif who makes big promises! Why have you returned, boy? To make excuses for your failure?'

'Oh, I found Medusa.' Perseus kept his voice calm and level. He raised the leather pouch. 'Here's her head, just as I promised. Now what exactly is going on?'

'It's simple!' the king said. 'Your mother has finally agreed to marry me!'

'No, I haven't!' Danaë screamed. One of the guards covered her mouth. Some of the crowd – the same ones who had mocked Perseus when he left on his quest – laughed nervously.

Andromeda slipped her hand into Perseus's. 'Time to cover my eyes, babe? Because that king over there needs killing.'

'Agreed,' Perseus said. 'Polydectes, you will never marry my mother. You're not worthy of her, or of being king. Give up your crown and I'll let you go into exile. Otherwise –'

'Ridiculous!' the king shrieked. 'Guards, kill him!'

A dozen soldiers levelled their spears and formed a ring around Perseus and Andromeda.

'Don't do this,' Perseus warned them. 'I'll turn you to stone.'

'Yeah, right!' the king yelled. 'Bring it on!'

Which, again, is a terrible last statement to be carved on your tombstone.

'Anyone who is with me,' Perseus yelled, 'close your eyes now!'

Andromeda, Danaë and Dictys closed their eyes as Perseus brought out the severed head of the Gorgon.

A crackling sound spread over the room. Then there was absolute silence.

Perseus put away Medusa's head. He opened his eyes. The entire crowd (except for his friends) had been turned to stone, which meant the price of marble statuary on Seriphos was going to crater.

Polydectes sat on his throne, frozen mid-scream. The guards looked like oversized chess pieces. The snotty nobles who had laughed at Perseus would never laugh at anyone again.

'Well, that was awesome.' Andromeda kissed her husband. 'Good job.'

Perseus made sure his mother was okay. She gave him a big hug. Then he pulled the old fisherman Dictys to his feet.

'Thank you, my friend,' Perseus said. 'You were always kind to us. You're a good man. Now that your brother is dead, I want you to be king of Seriphos.' He called out to the throne room. 'Any objections?'

None of the frozen nobles said anything.

'I . . .' The fisherman looked bewildered. 'I mean, thank you, I guess. But what about you, Perseus? Shouldn't *you* take the throne?'

Perseus smiled. 'Seriphos has never been my home. Argos is where I was born. That's where I will become the king.'

He left his mom in Seriphos, because she had no desire

to go back to her childhood home. (Can you blame her?) He promised to text and Skype as much as possible, because he was a good son. Then he and Andromeda flew off to the Greek mainland.

As it turned out, Perseus's grandfather – you remember old Acrisius with the bronze cell and the screaming and the yelling? – got advance warning of his grandson's plans. I don't know how. Maybe he had a prophecy or a bad dream. By the time Perseus got there, Acrisius had fled the city.

Nobody objected as Perseus and Andromeda became the king and queen of Argos. They had a wonderful marriage and loads and loads of children. Perseus gave his magic items back to Hermes (because you can't be greedy about stuff like that) and gifted the head of Medusa to the goddess Athena, who liked it so much she had it bronzed at the centre of her shield, the Aegis, to terrify her enemies when she charged into battle.

At this point maybe you're wondering about the prophecy that started the whole story. Wasn't Perseus supposed to kill his grandfather?

He did, later on. And it was a total accident.

Several years after Perseus became king, he was attending these athletic games in a neighbouring kingdom. A bunch of nobles were competing to show off their coolness and win sweet prizes. Perseus signed up for the discus throw.

The old king Acrisius happened to be there. He'd been hiding in the kingdom for a while, disguised as a beggar, but he made his way to the front of the crowd to watch the games, because they reminded him of the good old days when he'd been a king, not living in constant fear for his life.

Perseus got ready for his turn. If you've never seen a discus, it's basically a three-pound metal Frisbee. The idea is to chuck it as far as you can to prove how strong you are.

Acrisius hadn't seen his grandson since Perseus was an infant. He didn't know who the athlete was until the announcer called, 'Give it up for Perseus of Argos!'

The old man's eyes widened. He muttered, 'Oh, crud.' Or maybe something stronger.

Before Acrisius could get away, Perseus tossed his discus. A freak gust of wind caught it and hurled it straight at Acrisius, killing him instantly.

'OUCH!' the crowd yelled.

Perseus felt terrible, having killed an old man like that. But once Ancient Greek CSI identified the body as Acrisius and the death was ruled an accident, Perseus decided it was the will of the gods. He went back home to Argos and had more kids with Andromeda.

They had such a big family that half of Greece claimed to be descended from Perseus. One of his sons, Perses, supposedly started the line of Persian kings. One of his daughters was named Gorgophone. Like, seriously, *why*? Doesn't that mean *Sounds like a Gorgon*? Was she named after his emergency hotline? *Quick, King Perseus, you've got a call on the Gorgophone!*

His most famous descendant was a guy named Hercules.

We'll get to him later.

Right now, let's leave Perseus enjoy his happy ending with lots of hugs from Andromeda and lots of little demigod babies.

Because I want to prove that Andromeda's mom Kassiopeia was *not* the worst mother-in-law in history – that honour belongs to the love goddess Aphrodite. She made life so tough for a girl named Psyche . . . well, if you've got the stomach for fighting dragons, enduring torture, taking a trip to Hades and facing a herd of killer sheep, read on..

It's not pretty.

PSYCHE NINJAS
A BOX OF BEAUTY
CREAM

IT MUST SUCK TO BE BORN SUPER GORGEOUS.

No, I'm serious. Think about it.

Psyche should have had a happy childhood. Her parents were the king and queen of a Greek city. She had two older sisters, so the pressure was off about how well she did in school and who she would have to marry. She should've been able to kick back, enjoy being the baby princess and live life however she wanted.

Unfortunately, she was beautiful.

I'm not talking about normal human-level beauty. Her sisters were *normal* beautiful. If Psyche had been as attractive as them, or even slightly more attractive, that would've been okay.

But, as soon as Psyche became a teenager, she went from being 'That little kid is so adorable!' to 'Oh, my gods. Oh, WOW. She is SUPER HOT!'

She couldn't open her bedroom window without a hundred guys gathering in the street below, clamouring and applauding and throwing flowers (which really hurt if they happened to smack her in the face). Whenever she walked through town, she had to take four bodyguards with her to keep admirers away.

She wasn't stuck-up about it. She didn't feel like she was better than anyone else. She didn't want the attention. In fact, she wished she was a normal girl with normal looks, but she couldn't exactly complain to anyone about her problems.

'Oh, poor you!' her friends would say, their faces green with envy. 'You're too gorgeous! That must be a terrible burden.'

The older she got, the more trouble she had keeping friends. Everyone at school started treating her cruelly. They excluded her and spread rumours about her, because that's what people do when they feel threatened. But I guess if you've ever been in any school anywhere, you already know that.

Psyche's two sisters were the worst. They pretended to be nice, but behind her back they said the meanest things and encouraged everyone else to be mean, too.

Oh, well, you're thinking, *at least being super gorgeous she could have any guy she wanted, right?*

Wrong.

Psyche was so beautiful – so intimidatingly awesome – no guy dared to ask her out. They admired her. They threw flowers. They sighed and gazed at her face and drew pictures of her during study hall, but they loved her the way you would love your favourite song or a fantastic movie or the best pictures on DeviantArt. She was *above* reality – perfect because she was unattainable, unattainable because she was perfect.

Psyche's parents kept waiting for marriage offers to roll in. None did. Her sisters, who were just regular-old mortal beautiful, got married to rich husbands who were kings of other towns, but Psyche remained in her parents' palace, all alone, without friends or a boyfriend or anything.

This made Psyche miserable, but it didn't stop the adoration of the crowds.

By the time she was seventeen, the townsfolk had constructed a life-size marble statue of her in the public square. Legends started spreading that she wasn't even human. She was a goddess come down from Mount Olympus – a second Aphrodite, an even *better* Aphrodite. People from the surrounding kingdoms started to visit, hoping to catch a glimpse of her. Her hometown got rich off Psyche-centred tourism. They made T-shirts. They offered guided tours. They sold a full line of cosmetic products guaranteed to make you look like Psyche!

Psyche tried to discourage this. She was pious and smart (qualities no one ever seemed to notice since she was also beautiful). She always said her prayers and left offerings at the temples, because she didn't want to upset the gods.

'I'm not a goddess!' she would tell people. 'Stop saying that!'

'Yeah,' they muttered as soon as she left. 'She's a goddess, all right.'

Psyche's popularity went viral. Soon throngs of people from all around the Mediterranean were making pilgrimages to see her rather than going to the temples of Aphrodite.

You can probably guess how that went over with Aphrodite.

One day the goddess looked down from her personal

beauty spa on Mount Olympus, expecting to see hordes of adoring fans at her main temple on her sacred island of Cythera. Instead, the temple was deserted. The floor was caked with dust. The altar was empty. Even the priests were gone. A sign on the door read: GONE 2 WORSHIP PSYCHE. BBL.

'What's going on?' Aphrodite bolted upright, nearly ruining her manicure. 'Where is everyone? Why is no one worshipping me? Who is Psyche?'

Her servants didn't want to tell her because they'd seen the goddess get angry before, but it didn't take long for her to find out. A few minutes watching the mortal world, a couple of hashtag searches, and she knew all about the upstart Psyche.

'Oh, Hades, no,' Aphrodite growled. 'I am the most important and beautiful goddess in the universe, and I'm getting upstaged by a mortal girl? Eros, get in here!'

According to some legends, Eros was even older than Aphrodite. According to other legends, he was Aphrodite's son. I don't know which is true, but in this story Aphrodite definitely treats him as her son. Maybe he was, or maybe Aphrodite just *thought* he was, and Eros was too afraid to correct her. Either way, the dude was the god of romantic love, kind of the male counterpart to Aphrodite. He's better known by his Roman name, Cupid.

Does that mean he was a chubby Valentine baby with teeny wings, a tiny bow and cute little arrows? Not so much.

Eros was devilishly handsome. All the ladies wanted his photo as their home screen. You want details? Sorry, I've got none. Like Aphrodite, he sort of appeared however you wanted him to appear. So, ladies, imagine your perfect guy . . . and that's what Eros looked like.

He sauntered into his mom's audience chamber, rocking the skinny jeans and the fashionably ripped T-shirt, his hair tousled perfectly and his eyes gleaming with mischief, his theme song, 'I'm Too Sexy', playing in the background. (I'm making that up. I wasn't actually there.)

'What's up?' he asked.

'*What's up?*' Aphrodite screeched. 'Have you heard about this girl Psyche? Are you even paying attention to what's going on in the mortal world?'

'Uh . . .' Eros rubbed his handsome chin. 'Psyche? No. Doesn't ring a bell.'

Aphrodite explained how Psyche was stealing all her followers and their offerings, as well as the headlines in the gossip magazines.

Eros shuffled nervously. He didn't like it when Aphrodite got upset. She tended to destroy things with pretty pink explosions. 'So what do you want me to do about it?'

Aphrodite glared at him. 'What do I want you to do? *Your job!* Your arrows cause mortals to fall in love, don't they? Find this girl and teach her a lesson. Make her fall for the most disgusting, horrible man in the world. Perhaps a smelly old beggar. Or a violent murderer – I don't care about the details. Surprise me! Be a good son! Make her regret her beauty!'

Of course, Psyche already regretted her beauty, but Aphrodite didn't know that. The idea would not have computed in her immortal brain.

Eros flapped his feathery white wings. (Oh, yeah. He had huge wings. Did I mention that?) 'I'm on it . . . uh, Mom. Don't worry.'

Eros flew out of Aphrodite's Day Spa. He spiralled down towards the mortal world, anxious to complete his mission. He was curious to find this girl and see what the fuss was about. He absolutely adored shipping people with unlikely partners. Maybe he'd make her fall in love with a used-chariot salesman, or some geezer with an infectious skin disease. That would be hilarious.

'Oh, yeah,' Eros chuckled to himself. 'Psyche's going to wish she never saw me!'

It turned out he was right, but not in the way he imagined . . .

Meanwhile, down in the palace, Psyche hated her life.

Her sisters were married and gone. She had no friends. She was alone with just her parents and a bunch of bodyguards. She spent most of her time in bed with the shades drawn and the covers up over her head, weeping and heartbroken.

Naturally, her parents were concerned. Also, they'd been hoping to make a good marriage for her, because that brought lots of bennies like military alliances and positive buzz in the media. They didn't understand how such a beautiful, famous daughter, the Next Aphrodite, could be so miserable.

The king came to visit her. 'Honey, what's wrong? What can I do?'

Psyche sniffled. 'Just let me die.'

'I was thinking more along the lines of a cup of hot cocoa. Or a new teddy bear?'

'Daddy, I'm seventeen!'

'I tell you what. How about I go to Delphi and consult the Oracle? The god Apollo should be able to advise us!'

Did I mention that going to Delphi is usually a bad idea?

The king went anyway. He asked the Oracle how to get his daughter a good husband.

The Oracle lady inhaled some volcanic vapour and spoke in a deep male voice – the voice of Apollo.

'Despair, King!' she bellowed, which is never the opening line you want to hear. 'Your daughter shall marry no mortal. She is destined to marry a monster – a fierce, barbaric beast even the gods fear! Dress her for her wedding as you would dress her for her funeral. Take her to the tallest spire of rock in your kingdom. There she shall meet her doom!'

DOOM! DOOM! DOOM! echoed through the cavern.

The Oracle's voice returned to normal. 'Thank you for your offering. Have a nice day.'

Once the king returned home, he went to see his daughter. 'Honey . . . I have some good news and some bad news. The good news is you're going to get a husband.'

When Psyche heard the prophecy, she became still and quiet, which was scarier to her parents than the weeping. She accepted her fate. She'd asked to die, hadn't she? Apparently the gods had granted her wish. She was going to marry a monster, and she assumed *marry* was a euphemism for *get torn apart and devoured as part of the monster's balanced breakfast.*

Her parents wept, but Psyche took their hands. 'Don't weep for me. This is what happens when mortals challenge the gods. I should've put a stop to the "New Aphrodite" nonsense sooner. I *knew* it was going to cause trouble. I'm no goddess. I'm just a girl! If my death puts things right again, and spares the city from the wrath of the gods, then I'm okay with that. It'll be the first good thing I've ever done with my life.'

Her parents felt horrible. But they'd got direct orders from the god Apollo, and you can't ignore Apollo unless you want to get vaporized by a rain of fiery death arrows.

When news got out, the whole city went into a state of mourning. Their divinely beautiful princess, the goddess of love reborn, was going to be sacrificed to a monster on the tallest rock spire in the kingdom. This would *not* be good for the local Psyche™ cosmetics industry.

Psyche's parents dressed her in a black silk funeral gown. They covered her face with a black bridal veil and put a bouquet of black flowers in her hands. They escorted her to the edge of the kingdom, where a five-hundred-foot spire of rock jutted into the sky. Centuries ago, narrow steps had been carved around it so it could be used as a watchtower. Psyche climbed these steps alone until she reached the top.

Here goes nothing, she thought, looking at the rocky ground far below. I hope I get reborn with average looks. Or ugly. I would love to be ugly for a change.

She felt no fear, which kind of surprised her. In fact, for the first time in years, she felt at peace. She waited for a moment to see if some monster would swoop out of nowhere and bite her in half. When that didn't happen, she decided to take matters into her own hands.

She jumped.

As far as her parents could tell from their vantage point behind the spire, Psyche had plummeted to her death. They never found her body, but that didn't mean anything. It was a windy day, and they were too upset to launch a full-scale search. Besides, if Psyche *hadn't* died, that meant the monster of the prophecy had taken her, which was even worse. The king and queen returned home, broken-hearted, convinced they would never see their beloved daughter and favourite tourism magnet again.

The end.

Not really.

In the long run, Psyche would've suffered less if she had died, but she didn't. As she fell from the rock, the winds swirled around her. Forty feet from the valley floor, they slowed her fall and lifted her up.

'Hi,' said a disembodied voice. 'I'm Zephyrus, god of the west wind. How ya doing today?'

'Um . . . terrified?' said Psyche.

'Great,' said Zephyrus. 'So we have a short flight this morning, heading over to my master's palace. Weather looks good. Maybe a little turbulence on our initial ascent.'

'Your master's palace?'

'Please remember to keep your seat belt fastened and don't disable the smoke detectors in the lavatory.'

'What language are you speaking?' Psyche demanded. 'What are you talking – AHHH!'

The west wind swept her away at a thousand miles an hour, leaving behind Psyche's stomach and a trail of black flower petals.

They touched down in a grassy valley blanketed with wildflowers. Butterflies flitted through the sunlight. Rising in the distance was the most beautiful palace Psyche had ever seen.

'Thanks for flying with us today,' Zephyrus said. 'We know you have a lot of options when choosing a directional wind, and we appreciate your business. Now, you'd better get going. He'll be waiting.'

'Who –?'

But the air turned still. Psyche sensed that the wind god was gone.

Nervously, she approached the sprawling white villa. Gardens and orchards surrounded the property. A clear stream wended through flower beds. Shady arbours were laden with honeysuckle.

Psyche passed through the main doors into a living room with a panelled cedar-and-ivory ceiling, walls etched in silver geometric patterns and a mosaic floor made of precious jewels. Comfy white couches faced a low table filled with bowls of luscious fruit, steaming fresh bread and pitchers of ice-cold lemonade.

And that was just the first room.

In amazement, Psyche wandered through the palace. She found atriums with rose gardens and glittering fountains, bedrooms with the finest linens and fluffy feather pillows, libraries full of scrolls, an indoor swimming pool with a water slide, a gourmet kitchen, a bowling alley, a home theatre room with overstuffed reclining seats and a popcorn machine – this place had it *all*. It made her family's royal palace back home look like one of those nasty portable classroom buildings.

She opened a random closet. Stacks of gold bars gleamed inside. She opened another closet. Tupperware bins were neatly labelled DIAMONDS, EMERALDS, RUBIES, BOW TIES, FEZZES and SAPPHIRES. So many riches – the contents of any broom closet in the palace would be enough to buy a private island and your own army to defend it.

'Who lives here?' Psyche wondered aloud. 'Who owns all this stuff?'

Right next to her, a woman's voice said, 'You do, mistress.'

Psyche jumped, knocking over a large vase that shattered and spilled diamonds all over the floor. 'Who's there?'

'I'm sorry to startle you, mistress,' said the invisible woman. 'I am one of your servants. I only spoke because you asked a question. This is your palace. Everything here belongs to you.'

'But . . . But I –'

'Don't worry about the mess, mistress,' said the servant.

A gust of wind swept up the diamonds and the shards of broken vase and whisked them away.

'Anything you need, we will provide,' said the servant. 'I've drawn a nice hot bath for you. After that, if you're hungry, your private buffet line is open all day. If you require music, just ask. The invisible musicians know all your favourite songs. After dark, I will show you to your bedroom, and your husband will arrive.'

Psyche's throat twisted like a Twizzler. 'My husband?'

'Yes, mistress.'

'Who is my husband?'

'The lord of this house.'

'But who is the lord of this house?'

'Your husband, of course.'

Psyche took a shaky breath. 'We could go around in circles like this forever, couldn't we?'

'If you wish, mistress. I am here to serve.'

Psyche decided a hot bath would be good, because she needed to calm down.

After her soak in the tub (with a dozen choices of scented bath oils, accompanied by floating candles, thousand-jet

Jacuzzi whirlpool action and soothing music), invisible servants brought her the most beautiful, comfortable clothes she'd ever worn.

She ate the best dinner of her life while unseen musicians played her top ten tunes and the sun went down over the blooming apple trees in the orchard.

The knot in her stomach only got tighter.

Her husband would arrive after dark.

The Oracle had warned her parents: she was doomed to marry a monster, a barbaric beast feared by the gods themselves. But how could a monster live in a place like this? If he wanted her dead, why wasn't she dead already?

(By the way, if this whole thing is starting to sound like *Beauty and the Beast* – with the mysterious monster dude who lives in a cool palace with magic servants – that's no accident. *Beauty and the Beast* was totally based on Psyche's story. Just don't expect any singing teapots, because that ain't going to happen.)

Finally nightfall came. Psyche could have refused to go to bed. She could have tried to run away, but she decided that would only postpone her fate. After hours of wondering and worrying, it was almost a *relief* when it got dark. Besides, she had to admit she was a little bit curious. She'd never had a boyfriend, much less a husband. What if . . . what if he wasn't so bad?

The invisible servants guided Psyche to her bedchamber and gave her a nice warm set of My Little Pegasus pyjamas, the kind with footsies. She climbed into her huge bed, which was so soft it was like floating on air. (She knew about that thanks to her trip with Zephyrus.)

A breeze swirled through the room, snuffing out the candles and lamps. In total darkness, Psyche heard the door open. Bare feet padded across the marble. Something heavy sank onto the edge of the mattress.

'Hello,' said a man's voice.

He didn't sound monstrous. He sounded like a radio announcer. His tone was gentle and tinged with humour, as if he understood how ridiculous this first meeting was.

'I'm sorry for the drama,' he said. 'It was the only way I could arrange to meet you without . . . certain people noticing.'

Psyche found it difficult to talk, because her heart was lodged in her windpipe. 'Who – who are you?'

The man chuckled. 'I'm afraid I can't tell you my name. I'm not supposed to be here. I'm definitely not supposed to marry you. So, if you could just call me "husband", that would be great . . . assuming you're okay with marrying me.'

'I have a choice?'

'Look . . . I'm in love with you. I know that's insane, since we've just met, but I've been watching you for a long time. Not in, like, a stalker way.' He sighed. 'Sorry. I'm really messing this up.'

Psyche's feelings were hopelessly jumbled. She was used to people watching her. She'd endured that her whole life. 'You think you're in love with me because I'm beautiful?'

'No,' said the man. 'Well, yes. Of course you're beautiful. But I love you because of how you've handled it. You never let it go to your head. You tried to tell the people *no*. You kept your faith in the gods. I admire the way you endured your sadness and loneliness.'

She didn't want to cry, but her eyes stung. Nobody had ever

said anything so nice to her before. She was relieved to be in total darkness, where appearances didn't matter.

The man touched her fingers. Psyche was surprised to find that his hand felt warm and strong and very human.

'I can't even show you what I look like.' He sounded sad. 'If you knew my identity, our marriage would fall apart. You'd suffer terribly. It would ruin everything.'

'Why?'

'I – I'm sorry. You'll just have to trust me, if you can. I promise you this: I'll be a good husband. Whatever you need, just ask. But the ground rules are non-negotiable: we can only meet here, at night, in total darkness. Each morning, I'll be gone before the dawn. You can never know my real name. You can never look at me. Don't even try it.'

Psyche could feel her own pulse racing as she held his hand. 'What if I see you accidentally? What if there's a full moon or something –'

'Don't worry about that,' he said. 'The darkness is an extra precaution, but I'm also invisible. The only time you could potentially see me is when I'm asleep. While I'm sleeping, I can't will myself to be invisible. But as long as you don't do something silly like get up in the middle of the night, light a candle and intentionally look at me, we'll be fine. Psyche, I'm serious, though. You *don't* want to look at me. It would destroy us.'

Us. He said the word like it was a real thing. Like they were already a couple.

'I don't want to rush you,' he said. 'We can just talk. I know this is awkward.'

'Kiss me,' she said, her heart fluttering.

He hesitated. 'Are you sure?'

'You have lips, don't you? You're not, like, a bird monster or a zombie or something?'

He laughed under his breath. 'No. I have lips.'

He kissed her, and Psyche's insides melted into her My Little Pegasus footsies.

When he finally pulled away, she had to remember how to speak. 'That was . . . wow. That . . . wow.'

'Yeah,' he agreed. 'So . . .'

'Kiss me again, Husband.'

She could almost feel him smiling.

'You're the boss,' he said.

The next few weeks were great. Every day, Psyche chilled at the palace, enjoying her gardens and her indoor pool and her bowling alley. Every night, she couldn't wait for her husband to get home. He was the kindest, funniest, most amazing guy she'd never seen.

No way was he a monster. She'd touched his face. It felt like a perfectly normal human face – handsome, in fact. *Very* handsome. His arms were smooth and muscular. His . . . Well, you know what? I think that's good enough. I'm doing my best here, but I'm just not used to describing a dude from a lady's point of view. Sorry.

Psyche was happily married. 'Nuff said.

The only problem: she missed her family.

Why? Good question. Her sisters had always been mean to her, or at best, fake nice. Her mom and dad had always been clueless. They'd dressed her in a funeral/wedding dress and let her jump off a rock. But family connections are weird. Even if your relatives aren't particularly good to you, they're still your blood. You can't lose that connection completely. (And, believe me, I've got a few relatives on my dad's side that I would *love* to lose.)

Sometimes, when Psyche was sitting quietly in her garden, she thought she heard her family calling her name from far, far away. Once she heard her father's voice. Then her mother's. Mostly she heard her sisters, and they sounded distressed, which wasn't like them.

This made it hard for Psyche to enjoy her swimming pool, or her buffet lunch, or the invisible shoulder massages given by her invisible spa attendants.

One night Psyche asked her husband about the voices, because she was afraid she was going crazy.

In the darkness, he laced his fingers through hers. 'You're not going crazy, my love. Your father and mother haven't been doing well since you disappeared. They are sick with grief. Since your body was never found, they made your sisters promise to look for you. Every day, your sisters travel to that spire of rock where you jumped into the wind. They've been calling your name.'

Psyche's heart turned into a lump of granite. She'd been so focused on herself she hadn't considered how her family must be feeling.

'I have to go home,' she said. 'I have to see my parents.'

'You can't,' said her husband. 'If you leave this valley, you can never come back.'

'Why? Can't Zephyrus just –'

'It's not that simple.' Her husband's voice was full of pain, maybe even a little fear. 'Psyche, I'm trying to protect you.

You're under a death sentence from the gods. Well, one goddess in particular . . .'

Psyche had almost forgotten her troubles from being super gorgeous. 'You mean Aphro—'

'Don't say her name,' her husband warned. 'It's too easy to attract her attention. If you show yourself in the mortal world, all the adoration will start up again. The people will proclaim you a goddess. We'll both be in serious trouble. Everything we have here . . . our private world will be compromised. Please, just let your family believe you're dead.'

Psyche had never felt so torn. She was happy for the first time in her life. Despite the weird restrictions on their relationship, she had quickly grown to love her husband. She didn't want to mess that up. Plus the buffet line was pretty sweet.

On the other hand, her parents were sick from grief. Her sisters were searching for her daily, crying out her name. Psyche wasn't a selfish person. She didn't like turning her back on people. She couldn't enjoy her happiness knowing that others were miserable.

'What about a compromise?' she asked. 'I won't leave. But let my sisters come here.'

'Psyche . . .'

'I'll make them swear to secrecy! They'll only stay long enough to see that I'm alive and well. They'll just tell my parents, so they can stop worrying. That's it!'

'This is a very bad idea,' her husband said. 'Your sisters have always been jealous of you. If you bring them into our home, they will poison your thoughts. If you love me, please listen to me. This will ruin everything.'

She kissed his hand. 'You know I love you. I promise I'll

be careful. But you did say I should ask for whatever I needed. I need this.'

Reluctantly, her husband agreed.

The next morning, Psyche walked to the field of wild-flowers where she'd first landed. In the distance, she heard her sisters calling her name.

'Zephyrus,' she said, 'bring them here, please.'

Immediately her sisters came plummeting out of the sky, screaming and flailing their arms. They landed face first in the wildflowers. I guess Zephyrus didn't think much of them, or maybe they were flying economy class.

'Sisters!' Psyche said. 'Um, so glad to see you! Let me help you up!'

Ever had one of those urges to do something, like, *Oh, my gods, this is the best idea ever*, and as soon as you do it you're like, *What was I thinking?*

Psyche felt that way as soon as she saw her siblings. Suddenly she remembered how mean they could be. She started regretting her choice to bring them there. But it was too late now, so she tried to make the best of it.

Psyche gave them a tour of the palace. She explained how the wind had carried her there to meet her new husband. She apologized for not calling or writing, but there was this whole death-sentence-from-the-gods thing, and it was vitally important that the mortal world believe she was dead.

At first, the sisters were too stunned to say much. Over the course of the next few hours, they went from mystified to slightly relieved about their sister being alive to secretly outraged at how cool her new crib was. Psyche showed them the bowling alley, the indoor pool, the buffet, the endless bedrooms and gardens and living rooms, and a home theatre room with a popcorn machine.

'What's in here?' The eldest sister pulled open a closet door and was nearly crushed under an avalanche of gold bars, diamonds, rubies and bow ties.

'Oh, that's just storage,' Psyche said sheepishly.

The middle sister stared at the treasure, which was worth more than her husband's entire kingdom. 'You have many storage closets like this?'

'Um . . . I haven't counted. A few dozen? But that's not important!'

She offered each sister a private suite to freshen up in before lunch. The invisible servants treated them to hot baths and massages, haircuts and pedicures. They got new outfits that were fifty times more stylish than their old ones and jewellery worth more than their father's entire treasury.

Then they had peanut-butter and jam sandwiches on the veranda, because Psyche was all about PB & J.

'Who is your husband?' her eldest sister demanded. 'How can he afford all this?'

'Oh, um . . . he's a merchant.' Psyche felt bad about lying, but she'd promised her husband not to give away too many details – especially not the fact that he was invisible and only visited during total darkness. He was afraid that might freak out her sisters, though I can't imagine why.

'A merchant,' the middle sister repeated. 'A merchant who controls the wind and has invisible servants.'

'Well, he's very successful,' Psyche mumbled.

'Can we meet him?' asked the eldest sister.

'He's away . . . on business.' Psyche stood abruptly. 'Well, it's been wonderful seeing you! I really have to get back to . . . stuff!'

She loaded her sisters up with expensive presents and escorted them back to the edge of the valley.

'But, Psyche,' said the middle sister, 'at least let us visit you again. We'll bring you news from home. And . . . we miss you. Don't we, sister?'

The eldest sister nodded, trying not to dig her fingernails into her palms. 'Oh, so much! Please, let us visit again!'

'I'm not sure . . .' Psyche said. 'I promised my husband –'

'He wouldn't forbid a visit from your loving family!' The middle sister laughed. 'He's not a monster, is he?'

'Um . . . well, no –'

'Good!' said the eldest sister. 'Then we'll see you same time next week!'

Zephyrus carried the sisters away, but Psyche felt like *she* was the one trapped in a tornado.

That night, she told her husband about the visit. When he heard that the sisters wanted to visit again, he did not yell hooray and dance around the room.

'I warned you they would toy with your emotions,' he said. 'Don't have them back. Don't let them wreck our happiness. Besides –' he placed his hand gently on her belly – 'you have the baby to think about.'

Psyche's heart did a double flip. 'I – I'm going to –'

'Yep.'

'Are you sure?'

'Yep.'

'How?'

'I just know. Please, no more family visits. Forget your sisters.'

Psyche wished she could, but if she was having a baby, she should at least tell her family . . . shouldn't she? Also, her sister's question kept replaying in her head: *He's not a monster, is he?*

'I – I'm committed now,' Psyche said. 'I promise I won't let my sisters ruin our happiness. Just let them visit one more time.'

Her husband took his hand from her belly. 'I won't stop you.' His voice sounded heavy with regret.

Afterwards, for the first time, Psyche had trouble falling asleep in her comfortable new bed.

That same night, as soon as the west wind returned, Psyche's sisters to the rock spire, they started to whine to each other.

'Oh, my gods!' shrieked the middle sister. 'Did you *see* that mansion?'

'Did you see the gardens?' demanded the eldest sister. 'The bowling alley? The walk-in closets? What the Hades? I had to marry an old king with no hair and bad breath, and his house isn't *half* that nice.'

'Stop complaining,' said the middle sister. 'My husband has back trouble and terrible personal hygiene. He's repulsive! He certainly doesn't provide me with jewellery and invisible servants. And that popcorn machine –'

'Oh, gods, the popcorn machine!'

Both sisters sighed. You could almost see the green auras of envy glowing around their heads.

'We can't leave our sister in that place,' said the eldest. 'It's obviously some sort of trick or enchantment. Her husband probably *is* a monster.'

'Totally a monster,' the middle sister said. 'We have to find out the truth, for her own good.'

'For her own good,' the eldest sister agreed. 'Gods, I hate her so much right now.'

'I know, right?'

They went back to their parents' palace. Because the sisters were in the mood to be spiteful, instead of telling their mom and dad the truth, they reported that Psyche was dead.

'We saw the corpse,' the middle sister said. 'There wasn't much left, but it was definitely her. It was disgusting.'

'Disgusting,' the eldest sister echoed. 'We buried her. Really gross.'

This news broke their parents' hearts. Within three nights, the king and queen were both dead.

The sisters wept, but not too hard. Now they would get to divide the kingdom between the two of them. Besides, it served their parents right for letting their brat baby sister, Psyche, get all the attention and the best marriage.

Yeah ... those sisters. They were keepers.

At the end of the week, they once again travelled to the rock spire. The west wind picked them up and carried them to Psyche's secret palace of popcorn and diamonds. He didn't dump them face first in the grass this time, because Psyche had made him promise not to, but he got passive-aggressive revenge by not giving them a proper safety briefing.

Anyway, when they sat down to lunch with Psyche, the sisters were prepared.

'So,' said the eldest, 'how's that great husband of yours?'

'Oh, he's . . . great,' said Psyche.

The middle sister smiled encouragingly. 'What did you say he does for a living?'

Psyche blanked. She'd never been a good liar, and now she couldn't remember what she'd told her sisters. 'Well, he's a shepherd –'

'A shepherd.'

'Yes,' Psyche said meekly. 'A rich shepherd.'

Her eldest sister leaned forward and took her hands. She put on her best I-care-so-much-about-you look, even though she wanted to strangle the lucky, undeserving, infuriatingly gorgeous girl. 'Psyche, what are you not telling us? Last week you said your husband was a merchant. Now he's a shepherd. We're your sisters. Let us help you!'

'But . . . everything's fine.'

The two sisters exchanged a knowing glance.

'That's what people usually say when everything is *not* fine,' said the middle sister. 'Psyche, we think you're in danger. You haven't forgotten about the prophecy from the Oracle of Delphi, have you? You were doomed to marry a monster – a beast that terrifies even the gods. Prophecies *always* come true. Dad was constantly worrying about that. He talked about it non-stop right up until he died.'

Psyche choked on her lemonade. 'Wait. Dad is dead?'

'Yes. He died of sadness, because you wouldn't come visit him. But that's not important right now. You have to tell us: who is your husband, really?'

Psyche felt like someone was burying her up to her neck in sand. Her father was dead. Her sisters were trying to help her.

Prophecies were never wrong. But her husband's kind voice, his gentleness . . .

'I don't know who he is,' Psyche admitted. 'I'm not allowed to look at him.'

'*What?*' the middle sister said. 'Whoa, whoa, whoa. Back up and tell us everything.'

Psyche shouldn't have, but she confessed about her husband's invisibility, his night-time visits, his refusal to tell her his name. She told them about her unborn child, the My Little Pegasus pyjamas with the footsies – everything.

'It's worse than I thought,' said the eldest sister. 'You see what's happening, don't you?'

'No,' Psyche said.

'Your husband is a dragon,' said the eldest sister. 'Dragons can take human form. They can turn invisible and do all sorts of sorcery. I bet he's only kept you alive to fatten you up. Once your belly is nice and big –'

'Sister!' Psyche protested. 'That's impossible! Also sick!'

'But she's right,' said the middle sister. 'That happens all the time with dragons.'

'It – it does?' said Psyche.

The eldest sister nodded gravely. 'You have to save yourself! Tonight, when your husband is asleep, light a lamp or something. Check out his true form. I hope I'm wrong. Really, I do! But I'm not. Be sure you keep some sort of knife or razor handy. When you see his horrible monstrous face, you have to be quick. Cut off his head! Then call us back to the valley, and we'll help you get out of here.'

'We'll divide up all this lovely treasure,' the middle sister said.

'Although that's not important,' the eldest sister said.

'Not important at all,' the middle sister agreed. 'We only care about your safety and happiness, Psyche. We'll take you back home and find you a proper *mortal* husband, like ours.'

'Yes,' the eldest sister agreed, thinking, *A much older, smellier husband.*

'I – I don't know,' Psyche said. 'I can't –'

'Just consider what we've said,' the eldest sister urged. 'And for the gods' sake, be careful!'

Having thus advised Psyche to destroy her life very carefully, the sisters returned to the mortal world via Zephyrus Airways.

That night, Psyche made herself ready to do the stupidest thing in the history of ever. In one of the bathroom cabinets, she found a straight razor – one of those old-fashioned Sweeney Todd-looking things that would make a great weapon if you were, say, attacked by a giant feral pig (not that I would know anything about that). She hid the razor in her nightstand drawer along with an olive-oil lamp and a box of matches, or whatever they used to light stuff back then. Heck, I don't know.

As usual, her husband arrived after dark. All the lights went out and he sat on the bed and they talked for a while. *How was your day?/Oh, fine. My sisters didn't say anything that made me homicidally paranoid./Good, good. Love you. Goodnight.* Or something along those lines.

Around three in the morning, when she could tell from her husband's deep breathing that he was asleep, Psyche slipped out on her side of the bed. She retrieved the razor and lamp from her nightstand drawer. She lit the wick so a dim red glow spilled across the sheets.

Her husband lay on his side, facing away from her. Feather comforters were piled up at his back.

Wait . . . those weren't feather comforters. Psyche stared in amazement at the giant downy white wings folded along her husband's shoulder blades.

How was that possible? She'd never *felt* wings on his back before.

Also . . . if she'd managed not to notice his wings, what *else* might she have missed? What if his face wasn't as handsome – or as human – as it felt under her fingertips in the dark?

Your husband is a dragon, her sister's voice whispered in her head. *A beast that terrifies even the gods.*

Psyche's heart hammered against her sternum. Slowly she moved around the bed until she stood directly over her husband. The shadows receded from his sleeping face.

Psyche stifled a gasp.

Her husband was . . . unbelievably hot.

(Again, peeps, I'll leave the details to your imagination.)

He was amazing! So amazing, in fact, that Psyche's arms grew weak. The lamp trembled in her hand. The razor suddenly felt heavy.

Psyche didn't understand why her husband was worried about being seen. What did he have to hide?

Then she noticed something else – a bow and a quiver of arrows hanging from a peg over his nightstand.

His wings . . . His weapons . . . His face, too gorgeous for any mortal. Psyche suddenly understood.

'Eros,' she whispered to herself. 'My husband is Eros.'

Pro tip: Saying a god's name is not a good idea if you don't want to get their attention. Saying a god's name while you're standing over him with a razor and a lamp? Definitely a no-no.

Eros must have sensed her closeness. He muttered and turned in his sleep, startling Psyche. A single drop of hot oil sloshed from her lamp and sizzled on the god's bare shoulder.

'OW!' Eros lurched upright, and his eyes flew open.

Husband and wife stared at each other, momentarily frozen in the red light of the lamp. In a microsecond, Eros's expression changed from shock to regret to bitterness. He snatched up his bow and quiver, spread his wings and pushed Psyche aside.

'No!' Psyche dropped her razor and lamp. She lunged, just managing to grab the god's left ankle as he took off. 'Please! I'm sorry!'

Eros flew straight out of the window, dragging Psyche with him. As they passed through the garden, she lost her grip and tumbled. Despite himself, Eros hesitated. He alighted at the top of a cypress tree and looked down to make sure Psyche was okay. Not that it mattered now. Their relationship was over.

She lay crumpled on the ground, weeping and calling his name, but his heart had hardened. The single drop of oil had burned his shoulder so badly he could barely think through the pain.

'Foolish Psyche,' he said from the top of the tree. 'I warned you. By all the gods, I warned you!'

'Eros! Please, I didn't know. I'm sorry!'

'*Sorry?*' he shouted. 'I disobeyed my mother for you! I risked *everything*! Aphrodite ordered me to make you fall in love with the most despicable human being I could find.

Instead, *I* fell in love with you. I created this whole valley — the palace, the servants, *everything* — so I could hide you from my mother's gaze. We could have lived here in peace. But as soon as you saw me, as soon as you said my name — the magic was broken. Look!'

Behind them, the palace crumbled to dust. The gardens withered. The whole valley became a barren plain, desolate and grey in the moonlight.

'You listened to your sisters,' Eros said. 'They *wanted* this. They wanted you to be miserable. I warned you, but you chose to believe them instead of me. Now my mother will find out about you. It's only a matter of time. She'll see the truth. Neither one of us will escape her wrath. Run while you can, Psyche. She'll never stop until she hunts you down. You dishonoured her. Now you've dishonoured me.'

'I love you!' Psyche wailed. 'Please, we can make our marriage work. We can —'

Eros spread his wings and flew into the night, leaving Psyche heartbroken and pregnant and alone.

Uplifting story, right? Don't you feel awesome now?

But wait, it gets worse.

After Eros flew away, Psyche wandered in a daze. At the edge of the valley, she reached the banks of a river and decided to throw herself in and drown.

Now, kids, jumping into a river to drown yourself is *never* the answer. Especially if the river is, like, two feet deep, which it was. Psyche just sort of stumbled in and sat there bawling and looking silly.

It so happened that Pan, the satyr god of the wilderness,

was napping nearby after a three-day party. All the splashing and crying woke him up. He staggered to the river, saw a gorgeous girl floundering around and wondered if he was hallucinating.

'Hey, beautiful. *Hic!*' Pan leaned against a tree so he wouldn't fall over. 'You look – *hic!* – sad. Lemme guess. Don't tell me. Love problems, right?'

Psyche was so distraught she didn't even care that a drunken goat-man was talking to her. She nodded miserably.

'Well, don't drown yourself!' said the god. 'That's no solution. You know what you should do? Pray to Eros, the god of love! He's the only one who can help you!'

Psyche began crying her eyes out.

Pan stumbled backwards. 'Well . . . glad we had this little chat. I'll just . . . go over here now.' He quickly retreated. He had enough of a headache without the screaming and the drama.

Dawn came up, and Psyche started to calm down. Her misery didn't subside, but it became heavy and cold, slowly turning into determination.

'Maybe that goat-man was right,' she said. 'Eros is the only one who can help me. I need to find him and *make* him forgive me. I won't take no for an answer. But first . . .'

Her eyes took on a steely gleam. Probably a good thing no one else was around, because they would've called the Homicidal Maniac Hotline. 'First I have to thank my sisters for their *help*.'

Turns out Psyche had a cruel streak. It took a lot to make her angry, but the destruction of her marriage? That definitely did the trick.

She wandered across the countryside for days until she found the city-state where her eldest sister's husband was king. At first the guards wanted to turn Psyche away, because she looked like a homeless lady, but finally they realized who she was (they recognized her from the recent article '5 Hot New Goddesses to Worship!'). They brought her inside to see her sister.

'Oh, dear, look at you!' said the eldest sister, secretly delighted. 'My poor Psyche, what happened?'

'It's a long story,' Psyche said, wiping away a tear. 'I followed your advice, but it didn't go the way I expected.'

'Your husband? Is – is he a monster? Is he dead?'

'Neither.' Psyche sighed. 'I saw his true form. You're not going to believe this, but he's the god Eros.'

She described how amazing he was – every detail. She didn't have to fake her heartache. She told her sister the truth about what had happened . . . right up until the end.

'Before he flew away,' Psyche said, 'Eros told me he was dumping me. He said he would marry my sister instead. He called you by name.'

The eldest sister's eyes became the size of drachmas. If she'd had any doubts about Psyche's story, she now believed every word of it. It made total sense! Who else but the god of love would have a super-billionaire mansion like that with invisible servants and home theatre systems and a water slide? And Eros had called her by name! He obviously had good taste. He had seen past Psyche's silly gorgeousness. The eldest sister would finally have everything she deserved.

'Oh, Psyche,' she said, 'I'm so sorry. Will you excuse me a moment?'

The eldest sister ran out of the room. She stopped at her husband's audience chamber long enough to shout at him,

'I want a divorce!' Then she took the fastest horse from the stables and rode out of the kingdom.

She didn't stop until she reached the spire of rock where she'd first been swept away by Zephyrus. She climbed to the top and shouted, 'I'm here, Eros! Take me, my beloved!'

She jumped off and plummeted to her death.

Boy, did Zephyrus get a good laugh out of that. You should never try to board a flight until your group number is called. Everybody knows that.

Meanwhile, Psyche continued her travels. She found the kingdom where the middle sister lived and told her the same story.

'The weirdest thing?' Psyche concluded. 'Eros said he was going to marry my sister now. He mentioned you by name.'

Inflamed with desire, the middle sister ran out of the palace, commandeered a horse, charged to the rock spire and, with hope in her heart, launched herself to her death.

Cold of Psyche? I guess. But if anybody deserved to take a header off a five-hundred-foot rock it was those two ladies.

Having run out of sisters to destroy, Psyche wandered Greece, going from city to city, determined to find Eros. She checked his temples. She checked the roadside shrines. She checked the LA Fitness centres, the nightclubs and the single mingle Bible study groups where a love god might hang out. She had no luck.

That's because Eros was having his own problems.

When he'd left Psyche, his only plan was to get away from his shattered marriage, maybe find a cave to hide in for the next few centuries until Aphrodite got over her wrath. But the pain in his shoulder quickly became unbearable.

A single drop of hot oil shouldn't have hurt so badly. It burned into his central nervous system, corroding his godly essence. The pain was worse than anything he'd ever experienced . . . except perhaps the pain in his heart when he first set eyes on Psyche.

It's like the two things are related, Eros thought. It's like a *metaphor* or something!

(I put that in there so the English teachers would have something to make you write an essay about. Sorry. I did mention that I sold out for pizza and jelly beans, right?)

Anyway, Eros was so weak that he couldn't make it very far. He flew to Aphrodite's nearest vacation home, a villa on the shore of the Adriatic Sea and tumbled into his bedroom, crashing unconscious as soon as he hit the sheets.

You're thinking, *He was trying to avoid his mom, so he goes to his mom's house? That's smart.*

But I guess he was flying on autopilot. Or he wanted his own bed, the way you do when you're sick. Or he figured he might as well face his mom and get it over with.

Whatever the case, gossip quickly spread about Eros getting his heart broken by some mortal girl. Probably Zephyrus's wind spirits couldn't keep their mouths shut, because they were a bunch of airheads.

Aphrodite was vacationing on her sacred island of Cythera when she heard that her son had become the laughing stock of the cosmos. She sped off to find him – partly because she was concerned about him, but mostly because it reflected badly on her.

She arrived at her Adriatic palace and burst into Eros's room. 'Who is she?'

'Mom,' he grumbled from under the covers, 'don't you ever knock?'

'Who's the harlot who broke your heart?' she demanded. 'I haven't been disgraced this badly by a mortal since that Psyche girl a few months back!'

'Well, actually, about that . . .'

Eros told her the truth.

Aphrodite hit the roof. Literally. She blasted the ceiling to rubble with a pretty pink explosion, giving Eros the new skylight he'd always wanted.

'You ungrateful little boy!' she screamed. 'You were always trouble! You *never* listen. You mess with everyone's feelings, even mine! I should disown you. I should take away your immortality, your bow and arrows, and give them to one of my manservants. Any mortal slave could do your job. It's not that hard. You never apply yourself. You never follow directions. You –' Blah, blah, blah.

And on and on like that for about six hours.

Finally she noticed that Eros's face was sweaty and pale, which you don't normally see with an immortal. He was shivering under the blankets. His gaze was unfocused.

'What's wrong with you?' Aphrodite moved to the side of his bed, pulled back the covers and saw the festering, steaming wound in his shoulder. 'Oh, no! My poor baby!'

Funny how a mom's mood can change like that. She wants to strangle you, then *BOOM!* – a little life-threatening injury and she's cooing about her poor baby.

She brought him a cold washcloth, some rubbing alcohol,

a bandage and some chicken-soup-flavoured ambrosia. She summoned Apollo, the god of medicine, who was mystified by the wound.

'Normally you don't see this from a drop of hot oil,' he said.

'Thank you, Doctor Amazing,' Aphrodite grumbled.

'No problem!' Apollo said. 'Now, I have to get back to my groupies . . . I mean my concert on Mount Olympus.'

Nothing seemed to help Eros's wound, not even Aphrodite's magical beauty cream, which usually cleared up blemishes right away.

Aphrodite made Eros as comfortable as she could. Then she turned her attention to a blemish she *could* eliminate – that mortal witch Psyche, who had caused all this trouble.

She was about to leave when her front doorbell rang. The goddesses Demeter and Hera had arrived with flowers and balloons and sympathy cards.

'Oh, Aphrodite!' said Hera. 'We heard all about Eros.'

'Yes, I'm sure you did,' Aphrodite muttered. She imagined all the other goddesses were delighted to learn about her new family scandal.

'We're so sorry,' Demeter said. 'Is there anything we can do?'

A few rude suggestions popped into Aphrodite's mind, but she kept them to herself. 'No, thank you,' she managed. 'I'm going to find this mortal girl Psyche and destroy her.'

'You're angry,' Hera said, because she was perceptive like that. 'But has it occurred to you that the girl might be *good* for Eros?'

Aphrodite became very still. 'Excuse me?'

'Well, Eros is a grown man,' Hera continued. 'The right woman might help him to settle down.'

Demeter nodded. 'His happiness might even heal that wound in his shoulder. Apollo told us the burn wasn't responding to godly medicine.'

Aphrodite's eyes glowed pink with anger.

The other goddesses knew they were taking a chance, so why did they risk getting on Aphrodite's naughty list? Simple. They were more afraid of Eros. They saw this as a chance to get on his good side.

Eros was random. He was dangerous. He could shoot you with one of his arrows and mess up your entire life by making you fall in love with an ugly mortal or a pair of bell-bottom jeans or *anything*. That prophecy about Psyche marrying a monster? It applied to Eros just fine. Everybody was scared of him, even the gods.

Aphrodite glared at Demeter and Hera. 'I am going to destroy Psyche. No one will get in my way. *No one.* Understand?'

She stormed out of the palace and started her search.

Fortunately for Psyche, Aphrodite really sucked at searching.

If she'd been looking for her hairbrush or her favourite pair of pumps, that would've been easy. But looking for a mortal girl in a world full of mortals? That was *hard*. And *boring*.

She combed all the cities of Greece, flying overhead in her golden chariot pulled by giant doves. (Which I find kind of creepy. Does that seem romantic to you – getting pulled around by big white birds the size of Ford pickups? And the poop those things must've dropped . . . Okay, I'll stop.)

Aphrodite kept getting distracted by sales at the mall, or cute guys, or the shiny jewellery and dresses that the mortal girls were wearing this season.

Meanwhile, Psyche kept trudging along, searching for her husband in all the most remote shrines, temples and LA Fitness centres.

By this point, her pregnant belly was starting to show. Her clothes were torn and muddy. Her shoes were falling apart. She was constantly hungry and thirsty, but she would not give up.

One day she was roaming through the mountains of northern Greece when she spotted the ruins of an old temple. Hey, she thought, maybe this is a temple of Eros!

She struggled up the steep cliffs until she reached the abandoned building. Sadly, it wasn't a temple of Eros. Judging from the sheaves of wheat carved on the altar and the amount of dirt on the floor, it was a temple of Demeter that hadn't been used in decades.

What was a temple to the grain goddess doing on a barren mountain in the middle of nowhere? I'm not sure, but Psyche looked at the dusty altar, the broken statues lying across the floor, the graffiti on the walls, and she thought, I can't leave the place like this. It isn't right.

Despite all her problems, Psyche still respected the gods. She found some supplies in the janitor's closet and spent a week cleaning the old temple. She scrubbed off the graffiti, polished the altar and repaired the statues with some strategically placed duct tape.

As soon as she was done, a voice spoke behind her. 'Good job.'

Psyche turned. Standing at the altar was the goddess

Demeter. She wore green-and-brown robes, and she had a crown of wheat on her head and a golden scythe in her hand. Psyche fell to her knees in reverence, which is a good idea when you're facing a goddess with a scythe.

'O great Demeter!' she cried. 'Perhaps you can help me. I need to find my husband, Eros!'

Demeter winced. 'Yeah . . . about that. Aphrodite is out for your blood, girl. She won't rest until you are destroyed, and I can't cross her. Honestly, I would love to help you. If I ever get the chance to do something, like, off the record, I will. But you'll have to find Eros on your own.'

Some people might've gone mad. Psyche just lowered her head. 'I understand. I will keep looking.'

Deep down, she knew she would have to solve her own problem. She'd messed up, and no goddess could fix that for her. Just because she'd cleaned Demeter's temple, Psyche didn't expect a reward. She'd done it because it was the proper thing to do.

I know. Weird concept, right? But the girl was kinda heroic that way.

The goddess disappeared, and Psyche kept travelling. A few days later she was walking through a forest when she came across an abandoned shrine in a clearing. From the faded inscriptions and the ivy-covered statues, Psyche guessed it had once been a shrine to Hera.

I can't leave it like this, Psyche thought. (Me, I would've have drawn eyeglasses and moustaches on all the statues and run away. But Hera and I have a history.)

Psyche cleaned up the altar, pulled the ivy off the statues and did her best to make the shrine nice again.

When she was done, Hera appeared before her in a glowing white gown, a cloak of peacock feathers over her shoulders. In her hand was a staff topped with a lotus flower. 'Well done, Psyche. You even cleaned in the corners. Nobody does that any more.'

Psyche fell to her knees. 'Queen Hera! I expect no reward, but I am alone and pregnant and being hunted by Aphrodite. Could you protect me, just for a little while, until my child is born? I know you are the goddess of all mothers.'

Hera grimaced. 'Ouch. No can do, my child. Aphrodite is absolutely *crazy* about killing you. If she ever stops getting distracted by clearance sales, she'll tear you limb from limb. Perhaps one day I'll have the chance to help you in some subtle, secret way, but I can't protect you now. There's only one solution to your problem. I think you know what it is.'

Psyche rose. She was so weary she could barely think straight, but she understood what Hera was saying.

'I have to face Aphrodite,' Psyche said. 'Woman to woman.'

'Right. Good luck with that,' Hera said, and courageously disappeared.

Psyche continued her journey, but now she had a different focus. She went looking for the palace of Aphrodite.

Eventually Psyche found the right place: the big white villa on the shore of the Adriatic, with great views and lovely gardens all around. The place reminded Psyche, painfully, of the palace she'd shared with her husband.

She knocked at the big polished bronze doors.

When a servant answered and saw who it was, his jaw dropped.

'You came here on *purpose?*' he asked. 'Okay. I'll take you to the mistress. Just let me put my football helmet on first, in case she starts throwing stuff – like furniture, or me, or you.'

He brought Psyche to Aphrodite's throne room, where the goddess was resting after another boring search for Psyche. When Aphrodite saw the girl she'd been looking for walk in, it was the most annoying thing ever – like when you spend all morning searching for your glasses and you find them on your head. (I don't wear glasses, but my buddy Jason does. It's pretty funny when he loses them like that.)

'YOU!' Aphrodite charged at Psyche. She started kicking the poor girl, pulling her hair, raking her with her fingernails. The goddess probably would've killed her, but once she saw that Psyche was pregnant she couldn't quite bring herself to do that.

Psyche didn't fight back. She curled into a ball and waited for Aphrodite's rage to subside.

The goddess stopped to check her fingernails – because tearing a mortal to shreds can totally ruin your manicure – and Psyche spoke.

'Mother-in-law,' she said, 'I have come to face my punishment for mistrusting my husband – whatever you think is appropriate. I will do anything to prove I love him and win his forgiveness.'

'*Forgiveness?*' the goddess screamed. 'I don't recognize your marriage. I certainly don't recognize you as my daughter-in-law! But punishment I can certainly arrange. Guards! Take this mortal girl to my dungeon! I do have a dungeon, don't I? Whip her, torture her and bring her back to me. Then we'll see how I feel about *forgiveness.*'

The guards did what they were told. It was nasty. They didn't kill Psyche, but when they brought her back she was beaten up so badly she was hard to recognize. Aphrodite was a wonderful host like that.

'Well, girl?' the goddess demanded. 'Do you still wish to prove yourself?'

Amazingly, Psyche struggled to her feet. 'Yes, Mother-in-law. Anything.'

Aphrodite couldn't help being a little impressed. She decided to give Psyche a series of challenges – impossible ones, so she would still fail and die, but at least nobody could say later that Aphrodite didn't give her a chance.

(Except me, telling you right now: Aphrodite didn't give her a chance.)

'I will test you,' announced the goddess, 'to see if you are worthy of my forgiveness and my son's love. You're so *ugly*, the only way you could make a good wife is by being a good housekeeper. Let's see how well you can organize a pantry.'

Totally sexist challenge? Yeah. Totally Aphrodite? Pretty much.

She dragged Psyche to her godly kitchen and ordered the servants to dump out every sack of grain in the storeroom – barley, wheat, oats, rice, organic quinoa, whatever. Pretty soon the kitchen was buried in a blizzard of fibre.

'Sort out these grains,' Aphrodite ordered. 'Put all of them back in the proper bags before dinnertime. If you fail, I'll kill you. Or you can just admit defeat now and I'll go easy on you. I'll toss you into exile. You will NEVER see my son again, but at least you'll still have your miserable life.'

'I accept the challenge,' Psyche said, though looking

at the mountain of grain she didn't see how she could possibly succeed.

Aphrodite left in a huff to get her nails redone.

Psyche began sorting. She'd only been at it for a few minutes – quinoa, barley, dust bunny, oat – when an ant skittered towards her across the kitchen counter.

''Sup?' said the ant.

Psyche stared at it. 'You can talk?'

'Yeah. Demeter sent me. You need some help here?'

Psyche wasn't sure how a single ant could help, but she said, 'Uh, sure. Thanks.'

'Okay. But if anybody asks we were never here.'

'*We?*'

The ant let out a taxi whistle. 'All right, boys, we're on the clock!'

Millions of ants swarmed out of the skirting boards and set to work, sorting the grains into various bags. In about an hour, the whole kitchen was clean and tidy and the cupboard was back in order. The ants had even filled a new bag and neatly labelled it DUST BUNNIES AND OTHER FOUND OBJECTS.

'Thank you so much,' said Psyche.

'Shhh,' said the ant. 'You never saw us.'

'Never saw who?'

'Good girl,' said the ant. The entire colony wriggled back into the skirting boards and disappeared.

When Aphrodite returned, she was stunned. Then she got angry. 'I'm not a fool, girl. Obviously you didn't do this on your own. Some goddess helped you, eh? Someone wants to see me embarrassed! Who was it?'

'Um . . .'

'It doesn't matter!' Aphrodite yelled. 'You cheated, so this wasn't a fair test. You've earned yourself one night of rest on the kitchen floor and a crust of bread for dinner. In the morning, we'll find you a harder challenge!'

Psyche spent the night on the floor. Little did she know that in the same mansion, only a few rooms away, Eros was writhing in agony because of his wounded shoulder and (METAPHOR ALERT!!!!) his wounded heart. Aphrodite hadn't told him about Psyche's visit, but Eros could sense her presence, and it made his pain even worse.

In the morning, after another nutritious crust of bread for breakfast, Psyche got her second quest.

'I need wool,' Aphrodite announced. 'Any wife must be able to sew and mend clothes, and that requires good material. At the western edge of this valley, by the river, you'll find a herd of sheep. Fetch me some of their wool. Return before nightfall or I will kill you! Unless you want to give up now, in which case —'

'I know the drill.' Psyche's bones ached and her eyes were dim from hunger, but she bowed to the goddess. 'I'll get you your wool.'

Aphrodite forgot to mention a few details about the sheep. (Probably just slipped her mind.) For instance, their wool was pure gold. Also, the sheep had sharp horns, pointed teeth, poison bites and steel hooves as deadly as battering rams. (Get it? Rams?)

Psyche stood for a while in the morning sun, watching from a distance as the sheep destroyed and devoured any animal that came close — hedgehogs, rabbits, deer, small elephants. The pasture was pleasingly decorated with bones and human skulls.

Psyche realized it would be impossible for her to even get near the herd.

'Well . . .' She glanced at the river. 'I wonder if *that* water is deep enough to drown in.'

'Oh, don't do that,' said a voice. It seemed to come from behind a cluster of reed plants at the river's edge.

'Who are you?' asked Psyche. 'Come out from behind those reeds!'

'I can't,' said the reeds. 'I *am* the reeds.'

'Oh,' Psyche said. 'Are you going to lecture me about drowning myself?'

'Drowning is never the answer,' said the reeds. 'But mostly I'm going to give you tips on wool gathering, because Hera asked me to help you.'

Psyche relaxed. Talking to a reed plant about wool gathering was the least unusual thing that had happened to her recently. 'Thank you. Go ahead.'

'As you can guess, if you go near those sheep now, they'll tear you apart. But in the late afternoon, when it's nice and hot, they'll get sleepy and slow. They'll gather under the shade of those big plane trees on the left. You see the ones?'

'Those trees that look nothing like planes?'

'Those are the ones. When that happens, sneak over to the thorn bushes on the other side of the meadow. You see them?'

'The ones I can't see the thorns of because they're too far away?'

'You're a quick learner. Shake those thorn bushes, and your problems are solved.'

'No disrespect, O Wise Marsh Grass, but how will shaking thorn bushes solve my problems?'

The reeds said nothing. They had gone back to being regular, non-advice-giving plants.

Psyche figured she should attempt the plan. If Hera was trying to help her, it would be rude not to. She waited until the afternoon. Sure enough, the killer golden sheep gathered for a snooze in the shade of the plane trees.

Psyche crept to the other side of the meadow. She shook the nearest thorn bush and little tufts of gold wool fell from the branches. The sheep must have been using the thorn bushes as back-scratchers. Psyche went along as quietly as possible, shaking golden wool out of the bushes, until she had as much as she could carry. Then she hurried back to Aphrodite's palace.

When Psyche arrived, the goddess of love was eating her usual dinner: three pieces of celery and a cappuccino-flavoured protein shake (which may explain why she was always in a foul mood). She looked at the golden wool and wasn't sure if she felt outraged or awestruck. She settled for acting cold and indifferent, which was her default setting when it came to other women.

'That's not much wool,' said the goddess. 'Also, I can't imagine you were smart enough to figure out how to gather it without some god helping you. Who was it this time?'

'Well, there was this bunch of reeds –'

'It doesn't matter!' Aphrodite cried. 'You're a vile creature. Just talking to you makes me want to take a shower.'

She picked up a water pitcher and dumped out the contents. 'A good wife should be able to provide fresh water for her household's bathing needs. Your third quest: A mile north of here is a tall mountain with a waterfall crashing down the side of the cliffs. At the very top is a sacred spring – one of the headwaters for the River Styx, which eventually flows into the Underworld. Fill this pitcher from the spring. Not the bottom of the falls! I will know if you cheat. Bring back the water while it is still ice cold. Otherwise –'

'You'll kill me,' Psyche said wearily. 'And, no, I won't give up. I still love your son. I will do anything to win his forgiveness. I'll be right back with your Styx water.'

Little did either woman know, Eros had been eavesdropping. From his bedroom down the hall, he'd heard voices in the dining room. Somehow he knew that one of them belonged to Psyche. Despite the excruciating pain in his shoulder, he dragged himself out of bed and limped down the hall, then peeked out from behind the door to see what was happening. The sight of Psyche immediately lifted his spirits. His shoulder wound felt a little better. This annoyed Eros, but he couldn't help it. He still loved her.

When he heard his mother giving Psyche the waterfall quest, he felt horrible. The waterfall quest was impossible! Aphrodite could be such a . . . well, such a lot of things a son shouldn't call his own mother.

Eros was also impressed by Psyche's determination to win back his love.

He wanted to march into the dining hall and demand that his mother stop with the stupid Iron Housewife quests, but he couldn't because 1) he was still so weak he would fall on his face and pass out, and 2) he looked awful and didn't want Psyche to see him like this.

(Psyche looked pretty bad herself, but Eros didn't think so. Funny how love will do that. Once I saw *my* girlfriend with the cutest case of rat's-nest hair and . . . Sorry. I got distracted.)

Eros stumbled back to his bedroom. He went to the window and called out to the heavens, 'Lord Zeus, listen up! I've done you a few favours over the years. Now I need a favour from you!'

Meanwhile, Psyche found her way to the foot of the mountain. She gazed up at the slick vertical cliffs and realized that her loving mother-in-law had once again given her a job no mortal could do. Hooray!

From the top of the falls, about half a mile up, sheets of water cascaded down, roaring in a voice that sounded almost human: *TURN BACK! DON'T THINK ABOUT IT! THIS WATER IS SO COLD YOU DON'T EVEN WANNA KNOW!*

Aphrodite hadn't lied; this place was one of the earthly headwaters for the River Styx, and that made it deadly to any mortal. Just being near the falls filled Psyche with despair. Maybe she could've forced herself to fill the pitcher from the bottom of the waterfall . . . but making it to the top? No way.

Aphrodite had specifically asked for water from the top, and Psyche wasn't tempted to cheat. Not because she might get caught, but because it wasn't in her nature. (Again, I know – weird concept. But that's a hero for you. Crazy bunch, those heroes.)

As she stood looking at the falls, a huge bird spiralled out of the clouds. Psyche realized it was a golden eagle – the sacred animal of Zeus.

The eagle landed on a nearby rock. ''Sup?' it said.

'Uh, hi,' said Psyche. 'Are you from Zeus? I'm pretty sure I didn't fix up any of his shrines lately.'

'Relax,' said the eagle. 'You have a powerful friend who

pulled in a favour from the big guy. I admire your spirit, but unless you've got wings, you'll never get that water on your own. Gimme your pitcher.'

The eagle snatched it up and soared to the top of the waterfall. He filled the pitcher with ice-cold supernatural Styx water – fresh from the source! – and flew it back to Psyche.

'There ya go,' said the eagle. 'I'd give you a lift back to the palace, but it's best if Aphrodite doesn't see me. Peace out.'

The eagle flew away.

When Psyche returned to Aphrodite's dining table with a pitcher of ultra-frosty refreshing death water, the goddess was stunned.

'No way,' said Aphrodite. She washed her hands with the water, which is something only gods can do without a whole lot of pain. (Trust me on that.) Aphrodite tried to find something wrong with the water, but she couldn't. She sensed it had come from the top of the falls, just as she had requested.

'What is this sorcery?' The goddess narrowed her eyes. 'How have you passed all my tests, Psyche?'

'Oh . . . you know. Persistence. Clean living. Can I have my husband back now?'

Psyche figured three tests were enough. I mean, that's the usual deal, right? *Do these three things. Answer these three questions. Defeat these three Gorgons. Eat these Three Little Pigs.* Important stuff comes in threes.

But Aphrodite didn't know that. Or maybe she just wanted to make this story extra hard for demigods who might be trying to tell it in the future. (Thanks, lady.)

'Fourth quest!' she shrieked.

'What?' Psyche demanded. 'Come on!'

'Do this last thing for me,' the goddess said, 'and you will prove yourself a worthy wife for my son. Or, if you want to give up –'

'You are so annoying,' Psyche muttered.

'What was that?'

'I said I'd better get going,' Psyche said. 'What's the quest?'

'Obviously, the *most* important quality for a wife is beauty,' said Aphrodite, in her obviously stupid way. 'I've been so busy caring for my wounded son –'

'Eros?' Psyche interrupted, because she had no idea he was in the palace. 'He's wounded? He's in trouble?'

The goddess arched an eyebrow. 'Thanks to you. That drop of oil you spilled on his shoulder has been burning away his essence, just like your betrayal did! It's almost like a limerick.'

Psyche blinked. 'I think you mean a metaphor.'

'Whatever.'

'I must see him!' Psyche insisted. 'I must help him!'

'Oh, *now* you want to help him. I'm his mother and I have it under control, thank you very much. As I was saying, the most important quality for a woman is beauty. I've been so busy caring for my son that I've run out of my famous magical beauty cream. I've used it all up, and I need some more.'

'Wait . . . you tried to cure Eros with beauty cream?'

'Duh!' Aphrodite rolled her eyes. 'Anyway, I need more, but it's out of stock at, like, *every* store, so I need a proper substitute. The only goddess who has cosmetics I can use without my face breaking out is Persephone.'

'The queen of the Underworld?' Psyche's knees shook. 'You – you want me to –'

'Yes.' Aphrodite savoured the fear in Psyche's eyes. 'Pop down to the Underworld and ask Persephone if I can borrow a little of her beauty cream. You can put it in this.'

The goddess snapped her fingers. A polished rosewood box with golden filigree appeared in Psyche's hands. 'Last chance to give up and go into exile.'

Psyche did her best to hide her misery. 'No. I'd rather die trying to win back Eros's love than give up. I'll get you your beauty cream.'

'Make sure it's the unscented kind,' Aphrodite said. 'Hypoallergenic. And hurry. There's a new play on Mount Olympus tonight. I need to get ready.'

Psyche trudged out of the palace on her final quest.

Meanwhile, Eros had been listening behind the door again. He was still too weak to do much, but he couldn't believe how horrible his mother was being. He *had* to help Psyche. After all she'd been through trying to apologize to him, trying to win him back . . . He'd been such a fool. He should've confronted his mother in the first place and demanded the right to marry the mortal princess. He couldn't let Psyche face this last challenge alone.

Since he lacked physical strength, he sent his spirit out into the world, hoping he could at least find a way to communicate with his beloved.

Psyche drifted around with no real destination in mind. It's not like the entrance to the Underworld showed up on GPS. Finally, at the edge of a dark plain, she came across an old crumbling watchtower and decided to climb it. Maybe she'd be able to see something from the top.

Standing at the edge of the parapet, she remembered the rock spire from which Zephyrus had picked her up and spirited her away. That seemed like so long ago. (Girl's right, too. That was, like, forty pages back or something.)

Psyche thought how easy it would be to step off into nothingness and end her suffering. That would be *one* way to the Underworld – probably the only way she could manage. But she had her unborn baby to think about. And she hadn't come this far only to give up. Plus, her last half dozen suicide attempts hadn't worked out so well.

'Don't do it,' said a voice, rumbling from the stones at her feet. 'Jumping off towers is never the answer.'

Psyche stepped back from the edge. 'Hello? Is – is that the tower speaking?'

'Yes,' said the tower, resonating like a giant stone tuning fork. 'I am the tower.'

Something about the voice sounded familiar, though . . .

Psyche's heart leaped with joy. 'Eros? Is that you?'

A moment's pause.

'No,' said the voice, now in falsetto. 'I don't know any Eros. Just listen . . .' The tower cleared its throat (or whatever towers have instead of throats. Stairwells?).

In a deeper tone, it continued. 'Head towards the city of Sparta and find Mount Taenarus. At the base of the mountain, you'll see a volcanic fissure that's a breathing vent for the Underworld. It won't be easy, but you can climb down that way to Hades's domain.'

'Oh . . . okay.'

'Before you climb down, be sure you pick up two honey-flavoured rice cakes and two drachma coins. You can get the rice cakes in Sparta, or I think there's a convenience store off the highway around Exit Forty-three.'

'Um, all right. What do I do with that stuff?'

'You'll know when the time comes. But listen, don't let anything stop you until you reach Persephone. My mom will put up all sorts of distractions.'

'Your mom?'

Another hesitation. The voice went falsetto again. 'Obviously, towers don't have moms. I meant your mother-in-law, Aphrodite.'

Psyche was sure now that her estranged husband was trying to help her. She loved him for that. Even his falsetto voice was kind of cute. But she decided to play along. 'I'm listening, O Great Tower, who in no way resembles my wonderful husband.'

'Okay, then,' said the voice. 'As I was saying, Aphrodite will create distractions to test your resolve. She knows you are kind and helpful. She will try to use that against you. No matter who asks you for help on your journey, don't listen to them! Don't stop!'

'Thank you, Tower. If you were my husband, Eros, which of course you aren't, I would tell you I love you deeply and I'm very sorry. Also, how's the shoulder?'

'It hurts pretty bad,' said the tower. 'But I think . . .' Falsetto: 'Towers don't have shoulders, silly.'

The tower went silent. Psyche kissed the parapet. Then she

started off on her super-fun journey to Mount Taenarus and the Underworld.

Can we talk about this for a second?

A lot of heroes have journeyed to the Underworld. I'll tell you about some of them later. Most were dudes with swords and big attitudes. Heck, *I've* journeyed to the Underworld with a sword and a big attitude.

But Psyche made the journey with nothing but two rice cakes and a couple of drachmas. And she did it while she was seven months pregnant.

Respect.

As she was climbing down the narrow ledges inside the volcanic fissure, she happened to pass a lame ass-driver.

(Don't look at me funny. That's exactly what the old stories called him: a lame ass-driver. The dude was lame, like crippled. He was leading an ass, like a donkey. What did you *think* I meant?)

Anyway, Psyche thought it was weird to see a crippled dude in a volcanic vent, just hanging out with his ass. (I'm not going to laugh. Nope. Not even a little.)

The guy called out to her, 'Hello there, girl! You look kind and helpful. My ass has dropped some of its load . . . by which, of course, I mean that my donkey has dropped some of the firewood it was carrying. Could you help me gather up these sticks and put them back on my ass?'

I guess Aphrodite was testing Psyche to see if she would get distracted helping the dude. Either that or she was trying to make Psyche laugh so hard she would fall into the chasm.

But Psyche didn't respond to the guy. She remembered Eros's warning and kept climbing.

The ass-driver disappeared like a mirage, which was a relief to Psyche and all the parents reading this book, because things were getting a little inappropriate there.

Moving along . . .

Psyche reached the bottom of the chasm and trudged through the dark wastelands of the Underworld until she came to the banks of the River Styx – a gloomy black expanse shrouded in icy mist.

At the shore, the daimon boatman Charon was loading the souls of the dead into his ferry. He glanced at Psyche. 'Living, eh? Sorry, love. Too much red tape required to get you across.'

'I have a coin.' Psyche pulled out one of her drachmas.

'Hmm.' Charon loved shiny money. The dead usually gave him coins they'd been buried with under their tongues. By the time Charon collected them, the coins were nasty and corroded and had dead-person spit all over them. 'Right, then. Let's just keep this trip on the quiet, shall we?'

When the ferry was in the middle of the river, Psyche made the mistake of looking over the side. From the depths of the water, an old man surfaced, flailing his arms. 'Help me!' he cried. 'I can't swim!' Psyche's gentle heart made her want to pull him out, but she figured this was another test.

Eyes on the prize, she told herself. *Eros needs me.*

The old guy made a few gurgling noises and disappeared under the surface, which served him right. Everybody should know better than to go swimming in the Styx without inflatable armbands.

On the other side of the river, the black walls of Erebus

rose in the gloom. Psyche disembarked from the ferry and immediately noticed an old woman on the beach, weaving a tapestry on a loom.

That's pretty random, Psyche thought. This must be another test.

'Oh, please, dearie,' said the woman, 'help me weave for just a little while. My fingers are sore. My eyes are tired. Surely you can spare a little time for an old lady?'

It hurt Psyche, because the woman's voice reminded her of her own mother, but she kept walking.

'Well, fine!' the old woman cried. 'Be that way!'

She disappeared in a puff of smoke.

At last, Psyche reached the iron gates of the Underworld, where the souls of the dead streamed through like cars on the Jersey Turnpike. Sitting in the middle of the gateway was Hades's pet, the three-headed monster Rottweiler named Cerberus.

Cerberus snarled and snapped at Psyche, knowing she was human and would make a tasty meal.

A tasty meal, Psyche thought. When she was a little girl, back at the palace, she would always sneak table scraps to the dogs. They had loved her for that.

'Hey, boy,' she said, trying to hide her fear. 'Want a treat-treat?'

Cerberus's three heads all tilted sideways. He liked treat-treats.

Psyche tossed one of her honey rice cakes. While the three heads were fighting over it, she slipped inside the gates.

Getting through the Fields of Asphodel took her a while – what with the chattering shades of the dead, the Furies and the zombie border patrol – but finally Psyche reached the palace of Hades. She found the goddess Persephone in her garden, having tea in the gazebo in a grove of skeletal silver trees.

The goddess of springtime was in 'winter mode'. Her dress was pale grey and green – the colour of frost on grass. Her eyes were watery gold like the December sun. She didn't seem surprised to see a seven-months-pregnant mortal lady stumbling into her garden.

'Please, sit,' said Persephone. 'Have some tea and scones.'

Tea and scones sounded great to Psyche since she'd been living off Aphrodite's stale bread crusts, but she'd heard too many stories about eating food in the Underworld.

'Thank you, no,' she said. 'My lady Persephone, I have an unusual request. I hope you can help me. Aphrodite wonders if she can borrow some of your beauty cream.'

Behind Persephone, a patch of purple flowers wilted. 'Excuse me?' said the goddess.

Psyche explained her problem with Eros. She did her best not to cry, but she couldn't disguise the pain in her voice.

Persephone sized up this mortal woman. The queen was fascinated. Persephone had had her own marriage problems. She'd had her share of run-ins with Aphrodite, too. She guessed that the love goddess had sent Psyche here, hoping Persephone would get mad enough to kill her.

Well . . . Persephone wasn't going to do Aphrodite's dirty work for her. If the love goddess wanted to borrow some magic, though, Persephone had just the thing.

'Open the box,' Persephone said.

The goddess breathed into her own hand. Light collected in her palm like quicksilver. Persephone poured it into the rosewood box and closed the lid.

'There you are,' said Persephone. 'But this is important, child: do *not* open the box. What is inside is only for Aphrodite. Do you understand?'

'I understand,' said Psyche. 'Thank you, my lady.'

Psyche felt elated. Finally! She retraced her steps through the Underworld, using her second rice cake to distract Cerberus and her second drachma to pay Charon for passage across the river. She climbed back to the mortal world and began the long journey to Aphrodite's palace.

When she was halfway there, she was struck by a sudden thought.

'What am I doing?' Psyche said to herself. 'If this works, I'll get Eros back, but will he *want* me? I look *awful*. I'm exhausted, I've been living off breadcrumbs, my clothes are in rags and I haven't had a bath in, like, seven months. I've got a box full of godly beauty, and I'm about to give it all to Aphrodite, who doesn't even need it. I should take a little bit for myself.'

Foolish? Maybe. But cut her some slack. Psyche had been questing non-stop for months. She was sleep-deprived and food-deprived and probably wasn't thinking straight. Besides, the closer you get to the end of something, the more you tend to get reckless and make mistakes, because you want to be done with them. (Whoops. I mean *it*.)

Also – and I'm going out on a limb here – I think Psyche's fatal flaw was insecurity. She had a lot of courage and many other great qualities, but she didn't trust herself. She didn't believe that someone like Eros could love her for who she was. That's how her sisters had managed to manipulate her. That's why she opened the box of beauty.

Unfortunately, Persephone hadn't put any beauty in the box. She'd filled it with pure Stygian sleep – the essence of the Underworld. Persephone had meant it for Aphrodite as a little thank-you for involving Persephone in her problems.

I'm not sure what the stuff would've done to a goddess like Aphrodite – maybe put her in a coma, or made her face go numb so she'd talk funny for a few weeks. But when Psyche opened the box the Stygian sleep filled her lungs and made her pass out instantly.

Her life began to ebb.

Back at Aphrodite's palace, Eros's shoulder began to throb like someone was digging into it with a hot knife. He knew something was wrong with his wife. Despite the pain, he rose from his sickbed and found that some of his old strength had returned. His soul had begun to heal after he had talked to Psyche in the great falsetto tower exchange. He spread his wings, launched himself out of the window and flew to Psyche's side.

He cradled her unconscious form in his arms. 'No, no, no. Oh, my beloved, what have you done?'

He gathered her up and flew straight to Mount Olympus. He barged into Zeus's throne room, where all the gods were assembling to see a new play Apollo had written entitled *Twenty Awesome Things About Me*. (Don't look for it on Broadway. It closed after opening night.)

'Lord Zeus!' Eros yelled. 'I demand justice!'

Most gods knew better than to storm in and demand things from Zeus. Especially not justice. Zeus didn't exactly have a surplus of that.

Nevertheless, even the King of Olympus was a little scared of Eros, so Zeus beckoned him forward.

'Why have you brought this mortal into our midst?' Zeus asked. 'She's kind of hot, I grant you, but she's also very pregnant and it looks like she's dying.'

At that moment, Aphrodite arrived for the play. She sashayed into the throne room expecting everyone to compliment her on her new dress, only to find all the gods focused on Eros and Psyche.

Oh, my gods, thought Aphrodite. I don't believe this. Even smelly and unconscious, that girl *still* gets all the attention!

'What is going on?' the goddess demanded. 'That girl is *mine* to torture.'

'Chill, Aphrodite.' Zeus nodded to Eros. 'Speak, god of love. What's the scoop?'

Eros told the gods the whole story. Even the Olympians were moved by Psyche's bravery. Yes, she'd made a few mistakes. She'd looked on Eros's true form. She'd opened a box meant for Aphrodite. But she'd also shown faithfulness and determination. Most important, she'd shown proper reverence for the gods.

'Ridiculous!' Aphrodite shrieked. 'She didn't even complete her last quest! That box was not full of hypoallergenic beauty cream!'

Eros scowled. 'She is my wife. You need to accept that, Mother. I love her and I will not allow her to die.'

Zeus scratched his beard. 'I want to help, Eros. But she's pretty far gone with the Stygian sleep. I'm not sure I can bring her back to her old self.'

Hera stepped forward. 'Then make her a goddess. Psyche has earned that. If she will be Eros's wife, it's only fitting.'

'Yes,' Demeter agreed. 'Make her a goddess. And I don't expect any favours from Eros, even if it was totally my idea.'

'And my idea,' added Hera.

Aphrodite protested, but she could tell that the Olympian Council was against her. She grudgingly gave her approval. The Olympian vote was unanimous.

When Psyche opened her eyes, her body coursed with new-found power. Godly ichor ran through her veins. She found herself dressed in shimmering gossamer robes, and she had wings like a butterfly (which was a little weird, but whatever). She embraced her husband, Eros, who was now fully healed and happier than he'd ever been.

'My love,' he said. 'My wife for eternity!'

'I am still the boss?' she asked.

Eros laughed. 'You are definitely the boss.'

They kissed and made up, and Psyche became the goddess of the human soul – the one who looks out for us when we need a little strength and understanding, because she understands human suffering better than any other god.

She gave birth to her daughter, Hedone, who became the goddess of pleasure. You've got to admit, after all Psyche went through, she deserved a little pleasure.

So there you go. The end.

Wow . . . here I promised you all this death and suffering, and I give you two happy endings in a row. What's up with that?

How about we turn to a total car wreck of a demigod: a kid who crashed and burned and destroyed half the world. Let's visit Phaethon. He'll restore your lack of faith!

PHAETHON FAILS DRIVER'S ED

THIS DUDE WAS CURSED AS SOON AS HIS PARENTS named him.

I mean, *Phaethon*? In Ancient Greek, that means *The Shining*. His dad was the sun god, so I guess it makes sense. Still, any kid named after an old movie with Jack Nicholson as a psycho axe-murderer – that kid is not going to have a happy life.

His mom, Clymene, was a water nymph who lived among humans. She had a house on the banks of the River Nile, way down in Egypt. She must've been super beautiful, because Helios, the Titan of the sun, fell in love with her, and he pretty much had his pick of the ladies.

Helios spent every day cruising the sky in his sun-chariot chick magnet, checking out all the hot *chiquitas*. After sunset, he'd put on his disco outfit and hit the nightclubs. The girls couldn't resist his Titanish good looks, his power, his fame.

'You look so familiar,' the ladies would say. 'Are you on television?'

'I drive the sun,' Helios would tell them. 'You know, that big ball of fire in the sky?'

'Oh, my gods! That's where I've seen you!'

Once he met Clymene, Helios settled down and became a one-nymph man. (At least for a while. Gods don't do 'Till death do us part.') They had seven daughters together, and I don't know if they were septuplets or different ages or what, but *dang*, that's a lot of daughters. Nobody could remember their individual names, so they were just called the *Heliades*, meaning the *daughters of Helios*. They had matching sequinned jackets, like a gymnastics team, and everything.

Finally, Helios and Clymene had a son, Phaethon. No surprise: because he was the baby and the only boy, he got all the attention.

By the time Phaethon was old enough to remember anything, Helios was out of the picture. Sort of like: *Well, Clymene, it was nice having eight kids with you. Have fun with them! I'm going back to cruising in my chick magnet.*

That's a god for you.

Still, Phaethon loved hearing his mom's stories about Helios. Clymene always told Phaethon that he was more special than any other boy, because his father was an immortal.

'Look, Phaethon!' she said one morning when he was about three. 'There is your father, the sun god!'

'Fun god?'

'*Sun* god, dear. He is riding his chariot across the sky! No, don't look directly at him. You'll burn your retinas.'

His sisters might have been jealous of their baby brother, but they couldn't help liking him. He was just too cute, the way he would skip around the house yelling, 'Ima fun god! Ima fun god!' He loved doing dangerous things, like running with knives, sticking pennies in electrical outlets and driving his tricycle over the speed limit.

The seven Heliades quickly learned to look out for him. In fact, the people in town started calling them the seven 'Helio-copters', because they were always hovering around Phaethon. The kid grew up with eight ladies doting on him, which can give a guy a big head.

As he got older, Phaethon became obsessed with chariot racing. Why? Duh. His dad had the best chariot in existence. Unfortunately, his mom wouldn't allow him to race. She was a total freak about the dangers of sports. Whenever he went to just *watch* a chariot race, she made him wear a safety helmet, because you never knew when one of those drivers might lose control and crash into the crowd.

By the time he was sixteen, Phaethon was *really* frustrated with his overprotective mom and his seven helicopter sisters. He was determined to get his own chariot.

One day after school he went down to the track. A local prince, this dude named Epaphos, was showing off his new ride – a Mark V Zephyr with bronze radials, low-rider hydraulics and sequencer lights on the horses' yokes – the whole package. A crowd had gathered around him. All the dudes were like, *Whoa!* and all the girls were like, *You're so awesome!*

'It's no big thing,' Epaphos told his admirers. 'His Majesty – that would be my *dad* – he pretty much gives me whatever I want.'

Maybe you've known a few princes, or dudes who *think* they're princes. They can be jerks.

Inside, Phaethon boiled with jealousy and anger, because he knew that Epaphos's chariot cost more than most people would make in a lifetime. And in a few weeks the prince would get bored with his new toy, and it would end up gathering dust in the royal garage.

Epaphos let his groupies take turns holding the reins, feeding carrots to his horses, or triggering the retractable blades on the wheels.

'It's the best chariot in the world,' he said nonchalantly. 'Nobody has one better. But whatever.'

Phaethon couldn't stand it any more. He shouted over the crowd, 'It's garbage!'

The crowd went silent.

'Who said that?' the prince demanded.

Everybody turned and pointed at Phaethon, like, *Nice knowing you, buddy.*

Phaethon stepped forward. He held his head high, despite the fact that he was wearing a safety helmet with reflective decals. 'You call that the best chariot in the world? It's a hunk of junk compared to my father's chariot.'

Epaphos raised an eyebrow. 'You're *Phaethon*, aren't you? The one with the seven cute babysitters . . . I mean, sisters. You live in that, ah, humble house by the river.'

The spectators snickered. Phaethon was handsome and reasonably smart, but he wasn't popular. He had a reputation for being arrogant. Also, he didn't make many friends at school because his mom wouldn't let him participate in sports – at least not without a helmet, full padding, a life vest, a first-aid kit and a water bottle.

Phaethon kept his eyes on the prince. 'Epaphos, your dad may be the king, but my father is Helios, the god of the sun. His chariot would melt yours into a slag heap.'

He spoke with such confidence that the crowd backed away. Phaethon *did* look like a demigod. He was tall and muscular, with the upright bearing of a charioteer. His bronze skin, curly dark hair and regal face made it seem possible that he was telling the truth . . . His anger even made his eyes glow with internal fire – or was that a trick of the light?

Epaphos just laughed. 'You . . . a son of Helios. Tell me, where is your father?'

Phaethon pointed to the sky. 'Up there, of course. Driving his chariot.'

'And he comes home to your hut on the river every night, eh?'

'Well, no . . .'

'How often do you see him?'

'I've never actually seen him, but –'

'So how do you know he's your father?'

'My mother told me!'

The crowd began to laugh again.

'Oh, my gods,' said one of the girls.

'*So* lame,' said another.

Epaphos ran his hands along the custom bronze detailing on his chariot. 'Your mother . . . the same lady who makes you wear that stupid helmet everywhere?'

Phaethon's face stung. 'Concussions are serious,' he muttered, though his confidence was faltering.

'Did it ever occur to you,' said the prince, 'that your mother is lying? She's trying to make you feel better because you're a lowlife nobody.'

'That's not true!'

'If your father is Helios, prove it. Ask him to come down here.'

Phaethon looked up at the sun (which you should never do without proper eye protection, as Phaethon's mother had told him a million times). Silently he prayed to his father for a sign.

'Come on,' Epaphos goaded him. 'Make the sun zigzag for us. Make it do loops! My chariot can do wheelies at sixty miles an hour, and the horn plays "La Cucaracha". Surely the sun can do better than that!'

The crowd howled with delight.

Please, Dad, Phaethon pleaded, *help me out here.*

For a second, he thought the sun might be getting a little brighter . . . but no. Nothing.

Phaethon ran away in shame.

'That's right, shiny boy!' the prince yelled after him. 'Run home to your mommy and sisters. They probably have your bib and baby food ready!'

When Phaethon got home, he slammed the door of his room. He turned up his music too loud and threw his textbooks against the wall over and over. (Okay, I'm just guessing about that, but when *I'm* in a bad mood, nothing feels quite as good as turning *Fun with Algebraic Equations* into a Destructo-Frisbee.)

Phaethon's seven sisters gathered outside his door, asking him what was wrong. When he wouldn't answer, they ran to get their mother.

Finally Clymene got Phaethon to come out. He told her what had happened with Prince Epaphos.

'Oh, honey,' Clymene said, 'I wish you would wear sunscreen when you go to the racetrack.'

'Mom, you're missing the point!'

'Sorry, dear. Would you like a grilled cheese sandwich? That always makes you feel better.'

'I don't want a grilled cheese sandwich! I want some proof that my father is Helios!'

Clymene wrung her hands. She had always suspected this day would come. She'd done her best to keep her son safe, but stern warnings and protective padding could only go so far. Sooner or later, trouble always finds a demigod. (Trust me on that.)

She decided to try one last thing to placate him.

'Come with me,' she said.

She led Phaethon outside. In the middle of the street, Clymene raised her arms to the afternoon sun sinking behind the palm trees.

'Hear me, O gods!' she shouted. 'My child Phaethon is the son of Helios, lord of the sun!'

'Mom,' Phaethon muttered, 'you're embarrassing me.'

'If what I say is a lie,' Clymene kept shouting, 'let Helios strike me down with a bolt of fire!'

Nothing happened. It would've been kind of cool if Helios had reacted one way or the other, but gods don't like being told what to do, even if it's something fun like striking people with bolts of fire.

Clymene smiled. 'You see, my son? I'm still alive.'

'That's not much proof,' Phaethon muttered. 'I want to *meet* my dad. I want to hear the truth from him!'

Clymene's heart felt close to breaking. She realized it was time to let her son choose his own path, but she didn't want to. She wanted to wrap him in blankets and store him safely forever in a box of Styrofoam peanuts. 'Oh, Phaethon . . . Please, don't. It's a dangerous journey to the palace of Helios.'

'So you know the way! Tell me!'

Clymene sighed. 'If you must go, walk due east towards the horizon. At the end of the third night, you will reach the palace of the sun. Only travel at night, not during the day.'

'Because during the day my dad is driving his chariot across the sky. He's only home at night.'

'Right,' said Clymene. 'Also, it's really hot during the day. You'll get dehydrated.'

'Mom!'

'Just be careful, dear. Don't do anything rash!'

Phaethon had heard warnings like this a million times, so it just rolled right off his safety helmet.

'Thank you, Mother!' He kissed her goodbye. Then he hugged each of his seven sisters, who wept to see him go off alone without travel immunizations, water tablets or even training wheels.

As soon as he was out of sight, Phaethon threw away his safety helmet. Then he ventured off to find the palace of the sun, where he was sure he would win fame and glory.

Fame, yeah. Glory? Not so much.

For three nights he walked east from the River Nile. Now, if most people did that, they'd run into the Red Sea and a whole bunch of fancy beach resorts. Phaethon, being the son of Helios, managed to find his father's magical palace at the edge of the horizon, where every day Helios started his cruise for hot chicks – I mean, his glorious ascent into the sky.

Phaethon arrived at about three in the morning. Even in the pre-dawn darkness, he had to put on his sunglasses to deal with the blazing light of the palace. The parapets glowed like molten gold. Flames encircled the Celestial bronze columns that lined the facade. Etched on the silver gates – designed by Hephaestus himself – were scenes of mortal life that moved like video images.

As Phaethon approached, the doors swung open. Inside was an audience chamber the size of a sports arena. Various minor gods, the court attendants of Helios, mixed and mingled while they waited to start their daily duties. The three Horae, the goddesses of the seasons, sipped coffee and ate breakfast tacos. A lady in shimmering blue-and-gold robes – Hemera, the goddess of day – chatted with a beautiful winged girl in a rose-coloured gown. Phaethon guessed she must be Eos, the rosy-fingered goddess of the dawn, because she had the reddest hands he'd ever seen. Either that or she'd been finger-painting with blood, in which case Phaethon didn't want to know.

In another corner stood a whole crowd of guys in matching blue overalls with different times painted on their backs – 12:00 P.M., 1:00 A.M., 4:00 P.M. – and the words SCRUB TUB. Phaethon guessed they were the gods of the hours.

Yeah, every hour of the day had a minor god. Can you imagine being the god of two p.m.? All the schoolkids would hate you. They'd be like, *Can it please be three thirty? I wanna go home!*

In the centre of the room, the Titan Helios sat on a throne constructed entirely of emeralds. (No, he wasn't showy at all. Dude probably had a toilet made out of diamonds, too. You'd go blind every time you flushed it.)

His purple robes showed off his tan. A wreath of gold laurels crowned his dark hair. He smiled warmly (well, he was the sun; he did everything warmly), which helped offset the creepiness of his eyes. His pupils blazed like pilot lights for industrial ovens.

'Phaethon!' he called. 'Welcome, my son!'

My son. Those two words made Phaethon's entire life. Pride filled him with warmth, or maybe he was just getting a fever from the throne room, where the thermostat was set to, like, a hundred and twenty Fahrenheit.

'So it's true?' he asked in a small voice. 'I am your son?'

'Of course you are!' said Helios. 'Come here. Let me look at you!'

Phaethon approached the throne. The other gods gathered around, whispering comments like, *He's got his dad's nose. Nice posture. Handsome young man. Too bad he doesn't have flaming eyes.*

Phaethon felt dizzy. He wondered if coming there was such a good idea. Then he remembered Epaphos making fun of him, doubting his parentage. *Stupid prince with his stupid low-rider chariot.*

Phaethon's anger gave him renewed courage. He was a

demigod. He had every right to be here. He stood up straight
and met his father's blazing eyes.

Helios regarded his son. 'You have grown into a fine young
man. You deserve the name *The Shining*. And by that I mean you
are young and strong and handsome, not that you are associated
in any way with that psycho axe-murderer movie.'

'Um, thanks . . .'

'So, my son,' said the god, 'why have you come to see me?'

A bead of sweat trickled down Phaethon's cheek. He was
tempted to answer, *Because you never come to see me, you jerk,* but he
guessed that wouldn't go over too well.

'Father, I'm proud to be your son,' Phaethon said. 'But
back home no one believes me. They laugh at me. They claim
I'm lying.'

Helios scowled. 'Why don't they believe you? Didn't they
notice that I refrained from incinerating your mother when she
made that oath?'

'I don't think that convinced anyone.'

'Don't they know that your name means *The Shining*?'

'They don't care.'

'Mortals! There's no pleasing them.'

Helios brooded. He hated the idea of his kid getting
teased at the racetrack. He wanted to help Phaethon, but he
wasn't sure how. He should've gone for something easy, like a
signed note, or a father-and-son photo on Instagram. Maybe he
could've dragged a promotional banner behind the sun chariot:
PHAETHON IS MY SON. DEAL WITH IT.

Instead, Helios did something rash.

'To prove I am your father,' said the god, 'ask me one favour,
anything at all, and I will grant it.'

Phaethon's eyes lit up (not literally, like his dad's, but almost that bright). 'Really? Do you mean it?'

Helios chuckled. *Kids today . . .* He figured Phaethon would ask him for a magic sword or NASCAR tickets or something. 'I promise on the River Styx.'

There it is again, that promise you should never make, and which gods and heroes always seemed to blurt out at the worst possible moment.

I understand why Helios did it, though. Like a lot of godly dads (and mortal dads, too) he felt guilty about not spending enough time with his kids. He tried to compensate with an expensive present – in this case, a *way* stupid promise.

Phaethon didn't hesitate. Ever since he was a little boy, he'd wanted only one thing. He'd dreamed of it his whole life.

'I want to drive the sun chariot tomorrow!' he announced. 'For one day, all by myself!'

A record-needle scratching noise filled the throne room as all the gods whipped their necks around like, *Say what?*

Helios's godly jaw dropped. His godly butt felt uncomfortable on his emerald throne.

'Whoa, whoa, whoa.' He tried for a laugh, but it sounded more like somebody choking to death. 'Kid, let's not go crazy here. Pick something else. Seriously, that's the *only* thing I can't give you.'

'You promised *anything*,' Phaethon said. 'You didn't put an asterisk next to it.'

'The asterisk was implied! Come on, kid. The sun chariot? It's too dangerous! How about a nice set of Matchbox chariots?'

'Dad, I'm sixteen.'

'A *real* chariot, then! I'll give you one that's way better than all the other kids'. The Mark V Zephyr has bronze radials and –'

'Dad!' said Phaethon. 'Will you honour your promise or not?'

Helios felt trapped – worse than the time he blew a wheel at four o'clock and was stuck waiting for roadside assistance in the middle of the afternoon sky. 'Phaethon, okay, I promised. I can't back out. But I *can* try to talk some sense into you. This is a bad idea. If there was a god of bad ideas, he'd paint "letting a mortal drive the sun chariot" on his shield, because it's the ultimate bad idea.'

Phaethon's excitement didn't waver. For sixteen years his mother and sisters had been telling him that everything he wanted to do was a bad idea – too dangerous, too risky. He wasn't going to be dissuaded now.

'Let me drive the sun chariot,' he said. 'It's the only thing I've ever wanted. It's my dream!'

'But, son . . .' Helios looked around at his courtly attendants for help, but they were all suddenly very interested in their breakfast tacos. '*Nobody* can handle the heat of the chariot except me. Even Zeus couldn't do it, and he's the most powerful god of all. My four horses are almost impossible to control. Then there's the course. At first you climb straight up, like the craziest roller coaster ever. At the top, you're so high up, you're scraping against the heavens; and all those starry constellation monsters might attack you! Then there's the descent, which is the most terrifying, super-horrible adrenalin rush . . . I'm not convincing you, am I?'

'It sounds awesome!' Phaethon said. 'When can I start?'

'Let me drive you instead. You can ride shotgun and wave and throw candy.'

'No, Dad.'

'Let me train you for a few months before you take the reins. Or a few centuries. Going tomorrow – that's nuts.'

'No.'

Helios heaved a sigh. 'You're breaking my heart, kid. All right. Come on.'

The sun garage wasn't one of those garages that get crammed with storage boxes, broken furniture and old Christmas decorations. The marble floor was spotless. The horse stables were freshly scrubbed. The pit crew of hour gods rushed around in their matching Scrub Tub uniforms, polishing the chariot's trim, vacuuming the interior and yoking the elephant-size fiery horses to the draught pole.

The chariot's wheels stood twice as tall as Phaethon. The axle and rims were solid gold, with silver spokes and Maserati brake pads. The sides of the carriage were inlaid with Hephaestus's metalwork – fluid images of Mount Olympus in various hues of gold, silver and bronze. The black-leather interior had a tricked-out stereo system, twenty-four-carat drink holders and a pine-tree-shaped air freshener hanging from the rear-view mirror.

Phaethon was anxious to climb aboard, but when he grabbed the rails the metal burned like a stovetop.

'Hold up.' His father took out a bottle of what looked like sunscreen. 'Let me put this on you so you don't burst into flames.'

Phaethon squirmed impatiently while Helios applied magic

lotion to his face and arms. He'd had to go through this when he was little. While all the other kids were playing on the banks of the Nile, his mom would slather him up and give him stupid lectures about the dangers of sunstroke or crocodiles or whatever. So annoying!

'There,' said Helios. 'That should prevent instant death. Once the wheels start turning, the chariot's temperature goes up to about three hundred degrees Fahrenheit, and that's inside, with the AC on full blast.'

'It can't be *that* hot,' Phaethon said, though his palms were covered with blisters.

'Listen, kid, we don't have much time before sunrise. I'll try to give you some tips to save your life.'

'Whoa!' Phaethon climbed into the carriage and ran to the dashboard. 'You have built-in Bluetooth?'

'Phaethon, please!' Helios jumped in next to him, just in time to stop him from firing the rocket thrusters. 'Don't touch the buttons! And, whatever you do, don't whip the horses to go faster.'

'There's a whip? Cool!' Phaethon grabbed it from its holster. He flicked the golden lash and tongues of fire curled into the air.

'Don't use it!' Helios pleaded. 'The horses will go plenty fast enough. By the way, their names are Blaze, Dawn, Fire and Flame. *Don't* call them Donner, Blitzen, Comet and Cupid. They hate that.'

'Why?'

'Never mind. If you have to slow them down, use the reins. Keep a firm hand, or they'll know you're inexperienced. They'll start to misbehave.'

'Oh, please,' said Phaethon. 'These horses look like sweethearts.'

The stallions shook their fiery manes. They exhaled plumes of volcanic ash and clopped their hooves, scorching the marble floor.

'Um, sure,' Helios said. 'Most important — stick to the *middle* of the sky. Once you're up there, you'll see my tracks — kind of like vapour-trail skid marks. Follow those. The horses know the way. Don't go too high or you'll set the heavens on fire. Don't go too low or you'll destroy the earth.'

'Got it.'

'Don't go too far north or too far south. *The middle of the sky.* As long as you do that, and you don't do anything stupid, there's a small percent chance you might live.'

To Phaethon, all of this was the usual blah, blah, blah. His mom and sisters had been lecturing him since the beginning of time. All he could think about was that sweet fiery whip, those awesome smoking horses and how epic he would look driving this golden chariot into the morning sky.

The alarm tone went off on Helios's smartphone: 'Here Comes the Sun'. He climbed out of the carriage.

The dawn goddess, Eos, ran into the garage. She hit a button on the wall and the garage door rolled up. A spotlight switched on, illuminating the early morning sky. Eos put her rosy-coloured hands over the light and started making shadow-puppet designs. Phaethon had never realized the daily sunrise was such a weird gig.

'Last chance,' Helios implored his son. 'Please, don't do this.'

'I'll be fine, Dad! Jeez! I'll bring your chariot back, not a scratch.'

'No loud music. And keep your hands on the reins. And if you have to parallel park –'

'See you, Dad! Thanks!' Phaethon flicked the reins. 'Giddyap!'

The horses lurched forward, pulling Phaethon and the chariot into the sky as Helios yelled after him, 'The insurance card is in the glove compartment!'

The ride was even more awesome than Phaethon had imagined.

He whooped and hollered and did his happy dance as the chariot shot upward at a billion miles an hour.

'YEAH, BABY!' he shouted. 'Who's the sun? I'm the sun!'

The horses were already going crazy. Blaze, Dawn, Fire and Flame didn't appreciate how lightly Phaethon held their reins. They weren't big fans of his happy dance, either. They ran at twice their normal speed but, since they were climbing straight up and since Phaethon had never driven the chariot before, he didn't realize anything was wrong.

The folks down on the earth must have noticed, though. They woke up at, like, six a.m. Twenty minutes later it was lunchtime.

The chariot levelled out at the top of the sky. Phaethon's excitement started to level out, too. He gazed at all the dashboard buttons he wasn't supposed to push. He kept one hand on the reins and rummaged through his dad's CDs, looking for some non-lame music, but the selection was hopeless: 'Good Day, Sunshine', 'Walking on Sunshine', 'You Are the Sunshine of My

Life' – the sun-related oldies just kept on coming.

Phaethon tried to concentrate on the smoky trail of wheel marks across the sky, following them the way his dad had told him to; but that got monotonous after, like, five minutes. Besides, even with the AC on full blast, even with his magical sunscreen, the chariot was *hot*. Soon Phaethon felt sweaty and cranky and fidgety.

'I'm bored,' Phaethon said. 'This is boring.'

That may sound unbelievable, but I can relate. Most demigods are ADHD. No matter how awesome or terrifying an experience, after a few minutes we're ready for something else. Still . . . when you're hurtling through the stratosphere in a million-degree fiery death chariot, saying 'I'm bored' might be tempting fate just a teensy bit.

Phaethon looked down at the earth far below. The view was scary amazing. He'd never been so high up. No mortal had, since this was before aeroplanes and whatnot. He was pretty sure he could make out the blue line of the River Nile. His hometown would be in the middle, right about there.

'Hey, Epaphos!' he shouted down. 'How do you like *this* ride?'

But of course Epaphos couldn't hear him. Nobody at home would know Phaethon was driving the sun. In a few days, after the most thrilling experience in his life, Phaethon would return and brag about it, and no one would believe him. He'd be right back where he started – ridiculed, shunned, forced to wear a safety helmet and a life jacket for the rest of his sheltered, boring life.

'Unless . . .' He grinned. 'Unless I did something unusual that would prove it was *me* driving the chariot.'

The horses had reached the zenith of their path. The sky above was black. The air was thin, but I don't think you can blame a lack of oxygen for what Phaethon did next.

His fatal flaw was recklessness. That's pretty obvious.

Sure, you can accuse his mom and sisters of being over-protective. Maybe their obsessive worrying made Phaethon reckless. Or maybe they understood him well enough to know what would happen if they ever stopped looking out for him.

Whatever the case, Phaethon decided it would be a great idea to fly low enough over his hometown that he could shout to the folks and make it clear he was in the driver's seat.

'Dive!' he told the horses.

The horses were already running way too fast. They were confused and annoyed that their driver didn't have his normal steady hand on the reins. But they knew their usual path, and they stubbornly stuck to it.

Phaethon grabbed the whip. He flicked it, lashing tongues of fire across the horses' backsides. 'Dive!'

The horses snorted and whinnied, like, *You asked for it, buddy.*

They dived. Fortunately, Phaethon's left hand was wrapped around the reins. Otherwise, he would've flown out of the back of the chariot along with the whip, the floor mats and his dad's CD collection.

He screamed as he became the first human to experience zero-G, but part of him was thrilled. He could see his town clearly now – the houses, the palace and the racetrack all coming into focus as he hurtled towards the earth.

'They're going to notice me!' he shouted.

They noticed, all right. Their first clue was when the palm

trees burst into flames. Then the River Nile began to boil. The thatched roofs of the houses caught fire. Phaethon watched in horror as the entire northern part of Africa, which had always been green and lush, withered and burned, turning into a vast desert.

'No,' he murmured. 'No, no, no! Up! Go up, Comet or Blitzen or whatever your names are!'

The horses didn't like that. They bucked and turned, shaking the chariot from side to side, hoping to spill their stupid teenage driver.

More by luck than design, they banked up and to the north. They climbed into the sky above Europe. As they got higher, the northern parts of the continent began to freeze. Snow collected on the mountaintops. Glaciers expanded across the landscape, swallowing entire towns. The temperature inside the chariot became uncomfortably cool, which was not good, considering it was supposed to be three hundred degrees Fahrenheit. Frost formed on the yokes of the horses. Their fiery breath turned to steam.

Stars appeared in the midday sky – monstrous constellations in the shapes of a rampaging bull, a coiled serpent, a scorpion poised to strike.

I'm not sure what Phaethon saw up there in space, but it drove him mad with terror. He realized, too late, that he should never have asked to drive this chariot. He wished he'd never been born.

Please, he prayed, *just let me go back to my family. I'll never misbehave again.*

Down on the earth, the mortals were praying, too. The shortest morning in history had turned into the longest, worst afternoon ever. The southern parts of the earth were scorched and barren. The northern parts were frozen and icy. People were dying. Crops were burning. People's vacation plans were ruined. Meteorologists were curled into the foetal position on the TV studio floor, sobbing and cackling hysterically.

According to some versions of the story, Phaethon's little joyride also burned the people of Africa so their skin became darker. I don't know about that. I guess the Greeks were trying to explain why people have different skin colours, but I think it's just as likely that humans were originally dark and some god of laundry washed the Europeans with Clorox by accident and they got all bleached out.

Anyway, Phaethon was now totally out of control. The sun did loops through the sky and zigzagged around. The mortals screamed prayers to the king of the gods: 'Hey, Zeus! We're dying down here! A little help?'

Zeus was sitting in his throne room, engrossed in the latest issue of *GQ* (*God Quarterly*), but when he heard so many humans calling his name he glanced out of the window.

'Holy me!' He saw cities burning, people dying, seas boiling, his temples crumbling to dust. 'My temples! Noooo! Who's driving the sun?'

He used his super godly vision to zoom in on the chariot. He quickly realized that the scrawny dude at the reins was not Helios. 'Oh, I hate student drivers. Hey, Ganymede! Get in here!'

The king's cup-bearer poked his head around the corner. 'Yeah, boss?'

'Bring me one of my lightning bolts. They're over by the end table in the hallway, next to my keys.'

'What size lightning bolt?'

'Bring me a number ten.'

Ganymede's eyes widened. Zeus hardly ever busted out the number tens. They were for special occasions, like weddings and Armageddon. A minute later, Ganymede came back, lugging a Celestial bronze cylinder the size of a booster rocket.

Zeus hefted it and took careful aim. He would need to hit the driver without destroying the chariot. He wasn't sure what would happen if he blew up the sun, but he doubted it would be good. Still . . . that chariot was out of control. It was destroying his temples and some of his favourite statues of himself. Drastic measures were called for.

Phaethon's last thought as he was blasted out of the sky? *AHHHHHHHHHH!*

Though maybe, just a little, he was also thinking: *Thank the gods.*

At the end, he knew his joyride had to stop. He was endangering his family and the entire human race. He was scared out of his mind. No roller coaster can go on forever, even a super-terrifying adrenalin rush of fiery doom.

A bright flash and it was all over for Phaethon. Zeus knocked the kid clean out of the chariot. His body fell to earth as a fiery comet.

Without their annoying driver, the horses dragged the sun chariot back to their stables. Blaze, Dawn, Fire and Flame figured they would be rewarded for a good day's work with fiery carrots and molten oats.

After the Day of the Loopy Sun, life was never the same.

The gods held an emergency council to review safety

regulations for drivers. Helios mourned his son. His heart turned bitter. Rather than blaming himself for letting Phaethon drive, he blamed Zeus for killing the boy. Funny how gods (and people) do that sometimes.

'I will never drive the sun again!' Helios declared. 'Let someone else take over this stupid job!'

Maybe that's when people started thinking of Apollo as the sun god, because Helios quit without unemployment benefits or a severance package or anything. Or maybe the gods pleaded and threatened and Helios kept his job for a while longer. Either way, Helios never again let one of his kids borrow the chariot or mess with his CD collection.

As for Phaethon's burning body, his poor mother and seven sisters watched it fall past the northern horizon.

Clymene knew her son was dead. No one survives Zeus's lightning. But the seven Heliades decided they couldn't rest until they found their brother's body.

For months they travelled until they arrived in the wilds of northern Italy. There, near the swampy mouth of the Po River, they found their brother's final resting place.

Zeus's lightning had somehow turned the demigod into a never-ending fuel source. His body smouldered and smoked but never disintegrated. He had plunged into a small lake and become lodged at the bottom. There he lay, boiling eternally, heating the lake and generating bubbles of noxious gas that popped on the surface and made the whole area poisonous. Even birds that flew over the lake would drop dead.

The seven Heliades stood at the shore and wept. There was no way they could retrieve Phaethon's body, but they refused to leave. They wouldn't eat or drink. Finally Zeus took pity on them. Even though Phaethon had been kind of an idiot, the king of the gods appreciated the sisters' loyalty to their brother.

'You will stay with him forever,' Zeus decided. 'You will stand as a reminder of what happened on the Day of the Loopy Sun.'

The sisters changed shape. Their clothes hardened into tree bark. Their toes elongated, turning into roots. Their hair stretched out, reaching skyward to become branches and leaves. Their tears became golden sap, which hardened into amber.

That's why the Greeks called amber 'the stone of light' – because it was formed from the tears of the daughters of the sun.

Today, nobody knows exactly where that lake is. Maybe it sank into the sea or the marshes. But back in the day, maybe a hundred years after the Loopy Sun incident, another hero named Jason sailed up the River Po on his ship, the *Argo*. During the night, he heard the trees weeping – a ghostly wail that drove his crew insane with fear. The fumes from the lake were as poisonous as ever. An eerie golden light glowed at the bottom of the lake, where the body of Phaethon still smouldered. But we'll talk more about Jason later.

Anyway, now you know why Phaethon never got his driver's licence.

Moral of the story? *Destroying the earth will get you pulled over real fast.*

Or maybe: *Don't make stupid promises to your kid.*

Or maybe: *If your mom seems overprotective, it's possible she knows you better than you think.* (I had to put that in there. My mom is nodding and muttering, 'Thank you.')

So that's Phaethon. A nice unhappy ending with tons of death.

Feel better?

Good.

Because we're not done yet. The male heroes didn't have a monopoly on carnage and destruction. Let's go out to Amazon country and meet a sweetheart of a killer named Otrera.

OTRERA INVENTS THE AMAZONS (WITH FREE TWO-DAY SHIPPING!)

E DON'T KNOW MUCH ABOUT OTRERA FROM the old stories.

Those Ancient Greek dudes didn't care where Otrera came from or what made her tick.

Why would that be?

1) She was a woman.

2) She was a scary woman.

3) She was a scary woman who killed Ancient Greek dudes.

Originally she lived in the northern lands around the Black Sea – the same general area that would later produce great humanitarians like Attila the Hun. Who were Otrera's people? We don't know. That's probably because she killed them all. We just know that at some point she decided her life as a Bronze Age housewife sucked. She decided to do something about it.

Maybe you're wondering: what would make an average lady go crazy, kill all the men of her tribe and found a nation of homicidal women?

Did I mention that being a Bronze Age housewife sucked?

If you were a woman back then, this was your best-case scenario: you might be born in Sparta. Any time Sparta is your best-case scenario, you are truly stranded up Poop Creek without a paddle. At least in Sparta women could own property. They were respected as the mothers of warriors. Young girls could serve as acolytes in the temple of Artemis and, to please the goddess, help whip the male human sacrifices so their blood stained the altar. (For more details, see: *Spartans: Complete Freakazoids.*)

If you were born female in Athens, the cradle of democracy, you were almost as badly treated as a slave (and yeah, they had slaves). You couldn't own property. You couldn't vote in the assembly. You couldn't run a business. You weren't even supposed to go to the agora – the community market and outdoor mall – though a lot of women did anyway, because, you know, the lemon chicken at the food court was pretty tasty.

Basically, women couldn't do anything except stay home, cook food, clean the house and look pretty – preferably all at the same time. Now, me – being an awesome modern demigod dude – I can do all that easily. But not everybody can pull it off.

(My girlfriend, Annabeth, is reading this over my shoulder and laughing. *Why are you laughing?*)

Athenian women couldn't even choose who they married. That was true for most women back then. When you were a child, your parents were your guardians (read: your *dad* was your guardian, because your mom was just there to teach you how to clean and cook and look pretty). Your father made all your decisions for you.

Oh, you don't like his decisions? Well, your options are getting beaten, killed or sold into slavery. Take your time choosing.

Once you were old enough to marry – and by that I mean like twelve or thirteen – your dad would pick your husband for you. The lucky guy might be older. He might be ugly. He might be fat. But don't worry! Your dad would make sure your husband had the proper social standing so it would reflect well on your dad's reputation. Your dad would pay your husband a dowry – a price for taking you. In exchange, your husband would be your dad's ally in his political and business dealings. So, while you're sitting at home, cooking and looking pretty for your old, ugly, fat husband, you can take comfort in knowing it was the best match for your father's interests.

As a married woman, your husband became your guardian. He made all the decisions for you, just like your dad used to do.

Oh, you don't like his decisions? See your options for punishment above.

Starting to feel like a homicidal woman yet?

Then maybe you can understand what motivated Otrera. Because the stuff I just described for Athens and Sparta? In the northern lands, where Otrera was born, life was harsher and conditions for women were ten times worse.

When Otrera snapped, she snapped in a *big* way.

Ever since she was a kid, Otrera's favourite gods were Artemis and Ares. Artemis was the protector of young maidens, so that makes sense. Artemis didn't need no stinking man to take care of her, which appealed to Otrera. If her people were anything like the Spartans, I bet when Otrera was young she served as a junior priestess for Artemis. I can totally see her whipping human-sacrifice guys until they bled all over the altar.

Hey, she would've thought, this whipping men and making them bleed? This is fun!

Otrera didn't want to become a full-time follower of Artemis, though. That would've meant swearing off men forever. Nuh-uh. Otrera *liked* guys — when they weren't ordering her around. Later she would have plenty of boyfriends. She even gave birth to a couple of daughters. More on that in a sec . . .

Her other favourite god was Ares, the war dude. A god like Ares made sense to Otrera. She lived in a harsh country. Life was brutal. You want something, you kill for it. You get angry, you punch someone in the face. Simple. Direct. Bloody. Fun!

Like most places back then, Otrera's town was controlled by men. Women had no rights. They definitely weren't allowed to fight, but at some point Otrera got frustrated being her husband's laundress/cook/floor scrubber/eye candy. She decided to teach herself self-defence just in case . . . well, in case she needed it some day.

At night she sneaked off into the woods with her husband's sword and bow. She taught herself to spar by hacking at trees, imitating the moves she'd seen the young male soldiers use. She taught herself to shoot until she could take down a wild animal in the dark at two hundred yards. Once Otrera felt confident in her abilities, she sought out other townswomen who were just as frustrated as she was. They were tired of their old, smelly, fat husbands telling them what to do, beating them or killing them or selling them into slavery if they complained.

Otrera secretly began teaching her friends how to fight. In the woods at night, they learned the hunting skills of Artemis, but they also prayed to Ares for strength and courage in battle. Worshipping both gods together was an unusual mix, like, *Artemis tells us men are stupid brutes. Therefore, let us worship Ares, the stupidest manly brute of all.* But the combo was effective. Otrera and her followers soon became vicious and fearless.

For a while, they pretended everything was normal at home. Then one day something happened that made Otrera go nuclear. I don't know what. Maybe her husband ordered her to get him a beer from the fridge one too many times. Maybe he yelled at her for not being pretty enough while she was scrubbing the floor.

Otrera calmly retrieved her husband's sword from the closet. She hid the blade behind her skirts and walked over to where her husband was sitting.

'I want a divorce,' she said.

Her husband belched. 'You can't have a divorce. I make all the decisions for you. You belong to me. Also, nobody has invented divorce yet!'

'I just did.' Otrera whipped out the sword and cut off her husband's head. He never asked her for another beer, but he did get blood all over the floor that Otrera had just finished mopping. She hated it when that happened.

Her sword in hand, Otrera stepped outside her hut. She made a cawing sound like a raven – the sacred bird of Ares. Her followers heard the signal. They retrieved their swords and daggers and meat cleavers, and being a man suddenly became the most dangerous occupation in town.

Most of the males were either killed or put in chains. A few lucky ones escaped. They ran to the nearest town and explained what had happened.

You can imagine how that conversation went:

'My wife pulled a sword on me!'

'And you *ran away?*'

'She was crazy! The ladies killed everyone!'

'Your housewives killed all your best warriors? What kind of men are you? We'll go teach them a lesson!'

The guys from the neighbouring town marched to Otrera's village, but they didn't take the expedition very seriously. After all, they were going to fight *women*. They figured they'd walk in, administer a few spankings, have a few beers, then take the prettiest women as slaves and go home.

It didn't work out that way. Otrera had set tripwires and snares along the road. She'd built a barricade at the gates, fully manned (or womanned) by her best archers and sword fighters. The guys showed up. Otrera's followers slaughtered them.

Otrera marched to the neighbouring town. She liberated the women, recruiting those who wanted to join her and letting the rest go free. The remaining men she killed or enslaved. A few terrified survivors fled to nearby villages, spreading the word about the crazy woman Otrera and her band of merry murderesses.

The next town's men tried to stop her. Her warriors slaughtered them. Rinse and repeat. Soon Otrera found herself in control of a dozen towns, with a fledgling army of vicious women ready to follow her to glory. They were highly motivated to fight, because if they ever lost their male enemies would have no mercy. The women wouldn't be treated as prisoners of war. They'd be beaten, sold as slaves and *then* killed. The whole trifecta!

Otrera was still learning how to organize her troops when the menfolk of the neighbouring cities started to take her seriously. The men mustered an actual, no-nonsense army – thousands of hardened veterans with real weapons and no illusions about beer and spankings.

Otrera's scouts warned her what was up.

'We need more time,' Otrera said. 'We haven't trained our women properly. Besides, this country is harsh and barren and it really sucks. It's not worth defending. Let's migrate to a richer land and carve out our own queendom!'

That sounded a lot better to her followers than an all-out war they might not win. The entire tribe of warrior women, along with their slaves and captured loot, their children and their barnyard animals and their favourite knick-knacks, migrated to the other side of the Black Sea, to the northern coast of what is now Turkey. Glory awaited them! Also, a whole lot of blood and some flesh-eating birds . . .

Otrera founded a new capital city called Sinope near the Thermodon River. She trained her armies and gathered recruits, gradually expanding her territory and discovering where all the best restaurants were.

She'd set up her kingdom in a good spot – northeast of the Greeks, northwest of the Persians, in what was a no-man's-land. (Get it? No men?) Whenever she conquered a new town, she was careful to leave no male survivors. That way, word was slow getting out. By the time her neighbours figured out she was a threat, it was too late. The new nation was firmly entrenched.

They raised their terrible banner — a stick-figure guy with a big X through him. They became known and feared across the world as the Amazons.

Why were they called Amazons? Nobody's sure.

It doesn't have anything to do with the Amazon River down in Brazil. (Man, that confused me for years before Annabeth set me straight. I had this image of women warriors hanging out in the rainforest with parrots and monkeys and piranhas.) The ancient Amazons also have nothing to do with any modern company that might have the name Amazon, nor is that company a secret front for their plans for world domination. (*Cough.* Yeah, right. *Cough.*)

Some Greeks thought the name Amazon came from the word *amazos*, which means *without a breast*. They somehow got the idea (SERIOUS GROSS-OUT ALERT) that Amazon women removed their own right breasts so they could shoot a bow and throw a spear better.

Okay, first of all, no. Just no. That's not only gross; it's dumb. Why would the Amazons do that? I mean, yeah, they were serious battle-hardened killers, but you can shoot a bow or throw a spear just fine without . . . you know.

Also, if you look at any ancient statue or picture of the Amazons, there's no evidence that the Amazons were, um, lopsided.

Finally, I have met Amazons myself. They are not into hurting themselves unnecessarily. Other people? Sure! But not themselves.

A few Greek writers realized this was a bonehead theory. One dude, Herodotus, called Otrera's people the *androktones* instead, which means *man-killers*. Homer called them the *antianeirai*, meaning *those who fight like men*. Both of those terms are a lot more accurate than *those who did a big owie so they could shoot a bow better*.

Me, I like the theory that *Amazon* comes from the Persian term *ha-mazan*, which means *warriors*. I like that theory because Annabeth likes that theory, and if I don't like what she likes she gets all *ha-mazan* on me.

Anyway, the Amazons had arrived, loud and proud. They got stronger and more numerous as they raised their next generation of girls to think and act like warriors.

You're wondering: wait, it was a nation of all women. How did they have a next generation? Where did all the cute little Amazon killer babies come from?

Well, the Amazons had male slaves. I mentioned that, right? Some of those guys became the first househusbands, and they had just as many rights and privileges as women did in other countries, meaning none. Real nice.

Also, the Amazons had this weird arrangement with a neighbouring tribe called the Gargareans. The Gargareans lived on the opposite side of this huge mountain northeast of Amazon country. They were an all-male tribe, which I don't get. Seriously, a tribe made entirely of dudes? You *know* the laundry never got done, the living room was a disaster zone and the leftovers in the fridge smelled worse than Phaethon lake gas.

You'd think an all-male tribe would be the Amazons' worst enemy, but apparently not. Ever heard the old saying *Good fences make good neighbours?* Me neither. According to Annabeth it means something like *Don't touch my stuff and we'll get along fine.* In the case of the Gargareans and the Amazons, a big mountain made an *excellent* neighbour. The two groups never bothered each other. Once a year, by mutual agreement, they had a big potluck dinner and sleepover party on the mountaintop. Amazons got chummy with Gargareans. And what do you know? About nine months later, a whole lot of Amazons had cute little killer babies.

They kept the girls and raised them to be the next generation of warriors. The boys . . . well, who needed the boys?

The Amazons sent the strongest and healthiest ones to the Gargareans to raise. If Otrera thought the baby was too sickly and weak (he's a baby; how can he *not* be weak?), she would leave the little guy in the wilderness, exposed on a rock and let nature take its course. Harsh and cruel? Yep. Life was a lot of fun back then.

Otrera led her warriors on tons of successful campaigns across Asia Minor and into Greece. They founded two famous cities on the western coast of Turkey – Smyrna and Ephesus. Why they picked those names, I don't know. I would've gone with Buttkickville and Smackdown City, but that's just me.

They fought the Greeks so many times that if you go to Athens today you'll see tons of pictures of the Greek–Amazon wars. The pictures always show the Greeks winning, but that's just wishful thinking. Truth was, the Amazons scared the Cheez Whiz out of the Greeks. Otrera's warriors enslaved men. They fought like demons. And they definitely did not cook you dinner or scrub your floor.

Pretty soon the Amazon forces were so widespread they split into different tribes. Franchise towns started popping up all over the place. The Ancient Greek writers got confused when they tried to describe where the Amazons lived: 'They're over there. No, they're over there. THEY'RE EVERYWHERE!'

Otrera was still Queen of the Whole Enchilada (I'm pretty sure that was her official title). She ruled from her capital of Sinope, and if she called for a war all the Amazon factions obeyed. You didn't want to get on Otrera's bad side. Unfortunately, when dealing with men, that was the only side she had.

Okay . . . I take that back. She did fall in love with a guy once. Their romance was uglier than any wartime massacre.

One day, Otrera had just finished a hard day's work killing the neighbours. She and her warriors were walking along the shores of the Black Sea after a battle – looting dead bodies, enslaving survivors – when a red flash illuminated the clouds.

You do nice work, a deep voice rumbled from the sky. *Meet me at the island on the horizon. We have things to discuss.*

The Amazons weren't easy to scare, but that voice freaked them out.

One of the queen's lieutenants glanced at her. 'You're not going, are you?'

Otrera gazed across the water. Sure enough, a dark splotch of land was just visible on the horizon.

'Yes,' she decided. 'A flash of red light and a strange voice over the battlefield . . . Either we are all hallucinating from last night's casserole, or that was the god Ares talking. I'd better go see what he wants.'

Otrera rowed a boat to the island alone. On the shore stood the god Ares, seven feet tall in full bronze combat armour, with a flaming spear in his hand. His cloak was the colour of blood. His boots were speckled with mud and gore (because he loved to tap-dance over the corpses of his enemies). His face was ruggedly handsome, if you like that killer-Neanderthal look. His eyes glowed with pure fiery carnage.

'Otrera, we meet at last,' he said. 'Dang, girl, you're fine.'

Otrera's knees shook. It's not every day you meet one of your favourite gods. But she didn't bow or kneel. She was done bowing to men, even Ares. Also, she figured the war god would prefer a show of strength.

'You're not bad yourself,' she said. 'I like those boots.'

'Thanks!' Ares grinned. 'I got them at the army surplus store down in Sparta. They had this sale . . . But that's not important. I want you to build me a temple here on this island. You see that big rock?'

'What rock?'

Ares raised his spear. The clouds parted. A huge meteorite came hurtling down from space and slammed into the middle of the island. When the steam cleared and the dust settled, a black slab the size of a school bus was sticking upright out of the ground.

'Oh,' Otrera said. '*That* rock.'

'That's a sacred rock.'

'Okay.'

'Praying to the rock is basically a direct line to me. Build a stone temple around it. Every year, bring your Amazons here and sacrifice some of your most important animals.'

'Those would be our horses,' Otrera said. 'We use them in battle. They give us a huge advantage.'

'Horses it is!' Ares said. 'Do that for me, and I'll keep blessing you in combat. You'll keep slaughtering people. We'll get along great. What do you say?'

'Fight me.'

Ares stared at her with his nuclear-powered eyes. 'What?'

'We both respect strength. Let's seal the deal with a smackdown.'

'Wow. I think I'm falling in love with you.'

Otrera launched herself at the god. She slugged him across the face. They fell to the ground, kicking, gouging and doing their best to pulverize each other. It was love at first punch.

After they got through fighting, they decided to get married. From that day on, Otrera was known as the bride of Ares. It did wonders for her street cred. When enemy armies saw her riding towards them, they wet their bronze war breeches.

Otrera built a temple on the island, just like Ares had asked. To protect it, Ares sent a flock of killer birds that could shoot their feathers like arrows.

Every year, Otrera held a big festival on the island, sacrificing horses and talking to the large black rock. The killer birds didn't bother the Amazons, but if anybody else tried to approach the temple the birds shot them full of feathers and tore them apart with their sharp beaks. In other words, the temple didn't get a lot of out-of-towners.

Ares and Otrera had two daughters: Hippolyta and Penthesileia. Both names quickly shot to the top of the 25 Most Popular Baby Girls' Names for 1438 B.C.E. list. From then on, Amazon queens and even the Amazons in general were known as the daughters of Ares. Some were *literally* his daughters. The rest did their best to act like they were. *Aw, look! She's got her daddy's smile and his murderous rage. How cute!*

Ares was happy. The Amazons were happy. But one important person had been left out of the Amazon Temple-Building & Deity-Appreciation Programme: Artemis, Otrera's other favourite Olympian. Being a smart leader, Otrera figured she'd better show the hunter goddess some gratitude before it started raining silver arrows.

Otrera decided to build a temple to Artemis in the city of Ephesus, on the west coast of Turkey. She figured that would make it close enough for the Greeks to visit, since their islands were right across the Aegean Sea.

She didn't use arrow-shooting birds this time. Those tended to reduce tourist dollars. Instead, Otrera built the temple on a high hill so it could be seen from all over. She made it as beautiful as possible, with walls of aromatic cedar, floors of polished marble and ceilings inlaid with gold. In the centre of the sanctuary, a statue of Artemis was clad in a dress of amber teardrop ornaments so she glowed when light streamed through the windows.

Every year, Otrera hosted a big festival at the temple. The Amazons spent all day partying, doing ferocious war dances through the streets of Ephesus. They sacrificed jewellery to Artemis by draping it over the statue, so by the end of the festival Artemis looked like a hip-hop fashion model who'd been shopping at King Midas's Discount Gold Warehouse.

The temple was a hit – Otrera's greatest legacy. It outlasted her. It outlasted the Ancient Greeks. Heck, it almost outlasted the Roman Empire. It was destroyed a couple of times, but the Ephesians always rebuilt it. It was still around in Christian times when a dude named John went there to convert the locals.

The place was so famous it made the list of Seven Wonders of the Ancient World . . . along with the Egyptian pyramids and, um, those other ones. The first McDonald's? I forget.

The temple paid off for Otrera in more ways than tourist dollars. One time, it saved her and her entire army from death by grapes.

How it happened: this new wine god, Dionysus, was rolling through the mortal world with his band of followers, teaching everybody the wonders of partying, drunken savagery and a good Cabernet with dinner. If your kingdom welcomed Dionysus, great! If you tried to fight him, oops!

He was on his way to invade India, because that seemed like a good idea at the time, when he happened through the land of the Amazons.

When he met the first Amazon scouting party, he was delighted.

'Oh, hey!' he said. 'A nation of women? I can work with that. How about you girls party with us tonight?'

The Amazon scouts said, 'Sure, why not?'

They decided they liked wine. They joined Dionysus's group of super fangirls known as the maenads. Those ladies were mostly nymphs turned into wild party-hearty assassins who would rip the wine god's enemies to pieces with their bare hands. So imagine what would happen if the *Amazons* became maenads. Yeah, kinda like *The Texas Chainsaw Massacre* with no need for chainsaws.

Later, other groups of Amazons tried to stop Dionysus.

They weren't going to follow any *man*, especially since his army included a bunch of satyrs and drunken dudes who smelled like cheap Chardonnay.

The Amazons attacked. Dionysus used his godly powers to drive them insane and turn them into grapevines, and then stomped them to make more wine.

Otrera heard about these early defeats: some guy claiming to be a god, tromping through her kingdom and stealing her followers or turning them into deciduous fruiting berries. She decided to solve the problem in her usual diplomatic way.

'Kill them all!' she roared.

She summoned her entire army, which was a pretty impressive sight. Thousands of spears and shields glinted in the sun. Rows of mounted archers – the best cavalry in the world – prepared their flaming arrows.

The Amazons could destroy most enemies in a matter of minutes. Their reputation was so terrifying that other kingdoms would hire them as mercenaries to fight their wars. Usually, the other side would give up as soon as they saw the Amazons coming.

Over the years, Otrera had grown rich and powerful and confident. She figured she could wipe out a drunken mob, no problem.

Her fatal flaw? I'm thinking it was pride.

She forgot what had happened to those village guys who tried to smack her down in the old days. *Never* underestimate your enemy.

Dionysus was a god. It didn't matter how chummy Otrera was with Ares and Artemis; they couldn't help her against a fellow Olympian. The Amazons charged into battle and got thrashed. The maenads tore them apart with their bare hands. Satyrs whaled on them with clubs and old wine bottles. Every time Dionysus snapped his fingers, another battalion of Amazons went insane, turned into wombats or got choked to death in a thicket of grapevines.

Otrera quickly realized she was outmatched. She pulled her forces just before they were all destroyed. Then the Amazons fled for their lives.

Dionysus and his drunken army chased them halfway down the coast of Turkey. Finally, Otrera reached Ephesus and ran to the temple of Artemis. She threw herself in front of the goddess's statue.

'Please, Lady Artemis!' she begged. 'Save my people! Don't let them be destroyed because of my foolishness!'

Artemis heard her and intervened. Or maybe Dionysus just got bored and decided to go kill somebody else. The wine god's army turned away and marched off to India, leaving Ephesus alone. The Amazons were saved. Eventually, they rebuilt their army and managed to get all the squished grapes out from between their toes.

From then on, the temple of Artemis got a reputation as a refuge for women. Any woman who reached the altar and begged for protection would be shielded by the power of Artemis. No one could harm her. The priestesses of the temple and the entire town of Ephesus would fight for her if necessary.

After that, things settled down for Otrera. She retired to her capital at Sinope and ruled more or less in peace. She made alliances with her neighbours and brought safety and security to her people.

The only thing she couldn't protect Amazons from? Other Amazons. Like what happened with her two wonderful, bloodthirsty daughters . . .

As I said earlier, the great Ares–Otrera kickboxing marriage led to the birth of two daughters. Because of their parentage, they were both cute, sweet girls who liked glitter and ponies and frilly pink stuff.

Yeah, not so much . . .

Nobody knows exactly when Queen Otrera decided to retire, but after a while all the battles and enslavements and wild dance parties got tiring. She handed control of the Amazons over to her elder daughter, Hippolyta.

At first, Hippolyta did a good job. Her dad, Ares, was so pleased he gave her a magical suit of armour to wear for special events like bat mitzvahs and siege warfare. He also gave her a magical belt that made Hippolyta super strong.

Unfortunately, Hippolyta had the bad luck of meeting a guy named Hercules. More on that in a bit. For now, let's just say there was a big fight and the Amazons suffered their worst defeat since the invasion of the Wine Dude.

In the confusion of battle, Hippolyta was accidentally killed by her own sister, Penthesileia. The belt of the Amazons was lost (at least for a while). The Greeks got away. Penthesileia became the queen and, after mourning her sister's death, she rebuilt the Amazon army yet again.

Even though it was an accident, Penthesileia never forgave

herself for Hippolyta's death. She also never forgave the Greeks. Many years later, when the Trojan War broke out, she signed up to help Priam, the king of Troy, so she could crack Greek skulls and avenge her sister's death.

That didn't work out so well. Penthesileia fought bravely and slaughtered a bunch of great warriors, but eventually she got killed by the most famous Greek fighter of all – Achilles. When Achilles retrieved her body from the battlefield, he washed her wounds so she could have a proper funeral. He took off her war helmet, saw how beautiful the Amazon queen was and felt super depressed. It seemed like a waste that such a brave and extremely hot lady should die.

Achilles waited for the next big truce, when Trojans and Greeks got together to exchange bodies for burial. Those meetings must have been fun. *I'll trade you George here for Johnny and Billy Joe. Oh, wait. I think this leg belongs to Billy Joe. I'm not sure.*

Achilles presented the body of Penthesileia to the Trojans. He praised her bravery and beauty so much that one of his Greek comrades, a guy named Thersites, got annoyed.

A bunch of Thersites's friends had been killed by Penthesileia. He turned to Achilles and said, 'Dude, why are you praising her? She's an enemy and she's a *woman*. Are you in love with that dead girl?' (He called her something worse than a *girl*.)

Achilles gently set Penthesileia down. He turned to his comrade and backhanded Thersites so hard all his teeth flew out like tiny white salmon leaping from a red stream. Thersites fell down dead.

Achilles faced the Trojans. 'Please bury Penthesileia with honour.'

The Trojans, not wishing to get killed by major dental trauma, did what he asked.

I don't know if Otrera was still alive when her daughters died. For her sake, I kind of hope not. Even for a battle-hardened lady like Otrera, that would've been tough to deal with.

Otrera and her daughters became legends, though — some of the greatest women warriors of all time.

Maybe you're wondering why I included Otrera in this book, since it's about Greek heroes and technically she wasn't Greek. Maybe you're wondering whether she was really even a hero.

I'll admit she had her flaws: the occasional murder, a massacre here and there. She also liked Ares, which is just gross.

I have to get over my *own* prejudice, too. I had a run-in with Otrera once when she came back from the dead and tried to kill me. (Long story. Don't ask.)

But here's the thing. Women don't get a fair shake in the old stories. Even Otrera, the most famous, successful and powerful woman of the ancient world, hardly gets a mention.

I have to admire her guts. She went from being a downtrodden Bronze Age housewife to the queen of an empire. The Amazons became so famous we named a river in Brazil after them, along with that modern company that has absolutely no connection to the ancient Amazon nation. (*Cough*, ahem.)

To all the women she saved and trained for battle, Otrera was definitely a hero. She gave them hope. She gave them control over their own lives. Me, I would've gone a little easier on the whole beheading-husbands thing and I wouldn't have left baby boys in the wilderness to die, but she was a harsh lady living in harsh times.

So, yeah, I think she belongs in a book of Greek heroes.

If she gives you nightmares, the way she did those old Greek writers, well . . . just remember, the Amazons aren't around any more. They faded out of history thousands of years ago. (Wink, wink.) There isn't much chance they'll come after you. Like, a twenty percent chance at best. Maybe thirty percent . . .

While we're talking about dead people I've encountered, I guess I'd better tackle another difficult subject.

I gotta take a deep breath. This guy brings up some painful memories.

Okay. I can do this. Let's talk about Daedalus, the greatest inventor of all time.

DAEDALUS INVENTS
PRETTY MUCH
EVERYTHING ELSE

I HAVE TROUBLE WRITING ABOUT THIS GUY.

First off, my own experience with him doesn't jibe with the old stories. Of course, I wasn't there in Ancient Greece. Some of the stuff I know personally comes from dreams, which aren't always reliable. I'll do my best to tell you what Daedalus was like back in the day, but if that seems to contradict what you've read in my adventures that's because it does!

Secondly, I have a hard time getting into this guy's head because – and I know this will come as a shock to you – I have never been a genius.

Gasp! Percy, we thought you had an IQ of a billion!

Yeah, sorry to burst your bubble. Understanding a super-Einstein type like Daedalus isn't easy for me. I have enough trouble comprehending my girlfriend, and she's no slouch in the brainiac department.

Finally, well . . . Daedalus's life was just *so weird*.

I guess that's no surprise. The dude was descended from a handkerchief.

Maybe we should start with that. See, his great-grandfather Erikthonius was magically born from a rag Athena used to wipe Hephaestus's godly body fluid off her leg when Hephaestus tried to get too friendly. (For more info, see: *The Olympians: Completely Disgusting Stories*. Or, you know, that *Greek Gods* book I wrote.)

Since you can't have a better royal title than King Handkerchief, Erikthonius grew up to be the king of Athens. His offspring were demigod descendants of Athena and Hephaestus – the two most ingenious Olympians.

Daedalus himself was never in line to be king, but he made his Olympian great-great-grandparents proud. He quickly got a reputation for being able to build or repair just about anything.

Having trouble with your chariot's suspension? Daedalus can fix that.

Did your hard drive crash? Call 1-800-555-DAEDALUS.

You want to build a mansion with a revolving roof deck, an infinity pool and a state-of-the-art security system featuring boiling oil and mechanical crossbows? Piece of cake for the D-Man.

Soon Daedalus was the most famous man in Athens. His repair shop had a five-year waiting list for new clients. He designed and built all the best houses and temples and shopping centres. He sculpted statues so lifelike they would walk off their pedestals, blend in with the humans and become productive members of society.

Daedalus invented so many new technologies; every autumn the media went crazy when he presented his latest version of the Daedalus Chisel™, the Daedalus Wax Tablet™ and of course the Daedalus Spear™ with BronzeTip technology (patent pending).

The guy was a straight-up genius. But being a genius is hard work.

'I'm simply *too* popular,' Daedalus said to himself. 'I'm so busy fixing hard drives and inventing spectacular things I don't have any *me* time. I should train an apprentice to do some of the grunt work for me!'

It so happened that his sister had a son named Perdix. With a name like that, you know he must've got teased pretty bad on the playground, but this kid was *smart*. He had Athena's intelligence and Hephaestus's crafting skill. He was a real chip off the old hankie.

Anyway, Daedalus hired his nephew. At first Daedalus was delighted. Perdix could handle the most complicated repairs. He could look at a blueprint once and have it memorized. He even thought up some modifications for the Daedalus Spear™ 2.0, like the no-slip shaft and the customizable point that came in Sharp, Extra Sharp and Super Sharp. He was happy to give Daedalus the credit. Still, people started whispering, 'That young kid, Perdix – he's almost as smart as his uncle!'

A few months later, Perdix invented a contraption called the pottery wheel. Instead of making your pots by hand, which took forever and resulted in stupid lumpy pots, you could fashion clay on a whirling surface and make nice-looking bowls in just minutes.

People started saying, 'That kid, Perdix – he's even smarter than Daedalus!'

Clients began asking for Perdix by name. They wanted *him* to design their mansion's infinity pool. They wanted *him* to retrieve the data from their crashed hard drives. Glory and fame started slipping away from Daedalus.

One day Daedalus was at the top of the Acropolis – the huge clifftop fortress in the centre of Athens – checking the site of a new temple he had designed, when Perdix ran up with a big leather pouch slung over his shoulder.

'Uncle!' Perdix grinned. 'You have to see my new invention!'

Daedalus clenched his fists. At next week's press conference, he was set to announce the Daedalus Hammer™ and revolutionize the pounding of nails. He didn't need his upstart nephew stealing the spotlight with some annoyingly cool breakthrough.

'What is it now, Perdix?' he asked. 'Please tell me this isn't more nonsense about bigger displays for my wax tablets.'

'No, Uncle. Look!' From his leather pouch, Perdix pulled the jawbone of a small animal, with a row of sharp teeth still intact. 'It's from a snake!'

Daedalus scowled. 'That isn't an invention.'

'No, Uncle! I was playing around with it, running the teeth across a piece of wood, and I noticed they cut the surface. So I made this!'

Perdix took out a wide metal blade fixed to a wooden handle. One side of the blade was serrated like a row of teeth. 'I call it a *saw!*'

Daedalus felt like he'd been smacked between the eyes with a Daedalus Hammer™. He immediately realized the potential of Perdix's invention. Cutting boards with a saw instead of an axe would be easier, faster and more accurate. It would change the lumber industry forever! And, seriously, who *hasn't* dreamed of fame and riches in the lumber industry?

If the saw ever became a thing, Perdix would become famous. Daedalus would be forgotten. Daedalus couldn't allow this young whippersnapper to eclipse his reputation.

'Not bad.' Daedalus forced a smile. 'We'll run some tests when we get back to the workshop. First, I want your opinion on this section of the cliff. I'm afraid it's not stable enough to support my new temple.'

'Sure, Uncle!' Perdix trotted over to the edge of the parapets. 'Where?'

'About halfway down. Just lean over a bit and you'll see it. Here, let me hold your saw.'

'Okay.'

'Thanks.'

Perdix leaned over. 'I don't see —'

Daedalus pushed the boy off the Acropolis.

The exact details of how it happened . . . well, that depends on which story you believe.

Some say Perdix didn't actually die. As the kid fell, Athena took pity on him and turned him into a partridge. That's why *perdix* means *partridge* in Ancient Greek. Definitely the goddess didn't appreciate Daedalus murdering his nephew just because the boy had skills. Athena was all about cultivating new talent. And pushing smart kids off cliffs would lower the city's test-score averages. From there on out, she made sure Daedalus's life was cursed. No more big press conferences. No more media frenzy.

But, if Athena *did* grant Perdix new life as a bird, how do you explain the big mess where the kid hit the bottom of Acropolis Hill?

Daedalus saw it happen. He should have just walked away and feigned ignorance. *What? Perdix fell? You're kidding! That kid always was kind of clumsy.*

Guilt got the better of him.

He climbed down the cliff and wept over Perdix's body. He wrapped the remains in a tarp and dragged his poor nephew to the edge of town. He tried to dig a grave, but the ground was too rocky. I guess he hadn't invented the Daedalus Shovel yet.

A few locals spotted him. Before Daedalus could get away, a crowd gathered.

'What are you burying?' asked one guy.

Daedalus was sweating like a marathon runner. 'Oh, uh . . . it's a snake.'

The guy looked at the big wrapped-up lump. He nudged it with his foot and Perdix's right hand flopped out.

'I'm pretty sure snakes don't have hands,' the guy said.

Daedalus broke down in tears and confessed what he'd done.

The crowd almost lynched him right then and there. You can't blame them for being angry. Half of them had appointments with Perdix to fix their chariots the next week.

The crowd constrained themselves. They made a citizen's arrest and hauled Daedalus before the city judges.

His trial was the lead story on the Athenian News Network for weeks. His sister, Perdix's mom, argued for the death penalty. The thing was, Daedalus had done a lot of favours for wealthy citizens over the years. He'd built important buildings and patented many helpful inventions. The judges commuted his death sentence to permanent exile.

Daedalus left Athens forever. Everyone figured he'd go off and die in a cave somewhere.

But nope. For the murder he'd committed, Athena meant for Daedalus to live a long and tortured life. The inventor's punishment was just beginning.

Daedalus moved to the island of Crete, which happened to be Athens's biggest rival at the time. King Minos of Crete had the most powerful navy in the Mediterranean. He was always harassing Athenian ships and disrupting their trade.

You can imagine how the Athenians felt when they learned that their top inventor and hard-drive repairman was now working for King Minos. It'd be kind of like if all of America's best products were suddenly made in China.

Oh, wait . . .

Anyway, Daedalus arrived at Minos's palace for his job interview, and Minos was like, 'Why did you leave your previous position?'

'I was convicted of murder,' Daedalus said. 'I pushed my nephew off the Acropolis.'

Minos stroked his beard. 'So . . . it wasn't about the quality of your work?'

'No. I am as clever and skillful as ever. I just murdered someone.'

'Well, then, I see no problem,' Minos said. 'You're hired!'

Minos gave him tons of money. He set Daedalus up in a cutting-edge workshop in the capital city of Knossos. Soon

Daedalus's reputation was back, bigger and better than ever. He cranked out dozens of new inventions and built all the best temples and mansions in the kingdom.

He lived happily ever after for about six minutes.

The problem was, King Minos had daddy issues. He was the son of Zeus, which sounds like a good thing, but it didn't help him much as the king of Crete.

Long story short: the relationship between Zeus and Minos's mom, Europa, had started in a weird way. Zeus turned into a bull, coaxed Europa onto his back and swam away with her, carrying her across the sea to Crete. Zeus and Europa spent enough time together to have three kids. Minos was the oldest. But eventually Zeus got tired of his mortal girlfriend, the way gods always do, and he went back to Mount Olympus.

Europa married the king of Crete, a dude named Asterion. That worked out okay for a while. Asterion really loved Europa. They never had any kids of their own, so the king adopted the three little Zeus Juniors.

When Asterion died, Minos became the king. A lot of the locals grumbled about that. Minos was adopted. His real dad was supposedly Zeus, but they'd heard the same claim from plenty of others before. Every time some unwed girl in the city got pregnant, she was like, 'Oh, um, yeah. It was totally Zeus!' Minos's mom wasn't even from Crete. She'd illegally immigrated on a bull. Why should Minos be king?

Minos took this personally. He released his birth certificate showing he'd been born on Crete and everything, but the people didn't care.

He married a local princess, Pasiphaë, who was the daughter of the sun god Helios. Together, they had a whole mess of kids, including a smart, beautiful daughter named Ariadne. You would figure that having a son of Zeus for your king and a daughter of Helios for your queen would be good enough, but noooooo. Not for the Cretans. They were still like, *Minos is a foreigner. His dad was a bull. I think Minos is secretly working for the cattle!*

Minos decided he needed to do a better job of marketing his brand. People wanted to talk about his parentage? Okay! He was the son of Zeus and proud of it! Minos adopted the bull as his royal symbol. He had bulls painted on his banners. He had Daedalus design a giant mosaic bull for the throne-room floor and engrave golden bull heads on his throne's armrests. He got bull-patterned silverware, bull topiaries for the garden, even bull-patterned boxer shorts and fuzzy slippers shaped like cute little bull faces. Everybody who came to the palace on Wednesdays got a free bull bobblehead as a door prize.

Somehow the slippers and bobbleheads didn't convince his subjects of Minos's divine right to be king. They kept grumbling and not paying their taxes and whatnot.

Finally Minos decided he needed a big demonstration of his royal cred – something that would wow the Cretans and settle the matter once and for all. He called in Daedalus, since the inventor was the smartest guy in the kingdom.

'I recommend special effects,' Daedalus said. 'Flash powder. Smoke bombs. I could build a huge talking robot to carry you around town and announce to everyone how awesome you are.'

Minos frowned. 'No. I need a sign from the gods.'

'I can fake that!' Daedalus said. 'We'll use mirrors, maybe some guys flying around on invisible wires.'

'No!' Minos snapped. 'It must not be faked. It must be real.'

Daedalus scratched his head. 'You mean like . . . actually praying to the gods, in public, and hoping they send you a sign? I dunno, boss. Sounds risky.'

The king was adamant. He had a big platform constructed down by the docks. He called together the entire city population, then raised his arms to the crowd and shouted, 'Some of you doubt that I am your rightful king! I will prove that the gods support me! I will ask them to give me a sign!'

In the audience, somebody made a raspberry sound. 'That's no proof! You'll just ask your *daddy* for a favour.'

Minos blushed. 'No!' Actually, he had been planning to ask Zeus for a bolt of lightning, but now that plan was ruined.

'I will, um, pray to a totally different god!' He gazed out at the harbour and got an idea. 'Crete has the world's greatest navy, right? I will ask Poseidon, lord of the seas, to grant me his blessing!'

Please, Poseidon, Minos prayed silently. *I know we haven't talked much, but help me out here. I'll pay you back. Maybe you could make an animal miraculously pop out of the sea. I promise, as soon as this show is over, whatever animal you send, I will sacrifice it to you.*

Down at the bottom of the sea, Poseidon heard his prayer. He didn't really care about Minos one way or the other, but he liked sacrifices. He also liked people praying to him, and he never passed up an opportunity to look awesome in front of a major naval power.

'Hmm,' Poseidon said to himself. 'Minos wants an animal.

He likes bulls. I like bulls being sacrificed to me. Hey, I know! I'll send him a bull!'

The harbour churned with froth. Boats pitched at their moorings. A forty-foot wave rose up from nowhere, and riding the crest was a massive white bull. He landed on the docks, all cool and regal-looking, his head held high, his white horns gleaming.

'Ooohh! Ahhhhhh!' said the crowd, because it wasn't every day a bull surfed a gnarly peak into the harbour.

The Cretans turned to Minos and started cheering. The king bowed and thanked them and sent everybody home with commemorative bull-shaped coffee mugs.

The king's men put a rope around the bull's neck and led him to the royal bull pen. Later that evening, Minos and Daedalus went to inspect the animal, which was even more magnificent up close – at least twice as big and strong as any other bull in the royal herd.

'Wow,' Minos said. 'That's some bull! I think I'll keep him for breeding.'

Daedalus chewed his thumbnail. 'Um, are you sure, Your Majesty? If you promised to sacrifice the bull to Poseidon . . . well, keeping him wouldn't be the right thing to do, would it?'

The king snorted. 'You pushed your own nephew off the Acropolis. What do you know about right and wrong?'

Daedalus got a really bad feeling in his gut. Special effects he could control. The Olympian gods . . . well, even *he* hadn't invented a good machine for predicting how they would react. He tried to convince the king to sacrifice the white bull, but Minos wouldn't listen.

'You worry too much,' the king told him. 'I'll sacrifice one of my other bulls to Poseidon. He won't care! He probably won't even notice the difference!'

Poseidon cared. He noticed the difference.

When he realized Minos was keeping the beautiful white bull instead of sacrificing it like he had promised, Poseidon blew up like a pufferfish.

'Dude! Making that bull took me like *five seconds* of hard work! Okay, Minos. You think you're so great? You love bulls so much? You'll regret it. I'll make sure you never want to see another bull in your entire life!'

Poseidon could have punished Crete directly. He could've destroyed Knossos with an earthquake or wiped out the entire Cretan fleet with a tidal wave, but that would've only made the people of the island mad at *him*. Poseidon wanted to humiliate the royal family and make everyone disgusted with Minos and Pasiphaë, but he didn't want any blowback. He wanted the people of Crete to keep praying and sacrificing at his temple.

'I need a sneaky way to get revenge,' Poseidon decided. 'Let's see . . . who specializes in sneaky and embarrassing?'

Poseidon went to see the love goddess, Aphrodite, who was hanging out in her day spa on Mount Olympus.

'You won't believe this,' Poseidon told her. 'You know King Minos of Crete?'

'Mmm?' Aphrodite kept reading her fashion magazine. 'I suppose.'

'He dissed me! He promised to sacrifice a bull, and he didn't do it!'

'Mm-hmm?' Aphrodite scanned the ads for Givenchy bags.

'Also,' Poseidon said, 'that queen of his, Pasiphaë – you should've heard what she said about *you*.'

Aphrodite glanced up. 'Excuse me?'

'I mean sure, Pasiphaë is beautiful,' Poseidon said. 'But people are always talking about how lovely she is compared to you. And the queen never discourages them. Can you believe that?'

Aphrodite closed her magazine. Her eyes glowed a dangerous shade of pink. 'People are comparing this mortal queen to me? She *allows* it?'

'Yeah! And when was the last time Pasiphaë made a sacrifice at your temple, or called you the best goddess?'

Aphrodite ran through her mental list of sacrifices and prayers. She kept close track of which mortals paid her the proper respect. Pasiphaë's name wasn't anywhere in the top twenty.

'That ungrateful witch,' Aphrodite said.

To be fair, Pasiphaë really *was* a witch. She loved sorcery and potions. She was even more grasping and arrogant than her husband – basically not a nice person at all – but to blame her for not being an Aphrodite fangirl . . . well, that's like blaming me for not being a frequent flyer. Zeus and me – we try to stay out of each other's territory.

Anyway, Poseidon saw an opportunity for revenge, and he took it. I can't defend my dad's choice. Even the best gods can be vicious if you get on their bad side.

'You should totally punish her,' Poseidon suggested. 'Make the queen and king a laughing stock for failing to honour me . . . I mean, failing to honour *you*.'

'What did you have in mind?' Aphrodite asked.

Poseidon's eyes gleamed brighter than his Hawaiian shirt. 'Perhaps the queen should fall in love. She should have the most disgusting, embarrassing love affair of all time.'

'With David Hasselhoff?'

'Worse!'

'Charlie Sheen?'

'Worse! Minos's royal symbol is a bull, right? In his pens, he keeps a pure white bull that he loves more than anything in the world. What if the queen fell in love with that bull, too . . . ?'

Even for Aphrodite, the idea took a moment to sink in. 'Oh, gods . . . Oh, you don't mean . . . Oh, that's *sick*!'

Poseidon grinned. 'Isn't it?'

Aphrodite took some convincing. She went to the little goddesses' room, threw up, fixed her face and came back out. 'Very well,' she decided. 'This is an appropriate punishment for a queen who has never honoured me.'

'Or me,' said Poseidon.

'Whatever,' said Aphrodite.

The goddess went to work with her voodoo love magic. The next day, down on Crete, Pasiphaë was walking past the royal bull pens as quickly as possible to avoid the smell when she happened to glance at the king's prize white bull.

She stopped in her tracks.

It was true love.

Okay, folks. At this point, feel free to put down the book and run around in circles screaming 'EEEEWWWWW!' That's pretty much what I did the first time I heard this story.

Greek myths have a lot of gross stuff in them, but this right here is a major league retch-fest.

The thing is, Pasiphaë had done *nothing* to deserve it. Sure, she was an awful person who dabbled in dark sorcery, but we all have our faults! *She* wasn't the one who had failed to sacrifice the bull. *She* hadn't insulted Aphrodite.

It's kind of like the Fates were saying, *Okay, Minos, you did something bad? Well, see how you like it when we punish THIS RANDOM PERSON OVER HERE!*

Pasiphaë tried to shake her feelings. She knew they were wrong and disgusting. But she couldn't. She went back to her room and sat on her bed all day, reading books about bulls, drawing pictures of the bull until she ran out of white crayons, writing the bull's name on all her notebooks: BULL.

She struggled for weeks, trying to convince herself that she wasn't really in love with a fine specimen of livestock, but still she walked around in a daze, humming 'Hooked on a Feeling' and 'Milk Cow Blues'.

She tried to cure herself with spells and potions. Nothing worked.

Then, in desperation, she tried sorcery to make the bull like her. She found excuses to walk past the bull pen in her best dress with her hair done up nice. She muttered incantations. She poured love potions into the bull's trough. Nada.

The bull had absolutely no interest. To him, Pasiphaë was just another stupid human who wasn't bringing him fresh hay or waving a red flag in his face or doing anything interesting.

Finally, Pasiphaë sought out the help of the only person she considered even smarter than herself – Daedalus.

The inventor was in his workshop, looking over architectural drawings for the Knossos Football Stadium and Convention Centre, when the queen came in. She explained her problem and what she wanted him to do about it.

Daedalus glanced around, wondering if he was being secretly filmed for a reality show. 'So . . . Wait. You want me to do *what*, now?'

Pasiphae winced. Explaining it *once* had been embarrassing enough. 'I need to make the bull notice me. I *know* he'll love me back if I can just convince him –'

'He's a bull.'

'Yes!' the queen snapped. 'So I need him to think I'm a cow!'

Daedalus tried to keep his expression neutral. 'Um . . .'

'I'm serious! Use your mechanical super-duper know-how to make me a fake-cow suit. I'll slip inside, introduce myself to the bull, flirt a little, ask him where he's from, that sort of thing. I'm sure he'll fall in love with me!'

'Um –'

'It has to be an *attractive* fake-cow suit.'

'Your Majesty, I don't think I can –'

'Of course you can! You're a genius! What are we *paying* you for?'

'I'm pretty sure your husband isn't paying me for this.'

Pasiphaë sighed. 'Let me break it down for you. If you breathe a *word* of this to Minos, I will deny it. You'll be executed for spreading lies about the queen. If you refuse to help me, I'll tell Minos you made a pass at me. You'll be executed for that. The only way to avoid being executed is to *help* me.'

A line of sweat trickled down Daedalus's neck. 'I – I'm just saying . . . it isn't right.'

'You pushed your nephew off the Acropolis! What do you know about right and wrong?'

Daedalus really wished people would stop bringing that up. One little murder and they *never* let you forget it.

He didn't want to help the queen. A mechanical cow suit so she could chat up a bull? Even Daedalus had limits. But he also had his career and his family to think about. Since arriving on Crete, he'd got married. He now had a little boy named Icarus. Getting executed would make it difficult for Daedalus to attend his son's kindergarten back-to-school night. The inventor decided he had no choice. He began working on the most attractive fake-cow costume ever built by man.

As soon as the mechanical disguise was done, the queen slipped inside. Daedalus bribed the guards so they wouldn't notice anything strange about the inventor wheeling a fake cow from his workshop to the royal bull pen.

That night, the bull finally noticed Pasiphaë. This is a good time for all of us to put down the book again, run around in circles screaming 'Ewww!' and wash our eyes out with Optrex.

How did Aphrodite and Poseidon feel when their plan worked?

I hope they weren't sitting around Mount Olympus, high-fiving each other and saying, 'We did it!' I prefer to think they were staring in horror at the scene down in Crete and saying, 'Oh, gods . . . what have we done?'

Nine months later, a very pregnant Queen Pasiphaë was about to give birth.

King Minos couldn't wait! He was hoping for a son. He'd even picked out a name: Asterion, in honour of his stepfather, the former king. The people of Crete would love that!

Minor hitch in the plan: the boy was born a monster.

From the shoulders down, he was human. From the shoulders up, he had coarse fur, neck tendons like steel cables and the head of a bull. His horns started growing right away, which made it impossible to carry him around in a baby sling without getting gored.

The king wasn't as bright as Daedalus, but he figured out pretty quickly that the kid couldn't be his. The royal couple argued. They threw things. They screamed and yelled and chased off the servants, all of which must have been pretty upsetting for the poor baby.

No one was more horrified than Pasiphaë. Aphrodite's love curse had broken as soon as the baby was born. The queen was disgusted with herself, the gods and especially the baby. She confessed what had happened, but she couldn't explain her actions. How could she? Anyway, the damage was done. This wasn't something the royal couple could work through in marriage counselling.

Pasiphaë moved to a separate apartment in the palace. She lived under house arrest for the rest of her life. Minos was tempted to toss the monster baby into the sea, but something held him back – maybe the old taboo against killing your family, or maybe he had an inkling that the child was a punishment for *him*: a sick, twisted message from Poseidon. If so, killing the kid would only make the gods angrier.

Minos tried to hush up the details of the birth, but it was too late. Nursemaids, midwives and servants had all seen the baby. Nothing travels faster than bad news – especially when it happens to someone nobody likes.

The people of Crete were now *sure* that their king wasn't fit to rule. The mutant child was clearly a curse from the gods. The kid's name, Asterion, was an insult to the old king's memory, so the people didn't call him that. Everybody called the boy the *Minotaur* – the bull of Minos.

Minos turned bitter. He blamed everyone else – the gods, his wife, the bull, the ungrateful people of Crete. He couldn't punish them all. His popularity ratings were low enough as it was. But there was one person he *could* punish – someone who'd been involved in the plot and who made a perfect punching bag. He had Daedalus dragged before him in chains.

'*You*,' snarled the king. 'I gave you a second chance. I gave you a job, a workshop, R&D funding. And *this* is how you repay me? You have destroyed my reputation, inventor! Unless you can invent something that will make this right, I'll kill you slowly and painfully! Then I'll find a way to resurrect you and I'll kill you again!'

Daedalus was used to coming up with brilliant ideas. Normally he didn't have to do so while he was chained up and surrounded by guards with pointy swords, but he was highly motivated to think fast.

'We'll turn it into a positive!' he yelped.

Minos's stare was as cold as dry ice. 'My wife fell in love with a bull. She gave birth to a monster. You want to turn that into a positive?'

'Yes!' Daedalus said. 'We'll use that! Look, your people will never love you. That's obvious.'

'You're not making this better.'

'But we can make them *fear* you! Your enemies will tremble when they hear your name. Your own subjects will never dare cross you!'

The king's eyes narrowed. 'Go on.'

'Rumours about the Minotaur have already started to spread.'

'His name is Asterion.'

'No, sire! We embrace his monstrousness. We call him the Minotaur. We *never* show him to anyone. We let imaginations run wild. As bad as he is, we encourage people to think he's even worse. As he grows, we'll keep him locked away in the dungeons and feed him . . . I don't know, spoiled meat and Tabasco sauce – something to make him *really* angry. We'll throw prisoners in his cell from time to time and let the Minotaur practise killing them.'

'Wow,' said Minos. 'And I thought *I* was cruel. Keep talking.'

'Every time the Minotaur kills a prisoner, we'll give him a piece of candy. He'll learn to be a vicious, murderous beast! Once he's fully grown . . .' Daedalus got a light in his eyes that made even the king nervous.

'What?' Minos asked. 'What happens when he's grown?'

'By then, I'll be done building the Minotaur's new home. It'll be a prison like no other – a huge maze right behind the palace. The top will be open to the sky, but the walls will be tall and impossible to climb. The corridors will shift and turn. The whole place will be full of traps. And at the centre . . . *that's* where the Minotaur will live.'

Minos got a chill just imagining it. 'So . . . how would we feed him?'

Daedalus smiled. He was really getting into the whole evil genius thing now. 'Whenever you have someone you want to punish, you push them into the maze. You promise that if they can find their way out, you'll let them live, but I'll make sure no one can *ever* locate an exit. Eventually they'll get lost. They'll die of thirst or hunger . . . or the Minotaur will find them and eat them. Their screams will echo from the maze across the entire city. The Minotaur will become everyone's worst nightmare. No one will *ever* make fun of you again.'

Minos tapped his chin. 'I like your plan. Build this maze. We will call it . . . the Funhouse!'

'Erm, I was thinking something more mysterious and terrifying,' Daedalus said. 'Perhaps the Labyrinth?'

'Fine. Whatever. Now get to work before I change my mind and kill you!'

Daedalus put in more hours on the Labyrinth than he had on any other invention – more than the Daedalus Chisel™, the Daedalus Wax Tablet™, or even the Daedalus Food Processor™ that made mounds and mounds of julienned fries. He worked so hard that he neglected his family. His wife left him. His son Icarus grew up barely knowing his father.

For fifteen years Daedalus laboured, creating what looked like a trench-warfare playground in the backyard of the palace. Fortunately, it was a *really* big backyard. If you put the Mall of America, Walt Disney World and twenty football stadiums together, they would have all fitted inside the Labyrinth with room to spare.

Thirty-foot-tall brick walls zigzagged across the landscape. Corridors narrowed and widened, looping in curlicues, crossing and splitting. Some submerged underground and became tunnels. Others dead-ended or opened into gardens where every plant was poisonous. The walls shifted. Trapdoors and pits riddled the floors.

If you were sentenced to the Labyrinth, the guards would shove you inside. The entrance would vanish like it had never been there. The maze was so disorientating that as soon as you took three steps you'd be lost. The fact that you could see the sky just made it feel more claustrophobic. It was almost like the Labyrinth was alive – growing and changing and trying to kill you.

Believe me on this. I've been inside. It's not one of those places where you think, *When I grow up, I'm totally taking my kids here every summer!*

Daedalus completed his work just in time. The Minotaur was getting so strong that no cell in the dungeon could hold him. He had entered his teen years and, like a lot of us teens (myself excluded, of course), he could be sulky and angry and destructive. Unlike most teens, the Minotaur had sharp horns, blood-red eyes and fists the size of battering rams. Since he was a little kid, he'd been whipped, beaten and trained to kill. For a piece of candy, he would gladly tear a human apart with his bare hands.

Somehow, Minos managed to coax the Minotaur into his new home at the centre of Labyrinth – maybe by leaving a trail of Skittles. Once there, the Minotaur was ready to play his part as the most fearsome monster ever. At night he bellowed at the moon, and the sound echoed through the streets of Knossos.

Minos began throwing prisoners into the maze. Sure enough, they never came back. Either they got lost and died of thirst (if they were lucky), or they met the Minotaur, in which case their dying screams provided a lovely soundtrack for life in the big city.

The crime rate in Knossos went down ninety-seven percent. So did King Minos's popularity, but everyone was too scared of him and his monstrous son to say anything. Daedalus's plan had worked. He'd designed the most complicated, dangerous maze in human history. He'd turned Minos's disgrace into a source of power and fear.

For his reward, he was granted life in prison. Yippee! Minos locked Daedalus in his own Labyrinth, in a lovely suite of cells with a fully stocked workshop so he could keep making brilliant things for the king. The guards checked on him daily, using magical thread to find their way in and out of the maze, and made sure Daedalus wasn't up to anything funny.

To encourage the old man's cooperation, Minos kept Icarus a captive in the palace. Icarus was only allowed to visit his father every other Tuesday, but those visits were the highlight of Daedalus's miserable new life.

He wished he'd never heard of Crete or Minos or Pasiphaë. He never wanted to see another bull as long as he lived. Every night he had to listen to the Minotaur mooing and banging around next door. The Labyrinth walls rumbled and groaned as they shifted, making it impossible for the old man to sleep.

Being a genius inventor and all, Daedalus spent most of his time devising escape plans. Getting through the maze itself was no problem. Daedalus could navigate it easily. But the exit was locked and heavily guarded. Minos's army patrolled the perimeter 24/7. Even if Daedalus could somehow manage to slip out unnoticed, Minos controlled all the ships in the harbour. Daedalus would be arrested before he could ever board one.

To make matters worse, his son was the king's prisoner. If Daedalus fled, Icarus would be executed.

Daedalus needed a way to get off the island with his son – a way that didn't involve land or sea. The inventor began working on his greatest bad idea ever.

Daedalus's timeline got pushed up when the Labyrinth suffered its first jailbreak. A guy named Theseus pulled it off with a little inside help, but we'll get to that in a bit.

For now, let's just say it put Minos in a seriously bad mood. And when Minos got in a bad mood he tended to take it out on his favourite punching bag: Daedalus. The inventor figured he'd outlived his usefulness. His days were numbered. He sped up work on his amazing terrible idea.

He told no one about his plans except his son.

Icarus had grown into a sweet, handsome young man, but he was no inventor. He was no Perdix. Daedalus liked it that way. Icarus worshipped his dad and trusted him completely, so, when Daedalus told him they were breaking out of the Labyrinth together, Icarus did a happy dance.

'Awesome!' Icarus said. 'Are you building a bulldozer?'

'What?' Daedalus asked. 'No, that wouldn't work.'

'But you said "break out".'

'It's a figure of speech. There's no way to escape by land or sea. Minos has those routes covered. But there's one way he can't guard.'

Daedalus pointed at the sky.

Icarus nodded. 'Springs on our shoes. We will jump to freedom!'

'No.'

'Trained pigeons! We'll tie dozens of them to large lawn chairs and —'

'No! Although you're getting warmer. We'll fly out of here under our own power!'

Daedalus told him the plan. He warned Icarus not to talk about it and to be ready to leave when he visited the Labyrinth again in two weeks.

After Icarus left, Daedalus went to work. His forge glowed day and night as he smelted bronze and hammered out pieces of his new contraption. By this point, he was getting old. His eyesight wasn't as good as it used to be. His hands shook. His project required intricate sculpting and painstaking precision. After a few days he was wishing he'd gone with the pigeon-powered lawn chair idea.

Two weeks flew by.

When Icarus came back to visit, the boy was alarmed at how much frailer his father looked.

'Dad, the guards were acting funny,' Icarus warned. 'They said something about telling you goodbye and this being our last visit.'

'I *knew* it,' Daedalus muttered. 'The king is planning to execute me. We have to hurry!'

Daedalus opened his supply cabinet and pulled out his new invention — two sets of human-size bronze wings, each feather perfectly crafted, all the joints fully articulated.

'Whoa,' said Icarus. 'Shiny.'

'Do you remember our plan?' Daedalus asked.

'Yeah. Here, Dad, I'll attach your wings.'

The old man wanted to argue. He would have preferred that his son be ready to go first, but he was exhausted. He let Icarus fasten the straps on his leather harness, then use hot wax to fuse the wings into place on his back and arms. It wasn't a perfect design, but it was the best Daedalus could do on short notice with the supplies he had. The guards weren't about to let him have any *good* adhesive. With superglue or duct tape, Daedalus could have conquered the world.

'Hurry, son,' Daedalus urged. 'The guards will be bringing lunch soon . . .'

Or, if Minos really *had* decided to kill him, they might bring a guillotine instead of the usual cheese sandwich.

Icarus attached the last pinion to his father's wrist. 'There! You're ready to fly. Now do mine.'

The old man's hands shook. Several times, he spilled hot wax on his son's shoulders, but Icarus didn't complain.

Daedalus was about to do a final safety check when the workshop door burst open. King Minos himself stormed inside, flanked by guards.

The king looked at Daedalus and Icarus in their new bronze wings.

'What have we here?' Minos said. 'Giant bronze chickens? Perhaps I should pluck you and make soup!'

One of the guards laughed. 'Ha. Soup.'

'Icarus, go!' Daedalus kicked open the forge's floor vent. A blast of hot air from below lifted Icarus into the sky.

'Stop them!' Minos yelled.

Daedalus spread his wings. The hot wind carried him aloft. The guards hadn't brought bows, so all they could do was throw their swords and helmets while King Minos yelled and shook his fists. The inventor and his son soared away.

At first, the trip was awesome . . . kind of like the beginning of Phaethon's sun-chariot ride, except without the sun-related tunes or the built-in Bluetooth. Icarus whooped with delight as they glided away from Crete.

'We did it, Dad! We did it!'

'Son, be careful!' Daedalus cried, struggling to keep up. 'Remember what I told you!'

'I know!' Icarus swooped down next to him. 'Not too low, or the seawater will corrode the wings. Not too high, or the sun will melt the wax.'

'Right!' Daedalus said. 'Stick to the middle of the sky!'

Again, that might sound familiar from Phaethon's driver's education class. The Greeks were all about staying in the middle, avoiding extremes. They were the original nation of Goldilockses – not too hot, not too cold, just right.

Of course that doesn't mean they were any good at *following* the rule.

'I'll be careful, Dad,' Icarus promised. 'But first watch this! WOOHOO!'

He did loops and twirls. He dive-bombed the waves, then soared up and tried to touch the clouds. Daedalus yelled at him to stop, but you know us crazy kids. Give us wings and all we want to do is fly.

Icarus kept saying, 'Just one more time! These wings are great, Dad!'

Daedalus couldn't do much to stop him. The old guy was having enough trouble just staying aloft. Now that they were over the middle of the sea, he couldn't exactly stop to rest.

Icarus thought, I wonder how high I can go. Dad's wings will hold up. Dad is awesome! He's super smart!

Icarus shot into the clouds. Somewhere below, he heard his dad yelling, but Icarus was too busy enjoying the adrenalin rush.

I can touch the sun! he told himself. I can totally touch the sun!

He totally couldn't touch the sun.

The wax points melted. The bronze feathers began to moult.

With a loud metallic RRRIPP – like a bag of cans in a trash compactor – the wings peeled away. Icarus fell.

Daedalus screamed until his throat was sore, but there was nothing he could do. His son plummeted three hundred feet and hit the water, which from that height might as well have been tarmac.

Icarus sank beneath the waves.

In his honour, that stretch of water is still called the Icarian Sea, though why you'd want to be memorialized by the thing that killed you I'm not sure. If I ever bite it, please don't let them dedicate the Percy Jackson Memorial Brick Wall, the Percy Jackson Very Sharp Spear, or the Percy Jackson Memorial Sixteen-Wheeler Going a Hundred Miles an Hour. I would not feel honoured.

Heartbroken, Daedalus was tempted to give up. He could simply fall into the sea and die, joining his son in the Underworld. But his survival instinct was pretty strong. So was his instinct for revenge. Minos had driven them to this escape plan. Minos was responsible for his son's death. The king needed to pay.

The inventor flew on into the night. He had more things to invent, more trouble to cause and at least one really satisfying death to arrange.

Daedalus made it all the way to the island of Sicily, off the southwest tip of Italy. That's like five hundred miles from Crete, which is a long way for an old dude flapping metal wings.

When he landed, he was the first person ever to use that lame gag *I just flew in from Crete and, boy, are my arms tired!*

Fortunately, the Sicilians didn't apply the death penalty for corny jokes.

They took Daedalus to meet the local king, a guy named Cocalus, and the king couldn't believe his luck. Nobody famous ever came to Sicily!

'Oh, my gods!' The king leaped out of his throne. 'Daedalus? *The* Daedalus?' King Cocalus started fangirling all around the throne room. 'Can I get a photo with you? Will you sign my crown? I can't believe it! *The* Daedalus, in *my* kingdom. I have to tell all the neighbouring kings. They'll be *so* jealous.'

'Um, yeah, about that...' Daedalus explained that he'd just escaped from King Minos, who had the most powerful navy in the Mediterranean and would no doubt be looking for him. 'Maybe it's best if we keep my presence here on the down-low.'

Cocalus's eyes widened. 'Riiight. The down-low. Got it! If you work for me, you can have whatever you want. We'll keep your identity a secret. We'll give you a code name like ... Not-Daedalus! No one will suspect a thing!'

'Um –'

'Or how about Maedalus? Or Jimmy?'

Daedalus realized he had some work ahead of him. He'd have to make sure the royal brain didn't get pulled over for going under the speed limit. Still, it beat sitting in the Labyrinth.

Soon, Daedalus was the king's most trusted adviser. He could read entire sentences, spell words, even do maths. Truly, he was a wizard.

King Cocalus was as good as his word. (As long as you didn't ask him to *spell* his word.) He kept Daedalus's secret. He gave the old inventor a suite of rooms in the palace, a new workshop, even a good tool set from Ace Hardware in Athens, which was *not* easy to import.

Of course Sicily wasn't Crete. Cocalus didn't have nearly as much power or wealth as Minos, so Daedalus didn't have as many resources to work with. But he was *definitely* appreciated. He was the biggest thing that had ever happened in that part of the world. He sort of liked the attention.

Cocalus might have been a doofus, but the king's three daughters were all smart, with a ruthless streak. Daedalus thought they might make fine rulers some day. He began tutoring them on the basics of being a monarch – maths, reading, writing, warfare, basic torture, tax collection, advanced torture and tax collection with advanced torture. The princesses were quick learners.

Daedalus also did a ton of stuff for the locals. He introduced indoor plumbing. He built nice buildings. He taught the people how to tell if their clothes were on inside out. It was quite a Renaissance down there in Cocalus's kingdom. If you go to Sicily today, you can still see some of the stuff Daedalus built: the thermal baths in Selinus, a water reservoir in Hybla, an aqueduct and some fortifications in Camicos, the temple of Apollo in Cumae and don't miss the giant dancing bronze sloth in Palermo. (Okay, that last one isn't there any more, which is a bummer. It must've been awesome.) Daedalus became so popular that he started piling up gifts from the grateful people. Many Sicilians named their kids Jimmy or Not-Daedalus in his honour.

Daedalus figured that sooner or later the Cretan navy would come calling, so he built King Cocalus a new castle high on a cliff. Its one entry gate was at the top of a steep path, and four men could easily defend it against an entire army. On the downside, that made for a real bottleneck situation during rush hour.

For a while, life was good. Some nights, Daedalus could even sleep without having nightmares about Queen Pasiphaë in her fake-cow costume, or Icarus falling into the sea, or his nephew Perdix tumbling off the Acropolis.

But King Minos hadn't forgotten about the inventor. He gathered his fleet and slowly made his way around the Mediterranean, searching for Daedalus in every city. Minos was clever about it. Instead of banging on doors and threatening people, he set out bait that he figured Daedalus couldn't resist.

Minos said he was holding a contest to find the most ingenious person in the world. Whoever could thread a cord through a conch shell without breaking the shell would win eternal fame and an ass-load of gold. (By which I mean as much gold as could be carried by a strong donkey. Jeez, you people. What did you think I meant?)

Why did Minos pick the conch-shell challenge? Maybe he wanted to start a new fashion trend with extremely large seashell necklaces. If you've ever seen a conch shell, you know they're *really* curly on the inside. You can get your hand in partially, but it's impossible to coax a thread all the way through the spiral and out of the top – especially not with the technology they had back then.

Word of the contest spread. A lot of people wanted eternal fame. An ass-load of gold didn't sound too bad, either.

When Daedalus heard about the challenge, he just smiled. He had predicted that Minos would try something like this sooner or later.

He went to see King Cocalus. 'Your Majesty, about this conch-shell contest . . . I intend to enter it and win.'

The king frowned. 'But if you send in the winning entry, even if you do so under a fake name, won't Minos suspect it's you?'

'Yes.'

'But . . . then he'll come here. He'll demand to see the winner and –'

'Right.'

'Wait . . . you *want* him to come here?'

Daedalus realized he still had some work to do on the king's brain-speed capacity. 'Yes, my friend. Don't worry. I have a plan.'

Cocalus was a little nervous about confronting the most powerful king in the Mediterranean, but he loved Daedalus. He didn't want to lose his best adviser. He went along with what the inventor said.

First, Daedalus solved the conch-shell puzzle. That was

easy. He drilled a tiny hole at the top, where the shell came to a point. He put a little drop of honey around the edge of the hole. Then he found an ant and carefully tied a silken thread around the little guy's body. (Don't try this at home unless you've got tons of time, infinite patience and a very good magnifying glass.)

Daedalus nudged the ant inside the shell. The ant smelled the honey at the top and took off through the spirals, dragging the thread behind it. The ant popped out of the hole and – ta-da! – one threaded conch shell.

Daedalus gave the conch to King Cocalus, who sent it to Minos, whose fleet was now trolling off the coast of Italy.

A few weeks later, Minos received the shell, along with a note that read:

> *Solved your little puzzle. What else you got?*
> *Come and give me my reward.*
> *I'm in Cocalus's palace in Sicily.*
> XOX,
> *Not-Daedalus*

Minos saw through this clever pseudonym.

'It's Daedalus!' he cried. 'Quickly, we must sail for Sicily!'

His fleet anchored off the southern coast of the island. The place where he landed was immediately named Minoa in honour of the king's arrival. Like I said, not much happened in Sicily back then. Still, can you imagine every place you visit being named after you?

It'd be kind of annoying.

Mom: *Did you go to New Jersey last night?*

Me: *Um, no. Why do you ask?*

Mom: *Because there's a town named Percyopolis there now!*

King Cocalus sent messengers to greet Minos. They invited the king to the palace for a chat.

Minos looked up at the clifftop fortress with its narrow winding approach and its easily defendable gate. He realized it would be impossible to take by force. He guessed Daedalus must have constructed the place.

Minos gritted his teeth and decided to play along. Accompanied by a dozen guards and servants, he followed the messengers to King Cocalus's audience chamber.

The king sat nervously on his throne. Behind him stood three young redheaded ladies whom Minos assumed were the king's daughters.

'My friend Minos!' Cocalus said.

Minos scowled. He'd never met Cocalus. He didn't want to be friends. 'I understand someone at your court solved my puzzle,' he said.

'Oh, yes!' Cocalus grinned. 'My trusted adviser, Not-Daedalus. He's awesome!'

'Let's cut through the Mist, shall we?' Minos growled. 'I know you are harbouring the fugitive Daedalus.'

Cocalus's smile faded. 'Um, well –'

'How did he solve the conch-shell problem?'

'He, um . . . with an ant, if you can believe it. He tied a silk thread around the little guy, then coaxed it through the shell by putting a drop of honey at the other end.'

'Ingenious,' Minos said. 'Turn Daedalus over to me and we'll have no problem. Fail to do so and you will have Crete as an enemy. Believe me, you don't want that.'

Cocalus turned pale, which pleased Minos. He was *way* past the days of giving away free bobbleheads in the hope that people would like him. Now he was older and wiser. He just wanted to terrify and kill people.

One of King Cocalus's daughters inched forward. She whispered in her father's ear.

'What are you saying, girl?' Minos demanded.

The princess met his eyes. 'My lord, Daedalus is our teacher and friend. Turning him over to you would be treachery.'

Minos clenched his jaw. This girl defending the inventor reminded him of his own daughter, Ariadne – and that was a painful subject, as you'll find out in the next chapter.

'Princess, your loyalty is misplaced,' Minos warned. 'Daedalus also instructed *my* daughter. He poisoned her mind and she betrayed me to my enemies. Give me Daedalus now!'

King Cocalus cleared his throat. 'Of course, of course! But, um, there was some mention of a reward for solving the puzzle . . . ?'

Minos understood greed.

He clapped his hands and his servants brought forward several heavy chests – an ass-load of gold, minus the ass.

'It's yours,' Minos said. 'Give me Daedalus and I'll leave in peace.'

'Deal!' Cocalus wiped his brow with relief. 'Guards –'

'Father, wait.' The eldest princess set her hand on his arm. 'Your word is law. Obviously, we must do what King Minos asks. But shouldn't we entertain our guest properly first? He has travelled for many months. He must be weary. Tonight, let us give Minos a luxurious bath, fresh clothes and a feast. Then, in the morning, we will send him on his way with his prisoner and many presents.' She favoured King Minos with a flirty little smile. 'My sisters and I would be honoured to see to your bath personally.'

Zowie, thought King Minos. This could work.

He figured he'd won. He could see the greed and fear in King Cocalus's eyes. Sicily wouldn't dare risk a war with Crete. It *had* been a long, tiring trip, and he wasn't anxious to get back on a ship and sail home. Having three beautiful princesses prepare his bath and serve him a feast didn't sound so bad.

'I accept,' Minos said. 'Show me the hospitality of . . . Sicily.'

The three princesses escorted him to a lovely suite of rooms. They complimented him on his wealth, power and good looks. They convinced him to leave his guards behind. After all, he was among friends! What did a big, strong king have to fear from three girls?

They took Minos to the baths, where a steaming tub awaited, filled with fancy rose-scented bubble bath. As the old dude eased himself in, the princesses averted their eyes to protect their modesty (and also because he was old and hairy and gross and they didn't want to see).

'Ahhhh,' Minos said. 'This is the life.'

'Yes, my lord,' said the eldest princess. 'It's also your death.'

'What, now?'

She turned a knob. A hatch opened in the ceiling and a thousand gallons of scalding-hot water dumped on top of Minos. He wailed and shrieked and died in extreme pain.

Behind the towel rack, a secret door opened. Daedalus emerged.

'Well done, my princesses,' said the inventor. 'You were always quick learners.'

The princesses hugged him.

'We couldn't let Minos arrest you!' said the eldest. 'You can stay with us now. Continue to advise us!'

'Alas, my dear, I can't,' Daedalus said. 'The goddess Athena clearly isn't done cursing me. I have to move on before I bring more tragedy to this kingdom. But don't worry. You'll make excellent queens. And I have other plans . . .'

The old inventor embraced the loyal and murderous princesses. Then he disappeared into the secret passage and was never seen in Sicily again.

The princesses ran back to the throne room. Crying and screaming, they reported that their honoured guest Minos had accidentally slipped and fallen into the scalding-hot tub. The poor man had died instantly.

The Cretan guards were suspicious. When they saw the body of their king, he looked like he'd been boiled in a lobster pot. But what could they do? They were outnumbered at the palace. The fortress was too well protected for an all-out assault. To get proper revenge, they'd have to declare war, lay siege to the island and summon more troops from a thousand miles away. That was a lot of work for a king they'd never liked anyway. They decided to accept the princesses' story that the death had been an accident.

The Cretans sailed away in peace. Cocalus kept the ass-load of gold. His three murderous daughters lived happily ever after and became excellent at torturing and tax collecting.

And Daedalus?

Some stories say that he lived his last days on the island of Sardinia, but nobody is really sure.

Unless you've read some of my adventures. Then you might know what happened to the old guy. But, since we're sticking to the original myths and all, I'll have to leave it there.

Besides, my pet hellhound is getting really sad. She knows that I'm writing about Daedalus, her former master. Every time she hears his name, she starts to cry and chew holes in my armour.

So was Daedalus a hero? You tell me. The guy was definitely smart, but his ingenuity got him into trouble at least as often as it saved him. Comic book superheroes always get the same bit of advice: *Use your powers only for good.* Yeah . . . Daedalus didn't do that. He used his powers for greed and money and saving his own skin. But sometimes he also tried to help people.

Before you make up your mind, you should hear the other side of the story: what happened in the Labyrinth when a guy named Theseus came to town. It turned out Daedalus wasn't the only smart person in Crete, and Minos wasn't the only stone-cold killer. Ariadne and Theseus . . . they made quite a cut-throat team.

THESEUS SLAYS THE MIGHTY – OH, LOOK! A BUNNY RABBIT!

WANNA MAKE THESEUS MAD?

Ask him, 'Who's your daddy?'

He'll smack you upside the head *real* quick.

Nobody knows exactly who Theseus's father was. We're not even sure if he had one dad or two. The Ancient Greeks argued about it for centuries. They wrote essays and stories trying to figure it out until their brains exploded.

I'll try not to make your brain explode, but here's the deal:

The king of Athens was a dude named Aegeus. He had lots of enemies ready to take over his kingdom and no sons to carry on the family name. He really wanted a son, and so to get advice he decided – you guessed it – to visit the Oracle of Delphi.

Have you noticed how many of these stories have kings who wanted sons? I don't know what's up with that. You'd think no royal family ever had boys – like Greece was littered with kings standing on the side of the road holding cardboard signs that read:

WILL WORK FOR SONS.
PLEASE EXPLAIN TO ME HOW TO
HAVE BOY CHILDREN.
GODS BLESS.

They should have made a deal with the Amazons, since those ladies were throwing baby boys out with the recycling, but – oh, well.

Aegeus went to the Oracle and made the usual offerings.

'O Great Teller of the Future and Inhaler of Volcanic Gas!' said the king. 'Can I get a boy child over here, or what?'

On her three-legged stool, the priestess shuddered as the spirit of Apollo possessed her. 'Have patience, O King! Avoid women until you return to Athens. Your son shall have a noble mother and the blood of the gods, but he must arrive in his own good time!'

'What does *that* mean?'

'Thank for your offering. Have a nice day.'

That answer frustrated Aegeus. He grumbled all the way back to his ship and prepared for his long voyage home.

If you travelled overland, Delphi wasn't that far from Athens. But back then you *never* travelled overland, unless you were crazy or desperate. The roads were mostly muddy cow paths or treacherous mountain passes. The few usable stretches were infested with bandits, monsters and tacky outlet malls.

Because of this, the Greeks always travelled by boat — which wasn't exactly safe, just saf*er*.

To return to Athens, Aegeus had to sail all the way around the Peloponnese, the big dangly chunk of land that makes up the southern Greek mainland. The trip was a pain, but since Aegeus wanted to make it home alive he didn't have much choice. His enemies back home would *love* to catch him on the road, where they could ambush him, chop him into tiny pieces and make it look like the work of random monsters or enraged sheep.

So King Aegeus sailed around the Peloponnese. Every once in a while he docked at a city and had dinner with the local king. Aegeus would share his sob story and ask his host's advice about the Oracle's words. The local king would always be like, *Oh, you want a wife? I can totally hook you up. My niece is available!*

Everybody wanted a marriage alliance with a powerful city like Athens, but Aegeus remembered what the Oracle had said. He was supposed to avoid women until he got home. He kept declining offers for beautiful brides, which did not make him any less grumpy.

After weeks of travelling, he reached a little town called Troezen, about sixty miles south of Athens. All Aegeus had to do now was cross the Saronic Gulf and he'd be home.

The king of Troezen was a guy named Pittheus. Because his city was close to Athens, Pittheus and Aegeus knew each other pretty well and hung out sometimes, even though they had rival patron gods. Athens was all about Athena. Troezen's patron god was Poseidon. (They had good taste down there in Troezen.)

Anyway, the two kings got to chatting about the Oracle's prophecy.

Pittheus said, 'Oh, heck, you need a wife? I've got a single daughter – you remember Aethra, my oldest?'

'Dude, I appreciate it,' Aegeus said, 'but I'm supposed to avoid women until I get home, so –'

'Aethra!' called Pittheus. 'Get in here, would you?'

The princess swept into the dining hall. 'Hi.'

Aegeus's jaw hit his plate. Aethra was *all* kinds of gorgeous. 'Uh,' said Aegeus. 'Um, uh . . .'

Pittheus smirked. He knew his daughter had this effect on men. 'So, as I was saying, Aethra is single and –'

'B-but the prophecy,' Aegeus managed.

Pittheus scratched his kingly sideburns. 'The Oracle didn't say you shouldn't *marry* a woman, right? She said you should *avoid* women. Well, you've done your best. You've avoided women for weeks. You didn't *ask* to see my daughter. *She* found *you!* So I think we're good.'

Maybe Aegeus should have argued with that logic, but he didn't.

Right there in the dining room, they had a quick Vegas-style wedding – the priestess of Hera, the flowers, the Elvis impersonators, the whole bit. Then Aethra went back to her room to change into something more comfortable while Aegeus rushed off to reapply his deodorant, brush his teeth and await his lovely bride in the honeymoon suite.

How did Aethra feel about all this?

Pro and con. Like I said earlier, women back then didn't have much choice about who they married. Aethra definitely could've done worse. Aegeus wasn't a bad-looking guy. He and her dad were friends, which meant he would probably treat her well. Athens was a big powerful city, so that would give her a lot of street cred with the other Greek queens.

On the negative side, Aethra already had a secret boyfriend – the god Poseidon.

As Troezen's patron, Poseidon had first noticed the princess making sacrifices to him at the seaside. He'd decided to court her, because Aethra was super gorgeous. In no time she'd fallen for him.

Now that she was married to another guy, Aethra didn't know what to do.

After the ceremony, while her new husband was brushing his teeth, the princess slipped out of the palace. She ran down to the seashore and waded to the nearby island of Sphairia, where she and Poseidon usually met.

Poseidon was waiting for her in a hammock between two palm trees. He was rocking a Tommy Bahama shirt and Bermuda shorts while drinking a fruity beverage out of a coconut shell.

'Hey, babe,' he said. 'What's new?'

'Well . . . um, I got married.'

'Say what?'

Aethra told him what had happened. 'I – I suppose I could run away with you,' she offered hopefully.

Poseidon smiled. He liked Aethra, but not *that* much. Gods always moved on, eventually. This seemed like as good a time as any.

'No, no,' he said. 'Aegeus is a good guy, for an Athenian. He'll make you a fine husband. This will have to be goodbye for us, babe, but it's been great. Honestly!'

He snapped his fingers. A disco ball lowered from one of the palm trees. 'Last Dance' began playing in the background, because Poseidon was a total sucker for Donna Summer. Don't ask me. It's impossible to hang out in his palace without him playing that old disco stuff.

Anyway, they had one more quality evening together. Then Aethra hurried off to see her new husband, who must have been really careful about brushing his teeth, because he didn't notice how long his bride had been gone or the fact that she smelled like Sea Breeze aftershave.

Aethra and Aegeus spent their honeymoon in Troezen. Aegeus wasn't anxious to get home, since all he had waiting for him there were problems and enemies. After a few weeks, the king started having strange dreams about his new wife swimming across the Saronic Gulf with a baby boy in her arms.

Finally he asked Aethra about this.

She blushed. 'Well . . . I'm pretty sure I'm pregnant.'

'That's awesome!' said Aegeus.

'Except . . . I'm not sure if you're the dad.'

She confided to her husband about her fling with Poseidon.

Aegeus took the news better than you might expect. The gods were always falling in love with mortal princesses. He couldn't blame Aethra for being swept off her feet by an immortal hunk with supernatural good looks and limitless power. And he couldn't curse Poseidon without getting hit by a tsunami or swallowed by an earthquake.

'Okay, I understand,' said Aegeus. 'But if the child is a boy I am going to claim him as my son, all right?'

'What if it's a girl?' Aethra asked.

Aegeus sighed. 'Let's think positive. A boy would be awesome! I'll make some arrangements.'

'Arrangements?'

'You'll see.'

The next day, Aegeus took Aethra to a hill outside the city. At the crest stood a boulder the size of a two-car garage. A dozen of the king's men had wrapped ropes around the boulder and were harnessing them to a team of horses.

'Whoa,' Aethra said. 'You're going to move that rock?'

'Yeah, here's the deal.' Aegeus walked over to a shallow pit next to the boulder. He unbuckled his sword. 'This sword's hilt has the royal crest of Athens on it, see?'

'The owl and the olive branch?'

'Yeah. And those are my initials on the pommel. It's an excellent blade — Celestial bronze and everything.' He tossed the sword into the pit. 'I'm also burying these.'

From one of his servants, he took a polished wooden shoe box. He opened it for Aethra, and inside were . . . you guessed it. Shoes.

Aethra whistled. 'Those are some nice sandals.'

'Oh, yeah. Leather soles. Good-quality straps. Arch support. These shoes will last a lifetime.' Aegeus tossed the shoe box in the pit.

Now you might be wondering: what was the big deal about a pair of shoes? But back then good kicks were *super* hard to find. You couldn't just stroll into Foot Locker and score some Adidas. If you wanted to be a hero, making your way through monsters' lairs, vipers' nests and battlefields, you didn't want to go barefoot. You definitely didn't want to be slipping on blood and gore in a cheap pair of flip-flops. Good shoes could keep you alive just as well as a good sword.

Aegeus's men grabbed the ropes. The lines went taut. The team of horses strained. Very slowly, they dragged the giant rock until it covered the pit.

'There,' Aegeus said. 'If our child is a boy, wait until he comes of age and then tell him that I left him some gifts under this rock. If he can retrieve them, he is worthy of being my son. He should then make his way to Athens.'

Aethra frowned. 'You want *me* to tell him this? Where will you be?'

'My dear, you know those strange dreams I've been having? They're getting worse. If you come with me to Athens, I'm sure my enemies will kill you. They'll never allow you to give birth to my heir. Even if the child were born, he'd never be safe in Athens. It's best I return home alone and keep our marriage a secret. That way my enemies will think I've failed to have a son. They'll be content to wait for me to die. Once my son is old enough to defend himself, he can come to Athens and take his rightful place as the crown prince!'

'So you want me to stay here and raise the kid by myself for, like, sixteen, seventeen years.'

'That would be great. Thanks.' Aegeus kissed her. 'Well, my ship is waiting in the harbour. Love you! Have a good pregnancy!'

Aegeus sailed back to Athens and left Aethra in Troezen to wait for her child to be born.

She kind of hoped she would have a girl, because then she

could rest easy. Neither Aegeus nor Poseidon would care . . . being the enlightened feminist guys that they were. Aethra could raise her daughter in peace and not have to worry about shoes under boulders.

But if the child were a boy . . . well, Aethra at least hoped he would grow up to be a hero. Then both of his dads would be proud to claim him.

As you can probably guess, she had a boy, and the Greek storytellers spent the next thousand years arguing who his dad was. Some said Aegeus. Some said Poseidon. Some said he had *two* fathers, which I'm pretty sure is medically impossible. Then again we're talking about gods, so who knows?

As for Aethra, she raised her son by herself for the first seventeen years, which took a special kind of heroism.

Aethra's son was big and healthy, which you'd expect, since he had one or two powerful dads. She named him *Theseus*, meaning *the gathering*, maybe because she hoped he would gather all the people of Greece together into one big happy family. Or maybe because the kid was so high-energy that Aethra and a dozen nursemaids had to spend all day trying to gather him up.

Most demigods I've met have attention-deficit/ hyperactivity disorder. It keeps you alive on the battlefield, because you're so aware of *everything*. But Theseus was the original ADHD poster child. He was hyper in diapers. He was bouncing off the Corinthian columns. He was the super-caffeinated kid, the deficit demigod, the — well, you get the idea. The kid was a handful.

As he grew, he quickly ran out of things to do and bad guys to kill. All the monsters near Troezen? Toast. Bandits, murderers, evil geniuses trying to take over Ancient Greece? Forget it. They were dead before Theseus's naptime.

By the time he was seventeen, Theseus was so skillful in combat and so incredibly bored that his mom decided to send him to his father's city. She needed a break.

She led him to the hill with the huge boulder.

'My son,' she said, 'your real father is Aegeus, king of Athens. Or he might be Poseidon, god of the sea. Or possibly both.'

She tried to explain the details, but Theseus lost interest. 'What's with the rock?'

'Aegeus said that when you were old enough, I should bring you here. If you can figure out a way to move the boulder and retrieve the gifts beneath, you should seek out your father in Athens.'

'Gifts? Cool!' Theseus walked once around the boulder, then pressed his hands against the stone.

'Don't get a hernia,' his mother warned. 'Your father used a dozen men and a team of horses to –'

BOOM.

The boulder toppled over and rolled downhill.

Theseus had the attention span of a gerbil, but he was a genius at sizing up his opponents – even if that opponent was a large rock. He had noticed immediately that the boulder was lopsided and top-heavy on the left. Over the past seventeen years, the soil on that side had eroded. All Theseus had to do was give the stone a good push on the right and down it went.

Of course, Theseus wasn't so good at foreseeing consequences. The boulder barrelled through a nearby village, destroying several huts and scaring some pigs before rolling to a stop.

'Sorry!' Theseus yelled downhill.

He knelt by the pit where the boulder had stood. 'Nice sword. And — OH! SHOES!'

Theseus strapped on the sandals. He ran a few laps around the hilltop to break them in. 'These fit great!'

'Yes,' said his mother. 'They have excellent arch support. But, Theseus, about your destiny —'

'Right!' He leaped around like a ballet dancer. 'How do I get to Athens?'

'There are two routes,' his mother said. 'One is an easy trip by sea, directly across the Saronic Gulf.'

'Boring!' Theseus drew his sword and continued to jog in circles, slashing at imaginary enemies, though his mother had told him a thousand times not to run with sabers.

'The other way is by land,' Aethra said, 'which is extremely dangerous and infested with tacky outlet malls. The journey will take you many days and might get you killed.'

'Awesome!'

Aethra knew he would say that. He was always picking the most dangerous path, and she figured she'd better warn him of what lay ahead.

'I know of at least *six* deadly enemies on that road,' she said. 'I'll tell you about them. Try to pay attention.'

Theseus jumped about, slicing the air. 'Yeah, I'm totally listening!'

Aethra told him everything she knew. It was hard for her

to concentrate with Theseus doing his kung-fu sandal-fighter routine. She doubted he heard a word she said.

'Please, son,' she pleaded, 'the six villains along the road to Athens are *much* worse than the local bandits you're used to. They've made land travel between Troezen and Athens impossible for generations.'

'Then I will kill them and make the road safe!' Theseus kissed his mother and went running down the hill, waving his new saber. 'Bye, Mom! Thanks for everything!'

Aethra exhaled. Without Hurricane Theseus blowing through the palace, she might finally get a good night's sleep. She wasn't too worried about her son on the road. But the bandits and monsters? They had no idea what was coming their way.

It didn't take long for Theseus to find his first enemy, which was good, because he needed to burn off some energy.

He was sloshing down a muddy path, enjoying the scenic landscape of dead trees and burned-out villages, when he happened across a big ugly man standing in the road. Across his shoulder was a gleaming bronze club. Around his feet, the ground was littered with fuzzy smashed spheres, like mouldy cantaloupes.

As Theseus got closer, he realized the cantaloupes were human heads – all sprouting from the mud, still attached to bodies that had been buried upright. Apparently, the unfortunate travellers had been used for an evil game of Whac-A-Mole.

'Halt!' roared the guy with the club, which was stupid, since Theseus had already stopped to admire the bashed heads. 'Give me all your valuables! And then I will kill you!'

The bandit stood about seven feet tall. He was slightly smaller than an armoured truck, and his face was so ugly and swollen it looked like he washed it with fire ants. His arms rippled with muscles, but his legs were shrivelled and twisted, encased from thigh to ankle in bronze braces.

'I've heard of you!' Theseus said. 'You're Periphetes!'

See, he really *had* been listening to his mom's stories, which proves that you should never underestimate an ADHD hero. We soak up way more information than you might give us credit for. Running around while swinging a sword is just our way of concentrating.

Anyway, this guy Periphetes (pronounced *Pair-of-Feet-is*) was a demigod son of Hephaestus who had inherited his dad's strength and his deformed legs. He squinted so much that people sometimes thought he only had one eye and they mistook him for a Cyclops (no offence to my Cyclops friends and family).

Periphetes puffed up his huge chest. 'My legend precedes me! If you know who I am, you know it is useless to resist!'

'What's with all the heads?' Theseus asked. 'Did you bury them and then kill them, or —'

Periphetes laughed. 'I pounded them into the ground with my club! That's what I do! My nickname is the Clubber!'

'Oh.' Theseus scratched his armpit. 'I thought they called you the Clubber because you went to a lot of discos.'

'What? No! I am violent and terrifying and I smash people into the mud!'

'So . . . we can't hit some parties tonight, chat up the ladies, do some boogying?'

Periphetes scowled. He wasn't used to being asked to

boogie. 'I will rob you and kill you, puny boy. Those are nice shoes. Give them to me!'

He brandished his mighty club, but Theseus didn't tremble in terror the way he was supposed to.

'That is a *fine* club,' Theseus said. 'Is it wood covered with bronze?'

Pride warmed Periphetes's heart. He was a vicious murderer, but he was also a son of Hephaestus. He liked it when people appreciated his craftsmanship. 'Why, yes! A solid oak core wrapped in twenty sheets of bronze. I find it gives me a really good swing.'

Theseus scowled. 'Twenty sheets of bronze? C'mon, man. That would make it too heavy for anyone to carry.'

'I am strong!'

'Are you sure that's not Styrofoam wrapped in aluminium foil?'

'Yes! I'm sure!'

'Prove it. Let me check it out.'

Periphetes couldn't see any harm. He figured this puny boy would collapse under the weight of the club, which would be good for a laugh. He passed his club to Theseus. Instead of collapsing, Theseus swung it and smacked Periphetes upside the head, killing him instantly.

'Yep!' Theseus said. 'That's bronze over wood, all right! Thanks, man. I think I'll keep this.'

Periphetes didn't argue, since he was dead. Theseus slung his new favourite weapon over his shoulder and continued travelling, occasionally darting into the woods to look at squirrels, racing ahead to check out shiny objects in the road or stopping randomly to stare at bugs. That's where the old saying comes from: *Walk aimlessly and carry a big stick.*

I'm pretty sure that's how it goes.

As Theseus moved north, the smarter monsters and bandits got out of his way. The dumber ones got their heads smashed in.

After a few days, Theseus arrived at the narrow land bridge that connected the Peloponnese to the northern mainland called Attica. Since this was a natural choke point, it was also prime bandit real estate.

Theseus was strolling through a forest of tall pine trees when he saw a dude dressed like a lumberjack — jeans, flannel shirt, bushy black beard and a cap over his curly hair. Somehow, the guy had bent a fifty-foot pine tree and was pinning its top to the ground with both hands. The man grinned when he saw Theseus.

'Hello, stranger! My name is Sinis, and over there is my daughter, Perigune.'

A pretty young lady in a flannel dress peeked out from behind a tree. She waved nervously. Her expression said *Flee! Please!*

Theseus smiled at the lumberjack. 'Why are you holding a pine tree to the ground?'

'Oh, it's just a hobby of mine,' said Sinis. 'They call me the Pine Bender!'

'Catchy nickname.'

'Yeah, I like to challenge people. Anybody who can hold down a pine tree like I'm doing now can marry my daughter. Nobody yet has been able to do it. You want to give it a try?'

.Theseus came closer. He could see Sinis's limbs trembling. Holding down a fully grown pine tree, even for this dude with lots of muscles and lots of experience, was not easy.

Luckily, Aethra had told Theseus about Sinis, so he knew what to expect.

Sinis was a son of Poseidon. He'd inherited his dad's super strength and the ability to keep his footing in almost any situation – I guess because Poseidon was the Earthshaker and could make even the roots of the earth tremble. (*I* didn't inherit those traits from Poseidon, but I'll try not to be bitter.)

When Sinis was young, he had amused himself by bending tall trees and then letting them go, catapulting watermelons and cute forest animals into the stratosphere. He was a swell guy that way. Then he realized he could catapult *humans*. All he had to do was trick them or force them into holding the top of the tree when it was on the ground.

Over the years, he'd perfected his hobby. Sometimes he tied his victims' hands to the treetop so they couldn't loosen their grip. Sometimes he bent two trees at once. Then, since his hands were full, he would command Perigune to tie his victim's left arm to one tree and his right arm to the other. Then Sinis would let both trees go at once. Boy, that was super fun! You never knew how much of the victim would fly off in either direction.

'Interesting challenge,' Theseus said. 'Theoretically speaking, what happens if I decline?'

'Oh, well then, theoretically speaking, you'd be insulting my daughter's beauty, so I'd insist on an even tougher challenge.

I'd tie you to *two* pine trees, one to each wrist. I'd *force* you to hold them both down as long as you could. And when you eventually got tired – '

'Gotcha,' Theseus said. 'So I can hold down one pine tree for a chance at the beautiful girl. Or I can hold down two pine trees and win certain death.'

'You're a quick learner!'

'What if I just run away?'

Sinis laughed. 'Good luck with that. See all those skeletons littered among the pine cones?'

'I was wondering about those.'

'Those are the guys who declined my challenge. I've never lost in hand-to-hand combat, so fighting me is futile. And if you try to run . . . well, I'm deadly accurate up to three miles with a pine-tree catapult. I can peg you with a flying boulder or a moose.'

'I have no desire to be hit by a flying moose,' Theseus said. 'I'm up for the one-tree challenge!'

'Excellent! Come on over!'

Theseus put his club aside. He approached the Pine Bender and sized up the situation. He wasn't as strong as Sinis. He didn't have the ability to root himself to the earth. He didn't even have a plan. But he glanced over at the girl Perigune and his distractible brain started racing. *A girl in the trees. A girl. A tree. Trees have spirits. I'm hungry. Wow, Sinis smells bad. A dryad. I bet the dryads in these trees are really tired of getting bent. Hey, there's a chipmunk.*

'Any day now,' Sinis muttered, sweat trickling down his neck.

Theseus touched the branches of the pine with his fingertips. He thought, *Hello, in there. You want to get rid of this Pine Bender guy? Help me out.*

He wasn't sure if the dryad heard him, but he gripped the top of the tree.

'Got it?' Sinis asked. 'I want to be sure you have a firm grip.'

He was very courteous to people he was about to murder.

'Yeah,' Theseus said. 'I got it.'

'Okay, but just for safety . . .' Sinis carefully took one hand off the tree. From his back pocket he pulled a leather strap. He tied Theseus's left wrist to the tree, which isn't easy to do one-handed, but Sinis had had a lot of practice. 'There you go. Now you are properly buckled in for your trip. See you!'

Sinis jumped back. He expected the pine to spring skyward as usual, launching Theseus into orbit, probably minus his left arm.

The tree didn't move. Theseus held it firmly to the ground.

Maybe the spirit of the tree helped him. Also, Theseus was strong and smart. He knew how to apply the least amount of pressure to get the maximum results – like, for instance, to send a massive boulder rolling through a village.

He kept his feet firmly planted. His arms weren't even straining.

'So,' he said, 'how long do I have to hold this before I win your daughter?'

Sinis overcame his shock. 'I – I'm amazed you're still managing, little man. But you're only human. Eventually you'll run out of strength. Then you'll die.'

'Oh, I see,' said Theseus. 'In that case, I'd better get comfortable. This safety strap really chafes.'

He took one hand off the tree. The tree still went nowhere. He drew his sword and began sawing off the leather strap.

'What are you doing?' Sinis cried. 'If you think you can just step away from this challenge —'

'No, no. I'll keep holding the tree.' Theseus sheathed his sword. He continued to hold the pine with one hand. 'I can do this all day. How long do you want to wait?'

Theseus was betting that Sinis, being a demigod, was just as ADHD as he was.

Sure enough, in about ten seconds Sinis got impatient. 'This is impossible! What's your secret?'

'It's all about the grip,' Theseus said. 'Come here, I'll show you.'

Sinis edged forward.

'Okay,' Theseus said. 'See how the top of my hand is positioned?'

Sinis couldn't see through the pine needles unless he leaned over and looked directly down. When he did, Theseus let go of the tree. The pine sprang up, smacking Sinis in the face and knocking him out cold.

Hours later, the Pine Bender woke from a dream about flying moose. He was groggy. His mouth tasted like a Christmas tree. He realized he was lying spreadeagled on the forest floor.

Theseus's grinning face hovered above him. 'Good, you're up!'

'Wh-what —?'

'Listen, I was thinking about that two-tree challenge. I thought you could show me how it's done.'

Sinis struggled. His wrists were firmly bound. 'What have you done?'

'Well, I've got two pine trees bent to the ground right behind your head. I'm holding them both down with my foot. Your wrists are tied to them, so, if I were you, I'd get up and get ready.'

Sinis yelped. He struggled to rise, which wasn't easy with his hands tied. He had to do a sort of crab-walk somersault to get a grip on the trees. 'You can't do this!'

'Whoops!' Theseus stepped back, leaving Sinis to hold the pines.

Sinis had been bending trees all his life. He was super strong and could keep his footing in almost any situation. But now he was groggy and in pain. The two trees seemed to be actively fighting him, straining to be free. The pines felt . . . angry.

'How?' Sinis wailed. 'How could you possibly hold down both trees *and* tie me up?'

'I had help.'

The bandit's daughter peeped out from behind a tree. 'Hi, Dad.'

'Perigune, no! Release me!'

'Sorry, Dad. This handsome man won your contest, so I belong to him now. Bye!'

Theseus picked up his club. He and Perigune walked away, hand in hand, while Sinis screamed behind them.

'You sure you're okay with this, Perigune?' Theseus asked.

'Ugh, yes. My dad is horrible! It was only a matter of time before he flung *me* into the sky.'

'I wonder how long he can hold down those trees.'

From behind them came a stifled wail, followed by the

whoosh of two trees snapping upward and a sound like a five-hundred-pound bug hitting a windshield.

'Not long,' Perigune said. 'You want to get some dinner? I'm starving.'

They walked to the nearest town and spent a few nice days together. Some stories say that Perigune even had kids with Theseus, but I wasn't there, so I'm not going to gossip. After a while, Theseus explained that he had to keep travelling. He had business in Athens. Perigune had seen enough of the road and evil bandits, so she decided to stay put and make a new life for herself. They parted as BFFs.

After another lovely day in the wastelands, Theseus came to a village called Crommyon. In the town square, a crowd of locals was wailing and sobbing. Theseus wondered if they were upset because they had to live in a village called Crommyon. Then he realized they were gathered around the mangled body of an old man.

'What happened to him?' Theseus asked.

A boy looked up with tears in his eyes. 'It's that old lady and her pig!'

''Scuse me?' Theseus asked.

'Phaea!' the boy shouted. 'She lives out in the wilderness with her massive man-eating sow.'

'They're both monsters!' a woman cried. 'That sow has destroyed the entire countryside. It eats our crops, kills our farmers, knocks down our houses. Then that old lady Phaea comes along afterwards and loots our valuables.'

'I can fix that,' Theseus said. 'Let me kill the old lady and her pig.'

That may not sound like the most heroic promise, but the townspeople gasped and grovelled before Theseus as if he'd dropped from Mount Olympus.

He did look sort of like a god. He had a huge bronze club, an expensive sword and incredibly nice shoes.

'Who are you, O stranger?' one guy asked.

'I am Theseus! Son of Aegeus, king of Athens! Also son of Poseidon, god of the sea! Also son of Aethra, princess of Troezen.'

The peasants fell silent as they tried to do the maths.

'Never mind!' Theseus said. 'I will kill the bandit Phaea and her pet monster, the Crommyonian Sow!'

'Oh, please don't call it that,' said a farmer. 'We don't want our town to be immortalized because of a man-eating pig.'

And so the pig was forever after called the Crommyonian Sow, and that's the only thing the village is remembered for.

Theseus roamed the countryside, searching for the offending porker. She wasn't hard to find. Theseus simply followed the trail of dead bodies, trampled crops and burning farmsteads. The sow was as big as a barn, which was an easy comparison since she was standing in the shell of one, rooting around for dead farmers. Her mottled grey hide was covered with sword-size bristles. Her hooves were caked with splattered gore. And her smell . . . wow. Even from across the field, the stench almost knocked Theseus out. He doubted he'd ever be able to eat bacon again.

'Hey, pig!' he yelled. 'Tasty, yum, yum!'

Those were the magic words.

The pig turned, saw a juicy morsel of hero and charged.

I can tell you from personal experience, there is nothing

cute or funny about a charging giant pig. When you see those mean dark eyes and that toothy snout coming at you (oh, yes, they have teeth), all you want to do is run screaming to the nearest pig-proof bunker.

Theseus held his ground. At the last second, he dodged to the left and stuck the pig with his sword. The sow squealed in rage. She turned and charged again. This time Theseus dodged to the right.

Another thing about giant pigs: they aren't very smart and they can't turn worth crud. Don't ever try to parallel-park one. It won't work.

Theseus played matador until the pig was exhausted and bleeding from so many wounds, it just collapsed in the field. Then Theseus walked over, hefted his bronze club and said nighty-night to the Crommyonian Sow.

Theseus was wiping the pig blood off his club when he heard a shriek.

A fat woman in a sackcloth dress was hobbling towards him, a large battleaxe in her hands. Her skin was mottled grey. Her hair stuck up in a dark thicket of bristles.

'Are you related to this pig?' Theseus asked. 'Because you look —'

'That's my pet, you idiot!' the woman screamed. 'What have you done?'

'You must be Phaea.'

'Yes! And that pig made me good money in the banditry business!'

'Well, ma'am, I'm going to have to cite you for keeping livestock inside the Crommyon village limits. Also for killing, pillaging and being ugly without a licence.'

The woman raised her battleaxe. 'Die!'

Pro tip: if you come across a well-armed hero who has just killed a giant sow, it is not smart to yell 'Die!' and charge him with an axe.

Soon, Phaea was lying dead alongside her pig. Theseus cleaned his sword on her sackcloth dress. He could've gone back to Crommyon and told the people what had happened, but he figured they'd find out soon enough. Also, there really wasn't much to do in Crommyon once you'd killed the giant pig, so Theseus hit the road.

By this time, Theseus had developed a personal philosophy about killing things. He would only attack if he were attacked first. And, whenever possible, he would defeat his enemies the same way they tried to defeat him. Smack Theseus with a club? He'd take your club and kill you with it. Tie Theseus to a pine tree? He'd tie you to *two* pine trees. Not only was this system fair; it was fun. He only regretted that he couldn't kill Phaea with her own giant pig, but philosophy will only take you so far.

One afternoon Theseus was strolling along the top of a hundred-foot cliff (because heroes do that sort of thing). The sea glittered far below. The sun felt warm and pleasant on his face.

It was so peaceful and relaxing that Theseus started to feel antsy.

Fortunately, about fifty feet in front of him, a bandit jumped out from behind a rock and yelled, 'Stand and deliver!'

The guy was dressed in dusty black clothes, leather sandals

(not as nice as Theseus's) and a wide-brimmed black hat. A scarf covered the lower part of his face. He aimed a crossbow bolt at Theseus.

Theseus grinned. 'Man, am I glad to see you.'

The guy's crossbow dipped. 'You are?' he asked.

'Yeah! I was bored.'

The bandit blinked. 'Well . . . okay, then. This is a robbery! Give me all your goodies — that sword, that club, definitely those shoes. Those are nice shoes.'

'I don't suppose there's any way to avoid a confrontation here? Because I'm trying not to kill people unless they attack me.'

The bandit laughed. '*You* kill *me*? Good one! I tell you what: if you wash my feet as a show of respect, I won't kill you. I'll take your valuables, but you'll keep your life. That's the best deal you're going to get.'

The mention of foot-washing triggered Theseus's memory. 'Oh, my mom told me about you. You must be Sciron.'

The bandit puffed up his chest. 'Of course I am! I'm famous! Sciron, son of Poseidon! Number six on the Forbes list of Top Ten Richest Bandits!'

'Hey, I'm a son of Poseidon too,' Theseus said. 'You wouldn't rob a brother, would you?'

'Relatives are my favourite victims. Now, wash my feet! Right here at the edge of this cliff is good. Don't worry. I won't kick you off.'

Theseus peered over the edge. A hundred feet below, a massive round shape was moving under the waves. 'Is that a huge turtle down there?'

'Yes. That's my pet.'

'He doesn't eat humans, does he? For instance, if you kicked your victims off this cliff like you said you wouldn't do.'

'My turtle is a *she*. Her name is Molly. And of course she doesn't eat humans. What a silly idea!'

As if having a giant turtle named Molly wasn't already silly.

Sciron levelled his crossbow. 'Now, wash my feet or die! There're a bucket and rag behind that rock. And bring the disinfectant spray. You'll definitely need that.'

Theseus carefully set down his weapons. Sciron kept his crossbow trained on Theseus's chest as the hero retrieved the foot-washing supplies and knelt in front of the bandit.

'Have fun.' Sciron planted his left foot on a rock, positioning himself so Theseus would have his back to the sea. One swift kick and Sciron would be able to send him over the edge.

Fortunately, Theseus was expecting that.

He whistled as he undid Sciron's sandal straps. The bandit's toes were hairy and caked with unknown substances. In the crevices of his big toenail, green algae were close to developing an agricultural society.

The disgustingness of the feet distracted Theseus, but since he was *always* distracted, it didn't matter. He felt Sciron's leg tense. Just before the bandit kicked, Theseus dropped sideways. Sciron stumbled, off balance, and Theseus booted him in the butt, sending him over the edge.

'WAHHHHHHH!' Sciron flailed his arms, but, sadly, Poseidon's demigod children do not get the power to fly. The giant turtle's head broke the surface. She opened her huge maw.

'No, Molly!' Sciron cried. 'It's me!'

GULP.

Molly apparently didn't mind biting the hand that fed her . . . or swallowing the rest of him, either.

Theseus washed his own hands with antibacterial spray and continued on his way.

Finally he reached the end of the land bridge and crossed into Attica. (Annabeth tells me a narrow strip of land connecting two big chunks of land is called an *isthmus*. I can't pronounce that, but there you go, geography freaks.)

Theseus arrived at the city of Eleusis, which was famous for its temple of Demeter, but instead of selling Demeter-themed tourist junk and offering guided tours of the site, the locals were screaming and running around looking for places to hide.

'What's going on?' Theseus asked one guy.

'The king! He's insane! He wants to wrestle!'

Theseus frowned. His mom had warned him about Cercyon, the king of Eleusis. Apparently the guy was mean and strong and liked to kill travellers. But she hadn't said anything about wrestling.

Theseus made his way to the ceremonial hearth in the middle of town. Usually that was the safest place in any Greek city. Travellers and ambassadors would go there to pledge their peaceful intentions and accept the town's hospitality.

Now the town's hospitality consisted of a bear of a man stomping around the hearth in a glittering gold cape, gold spandex briefs and a mask with big eyeholes that looked suspiciously like a pair of underwear.

'WHO WILL WRESTLE ME?' roared the underwear man. 'I AM CERCYON, THE KING!'

'Wow,' Theseus said. 'Your outfit is shiny!'

'RAGH!' Cercyon randomly darted across the street to the temple of Demeter, punched his fist through a marble column and collapsed the entire front porch.

'Hey, now,' said Theseus, 'you shouldn't be damaging temples. Also, that can't be good for your fist.'

'I am Cercyon!' said Cercyon. 'Defeat me at wrestling and you can be the king! Otherwise I will kill you!'

The king paused like he'd forgotten what he was doing. Probably the strain of putting so many words together had overheated his brain.

Theseus considered what to do. Obviously King Cercyon had gone off the deep end. Maybe the gods had cursed him with insanity for all those years he'd been killing travellers and building up his evil reputation. Theseus didn't want to kill an insane person, but he also couldn't have Cercyon terrifying the locals, destroying temples and rampaging around in gold spandex shorts.

'So, if I beat you at wrestling,' Theseus said, 'I get to be king?'

'Yes!'

'Do I have to wear underwear on my head?'

'Yes!'

Theseus set down his sword and club. 'Do I have to kill you, or will you accept defeat if I just pin you down?'

'That will never happen,' Cercyon said, 'because I will break your spine!'

Theseus winced. 'I wish you hadn't said that. See, I've got this philosophy —'

'RAGGGGR!' Cercyon charged.

Theseus dodged the king's first attack. Cercyon was big and strong, but he was as clumsy as a giant sow. Theseus was familiar with those.

Cercyon charged again. This time Theseus sidestepped. He kicked Cercyon in the back, the way he'd done with Sciron. The wrestler stumbled into the hearth and came out screaming, his glittery cape on fire.

'Death!' Cercyon yelled.

Theseus put his back to the temple. As Cercyon barrelled towards him, Theseus dived between the big man's legs, and the wrestler obligingly ran face first into the marble wall.

The wall cracked. Cercyon's face didn't fare too well, either. He stumbled and collapsed. Summoning all his strength, Theseus picked up the groggy king and lifted him over his head.

Terrified townspeople came out of their hiding places. A crowd gathered as Theseus paraded the wrestler around the square.

'Give up, Cercyon,' said Theseus, 'and I'll spare your life.'

'Never,' mumbled the crazy man. 'Break . . . your spine.'

Theseus sighed. 'Well, folks, you heard him.'

He dropped the king over his knee in a total Bane-breaks-Batman move. Cercyon fell to the ground, dead.

Theseus ripped off the king's mask. He held it up for the people to see.

'Guys!' he yelled. 'You really should not follow orders from people who wear underwear on their heads! Also, the whole wrestling-to-the-death thing is stupid.'

'Hail, our new king!' someone cried.

'Oh, no,' Theseus said. 'I've got my own gig. Who's the smartest guy in town?'

The crowd hesitantly pointed to an old dude with a white beard, maybe the local philosopher.

'You're the king now,' Theseus said. 'Do a good job. Fix the temple. Dispose of this wrestler's body. And never wear an underwear mask.'

'I understand, hero,' said the old man.

So Theseus left the town of Eleusis in much better hands and with a lot less spandex.

Theseus was so close to Athens he could smell it.

I mean that literally. Back then, sanitation wasn't great. A city the size of Athens stank so bad you could smell it from twenty miles away.

Theseus was tired, though. The sun was going down. He figured he'd sleep on the road one more night and walk to Athens the next day.

He stopped at the worst, tackiest outlet mall on the entire highway. Outside the nearest shop, a big sign read: CRUSTY'S SLIGHTLY USED BEDS. STAY THE NIGHT WITH US!!

Theseus couldn't tell if the place was a hotel or a mattress store or what, but, with a sign like that, he couldn't resist checking it out. Plus, there were a lot of donkeys tied up in the parking lot, so he figured the place must be popular.

Strange thing: inside, he found no customers, just a dingy showroom with a low ceiling, guttering olive-oil lamps and two nasty old beds. One was about ten feet long. The other was about four feet long.

That must have really driven the Ancient Greeks crazy.

Like I said, they were a bunch of Goldilockses. They always wanted the middle option that was 'just right.' At Crusty's Slightly Used Beds, there wasn't one — just a bed that was way too long and a bed that was way too short.

'Welcome!' The proprietor emerged from behind a curtain at the back.

At first, Theseus thought it was Sciron's turtle, Molly. The guy had a huge leathery head with absolutely no hair. He wore a full-length black leather apron, like butchers wear, and as he walked over he wiped his hands like he'd just finished washing blood off them.

His name tag read: HI! I'M CRUSTY!

'You're Crusty?' Theseus asked.

'Why, yes, I am. My real name is Procrustes —'

'Which means the *Stretcher*,' Theseus noted. 'Okay. I've heard of you. I didn't recognize the name from just "Crusty".'

'Well, *Crusty* is easier for most people to remember. It looks better on the sign out front, too. Anyway, welcome to my humble mattress shop and motel! May I interest you in a slightly used waterbed?'

'Waterbed?'

Crusty snapped his fingers. 'Sorry. I forgot those haven't been invented yet. But I do have two lovely standard models. These are our most popular choices.'

'They are also your only choices,' Theseus observed.

Crusty chuckled. 'I can tell you're a smart customer. So which model appeals to you — the Crusty XL or the Crusty Nano?'

Theseus examined the larger bed. 'That's the XL? It's pretty long.'

'Yes, but don't worry! See those leather straps at the top and the bottom? If you don't fit exactly, I will stretch you until you do.'

'So you'll stretch me until I'm ten feet long. And if I can't survive that much elongation?'

'Well, you'll die, obviously. Those stains on the mattress are from previous customers who, um, came apart. I did say "slightly used".'

Theseus examined the smaller bed. The baseboard and headboard were caked with dried brown gunk.

'Your Crusty Nano looks kind of . . . crusty.'

'If you don't fit in the Nano, I just lop off the bits that hang out on either end.' Crusty whipped out a knife from his apron pocket. 'So what'll it be?'

'I suppose "just browsing" isn't an option.'

'Nope!'

'How's the firmness on the Nano mattress? I can't sleep if it's too soft.'

'Oh, it's excellent. A combination of memory foam and cushioned coils gives you perfect comfort for the few seconds you're alive.'

'Even for a big heavy guy like you?'

'Absolutely.'

'Sorry, but I have trouble believing that. I've been scammed before in these tacky outlet malls.'

Procrustes scowled. He hated having his merchandise questioned. 'I *never* lie about my products. Look!'

He sat down on the Crusty Nano. He bounced on the mattress. 'See?'

'Cool.' Theseus swung his club off his shoulder. He smacked Procrustes so hard, he fell sideways and banged his skull on the headboard.

When the storekeeper woke up, he was securely tied to the Crusty Nano. His head stuck out of the top. His feet dangled from the bottom. 'What is the meaning of this? I — I don't fit!'

'I can fix that.' Theseus whipped out his sword and helped Procrustes to fit perfectly in his own bed. That's where we get another old saying: *You made your bed, now lie in it, and if you don't fit we'll cut off your head and legs.*

Theseus spent the night in the Crusty XL, which was actually very comfortable if you could ignore the stains. In the morning he set off for Athens, ready to meet his royal father (as opposed to his godly father).

Things in Athens were not hunky-dory.

First problem: King Aegeus was getting old and weak. His influence extended about two feet beyond the royal palace. The rest of the city was ruled by rival gangs, headed by Aegeus's many enemies.

Who were these wonderful enemies? The king's relatives, naturally!

See, Aegeus had a younger brother named Pallas. (Not like Pallas Athena, the goddess; and yes, I know that's confusing.) Aegeus and Pallas never got along. Pallas wanted to be king. Since he was the *younger* brother, he got nada.

So Pallas spent his whole life complaining and having children — *fifty* sons, to be exact. How does someone even *have* fifty sons? Pallas must have had a dozen wives or one really advanced cloning machine. The kids were sort of his revenge on his brother, like *Oh, sorry, Aegeus. You couldn't have any sons? I have FIFTY. IN YOUR FACE!*

Anyway, his sons were known as the Pallantides, the sons of Pallas – kind of like the Sons of Anarchy, except without motorcycles. They'd all grown up to be major league jerks, and they all wanted their Uncle Aegeus dead.

They split into different gangs and took over various neighbourhoods. They had constant turf wars. Everybody in Athens was forced to pay protection money to one gang or another. If you pledged to the wrong group, you risked getting a javelin through the chest in a chariot drive-by.

By the time Theseus arrived in Athens, the fifty Pallantides had established their gangs and were just waiting for Aegeus to die. Afterwards they planned on having a good old-fashioned civil war and letting the strongest Pallantide come out on top. Because of this, the city was even more dangerous than the open highway. If Theseus strolled in claiming to be a son of Aegeus, he'd become a pincushion for arrows before he ever reached the palace.

Second problem: King Aegeus had found himself a new wife – a sorceress named Medea. I'll talk more about her in a later story. Anyway, she had promised Aegeus that her sorcery could grant him a male child, and the fifty Pallantides were not thrilled about that. They would've stormed the palace except the defences were good, the guards were well armed and there was a scary sorceress inside. So, even if Theseus got into the palace, Medea would kill him for messing up her plans.

Problem three: Athens was getting punked by a foreign superpower called Crete. Theseus didn't know much about Crete – just some ridiculous rumours about a half-bull, half-human monster who lived in a big maze. But, from overhearing conversations on the road, he learned that Athens and Crete had been hating on each other since before Theseus was born.

The way it started: one of King Minos's sons, Androgeus, had come to Athens twenty years ago for a local sports contest, and he was killed by some of the Pallantides.

Enraged, Minos summoned his navy and sailed to Athens. He besieged the city. He burned the harbour. He called on his father Zeus to send lightning and plagues and locusts and bedbugs.

Finally Aegeus was forced to surrender. Minos promised to lay off the destruction, but once every seven years Athens had to send their seven bravest young men and seven most beautiful young ladies to Crete as tributes, where they were fed to the Minotaur in the Labyrinth.

If you're thinking that sounds like *The Hunger Games*, that's because this story inspired that one. And, no, the Labyrinth wasn't televised, but only because Daedalus hadn't invented TV yet.

Anyway, the third seven-year cycle was coming to a close. Fourteen tributes were due to be chosen in a few months, and everybody was freaking out.

Sound like enough problems for one city?

Nope. They had an extra bonus problem!

A huge wild bull was also rampaging around the countryside near a suburb called Marathon. Nobody had been able to stop it. The Athenians were pretty sure the Marathonian Bull was a sign from the gods: *You people suck.*

'Wow,' Theseus said to himself. 'This place is seriously messed up. I love it! Lots to do!'

He wanted to get inside the palace and make sure his dad was okay, but that was harder than it sounded.

The guards were suspicious of assassins. They weren't letting anybody in. And of course claiming to be Aegeus's son would get Theseus killed in twenty different ways before he reached the throne room.

What I need, he thought, is a way to get an audience with the king without revealing my true identity.

He glanced at a nearby tavern, where the exterior wall was covered with leaflets. One of them read:

GET AN AUDIENCE WITH THE KING!*
KILL THE MARATHONIAN BULL!**
WIN FAME, RICHES AND DINNER
AT THE PALACE!***

*PALLANTIDES NOT ELIGIBLE.
**PROOF OF DEAD BULL REQUIRED.
***FAME MAY VARY. RICHES SUBJECT TO TAXES.
ALERT YOUR SERVER IF YOU HAVE FOOD ALLERGIES.

That's it! Theseus thought. I will kill the Marathonian Bull and win dinner at the palace. Also, I have no food allergies!

Theseus set off to find the bull, but as soon as he left the city a massive thunderstorm rolled overhead. The clouds looked like boiling ink. Lightning ripped across the sky. The rain stung so bad that Theseus felt like he was walking into a sandblaster.

On the side of the road, he spotted a little hut and rushed inside.

An old woman sat by the fire, stirring a pot of soup. She didn't look surprised to see him.

'Welcome, young one,' she said. 'Big storm, eh?'

'Yeah.' Theseus set down his club. 'You mind if I wait here for a while?'

'Not at all. Off to kill the Marathonian Bull, are you?'

Theseus blinked. 'How did you know that?'

'My name is Hecale. I used to be a priestess of Zeus. I know many things.'

'Oh . . .' Theseus was starting to think he should've wiped his feet before tromping inside. 'So . . . do you have any advice for me?'

Hecale chuckled. 'That bull is sacred to Minos, the son of Zeus. That's why Zeus won't let anyone kill it. That's also why the god sent this storm to stop you. If you promise to bring the bull back here after you capture it, I will sacrifice the animal to Zeus. That should please the lord of the sky.'

'Done!' Theseus said.

Immediately, the rain subsided. The thunder died. Theseus peeked outside and saw blue skies and heard birdies singing in the trees. 'Wow. That was fast.'

'Zeus doesn't mess around,' said Hecale. 'Now, remember your promise!'

When Theseus got to Marathon, he saw a white bull charging around the abandoned village, knocking over houses and smashing through fences.

Theseus probably could've killed the bull with his club, but he needed to bring it back alive for the priestess to sacrifice. He decided to build a trap. He sneaked into one of the few remaining barns and rigged up some snares using ropes and pulleys, and bales of hay for counterweights.

He opened the barn door and waited until the bull was within earshot.

'WOW!' Theseus yelled. 'There are some HOT COWS in this barn!'

The bull turned and snorted. He tilted his head, like *Hot cows, you say?*

'You can't have them!' Theseus yelled. 'They're all mine! I think I'll make hamburgers tonight! HAHAHAHA!'

He ran inside the barn.

The bull charged after him, determined to rescue the beautiful cows from their human tormentor. The bull's hooves hit the snares, which tightened around his legs, flipped him upside down and yanked him into the air. He thrashed and bellowed in outrage, but he couldn't escape.

Theseus made sure the bull was securely tied up. Then he lowered the animal into a wagon, found a couple of horses and carted the beast back towards the city.

He stopped by Hecale's hut like he'd promised, but the old lady had passed away during the night. Maybe it was a case of bad soup. Or maybe she'd lived just long enough to do her final task for Lord Zeus.

'Thanks, old lady,' Theseus said. 'I won't forget you. I'll take the bull to Athens and sacrifice it myself at the temple of Zeus.'

Before he left, Theseus buried Hecale. In her honour, he built a domed monument that stood in that spot for centuries, out in the middle of nowhere, as a reminder that good advice can come from strange places.

When Theseus returned to Athens, he made quite an entrance. The white bull weighed about five hundred pounds, but Theseus slung it over his shoulders and carried it through the city, attracting a crowd as he climbed the steps of the Acropolis to the temple of Zeus. He drew his sword and sacrificed the bull while people cheered and threw flowers.

The priest sent word to the palace: a young stranger had killed the Marathonian Bull. An hour later, a royal messenger brought Theseus an invitation to dinner.

Theseus was psyched! At long last, he would get to meet his father. He decided he'd wait until the middle of dinner and spring the news. *By the way, I'm your son!* Then, after he killed all his father's enemies, maybe they could catch a ball game together or something.

A hitch in the plan: the sorceress Medea had already figured out Theseus's identity. She had magic. She had spies. She'd learned about Theseus's exploits along the road to Athens, and she knew he was the son of Aegeus.

She couldn't allow Theseus to derail her scheme. She wanted a child of *hers* on the throne of Athens. So, before the congratulatory dinner, she approached old King Aegeus.

'Oh, Honey Bunny?' (Her pet name for him proves how evil she was.) 'I'm worried about this young hero who's coming to dinner. I think he's an assassin from the Pallantides.'

Aegeus frowned. He wasn't as sharp as he used to be, but he hated assassins. 'Well . . . what do you suggest?'

'Poison,' Medea said. 'When we toast the hero, we'll give him a cup of tainted wine.'

'Doesn't sound very hospitable. Isn't he our guest?'

'Dearest, you don't want to be killed before you and I can have a son together, do you?'

Aegeus sighed. Medea had been promising him a son for years. It never seemed to happen. Long ago, the king had met a truly fine woman, Aethra. He'd thought for sure *her* son would eventually show up from down in Troezen, but alas, he had never appeared. Now the king was stuck with a sorceress wife, a pack of enemies waiting for him to die and apparently an assassin who pretended to be a hero.

'Very well,' Aegeus said. 'Have the poison ready at dinner.'

When Theseus arrived, he was shocked at how old and feeble his father looked. He was less surprised by Medea, who glared daggers at him as they ate appetizers and chatted about the weather and the best ways to capture giant bulls.

The main course was roast beef, with a big goblet of wine to wash it down.

Theseus noted that the queen tensed up when the wine was set before him. He was really thirsty after so much small talk, but he decided to hold off on drinking.

'Roast beef looks great!' he said. 'But I should probably cut it into bite-size pieces. I'll use my sword, if you don't mind . . .'

Drawing a sword at dinner is usually bad etiquette, but Theseus went ahead and unbuckled the weapon and set it on the table. He unsheathed the blade and cut his meat.

The king's mind was hazy, but he recognized his own royal symbol and initials on the hilt. That sword . . . that was *his* sword. What had he done with it? Oh, right, he'd placed it under a big rock outside of Troezen for his son to retrieve.

This strong and handsome young man had his sword, which meant . . .

As Theseus reached for his wine goblet, the king shrieked and knocked it out of his hands. The poison spilled, hissing and steaming across the marble floor.

'My son!' Aegeus cried.

'Dad!' said Theseus.

'Medea!' the king snarled.

'Honey Bunny?' Medea leaped out of her chair and backed away from the dinner table.

'You *knew* who he was,' Aegeus said. 'You wanted me to poison my own son. You evil, twisted –'

'Now, dear, let's talk about this.'

'Guards, arrest her!'

Medea ran from the room with a dozen guards chasing after her. Somehow she managed to escape and flee the kingdom. Medea had had a lot of practice at fleeing kingdoms. But at least she was out of Aegeus's life.

The king tearfully embraced his son. They talked into the night. Theseus got the best guest room in the palace and slept in a bed even more comfortable than the Crusty XL. In the morning, father and son decided to visit the temples to give thanks for Theseus's arrival. Finally, the king had an heir!

Word quickly spread. The king would be venturing outside the palace for the first time in years. The fifty Pallantides realized they'd better act while they had the chance.

They got all their gangs together and split into two armies. Their plan was to wait until the king and Theseus and their guards were halfway to the temples. Then the two Pallantide armies would attack from either end, trapping the king in a pincer manoeuvre and destroying his whole party.

It was a good plan. I'm not sure even Theseus could've handled that many enemies at once.

Fortunately, the Pallantides had one servant, named Leos, who was still secretly loyal to the king. Leos ran to the palace at dawn and warned Aegeus and Theseus about what was up. Leos explained exactly where the armies would be lying in wait for the ambush.

Theseus got some armour from the royal supply room. He strapped on his sword, picked up his club and strode out of the palace. He found the first army of Pallantides sitting around in a dark alley eating pancakes, waiting for the royal procession to go by.

'Hi!' Theseus said cheerfully. Then he killed them all.

He didn't feel any remorse. They'd been planning to slaughter the entire royal party, so Theseus figured they got what they deserved. It was simple philosophy.

He strode through town, his lovely shoes now splattered in blood and syrup, until he found the second army of Pallantides in line at Starbucks, getting really impatient for their pumpkin spice lattes.

'Hi!' Theseus made the line a lot shorter by killing the entire army. Then he got a double cappuccino with extra foam and returned to the palace.

After that, the king had no trouble leading his procession to the temples.

He gave thanks to the gods for his new and extremely violent son. Everybody in Athens had a really good day, free from Pallantides gangs for the first time in decades.

Fun side note: that dude Leos who betrayed the sons of Pallas? Supposedly the folks in their hometown, Pallene, still can't stand to hear the word *Leo*. They never name their kids that, and if you are born under the zodiac sign Leo it's considered bad luck. I've got a friend named Leo. He'd love that story. He'd probably go to Pallene and introduce himself fifty times a day just to see how people would react.

Anyway, Theseus had made some pretty good progress on his checklist. He'd killed the Marathonian Bull. He'd chased off the evil sorceress queen. He had slaughtered all his dad's enemies in a single morning.

There was just one little dark cloud still looming on the horizon . . . and it looked a lot like a Minotaur.

A month after Theseus settled in as prince of Athens, the big seven-year Cretan lottery rolled around. Every young man and woman was required to register for a chance to win a free trip to Knossos, be wined and dined at the court of Minos and then be thrown into the Labyrinth for a photo op with the Minotaur, followed by painful death.

The people in Athens protested in the streets. Hey, I can't blame them. Their king was celebrating the arrival of his son, and everyone else was being asked to offer up their own children as tributes.

Theseus decided that wasn't right.

'Dad,' he said, 'I'm going to volunteer as a tribute.'

'*What?*' Aegeus tried to rise from his throne, but his legs were too shaky. 'Son, no! I just got you! I don't want to lose you!'

'Don't worry! The deal with Crete says that the tribute system stops forever as soon as one of us kills the Minotaur, right?'

'Yes, but –'

'So I'll kill the Minotaur. Easy!'

Aegeus wasn't sure it would be so easy, but Theseus was determined. It was the right thing to do. Also, Theseus hadn't killed any monsters or destroyed any armies in weeks, and he was *super* bored.

When the people heard that the prince had volunteered, they were amazed. They'd got cynical about politicians and their empty promises. Now this young guy was stepping up, risking his life along with the common folk. His popularity rating went up like seventy-five percent.

When the other tributes' names were chosen in the lottery, they didn't complain. They all rallied behind Theseus, who promised to lead them to Crete and bring them safely home again.

The night before the tributes set sail, King Aegeus had one last dinner with his son.

'Please, Theseus,' said the old king, 'do me one favour: usually, when the ship comes back from Crete, it has black sails because all the tributes have died. If you *do* manage to sail home, ask the captain to use a different colour sail. That way, as soon as I see the ship on the horizon, I'll know you are okay. When you dock we can have a big party in your honour.'

Theseus embraced his dad. 'Sure thing. What colour do you want?'

'Fuchsia,' the king suggested. 'With turquoise trim.'

'Um, how about white sails?' Theseus said. 'Those are easier.'

The king agreed, though white seemed a bit conventional.

The fourteen Athenian tributes gathered aboard their ship and sailed for Crete while their parents stayed behind on the docks, waving and trying not to cry. During the voyage, Theseus tried to keep the tributes' spirits up with bingo and shuffleboard, but everyone was nervous. They knew they wouldn't be allowed any weapons in the Labyrinth. No one had ever survived the experience. That made it hard to enjoy trivia night on the lido deck.

After three days at sea, they docked at Knossos. The capital's golden spires, marble temples, gardens and palaces made Athens look like a dump.

The tributes were met by jeering crowds waving bull flags and big foam hands that read CRETE IS No. 1! Except for Theseus, the fourteen teenagers had never been away from home before. They felt scared and overwhelmed, which was just the way Minos liked it.

Labyrinth Day was a huge PR win for him. It gave the people of Crete something to celebrate. They got to see the best and brightest of Athens's youth cringing in fear and totally humiliated before they were thrown to their death in the Minotaur's maze.

Theseus kind of ruined the effect. He smiled and waved and greeted the crowd as the tributes made their way to the palace. 'How ya doing? I'm Theseus. Hey, great to be here! Gonna kill your Minotaur. Okay, call me, babe. Lookin' good!'

The Athenians were brought to King Minos's palace for

the customary welcome dinner and get-to-know-you-before-you-die festivities.

King Minos was looking forward to some good old-fashioned grovelling from his guests. He loved grovelling. Again Theseus took the fun out of the dinner by daring to have fun. He laughed, told jokes and entertained the Cretan royal family with stories about his exploits on the road from Troezen. The story about Molly the giant turtle went over especially well. Theseus made a little Sciron doll out of bread sticks and tossed it across the table into the king's bowl of soup, yelling, 'NOOOO! MOLLLY!'

Minos's children laughed. Princess Ariadne happened to be sitting across from Theseus. She was fascinated by the handsome, funny, completely fearless Athenian prince. By the end of dinner, she was hopelessly in love with him. She couldn't bear the thought of him dying in the Labyrinth. Her dad was so annoying – maiming and torturing his subjects, throwing her mutant brother the Minotaur into that maze, always putting hot guys to death before she got to know them. Ugh!

King Minos, on the other hand, did not instantly fall in love with Theseus.

He decided the young hero needed to die even *before* the Labyrinth challenge. That would put the other tributes in the proper terrified mood. Otherwise Minos wouldn't get the full effect of their screaming when they were thrown into the Labyrinth. He loved the screams of Athenian youth. They soothed his fragile nerves.

'So, Theseus!' the king called across the table. 'I hear you are a son of Poseidon?'

'Yes, my lord!' Theseus said. 'I am blessed with two mighty fathers — one the king of Athens, the other the god of the sea.'

'How exciting,' Minos said. 'The *second* most powerful king in Greece and the *second* most powerful god. As you know, I am the king of the *most* powerful nation, and my father is Zeus.'

Minos was a twerp like that.

The king rose. He pulled off his royal signet ring — a band of gold set with a bull's head carved in sapphire. 'Shall we test your parentage, Theseus?'

Minos walked to the window. The dining room happened to be on the twentieth floor of the tallest tower, looking out over the depths of the sea. 'How about I throw this ring into the ocean and you dive for it? Then we'll know you are the son of Poseidon. After all your other exploits, I'm sure that's no challenge for you.'

The ring cost about a million drachmas, but what did Minos care? He had a dozen more just like it in his nightstand drawer. He guessed the newcomer would tremble in fear or make some lame excuse for why he couldn't jump out of a twentieth-storey window. But if he really *did* jump that would be funny.

Minos tossed the ring out of the window.

As usual, Theseus did the impulsive thing. *Shiny object moving quickly? Chase it!*

He ran to the window and launched himself into the air.

King Minos laughed. 'Well, so much for *that* Athenian.'

Theseus was halfway down when he wondered if he should've made some preparations . . . a parachute, or maybe a boogie board. He settled for a prayer.

'Hey, Poseidon,' he said. 'A little help?'

He hit the water. That should've killed him instantly, but instead he sliced easily into the depths. The currents carried him down to the ocean floor. He spotted a glittering bit of gold in the sand and grabbed the ring of Minos.

Theseus kicked upward and broke the surface. He didn't even feel winded. 'Thanks, Dad!'

The waves carried Theseus safely to shore. A few minutes later, one of the waiters in the royal dining hall came running up to the king. 'Um, sir, there's a wet guy at the door, says he has your ring.'

Theseus burst in. 'Ta-da! My lord Minos, I bring greetings from the *second* most powerful god, Poseidon. He says, "What else you got, loser?"' Theseus tossed the ring into the king's soup bowl.

The Athenians laughed. Even the Cretans smiled and snickered.

King Minos tried to keep his cool, but it wasn't easy. The veins on his forehead felt like they were about to explode.

'Dinner is over!' The king rose. 'Sleep well, tributes. Tomorrow, you face the Minotaur. And our dashing friend Theseus will have the honour of dying – I mean, *going in* first.'

Princess Ariadne couldn't sleep that night.

Her dad was *so* mean, putting the man she loved to death. She decided she couldn't stand it. She wrapped herself in a hooded cloak and sneaked out of her room to visit her mentor, Daedalus, who lived in a workshop in the Labyrinth, imprisoned there by order of the king.

Over the years, Ariadne had become friends with the old

inventor. He tutored her in maths and science. He listened as she complained about her parents (and you've got to admit her parents were *messed up*). Daedalus had built the Labyrinth, so he taught Ariadne how to navigate it safely — always go forward and to the right, and unravel a ball of string so you can find your way back out. At least once a week, she sneaked into the maze to visit the old man. Now she needed his advice to save her new boyfriend.

She arrived at the inventor's workshop and explained her problem. 'I have to help Theseus! I'll show him your navigation tricks so he can get through the maze. But how can he defeat the Minotaur?'

Daedalus tugged nervously at his beard. He liked Ariadne. He wanted to help her, but he had a feeling this would not end well for any of them.

Ariadne gave him the big sad puppy-dog eyes.

Daedalus sighed. 'Fine. Your boyfriend won't be allowed to bring any weapons into the maze, but the Minotaur has two perfectly good weapons on top of his head. Tell your boyfriend to borrow them. Also, the Minotaur's real name is Asterion.'

'Wow,' said Ariadne. 'I'd forgotten that.'

'Most people have. The Minotaur probably has. But Theseus might be able to use that name to confuse the monster. It may buy him a few seconds.'

Ariadne kissed the old man on the forehead. 'You're the best, Daedalus!'

Later that night, Theseus heard a knock on his door. He figured the guards were checking to make sure he hadn't jumped out of the window again. Instead, when he opened his door, he found the Princess Ariadne, her face flushed, a simple traveller's cloak over her royal gowns.

'I can help you get in and out of the Labyrinth,' she said. 'I'll tell you how to kill the Minotaur. But I have one condition: if you succeed, you've got to take me with you when you leave. I hate Crete!'

'I can work with that,' Theseus said.

Ariadne explained how to navigate the maze. She gave him a ball of thread. 'You'll find the Minotaur in the centre of the maze. If you call him by his real name, Asterion, you might confuse him long enough to get the initiative. You won't be allowed to bring any weapons, but Daedalus said you could use the monster's own horns against him.'

'Okay,' Theseus said. 'Or I could just use my hands. They're registered as lethal weapons in twenty-seven countries.'

The princess's eyes widened. 'Really?'

'No, I'm kidding. I'll use the horns. Thanks for the ball of string.'

The next morning, guards herded the fourteen Athenian tributes to the Labyrinth. The crowd of spectators was even bigger than usual. Everybody wanted to see how Theseus, the prince of Athens, handled his death sentence.

Theseus treated it like a party. He waved and smiled. He shook hands with the Cretans, kissed babies and stopped for photos with his admirers.

When he got to the entrance of the Labyrinth, he called his fellow tributes together for a huddle. 'I'll go in first,' he told them. 'I'll get to the centre, unravelling some string as I go. You guys just take it slow. Hold on to the string. Once I kill the

Minotaur, I'll backtrack, collect you guys, and we'll all go home alive. Ready? Break!'

The giant stone gates of the Labyrinth rolled open. The guards frisked the tributes for weapons, but nobody noticed Theseus's thread, which he'd wrapped around his waist like a belt.

Theseus yelled, 'Yeah, Labyrinth! Woohoo!'

He ran inside. The other Athenians followed, not quite as enthusiastically. The gates slammed shut, and the crowd outside waited for the first screams to pierce the air.

Theseus unwound his string. He tied one end to a torch sconce conveniently located by the exit. He reminded the other tributes not to stray too far.

'Just mingle,' he told them. 'Talk among yourselves. I'll be back soon.'

He headed into the maze.

The place was designed to be confusing. After four or five steps, Theseus would've been hopelessly lost, if not for his trusty string and Ariadne's instructions: *when in doubt, always go forward and to the right.*

He made his way past spring-activated crossbows, pits full of poisonous spikes, corridors filled with rotating blades and hallways lined with mirrors that made him look really fat or really skinny. Finally the maze opened into a circular arena like a rodeo ring.

The Minotaur was waiting.

Thanks to his diet of red meat, steroids, candy and Tabasco sauce, he'd grown to be eight feet tall. With his bullish shoulders, neck and head, and his blood-red eyes and glistening curved horns, he made the Marathonian Bull look like a newborn calf. He was pretty scary from the shoulders down, too. His arms and legs were swollen with muscles. He wore only a loincloth. And the guy hadn't had a bath or a manicure in twenty years.

The floor around him was strewn with broken chains and bones from all the prisoners he'd eaten over the years. Otherwise the arena was empty except for some hay to sleep on, a trough of dirty water to drink from, a hole in the ground for a toilet and a couple of old issues of *National Geographic* for reading material. No wonder the Minotaur was angry.

Theseus approached the bull-man. He wasn't sure if he felt terrified, fascinated or just sorry for the monster. 'Dude, your life must *suck*. You sure we have to fight? I could break you out of here and –'

'ROOOOAR!' The Minotaur charged. He'd been trained since birth to kill and hate. He'd been tortured, taunted and shunned. He wasn't about to trust a human now.

Theseus dodged, but the Minotaur was fast. His left horn scraped Theseus's chest and drew blood.

Theseus knew a lot of tricks for unarmed combat, but he quickly realized the Minotaur was stronger and smarter than any opponent he'd ever faced. He staggered back as the monster turned and charged again.

Theseus dived to the left. The monster anticipated it. The Minotaur backhanded Theseus across the arena.

Theseus groaned and clawed through the hay. Desperately, he grabbed a length of chain. As the Minotaur bore down on him, Theseus lashed out with the chain, wrapping the end around the monster's horn.

Instinctively the Minotaur pulled away. Theseus yanked back with all his strength, and the horn snapped off at the base.

'ARRROOOOOO!' The Minotaur stumbled, but the broken horn was more startling than painful.

The monster planted his feet. He balled his huge fists and glared at Theseus.

For the first time in his life, Theseus felt doubt. He clutched the monster's broken horn, but he wasn't sure he would have time to use the weapon. The monster was simply too fast and strong. Theseus would never get close enough without getting torn to pieces.

'Let's talk about this, man.' He slowly rose to his feet. 'Doesn't have to be this way. You're not all monster. You're part human.'

'RAGGR!' The Minotaur couldn't think of anything more insulting than being called a human. He ran at Theseus, determined to trample him into hero puree.

'Asterion!' Theseus cried.

The Minotaur froze as if he'd been punched in the snout. That name . . . He knew that name. His earliest memories . . . gentle voices. A woman, maybe his mother? A comfortable nursery with actual baby food, warm blankets, a fire in the hearth. The Minotaur remembered a life outside the maze. He had a fleeting, warm sense of being human.

And, in that moment, Theseus stabbed him in the gut with his own broken horn.

The bull-man thrashed and wailed. His screams echoed through every street in Knossos. He tried to grab Theseus, but the hero darted away.

The Minotaur chased after him, but his legs felt like lead. The pain in his gut grew worse. His vision swam. The monster fell to his knees and collapsed. His last vision was of Theseus standing over him, the hero's expression sad rather than triumphant.

'Rest easy, Asterion,' Theseus said. 'Go to sleep.'

The monster closed his eyes. As he died, he drifted into a dream of warm blankets and kind voices.

Theseus pulled the broken horn from the monster's gut. His clothes were soaked in blood. He wanted to tear down the Labyrinth brick by brick. He wanted to stab King Minos with Asterion's horn. But he had thirteen other Athenians to think about. He had promised to bring them home.

He found the end of his string and followed it back the way he'd come. He collected his fellow tributes until all fourteen of them stood at the maze's exit.

Normally, that wouldn't have done him any good. The guards weren't going to open the doors to let anyone out. But Princess Ariadne was waiting just outside the gates. She heard Theseus calling from within: 'Helllooooo? Minotaur gone bye-bye. Can we come out now?'

'Open the gates!' Ariadne told the guards. 'Your princess commands you!'

The guards did as they were told.

Theseus stepped out, followed by the other tributes. He raised the bloody horn so all the spectators could see. 'No more Minotaur! No more tributes!'

The crowd grew silent. They might have turned on him. Things can get ugly when the visiting team wins. But the truth was the Cretans liked brave heroes and dead Minotaurs a whole lot more than they liked King Minos.

The crowd exploded with cheering. They ripped up their bull banners. They chanted *THEE-SEE-US!* over and over as they lifted the hero and Princess Ariadne onto their shoulders and paraded them down to the docks, where the Athenians' ship waited. The city guards joined in the celebration. Ariadne's younger sibling Phaedra, who happened to be in the crowd, shouted to her sister, 'Wait, you're leaving Crete? TAKE ME WITH YOU!' So both princesses fell in with the Athenians.

There was absolutely nothing Minos could do except scream and stomp around his palace as the entire population of Knossos threw a party for Theseus, then escorted him to his ship for his return voyage with tons of gifts, Princess Ariadne and bonus princess Phaedra.

The ship sailed away that night. Their trip home was a massive three-day party. This time everybody played bingo. Trivia night on the lido deck got pretty wild.

If you want a happy ending, this would be a good place to stop reading.

Because, now that he was on top of the world, Theseus wasted no time turning into a dirtwad.

During the first night at sea, the Athenians were so busy partying that their ship ran aground on the island of Naxos. While the crew was doing repairs, Ariadne and Theseus had some kind of falling out. They'd been together less than twenty-four hours, but Theseus decided it wasn't going to work. Maybe Ariadne was more serious about the relationship than he was. Maybe she drooled in her sleep.

Anyway, Theseus told Ariadne he was going to leave her on Naxos and sail home without her.

Cold, right?

Even worse, he claimed that Athena herself had ordered him to do it in a dream. *Gee, honey, sorry, but a goddess told me I have to break up with you. Totally not my fault.*

Yeah. Sure, buddy.

Worst of all? He immediately started dating Ariadne's younger sister Phaedra.

Ouch.

Ariadne's heart was broken, but things worked out for her in the end. After Theseus sailed away, the god Dionysus stumbled across her on Naxos. He fell in love with her, married her, and made her immortal.

Ariadne wouldn't have wanted to marry Theseus anyway. As you'll see in a sec, he turned out to be a failure at Husbanding 101.

The Athenians' ship sailed on, but Theseus, distracted by all of the partying, made a typical ADHD mistake. He totally forgot about changing the colour of the sails to alert his dad that everything was okay.

The ship appeared in the harbour with black sails.

The people of Athens wailed and grieved. They assumed their tributes were dead, as usual. Old King Aegeus was watching from the tallest tower of the castle. When he saw that the sails weren't fuchsia (or white, whatever) he was so heartbroken he threw himself into the sea.

Unlike Theseus, Aegeus couldn't survive a twenty-storey fall. He died, and that part of the Mediterranean became known as the Aegean Sea after the old king.

Theseus docked in Athens. When he found out his dad was dead, he was totally bummed. They never even got to go to a ball game together.

On the bright side, Theseus was now king of Athens. He had destroyed all his family's enemies, found a new wife, Phaedra (who was way hotter than his other new wife, Ariadne), and ended the Athenian tributes to Crete forever.

For a while, King Theseus was super popular. The ship he sailed home on was turned into a floating tribute to him, with a nice café and gift shop. The ship stayed in the harbour for centuries. Each time a plank rotted, the Athenians replaced it, until pretty much every piece of the ship had been swapped out several times.

The local philosophers, who had way too much time on their hands, started debating the 'Theseus ship problem'. If you gradually replace every piece of an original with an exact copy, is it still the same object? I've wondered about that with celebrities who get too much plastic surgery. But Annabeth tells me I'm getting off track . . .

Theseus united Attica under the leadership of Athens. He had kids with Phaedra, and for a few years they were happy. But you know how it is when you're restless and bored – you can't leave well enough alone.

Of course, it wasn't all Theseus's fault.

He found a friend who was a bad influence – the kind of impulsive delinquent your mom always warns you about.

Usually, *I* am that friend. For Theseus, it was a guy named Pirithous.

Pirithous was the chieftain of the Lapiths – a northern Greek tribe so wild they hung out with centaurs. Believe me, centaur parties are *not* for the faint-hearted.

Pirithous kept hearing stories about the strong, brave king of Athens down south. For a while, you couldn't check the news without seeing headlines about *Theseus this* and *Theseus that*.

Pirithous got annoyed. 'He can't be *that* great. I'm going down there to call out this punk.'

He saddled his horse and rode to Marathon, where Theseus had captured the white bull long ago. Pirithous thought, *Theseus thinks he's cool for stealing one bull? I'm gonna steal every cow in town.*

And he did. He rounded up all the cattle in Marathon, because the Lapiths were great cattle thieves along with all their other fine qualities. Since Pirithous was a pretty scary guy, none of the locals tried to stop him.

'You want your cows back?' Pirithous said. 'Why don't you get your king to help you? Tell Theseus I'll be waiting for him.'

Pirithous herded the cattle north.

News of the cattle-rustling incident reached Theseus, and he couldn't let the insult go. He rode north all by himself. Pirithous wasn't hard to find, since that many cows leave behind a whole lot of patties.

When Theseus caught up to Pirithous, they trash-talked

one another for about an hour until they ran out of *your mama* insults. Then they had an epic smackdown. They broke rocks over each other's heads. They threw each other off cliffs. They wrestled and swung swords and tossed grenades, but they just couldn't kill one another. They were equally strong and fast and lucky.

Finally, exhausted, they sat down together and shared a bottle of wine.

'To Hades with it,' Theseus said. 'If we can't kill each other, we might as well be friends.'

There's demigod logic for you.

Unfortunately, Pirithous got Theseus into all kinds of trouble. Every weekend the two of them went carousing – drinking, getting into bar fights and destroying entire nations. Theseus forgot his old philosophy about only attacking when he was attacked. He forgot about only using as much force as his enemies used against him. He just let loose and killed everything in his path.

Theseus would drag himself into the palace on Sunday night, and Queen Phaedra would be like, *Where have you been?*

'Out.'

'Were you destroying entire nations with Pirithous again?'

'Leave me alone, woman! I was just trying to unwind. Gods!'

One time Theseus and Pirithous decided to make war on the Amazons, and Theseus ended up having a fling with Hippolyta, the Amazon queen. How that happened, I'm not sure, but they had a son together – Hippolytus. When the news got around, it didn't go over real well with Phaedra.

She decided to take the kids and move into a different palace. Theseus sulked for a while. Then he did what he usually did to cheer up: he went to hang out with the Lapiths.

While Theseus was there, Pirithous decided to marry a local girl named Hippodamia. I don't know why you would name your kid Hippo-anything, but allegedly she was beautiful. For the wedding, Pirithous invited all the neighbouring tribes, including the centaurs. Unfortunately, the centaurs got drunk and tried to kidnap the bride. Even among the Lapiths, that was rude. The wedding turned into a war. Pirithous and Theseus led the Lapiths against the Party Ponies and kicked their horsey behinds.

Theseus considered this one of his greatest victories. But it didn't do much for his reputation at home when he brought an army of rowdy Lapiths back to Athens and had a drunken, violent victory party at the Acropolis. The place was littered with severed centaur heads and party streamers for weeks.

Then Pirithous got a *really* bad idea. He decided he and Theseus should get new wives together.

'We're the best warriors in the world!' Pirithous threw his arm around his friend. 'We should – *hic!* – we should *totally* marry daughters of Zeus.'

As usual, Theseus didn't bother thinking this through. It was a shiny idea, and he jumped at it. 'Yeah, cool. But who and how?'

'Whoever, man! And we'll just kidnap them!'

'Awesome.'

'I'll help you snag a wife. Then you help me. Who do you want?'

Theseus chose the most beautiful girl he'd ever seen – a

daughter of Zeus named Helen. (As in Helen of Troy.) She was still too young to get married, but Theseus figured they would kidnap her and wait for her to get older. Disgusting and wrong? You bet. I did mention Pirithous was a bad influence, right?

They had no trouble kidnapping Helen. Theseus brought her to Troezen, where his mom, Aethra, was now the queen. He asked her to keep Helen on ice for a few years until she was of marrying age.

I have a feeling Aethra didn't think much of that idea, because later Helen got away from Troezen and grew up to marry someone else, but that's a whole other story.

Then Pirithous decided it was his turn to pick a wife. 'I know just the lady! Persephone!'

Theseus scowled. 'You mean, like . . . the Queen of the Underworld?'

'Yeah! We'll go to the Underworld and grab her. It'll be awesome!'

Like a numbskull, Theseus went along with it. They found an entrance to Hades's realm and battled their way into the Underworld, killing monsters and scaring ghosts. They intimidated Charon the ferryman into taking them across the River Styx.

They were almost to the palace of Hades when they got tired and decided to sit down for a few minutes on a couple of rocks. Theseus's eyes got heavy. He began to doze off. Then he realized taking a nap in the Underworld probably wasn't a good idea. He tried to get up, but his legs wouldn't move. His arms were frozen.

'Pirithous!' he cried. 'Help!'

He glanced over. His friend had turned entirely to stone. Hovering over Pirithous were three ugly bat-winged ladies with fiery whips – the Furies themselves.

'Serves you right for trying to kidnap our queen!' one of them hissed. 'Tourists!'

The Furies flew away, leaving Theseus frozen and helpless. He stayed there for months, with no company except ghosts, until finally another hero came by on a different quest and set him free.

That guy's name was Hercules. We'll get to him later on, after I've had my vitamins and fuelled up on pizza, because that dude did, like, *everything*.

Theseus finally got home to Athens, but he was never the same.

The people of Athens didn't love him any more. They were tired of his carousing and acting like a jerk. His estranged wife, Phaedra, had fallen in love with Theseus's own son, Hippolytus, who was now all grown up and ready to become king – which gets us into a whole *telenovela* level of weirdness.

When Theseus found out, he lost his cool. He killed his own son, which is a big bad smite-from-the-gods no-no. At that point he figured he'd better leave Athens permanently, before the locals lynched him.

Scorned and reviled, he travelled to the nearby island of Skyros, but the folks there didn't like him, either. The local king, Lycomedes, took Theseus into custody, and the townspeople literally voted him off the island. They dragged him to the top of the cliff and tossed him off. This time, Poseidon didn't save Theseus when he hit the bottom.

After Theseus died, his reputation was dirt for a whole

generation. Only later did people forget the bad stuff he'd done and start concentrating on the heroic deeds of his youth.

Me, I think Theseus got what he deserved, right in line with his own philosophy. Things started to go badly for him when he lost interest in Ariadne and dumped her. Eventually Athens lost interest in him and dumped him. You don't mess with karma.

Does his story have a moral? If it does, I have a sinking feeling it would apply to me. Being impulsive and hyper-attentive can be really helpful. ADHD can keep you alive. It can even make you a hero.

On the other hand, if you lose sight of the important things, if you get reckless and stupid and allow yourself to get distracted when you're on the verge of learning an important lesson —

OOH, A CHIPMUNK!

ATALANTA VS. THREE PIECES OF FRUIT: THE ULTIMATE DEATH MATCH

FOR YEARS I THOUGHT THIS LADY WAS THE CAPITAL of Georgia.

Then I figured out *Atalanta* and *Atlanta* were two separate words, and I wondered if maybe Atalanta was named after Atlanta because she really liked the Braves or Coca-Cola.

But nope.

Turns out the name Atalanta in Ancient Greek means *equal in weight*.

Makes sense. Atalanta was equal to any male hero. Actually, she was stronger and faster than most of them, but Greek men wouldn't have dubbed a woman *Better Than Us*. That would've hurt their pride. The best compliment they were willing to pay was *As Good as a Dude*.

Atalanta's parents didn't give her that name. They hated her from the moment she was born.

Her father, Iasus (pronounced *Yay Sauce*), was the king of Arcadia. Like a lot of Greek kings, he was obsessed with having sons to carry on the family name. Maybe with a name like King Yay Sauce he was touchy about not appearing macho enough. When his first child turned out to be a girl, he was so upset that he pulled a reverse Amazon. He took the newborn baby out into the wilderness and left her on a rock to die.

He did not win the award that year for World's Best Dad.

The little baby cried and screamed. I would too, if my dad threw me away. She had a strong pair of lungs, so it wasn't long before a huge she-bear lumbered out of the woods to see what the fuss was about.

That could have ended badly for the baby and deliciously for the bear.

Fortunately, this bear was a grieving mother. Her own cubs had just been killed by hunters. She found Atalanta mewling and squirming on the rock, and Mama Bear decided to raise the baby as her own. She carefully picked up Atalanta in her huge mouth and returned to her cave, where she suckled the child on yummy bear milk.

For her first few years, Atalanta grew up thinking she was a bear. She was healthy and strong. She learned to fear nothing except human hunters. At night, she snuggled into her mother's thick fur. During the day, she ate honey and rummaged through Dumpsters, or whatever bears did in Ancient Greece.

Life was great . . . until hunters came back to the area. One afternoon, while Mama Bear was out foraging, two guys crept into the cave, hoping to find some bear cubs they could kill for fur, or maybe capture and sell to a travelling circus. Instead, they found a human child napping on a bed of animal pelts.

'Dude, that's not right,' said the first hunter.

'We should get this kid out of here,' said the second hunter.

Their voices woke Atalanta. She snarled and bared her teeth.

'It's okay, girl,' said the first hunter. 'We'll rescue you.'

Atalanta did not want to be rescued. She clawed at the hunters' eyes and kicked them in the crotch, but the men were bigger and stronger. They kidnapped her and took her back to their village, which must have broken Mama Bear's heart. For the second time, humans had raided her home and family. She really needed a better security system.

The villagers did their best to raise Atalanta as a human. They taught her how to speak, wear clothes and eat with a fork. They discouraged her from mauling people and hibernating during the winter.

Atalanta adapted, but she never lost her wild edge. She preferred wearing fur pelts to dresses. Her fierce stare could make the most seasoned warrior back down. By the time she was fourteen, she could shoot a bow and wield a knife better than anyone in the village. She could outrun the fastest horse.

She grew taller and stronger than any woman the villagers had ever seen. With her bronze skin and her long blonde hair (a rarity in Greece), she was both gorgeous and terrifying. The villagers began calling her Atalanta, *equal in weight*, because no man could dominate her. Any who tried ended up dead.

It probably won't surprise you that her favourite goddess was Artemis, the virgin huntress. Atalanta never became an actual follower of Artemis, but she admired everything about the goddess: her self-confidence, her skill at hunting, the way she killed any man who even looked at her funny.

When she was sixteen, Atalanta wore out her welcome among the villagers. They started talking about marriage prospects for her, and Atalanta figured she'd better leave before she hurt somebody.

She moved back to the wilderness, where she could live like Artemis, without the company of annoying men. Atalanta never found her Mama Bear again, but she did find a cave that reminded her of home. It was halfway up a mountain, where a cold stream burst from the rocks and provided unlimited running water. Curtains of ivy covered the cave entrance, giving her privacy. The view from her front porch was pretty spectacular: a valley filled with wildflowers, forests of oaks and pines and no other humans in sight.

Her only neighbours were centaurs, who knew better than to bother her.

Well . . . mostly. One time, two young stallion bros named Rhoikos and Hylaios got drunk and decided it would be a super idea to capture Atalanta and force her to marry them.

Two centaurs. One Atalanta. Which of them would get to marry her? They hadn't planned that far ahead. They were drunk. They were centaurs. They didn't need no stinking plan.

They painted their faces red, wreathed their heads in grapevines and put on their grungiest tie-dyed Phish concert T-shirts. Usually that was enough to scare even the toughest humans. That afternoon, while Atalanta was out hunting, the centaurs hid in the trees near her cave, hoping to ambush her when she came home.

Atalanta came along with her bow and quiver, a deer

carcass slung over her shoulder. The two centaurs burst out of the woods, screaming and waving their spears.

'Marry me or die!' Rhoikos yelled.

He expected Atalanta to collapse in a puddle of tears. Instead, she dropped her deer carcass, calmly nocked an arrow and shot Rhoikos through the centre of his forehead. The centaur toppled over dead.

Hylaios roared in outrage. 'How dare you kill my friend?'

'Back off,' Atalanta warned, 'or you're next.'

'I will have you for my wife!'

'Yeah . . . that's not happening.'

Hylaios levelled his spear and charged. Atalanta shot him through the heart.

She dipped an arrow in centaur blood and wrote across their dead withers: NO MEANS NO. Then she left them to rot.

After that, the other centaurs gave her lots of space.

Atalanta would have been happy spending the rest of her life alone in those woods – eating nuts and berries, weaving baskets and hanging out with cute woodland critters, then tracking them down and killing them.

Unfortunately, her reputation began to spread. The centaurs gossiped. So did the villagers and occasional hunters who happened through her territory. They spoke of a wild blonde woman who ran faster than the wind and fired a bow with deadly accuracy. Some wondered if she was Artemis in human form.

Eventually, a guy sought out Atalanta – not for marriage, but for help with a giant feral hog.

So, if you read that other book I wrote about the Greek gods, you might recall a cute little monster called the Kalydonian

Boar, aka the Death Pig. Artemis unleashed this fifty-ton tank of angry pork on the kingdom of Kalydon because the king was a doofus and forgot to sacrifice to her.

Anyway, here's part of the story I didn't tell you.

The king's son, Prince Meleager, was the one who organized the kingdom's defences. He decided to host a pig hunt with all the best warriors in Greece.

Meleager was an interesting guy. When he was born, the Fates appeared to his mom and prophesied that he would live only as long as a particular piece of wood in the fireplace remained unburned. If that seems random, it's because it is. The Fates must have had a sense of humour. They loved playing practical jokes on mortals, like *Oh, my gods! Let's tell her that her son's life depends on a piece of wood. That'll be hilarious!*

Anyway, Meleager's mom snatched the wood out of the fireplace and kept it safe in a box. Because of that, Meleager grew up believing he was pretty much invincible. As long as the firewood was safe, he was safe. When the time came to hunt the Kalydonian Boar, Meleager wasn't afraid. The only way that pig could kill him was if it charged into the palace, found his mother's room, broke open her lockbox, took the magical firewood and learned to use matches. Wild boars weren't known for such behaviour.

But Meleager couldn't kill the monster on his own. Nor did he trust the skills of the others who had joined his celebrity pig hunt. That's why he decided to recruit Atalanta.

By this time, her legend had spread throughout Greece. Meleager was dying to meet her. He loved hunting. He loved beautiful women. A beautiful woman who was the best hunter in the world? That was too interesting not to check out.

For weeks he searched the wilderness until he met a centaur who gave him directions to Atalanta's cave.

'Just don't tell her I sent you,' the centaur pleaded. 'That lady is crazy!'

Meleager approached the base of the cliffs. He set down his weapons, then peered up at the curtains of ivy covering the cave entrance.

'Hello, Atalanta?'

The ivy rustled. A voice called down, 'There is no one here by that name.'

'Look, I just want to talk. My name is Meleager.'

The ivy parted. Atalanta stood on the ledge, her bow aimed at Meleager's head. With her flowing blonde hair, her fierce eyes, and her dress of animal pelts, she was even more beautiful than Meleager had imagined. Not many people can pull off the dead-animal look, but Atalanta totally rocked it.

'Go away,' she warned. 'Otherwise I'll shoot you in the face. I'm tired of men coming here asking to marry me.'

'I'm not here to marry you,' Meleager said, though his heart was pounding. His brain screamed, *Marry her! Marry her!*

He explained about the Kalydonian Boar and his pig-hunting party.

'We could really use your help,' he said. 'The hunter who brings down the boar will win riches and fame.'

'I don't care about riches,' Atalanta said. 'There's nothing to buy out here in the wilderness. I already have everything I need: shelter, clean water, food, pelts.'

'How about fame?' Meleager asked. 'This boar is a curse from Artemis. Only someone who has the blessing of the goddess could possibly kill it. If you bring down the monster, you'll prove yourself the world's greatest hunter, favoured by Artemis. Your name will live forever. You'll also make the male hunters in the group look like incompetent fools.'

Atalanta lowered her bow. She had no use for this prince, or his money, or his promises of fame. But making male hunters look like fools . . . that was tempting.

'If I join this hunt,' she said, 'I will tolerate no flirting from you. No attempts to marry me. If anyone else in your group makes a pass at me, I will most likely kill him.'

'Seems . . . fair,' Meleager said, though he was secretly hoping she would warm up to him. 'Welcome aboard!'

He led Atalanta back to his kingdom, sending messengers out ahead of him with the warning *ATALANTA IS COMING. DO NOT FLIRT WITH THE TALENT. SHE WILL PUT AN ARROW THROUGH YOUR HEAD.*

By the time they reached the palace, dozens of famous hunters had gathered: Ankaios, Mopsos, Kepheus . . . all the biggest, most unpronounceable names in hunting!

They'd got the warning about Atalanta, and they weren't exactly thrilled to see her. A beautiful woman they couldn't possess, who claimed to be better than they were at their chosen profession? Forget about it!

'You expect me to hunt with this *woman*?' Kepheus said. 'I am offended! I won't lower myself to such a contest!'

'Neither will I!' said Mopsos.

Atalanta snarled. 'Go home, then, all of you. At least I won't have to deal with your stench.'

The men reached for their knives.

'Guys!' Meleager pleaded. 'We have to work as a team. We need Atalanta's skills.'

'Ridiculous,' said Ankaios. 'I don't need any woman's help. I will single-handedly slay the boar!'

'Let's make a deal,' said Meleager. 'We hunt the boar together. No killing each other. No complaining about girl cooties. You'll all share the reward money and the glory. Whoever draws first blood from the beast will get a special prize. He – or she – will get to keep the monster's hide. That will decide who is the best hunter.'

I'm not sure why anyone would want a smelly giant boar's hide, but the hunters' eyes lit up with excitement. They all agreed to Meleager's terms.

The next day, they set out to find the boar. As they travelled, the other hunters gave Atalanta the cold shoulder, so she ate most of her meals with Prince Meleager. He tried very hard not to flirt with her. He asked about her early days. He sought her advice on the best ways to track and trap. Despite herself, Atalanta began to warm to the man. She'd never been around someone who was almost . . . well, respectful.

They might have become friends, or maybe more. But, before that could happen, Atalanta picked up the boar's trail. She found pig hoofprints the size of dustbin lids leading through a marsh. That was her first clue.

The hunters fanned out. They combed through the swamp, up to their waists in slimy water, their sandals sticking in the mud. Clouds of mosquitoes buzzed around their faces as they stood in marsh grass taller than their heads, making it impossible to see.

You'd think a giant boar would be easy to hear when it charged, but the Death Pig gave them no warning. It crashed through the reeds like a pork tidal wave, trampling Kepheus, impaling Ankaios with its tusks, and tossing Mopsos aside after his spear bounced harmlessly off its hide. The boar shot lightning from its mouth, which is especially nasty for the recipient if you're fighting waist-deep in swamp water. Soon twenty hunters were dead – fried, flattened or flayed. One hunter, Peleus, managed to throw his javelin, but he was so terrified his shot went wide and he accidentally killed his friend Eurytion.

The only person who kept her cool was Atalanta. As the creature rampaged, she stood her ground, drew her bow and waited for a shot. The wild boar turned towards Meleager, ready to blast the prince with lightning. Atalanta fired. Her arrow hit the creature's back with such force it penetrated the spine. The boar's back legs collapsed, instantly paralysed.

The Death Pig bellowed in pain, the way you might if an arrow went through your spine. It dragged itself through the swamp until Meleager stepped forward and plunged his sword through the monster's ribcage, piercing its heart.

The remaining hunters slowly recovered from their shock. They buried their dead. They bandaged their wounds. They skinned the boar, which must have taken forever. By the time they were done, everybody was hot, tired and grumpy.

'*I* should get the boar's skin,' said Mopsos who, miraculously, had survived. 'I threw the first spear.'

'Which did no damage,' Atalanta reminded him.

'We should all share the hide!' shouted Peleus.

Atalanta scoffed. 'You want a reward because you accidentally killed your friend?'

'Guys!' Meleager yelled. 'Atalanta drew first blood. Without her, I never would have brought down the boar. The hide rightfully belongs to her.'

Two of Meleager's own relatives stepped forward – his brother Toxeus and his uncle Plexippus. (And can we just take a moment to admire how bad those names are? Thanks.)

'You will regret this, brother,' Toxeus warned. 'Do not favour this wild woman over your own family.'

'I could never regret being fair,' Meleager said.

He presented the boar skin to Atalanta, who must have been thinking, *Gee, thanks. I've always wanted to make my own pigskin hot-air balloon.* But she was also sort of impressed that Meleager had taken her side.

The hunters headed back to the palace for what was supposed to be a celebratory dinner, but Meleager's relatives were in no mood to party. The more they drank, the angrier they got. *Stupid Atalanta. Stupid Meleager, giving her that boar's skin just because he's a sucker for beautiful women.*

It was true. Meleager *did* want Atalanta for his wife, but we'll never know whether that relationship would've worked out.

In the middle of dinner, Toxeus and Plexippus knocked Atalanta out of her chair. They took the boar skin and refused to give it back. The other hunters laughed and jeered until things degenerated into a brawl. Atalanta probably would've slaughtered them all, but Meleager acted first. He drew his sword and killed his brother and his uncle.

Meleager's mother, Queen Althaia, was horrified.

'I saved you when you were a baby!' she shouted. 'This is

how you repay me? You kill your own family members for the love of a *wild woman?*'

'Mother, wait –'

Althaia stormed out of the dining hall. She rushed to her bedroom, opened her lockbox and threw the piece of magical wood into the blazing fireplace.

The wood disintegrated into ash. Down in the dining hall, so did Meleager.

Atalanta was overcome with rage and grief. She wanted to slay everyone in the palace, but she was badly outnumbered. She knew she would be executed if she stayed, so she ran back to her cave, her eyes stinging with tears. She vowed never to return to the 'civilized' world. Humans were nothing but trouble. Bears, deer and squirrels were much easier to understand.

Unfortunately, the civilized world wasn't done with her.

The Kalydonian Boar Hunt made her more famous than ever. Her reputation spread. Finally her dad, King Iasus of Arcadia, decided it was time to bring his daughter home.

Maybe you're wondering how Iasus realized Atalanta was his daughter. I mean, there were no paternity tests back then. No birth certificates. Iasus wasn't the only guy in Ancient Greece who'd thrown away his infant daughter. She could have been somebody else's kid raised by wild animals. Happened all the time.

The stories are a little unclear, but apparently Atalanta and Iasus both visited oracles at about the same time and learned the truth.

Atalanta was on her way back home when she happened to

pass a local prophetess offering the usual tarot card readings, half-price love charms and divine wisdom from the gods. Atalanta was so shaken up by the Boar Hunt Family Massacre she decided she could use a little guidance.

'O Oracle,' she said, 'what will happen to me? Can I live in the wilderness without being bothered again? Can I get away with never being married?'

The Oracle spoke in a raspy voice. 'Huntress, you do not need a husband, and you would be happier without one, but marriage is a fate you cannot avoid. Even now, your father Iasus searches for you. He will not rest until you are wed to some suitable man. The best you can do is meet the challenge head-on and set your own terms for how you will marry.'

'Will that assure me of a happy marriage?'

'Oh, no. Marriage will be your undoing. You will lose your identity after you wed. That cannot be avoided.'

'That sucks,' Atalanta said. 'I hate prophecies.'

'Thank you for your offering,' said the Oracle. 'Have a nice day.'

Meanwhile, in Arcadia, King Iasus was also consulting an oracle, who confirmed his suspicions: the great huntress Atalanta was indeed his long-lost daughter, and she would soon come home to get married.

'That's awesome!' the king cried. 'I love prophecies! She's so famous now . . . I can use her to make an excellent marriage alliance. What do I need to do to retrieve her?'

'Just sit tight,' the Oracle said. 'Atalanta will return on her own.'

The king went back to his palace. A few days later, he was not surprised when Atalanta showed up at his gates. The guards escorted her in, and Iasus was impressed by what he saw. Atalanta was beautiful! Perhaps a little too large and muscular for a proper princess, but her flowing golden hair was a plus. She looked healthy and ready for childbearing. Yes, she was a fine specimen of marriageable female.

'My beloved daughter!' he said.

Atalanta scowled. 'Whom you left in the wilderness to die.'

'Well, obviously that was an oversight. But why dwell on the past? Let's talk about getting you married!'

Atalanta was tempted to put an arrow through the king's head. What a jerk!

Still . . . she recognized something of herself in Iasus. He had the same fierce smile, the same remorseless eyes. He didn't care about sentiment. He was only interested in what would help him survive. Atalanta understood that, even if it hurt. She started to wonder if she'd inherited her wildness from Mama Bear or from her royal father.

'I don't want to marry,' she said. 'But, since the Oracle has told me I can't avoid it, I'm going to set my own terms.'

The king frowned. 'The bride's father always sets the terms. *I* know which suitors can bring the most powerful and profitable alliances for the kingdom.'

'We do it *my* way,' Atalanta insisted.

'Or?'

'Or I take my chances and defy the Oracle. I kill you and all your guards. Then I go back to the wilderness.'

'Let's do it your way,' the king decided. 'How do we proceed?'

Atalanta smiled. 'Do you have a racetrack?'

'Of course. Every Greek city worth *anything* has a racetrack.'

'Meet me there in the morning. Spread the word: anyone who wants to be my suitor should show up wearing his best running shoes.'

King Iasus was tempted to ask questions, but he decided against it. Atalanta was gripping her bow like she meant business. 'Very well. Tomorrow morning.'

The king's messengers carried the news throughout Arcadia. The beautiful, terrifying princess Atalanta had returned to the kingdom. She was up for grabs at the racetrack. Bring your running shoes!

(Actually, most Greeks raced barefoot back then. They also raced naked. But, if it's all the same to you, I'm going to imagine them wearing Under Armour workout clothes and Reeboks.)

The next morning, a crowd jammed the arena. Everyone was curious to see Atalanta's strange and fitness-conscious way of choosing a husband. Fifty or sixty potential suitors gathered on the track – all young men from good families. Hey, who wouldn't want to marry a princess? And if they just had to win a foot race to win the bride – that was the easiest score ever!

Atalanta, King Iasus and his guards marched onto the field. Atalanta wore a simple white chiton cinched at the waist by a leather belt with two sheathed daggers. A single blonde braid hung down her back. She held up a long stick like a spear shaft.

The crowd fell silent.

'People of Arcadia!' Atalanta's voice easily filled the stadium. 'Here are my conditions for marriage!'

The crowd stirred nervously. The princess sounded more like she was dictating terms for a military surrender. She strode to the middle of the racetrack and planted the spear shaft upright in the clay surface.

'This three-cubit-long marker shall be the starting line and the finish line!'

(Maybe you're wondering what a cubit is, and why you should care. Measure from your elbow to the tip of your middle finger. That's a cubit in length, more or less. Why should you care? That I can't answer. I'm still trying to figure out the metric system.)

The potential suitors murmured among themselves.

'How many times do we have to run around the track?' one asked.

Atalanta's eyes gleamed. 'Just once.'

'That's easy!' said another. 'So we all race at once, and the winner gets to marry you?'

'Oh, no,' Atalanta said. 'I'm afraid you misunderstand. You don't race one another. Any man who wants to marry me has to race *me* – one-on-one.'

The crowd gasped. The suitors' jaws dropped.

Everyone started to whisper. *Race a girl? Is she serious? She does look pretty fast . . .*

'There's more,' the princess said. 'To make things easier on you, I will start twenty paces behind the starting post, so each suitor will have a head start.'

'Absurd!' one suitor shouted. 'A head start against a *girl*? This whole idea is insulting!'

He stormed off, along with a dozen other suitors.

The rest lingered, either because they were more open-minded or more desperate for a rich wife.

'So we race you one at a time,' another suitor ventured,

'with a head start of twenty paces. And the first guy to beat you across the finish line gets to marry you?'

'Correct,' Atalanta said. 'However, there's one last detail.' She drew her daggers. 'If I catch you before you cross the finish line . . . I'll kill you.'

'Ooooooh . . .' the crowd murmured.

They edged forward in their seats to see how the suitors would react. The morning race had just got interesting.

King Iasus fidgeted with his crown. He hadn't been expecting a death match. He hadn't had time to organize a proper betting pool.

Finally one of the suitors pulled off his racing shoes and threw them away. 'This is stupid! No woman is worth dying for!'

He tromped off, along with most of the others.

A few really stupid or brave suitors stayed behind.

'I'm in!' declared one. 'A race against a *woman*? That's the easiest challenge ever! Just don't fall on your own knives, baby. I wouldn't want my future bride to kill herself.'

'Any future bride of yours would be tempted,' Atalanta said. 'Let's see how fast you are.'

The crowd cheered as Atalanta and Dumbnuts (sorry, the brave suitor) took their marks. The king agreed to serve as referee.

Iasus shouted, 'Ready . . . set . . . go!'

The suitor took off at top speed. He made it ten feet before Atalanta caught him. Her bronze blades flashed. Dumbnuts fell dead at her feet.

'Anyone else?' Atalanta asked, not even winded.

You'd think the remaining suitors would've left the track, right? I mean, they'd *seen* how fast Atalanta could run. She'd pounced on that guy like a lioness taking down a deer. *Blink.* He was dead.

But three others dared to race her. Maybe they thought they were super fast. Maybe they really liked Atalanta. Maybe they were idiots. Within minutes, three more corpses decorated the racetrack. The fastest guy made it fifty feet.

'Anyone else?' Atalanta called.

The arena went silent.

'Okay, then,' she said. 'The challenge will remain open until someone manages to win. I'll be here same time next week if anybody cares to try.'

She wiped her dagger blades on the hem of her chiton, then strode out of the stadium. The king followed, relieved that the show was over and he would have time to organize betting for next week's race.

If Atalanta wasn't famous enough before, her reputation *really* got a boost after the death race. Suitors came from all over Greece to try their luck. Some chickened out when they saw Atalanta run. Others challenged her and died. Nobody made it even halfway around the track before getting butchered.

King Iasus was miffed that his daughter wasn't getting married. But on the bright side the races were great for tourism, and he was making a bundle from his bookies.

A few months later, a guy named Hippomenes happened to be in town on business. He was from a rich family in a city down the coast. His dad, Megareus, was a son of Poseidon, so obviously Hippomenes had excellent lineage. He'd also been trained in the hero business by the wise centaur Chiron, who tutored only the best. (Including me, not that I'm bragging. Okay, maybe I'm bragging.)

One morning, Hippomenes was wandering through town when he noticed that all of the locals were closing up shop and hurrying to the racetrack.

'What's going on?' he asked a shopkeeper. 'Seems a little early in the day for a siesta.'

The shopkeeper grinned. 'Atalanta has a new batch of suitors to murder . . . I mean, race.'

He explained about Atalanta's popular local reality show: *The Bachelor (Whom I'm About to Run Down and Eviscerate)*. Hippomenes wasn't sure whether to laugh or throw up.

'That's horrible!' he said. 'Those men must be idiots! No woman, no matter how wonderful, is worth a risk like that.'

'I guess you haven't seen Atalanta,' said the shopkeeper. Then he rushed off.

Hippomenes was overcome by curiosity. He followed the crowd to the stadium, where half a dozen new suitors had gathered to try their luck. Hippomenes couldn't believe so many men could be so stupid.

Then he saw Atalanta. She stood to one side doing some runner's stretches. In her simple white chiton, with her golden braid of hair, she was the most beautiful woman Hippomenes had ever seen. In a daze, he pushed his way through the crowd until he stood next the suitors.

'I have to apologize,' he told them. 'I thought risking one's life for any woman was ridiculous. Now that I've seen her, I totally understand.'

One of the suitors frowned. 'Yeah, that's great, buddy. Step aside. This week it's *our* turn.'

Atalanta overheard the exchange. She pretended not to look, but out of the corner of her eye she assessed Hippomenes: curly black hair, sea-green eyes, strong, graceful limbs. His voice was what really captured her attention. It was rich and pleasing and mellifluous (there's my big word for the week; thank you, SAT prep class), like the waterfall outside Atalanta's old cave. She felt unfamiliar warmth in her chest – something she hadn't experienced since Meleager took her side during the Kalydonian Boar Hunt.

She tried to clear her mind. She had a race to win and six suitors to kill.

King Iasus called the first runner to his mark. Atalanta took her starting position, twenty paces back.

Hippomenes watched, entranced, as Atalanta chased down her would-be husbands one after the other. She ran more swiftly than an arrow fired from a Scythian bow (translation: hella fast). She moved more gracefully than a leopard. And the way she whipped out her knives and butchered those suitors . . . Wow. What a woman!

If he'd had any sense, Hippomenes would've run away in terror. Instead, he fell hopelessly in love.

After the last race, as the crowd was dispersing, he approached the victorious princess, who was cleaning the blood off her knives.

'O beautiful princess!' Hippomenes said. 'May I dare to speak with you?'

Atalanta wasn't sure he was talking to her. She was sweaty

from running six races. Her face was blotchy from exertion, and her braid had come undone. Her feet were caked with clay. Her chiton was stained with the blood and tears of her dead opponents.

And this guy thought she was beautiful?

'You may dare to speak,' she said.

'Those suitors you raced against,' Hippomenes said, 'they were not worthy opponents. Where is the glory in defeating such men? Race me instead. *I* understand your worth.'

'Oh, you do, eh?'

Hippomenes bowed. 'My grandsire is Poseidon, lord of the waves. I know a force of nature when I see one. The others see only your beauty or your father's wealth. I look at you and I see the winds of a storm. I see the roaring current of a great river. I see the most powerful woman ever created by the gods. You need no husband trying to master you. You need an equal to share your life. Let me prove I am that man.'

Atalanta's heart stumbled against her ribs. She'd never been complimented in a way that felt so genuine.

'What is your name?' she asked.

'Hippomenes.'

'Do you go by Hippo?'

'I do not.'

'That's good. Listen, Hippomenes, I appreciate the sentiment, but I'm not worth the risk. I'm sure a hundred girls in this city would be thrilled to marry you. Do yourself a favour. Pick one of them. Turn around, leave and forget you ever saw me. I'd hate to have to kill the one courteous man in Greece.'

Hippomenes knelt at her feet. 'It's too late, princess. I've seen you now. I can't forget you.' He took her hand. 'I can only pray that my love is as powerful and uncontainable as you are. When do we race?'

An electric current raced through Atalanta's body. What was she feeling . . . sadness? Pity? She'd never been in love before. She didn't know how to recognize the emotion.

She wanted to deny Hippomenes the race, but her father stood nearby, watching like a falcon. His expression was clear: *You made the rules. Now you have to follow them.*

Atalanta sighed. 'Poor Hippomenes. I wish I could spare your life, but, if you are determined to die, meet me here next week, same day and time, and we will see who is faster.'

Hippomenes kissed her blood-speckled hand. 'Next week, then.'

As he left the stadium, the crowd parted around him in awe. No man had ever got that close to Atalanta and lived. Certainly nobody had ever dared to kiss her hand without having his face surgically removed.

Hippomenes's mind was racing. He knew he couldn't win Atalanta without divine help. His grandfather Poseidon was awesome in many ways, but Hippomenes doubted he could assist him in winning a foot race or a woman's heart. Maybe Poseidon could disrupt the race by causing an earthquake or a tidal wave, but that would kill thousands of people, which wasn't the sort of collateral damage Hippomenes wanted on his wedding day.

He asked around until he got directions to the nearest shrine to Aphrodite. It sat unused and neglected at the edge of town, I suppose because the folks in Arcadia were more interested in betting on death matches than in romance.

PERCY JACKSON AND THE GREEK HEROES

Hippomenes tidied up the shrine. He cleaned the altar, then prayed to the goddess of love.

'Help me, Aphrodite!' he cried. 'Love is the strongest force in the world. Let me prove it! I'm sure Atalanta loves me. I love her, but she worships the maiden goddess, Artemis. Show the world that *you* are the most powerful goddess! Help me win Atalanta's heart by winning this race!'

A breeze swirled through the shrine, filling the air with the scent of apple blossoms. A female voice whispered in the wind. *Hippomenes, my dear young man . . .*

'Aphrodite?' he asked.

No, it's Ares, chided the voice. *Of course it's Aphrodite. You're praying in my shrine, aren't you?*

'Right, sorry.'

I will help you win the love of Atalanta, but it will not be easy. I cannot increase your running speed. I have no control over sporting contests. Nike oversees that sort of thing, and she is such a bore.

'I am a fast runner,' Hippomenes promised. 'But Atalanta is faster. Unless there is some way to slow her down –'

I have just the thing. Three pieces of baseball-sized golden fruit floated into the shrine and settled on the altar.

'Apples?' Hippomenes asked.

Not just any apples. These are from my sacred tree in Cyprus. I flew them here especially for you!

'Wow, thanks.'

Shipping is free on your first order.

'So I'm supposed to get Atalanta to eat these?'

No, no. She'll give you a head start in the race, correct?

'Yeah. Like twenty paces.'

As you run, whenever Atalanta gets too close, drop one of these apples

278

in her path. She'll stop to pick it up, which will buy you a few seconds. You'll have three chances to slow her down. If you time it just right, you might make it across the finish line before she kills you.

Hippomenes stared at the apples. They might've been from a sacred tree, but they didn't look magical. They looked like regular Golden Delicious apples, $1.29/lb. at Safeway.

'Why would Atalanta stop to pick these up?' he asked. 'Does she need more fibre in her diet?'

The apples are impossible to resist, said the goddess. *Just like love. Just like me. Have faith, Hippomenes.*

'I will, goddess. I will do exactly as you say.'

One more thing: when you win Atalanta's heart, come back here and give me a proper sacrifice. Don't forget to give me the credit.

'Of course! Thank you!'

Hippomenes scooped up the apples and ran back to town. He had a lot of training to do before the race.

The next week, crowds packed the stadium again. The betting was heavy. King Iasus offered five-to-one odds that Hippomenes would make it halfway around the track; a thousand-to-one that he would actually win the race. The townsfolk couldn't wait to see how far this handsome, brave young man would get before he was slaughtered.

Atalanta hadn't slept well all week. She'd been tossing and turning, thinking about the Oracle's prophecy, remembering how Hippomenes had held her hand. Now she paced nervously on the track. Her knives felt heavier than usual.

Hippomenes, on the other hand, looked cheerful and confident. He strode up to Atalanta with a cloth bag hanging from his belt.

'Good morning, my princess!'

Atalanta frowned. 'What's in the bag?'

'Just some fresh fruit, in case I get hungry.'

'You can't run with that.'

'You run with knives. Why can't I run with a packed lunch?'

Atalanta suspected a trick, but she'd never made any rules about what the suitors could or couldn't carry. 'Very well. Run with your lunch. You'll die regardless.'

'Oh, no,' Hippomenes promised. 'By the end of the day, you and I will be married. I can't wait.'

Atalanta grunted and turned away. She was afraid she might be blushing. She walked to her starting position, twenty paces back.

King Iasus raised his arms. The crowd fell silent.

'Ready . . .' shouted the king. 'Set . . . go!'

Hippomenes shot from the starting post. He'd always been a fast runner. Now his life was at stake. More than that: his true love needed him. Atalanta was trapped in this race just as much as he was. He could tell she didn't want to kill him. He had to win for both of them.

He was a quarter of the way around the track, further than any other suitor had ever got, when he sensed Atalanta behind him.

He heard the hiss of a knife blade drawn from a leather sheath.

He thrust his hand into his pouch, grabbed the first apple and tossed it over his shoulder.

Atalanta dodged instinctively. Out of the corner of her eye, she saw a flash of gold as the apple sailed past.

What the Hades? she thought. *Did Hippomenes just throw a piece of fruit at me?*

She was so surprised she glanced behind her. Sure enough, a golden apple was rolling across the track. She knew she should keep running, but something about that apple lying in the dust seemed wasteful and sad. As the crowd roared in disbelief, Atalanta turned back and snatched it up.

Hippomenes was now a third of the way around the track.

Atalanta snarled in frustration. She didn't understand what had made her grab the fruit, but she wasn't about to lose the race because of a cheap trick. Apple in one hand, knife in the other, she poured on the speed, her feet ripping across the clay at the speed of whirring helicopter blades.

Hippomenes had just passed the halfway mark. The crowd was going wild. He couldn't hear Atalanta, and he didn't dare look behind him, but judging from the cheering and the chants of *KILL! KILL! KILL!* he guessed she was about to stab him in the back.

He tossed the second apple over his head.

Atalanta veered to avoid the fruit. But the sweet smell caught her nose, pulling her off course like she'd been hooked on a fishing line. She grabbed the apple before it hit the ground, but managing two apples and a knife while running wasn't easy, even for the world's best hunter. She lost valuable time.

Why do I need these apples? Atalanta wondered as she raced after Hippomenes. *This is stupid. I should just drop them!*

But she couldn't. The apples' smell and warm golden colour reminded her of her happiest days – eating honeycombs with Mama Bear in the forest, watching daffodils bloom near her cave by the waterfall, chasing the Kalydonian Boar with Meleager at her side. The apples also made her wistful for something she'd never known. Watching Hippomenes run in front of her, she fell into a sort of trance, admiring his strength and speed. It wouldn't be so bad spending her life with such a man.

Stop it! she scolded herself. *Run!*

She pushed herself like never before. Her feet barely touched the ground as she flew after Hippomenes. He was only fifty feet from the marker now, but she could still close the gap.

She was within striking distance when Hippomenes threw his last apple.

Atalanta had anticipated that. She told herself not to get distracted.

But as the golden fruit sped by her ear a voice seemed to whisper, *Last chance. This apple is everything you are losing: companionship, joy, true love. How can you simply run past and leave it lying in the dust?*

Atalanta lunged sideways. She grabbed the last apple as Hippomenes crossed the finish line.

The spectators surged to their feet, cheering with jubilation – especially those who had bet on Hippomenes at a thousand to one. Atalanta staggered up to him with three apples and a clean knife gathered in her skirt.

'Trickery!' she grumbled. 'Magic!'

'Love,' Hippomenes corrected. 'And I promise you my love is genuine.'

'I don't even like apples.' Atalanta dumped the golden fruit on the ground. She threw her arms around Hippomenes. His kisses tasted even better than honeycombs.

That night they got married at the palace. King Iasus wasn't in the best spirits, since the day's betting had nearly bankrupted him, but Atalanta and Hippomenes were deliriously happy.

They spent a blissful year together. Atalanta gave birth to

a son, Parthenopaeus, who later became a great warrior. (Some folks whispered that the boy's father was actually Meleager, or maybe even the war god, Ares, but I don't like to gossip.)

Atalanta and Hippomenes deserved to live happily ever after, don't you think?

They didn't.

Hippomenes was so head-over-heels in love with Atalanta that he forgot one teensy little detail: to make a sacrifice at the shrine of Aphrodite.

Sure, that was stupid. But come on! The guy was in love. He was distracted. You'd think Aphrodite of all people would understand.

But you don't short-change the gods without paying a price.

One spring afternoon, Hippomenes and Atalanta were riding back to town after a wonderful day of hunting. They happened to stop at a small shrine to Zeus and decided to have lunch there. They were just finishing their sandwiches when their eyes met. They were suddenly overwhelmed with how much they loved one another. Up on Mount Olympus, Aphrodite was working her magic – inflaming their emotions and taking away their common sense.

'Kiss me, you fool!' Atalanta cried.

'But this is a shrine to Zeus,' Hippomenes protested weakly. 'Maybe we shouldn't –'

'Who cares!' Atalanta tackled her husband. They started rolling around and smooching right in front of the altar.

Not such a good idea.

Zeus looked down from Mount Olympus and saw two mortals desecrating his shrine with their public display of affection. 'GROSS! THEY CAN'T DO THAT IN MY SHRINE! ONLY *I* CAN DO THAT IN MY SHRINE!'

He snapped his fingers. The two lovers instantly changed form. Golden fur covered their bodies. A shaggy mane ringed Hippomenes's neck. Their nails grew into claws. Their teeth became fangs. Atalanta and Hippomenes slunk off into the woods as a pair of lions.

According to some stories, a goddess named Cybele eventually harnessed those lions to pull her chariot, but most of the time Atalanta and Hippomenes prowled the wilderness, untamable and impossible to hunt, because as former hunters they knew all the tricks.

Some of their children are still out there: lions that can out-think humans . . . but I wouldn't recommend hunting them, unless you want to end up as a serving of demigod tartare.

And so the Oracle's prophecy came true: Atalanta *did* lose her identity after she got married. But at least she got to go back to the Great Outdoors, and she got to stay with her husband.

It could've been worse.

She could've ended up like the hero Bellerophon.

When that guy fell, he fell *hard*.

WHATEVER IT IS, BELLEROPHON DIDN'T DO IT

THE ANCIENT GREEKS CALLED THIS GUY Bellerophon the Blameless, which is funny, since he was always in trouble.

His real name wasn't even Bellerophon. He got that name after his first murder . . . but maybe I should back up.

In the old days, every Greek city wanted its own hero. Athens had Theseus. Argos had Perseus.

The city of Corinth didn't have jack. Their most famous native son was Sisyphus, who'd once tied up Death and got himself condemned to eternal punishment. That didn't make him a very good poster boy for the city.

After Sisyphus got dragged to the Underworld, his son Glaucus became the king of the city. He did his best to improve its reputation. He built a new palace. He sponsored a pro soccer team. He hung colourful banners along Main Street that read CORINTH: YOUR GATEWAY TO FUN!

Glaucus also married a beautiful princess named Eurynome. He hoped to have noble sons who would some day become great heroes and put Corinth on the map.

Only problem: the gods were still angry about Sisyphus. Zeus decreed that Sisyphus's children would never have sons of their own to carry on the family name. Zeus didn't want any more little Sisyphuses (Sisyphi?) running around Greece trying to cheat Death.

Because of that, Glaucus was unable to sire male children. Eurynome and he tried for years with no luck. The king was always fretting about it.

One night he paced the royal bedroom, wringing his hands. 'What can we do?' he asked his wife. 'How can I have an heir to the throne?'

'Well, we could have a *daughter*,' his wife suggested. 'Let her become queen.'

'Oh, please,' Glaucus said. 'I'm in no mood for jokes.'

Eurynome rolled her eyes. 'All right, then. What if we adopted a son?'

'The people would never accept an adopted king!'

'Hmm.' She gazed out of the bedroom window at the moonlit sea. 'In that case, perhaps I should seek divine help.'

'What do you mean?'

Eurynome smiled. 'Leave it to me, dear.'

The queen had always been a fan of the sea god, Poseidon. Clearly, she had good taste. The next evening, she went down to the beach and prayed. 'O great Poseidon! I have a problem! My husband cannot sire sons, but he really wants an heir. I could use your help, if you catch my meaning . . .'

Poseidon heard the beautiful queen asking for his assistance. He rose from the waves in all his glory, wearing only his swim trunks.

'Greetings, Eurynome,' said the lord of the sea. 'You want to have a son? Sure. I can help you out.'

That's my dad. Always thinking of the greater good.

Nine months later, Eurynome gave birth to a healthy baby boy. She named him Hipponous, because we don't already have enough people named Hippo in this book.

King Glaucus was delighted! He was sure the boy was his. The queen had prayed for a miracle. The gods had answered. Glaucus wasn't going to question his good fortune. The fact that his new son looked exactly like the mosaic portraits of Poseidon in the local temple was simply a coincidence.

As Hipponous grew, he got a reputation for being reckless. He was always in the wrong place at the wrong time. Once, he and his friends were roasting marshmallows at the royal hearth when he spilled too much oil on the fire and burned down the dining hall.

'It was an accident!' the prince wailed.

Another time he inadvertently goosed a sacrificial bull with his dagger and caused a stampede through the temple.

'It wasn't my fault!' he cried.

A few weeks later he was sitting on the royal docks, absently sawing on a rope because he was bored, when the rope snapped and his father's finest ship sailed out to sea with no crew.

'I didn't do it!' he said.

The prince's most famous oopsie: one year at his parents' New Year's Eve party he and his friends were throwing daggers at a bale of hay, trying to hit a bull's-eye, when somebody yelled, 'Hey, Hipponous!'

The prince turned and threw his dagger at the same time, because he wasn't very coordinated. His dagger hit a guy named Belleros in the chest, killing him instantly.

'It was an accident!' Hipponous sobbed.

Everybody agreed the death was not intentional. Nobody had liked Belleros very much anyway, so Hipponous didn't get into trouble. But people began calling the prince *Bellerophon*, which means *the killer of Belleros*. The nickname stuck.

Imagine living like that. You kill some dude named Joe. For the rest of your life, you have to answer to 'I Killed Joe'. Then you earn a title like 'the Blameless', so your name is basically 'I Killed Joe, But It Wasn't My Fault'.

The final straw came when Bellerophon was a teenager. By that time he had a little brother named Deliades. How did the royal couple have another son? Maybe Zeus decided to lift the curse. Or maybe Poseidon was still visiting the queen out of a sense of civic duty. Whatever the case, Bellerophon was teaching Deliades how to fight with a sword one afternoon. (I know. Terrible idea.)

In the middle of combat, Bellerophon said, 'Okay, Deliades, I'm going to attack on your right. Block the strike!'

Deliades blocked right. Bellerophon mistakenly swung left, because he still wasn't clear on the whole left/right thing. He killed his brother.

'It was an accident!' Bellerophon said.

At that point, his parents held an intervention.

'Look, son,' said King Glaucus, 'you can't keep having accidents. Killing your brother . . . that was not okay.'

'But, Dad —'

'I know you didn't mean it,' said Queen Eurynome. 'Nevertheless, my dear, your father and I have decided to send you away for a while before you *accident* us both to an early grave.'

'Send me away? But, Mom —'

'My friend King Proitos has agreed to take you in,' said the king. 'You will go to Argos and complete the rituals of purification to atone for your brother's death.'

'Rituals of purification?' Bellerophon sniffled. 'Do they hurt?'

'You'll spend a few months in mourning,' his dad said, 'praying to the gods. You'll be fine.'

'A few months? Then can I come home?'

'Maybe. We'll see.'

Bellerophon's lower lip quivered. He didn't want to cry, but he felt so unwanted. Sure, he burned down the occasional building and killed the occasional brother, but did his parents really have to send him away?

The next day he left town alone. He took the road, even though it was dangerous. He was so depressed and moved so slowly he only made it a few miles before sunset. He found a roadside shrine to Athena and decided to spend the night there.

Before he went to sleep, Bellerophon prayed to the goddess. 'Athena, I could really use some of your wisdom. My parents think I'm worthless. I destroy everything I touch. Should I just give up, or what?'

Weeping, he climbed onto the altar and went to sleep.

Normally, sleeping on a god's altar is not a good idea. You are likely to wake up as a ferret or a potted plant.

But Athena felt bad for Bellerophon. Even though he was a son of Poseidon, who wasn't exactly Athena's best buddy, the young man had potential to be more than a walking disaster.

While he slept, Athena appeared in his dream. Grey fog billowed around the altar. Lightning flashed. 'Bellerophon!'

Bellerophon's dream-self tumbled off the altar, knocking over a statue, which shattered on the floor. He shot to his feet. 'I didn't do it!'

Athena sighed. 'That's okay. This is only a dream. I heard your prayer, Bellerophon. You are *not* worthless. Your real father is Poseidon, god of the sea.'

Bellerophon gasped. 'Is that why I look like those mosaics?'

'Yes.'

'And why my mom enjoys the beach so much?'

'Yes. So stop feeling sorry for yourself. You can be a great hero if you just find your self-confidence.'

'I'll – I'll try, Athena.'

'To get you started, I have a present for you.' The goddess held up a contraption of woven gold straps.

'Is that a net?' Bellerophon asked.

'No.'

'A brassiere?'

Athena scowled. 'Think about it. Why would I give you a golden brassiere?'

'Um . . .'

'It's a bridle! The thing you put around a horse's head!'

'Oh, right.' Bellerophon had never paid much attention to bridles. Every time he tried to ride a horse, he either ran someone over or drove the horse through somebody's living room. 'So . . . I should find a steed to put this on?'

Athena began to wonder if appearing in this young man's dream had been such a good idea. He reminded her of Poseidon on his stormiest days: blowing around aimlessly, destroying things for no apparent reason. But she was here now. She had to try to steer the boy on a better course.

'Near this shrine,' she said, 'at a place called Peirene, you will find a freshwater spring. At this spot, Pegasus often comes to drink.'

'Whoa. *The* Pegasus?' Bellerophon had heard legends about the winged horse. Supposedly he had sprung from the blood of Medusa after Perseus cut off her head. Many heroes had tried to capture Pegasus. None had succeeded.

'That's right,' Athena said. 'How would you like to ride an immortal winged steed?'

Bellerophon rubbed his chin. 'Wait . . . If my dad is Poseidon, and Pegasus's dad is Poseidon, isn't the horse my brother?'

'Best not to think about that,' Athena advised. 'Just follow my instructions. As soon as you wake up, make a proper sacrifice to me and to your father, Poseidon. That will ensure our blessings. Then find the spring of Peirene, and wait until Pegasus lands. When he folds his wings to drink, you'll have to sneak up behind him and slip the bridle over his head.'

'Um, stealth isn't really my thing.'

'Do your best. Try not to kill yourself. If you can succeed in getting the bit into Pegasus's mouth, the magic of the bridle will instantly calm him down. He'll accept your friendship and take you wherever you want to go.'

'Awesome!'

'Just don't push your luck,' Athena warned. 'Heroes always push their luck when they get some cool gift like a flying horse. DON'T DO THAT.'

'Of course not. Thanks, Athena!'

The goddess faded into the fog. Bellerophon awoke from his dream, promptly toppled off the altar, and knocked over a statue, which shattered on the floor.

He looked up at the heavens. 'Sorry. That was an accident.'

The wind made a sound like an exasperated sigh.

Bellerophon walked to the nearest farm and spent all his travelling money on a young bull. He sacrificed the animal — half to Athena, half to Poseidon.

Then he set off to capture Pegasus with his magical golden brassiere.

The spring of Peirene gushed from a limestone crevice and spilled into a pool dotted with lotuses and water lilies.

Bellerophon crouched behind a nearby bush and waited for what seemed like hours. Probably because it *was* hours. He learned what most ADHD demigods know: we may be easily distracted, but if we're really interested in something we can focus like a laser beam. Bellerophon was really interested in capturing Pegasus.

At last a dark shape spiralled out of the clouds. Bellerophon thought it was an eagle, because it had the same gold-and-brown plumage. But, as it descended, Bellerophon realized the creature was much larger: a tan stallion with a rust-blazed muzzle and a twenty-foot wingspan.

Bellerophon didn't dare breathe as the horse landed. Pegasus pawed the grass. He folded his wings, approached the spring and lowered his head to drink.

Bellerophon crept forward with the golden bridle. Halfway across the meadow, he stepped on a twig.

Bellerophon froze. Pegasus looked over. The horse noticed the golden bridle and, being an intelligent animal, knew what was up.

Pegasus nickered. Bellerophon could have sworn the horse was saying, *Man, you are such a loser. All right, fine. C'mere.*

Bellerophon approached. Pegasus allowed him to put the golden bridle around his head. I'm not sure why Pegasus decided to cooperate, but it was a good thing for Bellerophon. He'd never bridled a horse before. It took him about six tries. At first, the poor horse had the throatlatch running across his eyeballs and the bit sticking out of his left ear, but eventually Bellerophon got it right.

Pegasus shivered as the golden bridle filled him with warm, tingly, happy magic. He whinnied softly, like, *Where are we going?*

'The city of Argos.' Bellerophon stroked the horse's nose. 'Oh, gods, you are amazing! You are the most incredible – Ow!'

Pegasus stepped on his foot, like, *Shut up and get on before I change my mind.*

Bellerophon climbed onto the stallion's back. Together they soared into the sky.

They made quite an entrance in Argos. It wasn't every day a Corinthian flew a horse through the window of the throne room. Fortunately, it was a big window. And nobody had invented glass panes yet. Otherwise it could've got messy. As it was, Pegasus got a tapestry cord tangled around his back hoof, ripped it off the wall, dropped Bellerophon at the royal dais, then flew out of the window again, the tapestry trailing behind him like an advertising banner.

King Proitos welcomed Bellerophon as an honoured guest. Anybody who could tame Pegasus (more or less) was okay in his book.

His wife, Anteia, was even happier to see the handsome young hero.

The queen was lonely. Her homeland, Lycia, lay far across the sea on the coast of modern-day Turkey. Her father had forced her to marry Proitos, who was much older, pot-bellied, and balding. She hated Argos. She hated being stuck with an old, gross husband. As soon as she saw Bellerophon, she fell in love with him.

Bellerophon spent several months at the palace. Every day he would go to the temples to pray, sacrifice and beg the gods' forgiveness for killing his younger brother. (Oh, and that other dude, Belleros. Him, too.)

Every night, Bellerophon would try to avoid Anteia. The queen flirted with him constantly and ambushed him whenever he was alone, but Bellerophon was pretty sure having an affair with the queen would not help him purify his soul.

As the weeks passed, Anteia got more and more frustrated. Finally, one night after dinner, she barged into Bellerophon's bedroom.

'What's wrong with me?' she demanded. 'Am I not beautiful enough?'

'Um . . . no. I mean, yes. I mean . . . you're married.'

'*So?* Aphrodite is married. It never stopped her from enjoying life!'

'I'm not sure that's a good comparison.'

'Will you kiss me or not?'

'I – I can't. It's not right.'

'Argh!'

Anteia stormed out of his room. She hated self-righteous young men, especially handsome ones who refused to flirt with her. She marched into the audience chamber, where her fat, old husband was snoozing on his throne.

'Proitos, wake up!'

The king flinched. 'I was just resting my eyes.'

'Bellerophon attacked me!'

Proitos frowned. 'He . . . he did? But he's always so polite. Are you sure it wasn't some sort of accident? He has a lot of accidents.'

'He chased me around his bedroom and tried to grab me!'

'What were you doing in his bedroom?'

'That's not the point! He tried to kiss me. He called me Babycakes and all sorts of horrible lewd names.'

Proitos wondered if he was dreaming. The queen wasn't making much sense. 'Bellerophon attacked you. He called you Babycakes.'

'Yes!' Anteia clenched her fists. 'I demand justice. If you love me, arrest him and execute him!'

Proitos scratched his beard. 'Look, dear, attacking the queen is a very serious crime. But . . . I mean, are you sure? Bellerophon doesn't strike me as that sort of person. He's the son of my old friend King Glaucus. Killing him would probably start a war with Corinth. Also, Bellerophon is a guest in my house. The gods frown on killing guests.'

Anteia snarled. 'You are so useless! If you won't kill him, send him to my father in Lycia. My father will definitely kill him!'

Proitos had no desire to kill Bellerophon, but he also didn't like the queen yelling at him. He had to live with her. She could be very unpleasant when she didn't get her way. 'If I sent him to your father for execution, how would that work exactly?'

Anteia tried to contain her impatience. Honestly, she had to explain *everything* to her stupid husband. 'You're Bellerophon's host, aren't you? You decide what he should do for his purification rituals and when he's finished, right?'

'Well, yes. In fact, I was about to declare his purification complete.'

'Tell him he has one more thing to do,' said Anteia. 'Before he can be purified, he must travel to Lycia and offer his services to my father, King Iobates.'

'But how does that get Bellerophon executed?'

'Give him a sealed letter of introduction for my father. Bellerophon will think it's just a bunch of compliments about him. But, in the letter, you ask Iobates to execute him. My father reads the letter. He kills Bellerophon. Problem solved.'

Proitos stared at his wife. He'd never realized how bloodthirsty she was. He had a hard time believing anyone would call her Babycakes. 'Okay, I guess that's a good plan . . .'

The next morning, Proitos summoned Bellerophon to the throne room. 'My friend, congratulations on nearly being finished with purification! You have almost earned the title Bellerophon the Blameless!'

'Almost?'

The king explained about the trip to Lycia. He handed Bellerophon an envelope sealed with wax. 'When you arrive in Lycia, present this to King Iobates. It will ensure that he gives you the proper welcome.'

Bellerophon didn't like the cold look in Queen Anteia's eyes, or the way Proitos's hand shook when he gave him the envelope, or the creepy organ music that was playing in the background. But Proitos was his host. Bellerophon couldn't question his orders without appearing rude.

'Uh, okay. Thanks for everything.' Bellerophon whistled for his steed.

Pegasus had been spending the last few months roaming free in the clouds, but when he heard Bellerophon's call he soared straight through the window and landed in the throne room.

Bellerophon bid his hosts goodbye, then flew off for Lycia to deliver his own death warrant.

Normally it would've taken weeks to sail from Argos to Lycia. Pegasus made the trip in half an hour – not even enough time for an in-flight beverage. As they glided over the Lycian countryside, Bellerophon noticed lots of fires – burned-out villages, blackened fields, swathes of smoking forests. Either Lycia had lost a war or National Barbecue Day had got really out of hand.

When Bellerophon arrived at the palace, King Iobates was quite surprised. It wasn't every day a Corinthian flew a horse through his window. The king was even more surprised when Bellerophon handed him a letter of introduction from his old, fat son-in-law, the king of Argos.

Iobates opened the letter. It read:

Dear Iobates,

Before you stands Bellerophon the Blameless. He has offended my wife, your daughter, by calling her Babycakes and other lewd names. Please kill him immediately. Thanks a bunch.

Yours,

Proitos

Iobates cleared his throat. 'This is ... quite an introduction.'

Bellerophon smiled. 'Proitos has been very kind to me.'

'Yeah. I'm guessing you haven't read this letter?'

'Nope.'

'I see ...'

Anger formed a hard clot in Iobates's throat. He wasn't angry with Bellerophon. The king knew his daughter Anteia quite well. She had a habit of flirting with young men, then asking to have them executed if they didn't return her affection. Iobates had hoped she would settle down once she married Proitos. Apparently she was still up to her old tricks. Now she wanted him to do her dirty work long-distance.

He studied Bellerophon. The young man seemed nice enough. He resembled the mosaics of Poseidon in the local temple, and Iobates figured that was not a coincidence. Bellerophon had also befriended the immortal horse Pegasus, which had to count for something.

Iobates decided he couldn't simply kill Bellerophon on the spot. That would be rude, messy and possibly get him into trouble with Poseidon.

The king had another idea. Perhaps he could solve two problems at once. He would give Bellerophon an impossible quest and let the Fates decide whether he should live. If Bellerophon failed, Anteia would be satisfied with his death. If he succeeded, Iobates's kingdom would benefit.

'Blameless Bellerophon,' he said, 'you have come here to complete your purification, yes? I have a task in mind for you. I'm not going to lie: it won't be easy. But you're a strong young hero. You have a flying horse. You might be just the man for the job.'

Bellerophon stood up straight. He wasn't used to being trusted with important missions. 'I would be happy to help, Your Majesty. It doesn't involve anything fragile, does it? My fine motor skills aren't the best.'

'No, nothing fragile. It involves a monster called the Chimera. Perhaps you noticed some fires as you flew into my kingdom.'

'I did. So it's not National Barbecue Day?'

'No. A foul supernatural creature has been destroying my villages, burning my crops, terrorizing my people. No one has been able to get close to it, much less kill it. According to a few eyewitness survivors, the monster is part lion, part dragon, part goat.'

'Part *goat*?'

'Yes.'

'The lion and dragon, I understand. Those are terrifying. But a goat?'

'Don't ask me. The local priests have been trying to discern where the monster came from. As near as they can figure, the Chimera crawled out of Tartarus. It's probably some spawn of

Echidna. Anyway, a neighbouring king, Amisodarus, had the bright idea of feeding the Chimera and trying to harness it for war. That didn't work out so well. The Chimera destroyed his kingdom. Now it's destroying mine. It radiates fear, spits poison and breathes fire hot enough to melt armour.'

'Oh,' said Bellerophon.

'So that's your task,' Iobates said. 'Go kill it. And thanks!'

Bellerophon had never been given such an important job before. All his life, people had been telling him *not* to do things: don't throw that dagger, don't spill that flask of oil, don't saw that rope. Now King Iobates, who barely knew him, was trusting him with the fate of his kingdom. What a nice guy!

Bellerophon was determined not to screw things up.

He jumped on Pegasus's back and flew out of the window.

They found the Chimera blowtorching a village about twenty miles south of the capital. Flying overhead, Bellerophon could understand why nobody had been able to give a good description of the monster. Anyone who got within a hundred feet would've been blasted to ashes.

(Just for the record, I have met the Chimera. At the time, it did *not* look the way Bellerophon saw it. Monsters often change appearance, so that's not a surprise. Also when I met the Chimera it was disguised as a Chihuahua named Sonny, which gets us into a whole new level of terrifying. But moving along . . .)

Bellerophon saw a creature about the size of a woolly mammoth. In the front, it had the head and forepaws of a lion. The back half of its body was scaly and reptilian, with dragon legs and a snaky tail that for some reason had a rattlesnake's head at the tip. The snake head lashed back and forth, snapping angrily at the air. Of course, if I was stuck on a monster's rear end, I'd be a little cranky, too.

The weirdest part of the monster was the goat head that poked straight up from its back like a periscope. It turned in almost a complete circle, spewing a hundred-foot-long column of fire.

'Wow,' Bellerophon muttered. 'What do you think, Pegasus? Can we dive-bomb that thing?'

Pegasus nickered as if to say, *Dunno, kid. I'm immortal, but you? Not so much.*

Like any good hero, Bellerophon had brought along a sword and a spear. He readied the spear, since it was slightly longer, and spurred Pegasus into a dive. They got about twenty feet above the Chimera before the goat head saw them and shot fire.

Pegasus banked so hard Bellerophon nearly fell off. The heat from the flames singed his arm hairs. The snake head spat a cloud of poison that made Bellerophon's lungs hurt. The lion's roar was so terrifying he almost blacked out.

Only his flying steed saved him. Pegasus soared upward, out of danger, leaving a spiral of burning horse feathers in his wake.

Bellerophon coughed the poison and smoke out of his lungs. 'That was too close.'

Pegasus snorted, *Ya think?*

As they circled above, the Chimera watched them. The rattlesnake head hissed on the end of its tail. The lion bared its fangs and snarled. But the goat head scared Bellerophon the most. That thing was a barnyard animal of mass destruction.

'We need a way to shut off those flames,' Bellerophon said.

'I could throw my spear down its throat, but it would just melt the point . . .'

Suddenly Bellerophon had an idea. He remembered getting into trouble as a boy for burning down the dining hall. Before he'd spilled that oil, he'd been roasting marshmallows, enjoying the way they toasted and melted on the stick, turning to gooey yummy messes.

Don't choke on those, his mother always said. *They'll clog up your throat and kill you.*

'Huh,' Bellerophon said to himself. 'Thanks, Mom . . .'

He scanned the ruins of the village. At the edge of Main Street, he spotted an abandoned blacksmith's shop. He urged Pegasus into another dive. As soon as they landed at the shop, Bellerophon leaped off and began searching through the rubble.

The Chimera saw them land. It roared and charged down Main Street as fast as its mismatched legs could carry it.

'C'mon, c'mon,' Bellerophon muttered. He yanked some fallen timber away from the forge. 'Aha!'

Next to the bellows sat a lump of lead the size of a pillow. Bellerophon could barely pick it up, but he staggered over to Pegasus and somehow managed to climb back on. They launched into the sky just as the Chimera sprayed the shop with fire.

Pegasus grunted, straining to fly with the new weight. *What's the deal with the lead pillow?*

'You'll see.' Bellerophon bored his spear point into the chunk of metal. Fortunately, lead is soft. He was able to impale it firmly like a giant heavy marshmallow on a stick. 'Pegasus, get me close enough to feed this to the goat.'

With pleasure, Pegasus nickered. He dived once more.

'Hey, Chimera!' Bellerophon yelled. 'You want a marshmallow?'

The monster's three heads looked up. The Chimera had never eaten a marshmallow before. They were incredibly hard to get in Tartarus. Sure enough, the mortal hero did appear to have a giant grey marshmallow on a stick.

The Chimera's three little brains had a brief argument over the pros and cons of accepting marshmallows from strangers. Bellerophon was only ten feet away when the goat head decided this was some sort of trick. Its mouth opened to melt Bellerophon's face off, but the hero chucked his lead-on-a-stick right down the goat's fiery throat.

Pegasus veered to one side as the goat head choked, molten lead filling its lungs. The Chimera staggered. The lion and snake heads writhed in pain.

Bellerophon jumped from Pegasus's back and drew his sword. Amazingly, he managed to do this without stabbing himself.

For the first time, Bellerophon felt like a true hero with working reflexes and motor coordination and everything. As the Chimera reared on its hind legs, ready to pounce, Bellerophon lunged underneath and drove his sword through the monster's belly. The Chimera collapsed, its rear-end rattlesnake head still thrashing.

'Boo-yah!' shouted Bellerophon. He held up his hand to high-five Pegasus. The horse looked at him like, *Please*.

For a souvenir, Bellerophon cut off the Chimera's goat head with its steaming lead-coated mouth. He took a couple of selfies with the monster's corpse. Then he rode Pegasus back to Lycia to tell King Iobates the good news.

The king was delighted that the Chimera was dead, but he was shocked that Bellerophon had come back alive.

'Now what am I supposed to do?' Iobates wondered aloud.

Bellerophon frowned. 'Your Majesty?'

'I mean . . . how can I possibly thank you enough? Well done!'

That night, the king threw a big party in Bellerophon's honour. They had cake and ice cream and clowns and magicians, though the king nixed the fire-swallowers as being in bad taste after the Chimera incident.

Iobates and Bellerophon talked through the night. The king decided he truly liked this young hero. Iobates didn't want to see him die, but he also wasn't quite ready to dismiss his daughter Anteia's letter asking for Bellerophon's execution.

Why? Maybe Iobates was worried that Bellerophon could present a threat to the kingdom. Or maybe Iobates was just a dad who hated saying no to his children, even if his children were sociopaths. Whatever the case, the king decided to give Bellerophon another challenge, just to make sure the Fates really wanted this hero alive.

'You know, Bellerophon,' he said over dessert, 'I have no right to ask you any more favours, but . . .'

'Anything, my lord!'

Bellerophon meant it, too. He'd never felt like a hero before, and he enjoyed it. The people loved him. The king's beautiful youngest daughter, Philonoe, had been flirting with him shamelessly, and he liked that, too. Most importantly, Iobates *believed* in him. The king had given Bellerophon a chance to prove himself. What a great guy!

'If I can help you in any way,' Bellerophon said, 'I will do it. Just name the favour!'

The crowd applauded and raised their glasses to Bellerophon.

Iobates felt like a real jerk, but he forced a smile. 'Well, this neighbouring tribe, the Solymoi – they've been causing all sorts of trouble on our eastern border. The Chimera killed my best men – except for you, of course – so I don't have much of an army. I'm afraid the Solymoi will overrun the whole country if they're not stopped.'

'Say no more!' said Bellerophon. 'I will fly over there tomorrow and sort things out.'

The crowd cheered. Princess Philonoe batted her eyelashes.

Iobates heaped praise on the young hero, but inside the king felt bad.

The Solymoi had never been conquered. They were blessed by the war god, Ares. In battle, they were absolutely fearless. Sending one guy to deal with them . . . that was suicide.

The next day, Bellerophon hopped on Pegasus and flew off to fight the neighbours. Maybe he surprised them from the air. Maybe he'd just found his self-confidence, the way Athena had advised him. Iobates believed in him, so he believed in himself. Anyway, Bellerophon landed in the middle of the Solymoi camp and slaughtered them. After Bellerophon killed about half the tribe and threw the rest into a panic, the chieftain begged for peace. He promised never to attack Lycia again. He and Bellerophon signed a peace treaty and took a few selfies together for posterity. Then Bellerophon flew back to the palace.

Again, King Iobates was amazed. The people of Lycia went wild with joy. That night they held another victory celebration. The princess Philonoe flirted with the young Corinthian and begged her father to arrange a marriage for them.

Iobates was torn. Bellerophon was turning out to be super helpful. He was brave and strong and truly blameless. He hadn't had a single accident since arriving in Lycia – no relatives killed, no dining halls burned down, not so much as an empty ship launched.

Still . . . Anteia had asked for the young man's death, and Iobates had trouble denying his homicidal eldest daughter anything. He decided to give Bellerophon one more dangerous challenge just to be absolutely, one-hundred-percent sure the hero had the Fates on his side.

'My wonderful friend Bellerophon,' said the king, 'I hate to ask, but there is one more threat to this kingdom . . . No, it is too dangerous, even for such a hero as you.'

'Name it!' Bellerophon said.

The crowd cheered wildly and banged their cups on the tables.

'Well,' said Iobates, 'this particular nation is making war on all the cities of Anatolia. Perhaps you've heard of the Amazons?'

The cheering died down. Bellerophon gulped. He had heard legends about the Amazons, all right. The name alone gave Greek children nightmares.

'You – you want me to fight *them*?'

'I wouldn't trust anyone else with this mission,' Iobates said, which was true. 'If you could just get them to back off, like you did with the Solymoi, that would be amazing.'

The next day Bellerophon flew off to battle. He couldn't believe he would be facing the Amazons, but Iobates believed in him, and Bellerophon couldn't let him down.

Bellerophon flew straight into the Amazon encampment. He laid waste to their army. The Amazons were paralysed by shock. They simply couldn't believe one stupid *male* could be so brave. By the time the Amazon queen was able to restore order, Bellerophon had killed hundreds of her best warriors.

The queen called for a truce. Bellerophon agreed to leave the Amazons alone if they stopped raiding Lycia. The Amazons signed a peace treaty, which they rarely did, but they respected bravery, and Bellerophon the Blameless obviously had it. The Amazons wouldn't take any photos with him, but that was okay. Bellerophon flew back to the palace in high spirits.

When he knelt before the king and announced his victory, Iobates did something unexpected.

The old man burst into tears. He slipped out of his throne, clasped Bellerophon's ankles, and blubbered, 'Forgive me, my boy. Forgive me.'

'Uh . . . sure,' Bellerophon said. 'What did you do?'

Iobates confessed the whole thing about Proitos's death warrant. He showed Bellerophon the letter. He explained that the quests had really been attempts to honour his daughter's wishes and get Bellerophon killed.

The hero might have got angry. Instead, he pulled the king to his feet.

'I forgive you,' Bellerophon said. 'Rather than kill me

outright, you gave me chances to prove myself. You made me a true hero. How could I be mad about that?'

'My dear boy!' Iobates was so grateful he arranged for Bellerophon to marry his daughter Philonoe. Bellerophon was named heir to the throne. Years later, when Iobates died, Bellerophon became the king of Lycia.

As for Anteia, she never got her revenge. When she heard that Bellerophon had married her younger sister and taken over her father's kingdom, she was so upset she killed herself.

And they lived happily ever after.

Hahaha. Not really.

By now, you've heard enough of these stories to know better. Bellerophon had one more major screw-up to get out of his system.

After he'd been king for many years, Bellerophon started to miss the good old days. The crowds didn't cheer for him like they used to when he killed the Chimera. Nobody remembered the way he'd defeated the Solymoi and the Amazons. When he told those stories at the royal banquets, his guests stifled their yawns. Even his wife, Philonoe, rolled her eyes.

Funny how that happens. New heroes come along. The old ones are tossed aside. We forget the bad stuff from the past. We get nostalgic for the good old days – burning down palaces, getting sentenced to death by crazed queens.

Bellerophon decided he needed one more adventure – a midlife-crisis quest to make everybody love him again and put some spice back in his life.

He would fly higher than any hero had ever gone. He would

visit the gods on Mount Olympus! He went to the palace's highest balcony and whistled for Pegasus.

The winged horse answered his call. They hadn't seen each other in years. Pegasus looked no different, being immortal, but the horse was kind of shocked by how much Bellerophon had aged.

Pegasus tilted his head. *What's up?*

'Oh, my friend!' said Bellerophon. 'We have one more quest to complete!'

Bellerophon climbed onto Pegasus's back and took the golden reins. Pegasus flew skyward, thinking they were off to fight Amazons or something.

Berellophon spurred him in the wrong direction – west. Soon they were racing over the Aegean Sea, climbing into the clouds.

Pegasus whinnied, like, *Um, where are we going?*

'Mount Olympus, my friend!' Bellerophon cried with glee. 'We're off to see the gods!'

Pegasus grunted and tried to turn. He'd flown to Mount Olympus before and knew it was restricted airspace. Mortals definitely did not have clearance.

Bellerophon held the reins steady. He forced Pegasus to fly higher and higher against his will. They'd always had a balanced relationship, the horse and Bellerophon, but now Bellerophon was calling the shots.

He'd forgotten Athena's warning from years ago: *Don't push your luck. DON'T DO THAT!*

All Bellerophon could think about was the glory he would achieve when he returned home with stories about the gods, and maybe some souvenirs for the kids.

Meanwhile, on Mount Olympus, Hermes was standing on one of the balconies, enjoying a nectar frappe, when he saw Bellerophon winging his way up from the earth.

'Uh, Zeus?' called the messenger god. 'Were you expecting a delivery?'

Zeus joined him on the balcony. 'Who is *that*? And why is he flying this way with that stupid grin on his face? Ganymede, fetch me a lightning bolt!'

Hermes cleared his throat. 'Ganymede is on lunch break, Lord Zeus. You want me to fly down there and smack the guy?'

'No,' Zeus grumbled. 'I have another idea.'

Zeus pulled a small tuft of vapour from the nearest cloud and fashioned a new kind of insect – the gadfly. If you've never seen one, you're lucky. It's basically the biggest, ugliest housefly you can imagine crossed with the nastiest, most bloodthirsty mosquito. It has razor-sharp mandibles designed to rip into horseflesh, which is why it's sometimes called a horsefly.

Zeus sent this new little bloodsucker down for its first meal. The gadfly bit Pegasus right between the eyes.

Pegasus was immortal, but he could still feel pain. The gadfly's bite was the worst thing he'd experienced since getting singed by super-goat flame breath.

The winged horse bucked violently. Bellerophon lost the reins. He fell off and plummeted several thousand feet to his death.

Pegasus felt bad about that. But, come on. Bellerophon should've known better than to fly to Mount Olympus. All it got him was an embarrassing death, and now the rest of us have to deal with gadflies.

On the bright side, Bellerophon and Philonoe had three

wonderful children. Of course their oldest son, Isandros, was later killed by Ares. Oh, and their oldest daughter, Laodameia, was killed by Artemis. Their youngest son, Hippolochos – he lived! But of course *his* son Glaucus (named after the old king of Corinth) was skewered by Ajax in the Trojan War. So yeah . . . basically Bellerophon and everybody related to him was murdered.

The end.

And, if you don't like it, remember I didn't make any of this up. You can just call me Percy the Blameless. It's totally not my fault.

CYRENE PUNCHES
A LION

As a demigod, I get a lot of questions: can Titans have demigod children? Has a mortal ever fallen in love with two different gods? What's the proper way to kill a lion with your bare hands?

Cyrene is great, because her story answers all that and more!

She was born in Thessaly, part of northern Greece. You might remember her tribe, the Lapiths, from Theseus's story. They liked partying, killing centaurs, watching Sunday football and destroying entire nations. The Lapiths were rough and rugged, so Cyrene grew up preferring spears to Barbie dolls and swords to Disney movies. Her friends knew better than to sing that song from *Frozen*, or she would pummel them unconscious.

I like Cyrene.

When she was young, her dad, Hypseus (possibly aka

the Hipster), became king of the Lapiths. His grandfather was Oceanus, the Titan of the seas, which proves that Titans can have demigod children. And Hypseus's dad was a river spirit. With those two godly connections, it's no wonder that Cyrene's body was made up of more than sixty percent water. That's a higher percentage than the average human. Not that I'm judging. I've got plenty of saltwater in my system.

(Annabeth says most of that saltwater is in my head. Very funny, Wise Girl.)

Anyway, Cyrene grew up dreaming of war and conquest.

She wanted to be a great fighter like her dad. She wanted to spend every Saturday slaughtering centaurs and every Sunday watching football with the guys! Unfortunately, Lapith women weren't allowed to do any of the fun stuff.

'Men wage war,' said her father. 'Women stay home. Just watch the sheep while I'm gone.'

'I don't want to watch the sheep,' Cyrene grumbled. 'Sheep are boring.'

'Daughter,' he said sternly, 'if no one is there to guard the flock, the sheep will get eaten by wild animals.'

Cyrene perked up. 'Wild animals?'

'Yes. Bears. Lions. Wolves. Occasionally dragons. All sorts of dangerous animals would love to eat our livestock.'

Cyrene grabbed her spear and her sword. 'I think I'll watch the sheep.'

And so, while King Hipster was off waging war against the neighbours, Cyrene stayed home and waged war against wild animals.

She had plenty to choose from. Back then, the hills and forests of Greece were full of vicious predators. Cougars, bears, mutant badgers . . . you name it. Cyrene didn't wait for the predators to attack her sheep, either. While her flock was grazing the craggy, windswept valleys, she patrolled the surrounding hills, seeking out and destroying any potential threat. She killed bears that were three times her size. She considered it a boring day if she didn't fight at least one dragon before lunchtime. She nearly drove the mutant-badger population to extinction.

Cyrene got addicted to danger. Her friends would invite her to parties and she'd say, 'Nah, I think I'll go kill some pumas.'

'You did that *last* night!' her friends would complain.

Cyrene didn't care. She barely slept or ate. She spent most of her time in the wilderness with her flocks, returning to the village only when she had to.

She was so good at her job the villagers eventually asked her to watch the cattle as well as the sheep. Cyrene was glad to. That meant more enticing targets for predators. She drove her herds to dangerous places, hoping to attract bigger and badder monsters to fight. The sheep and cows weren't even worried about it. They trusted Cyrene completely.

One cow would get a whiff of danger and ask another cow, 'What's that?'

'Oh,' the second cow would say, 'that's just a pack of wolves.'

'Won't they eat us? Should we panic and stampede?'

'No,' said the second cow. 'Watch.'

Cyrene came hurtling out of the darkness, wailing like a banshee, and slaughtered the entire wolf pack.

'Oh, cool,' said the first cow.

'Yeah, she's awesome. Want to chew some more cud?'

Cyrene was such a great hunter that Artemis herself took notice. The goddess gave her two fine hunting dogs as gifts. She tried to recruit Cyrene to join her followers, but Cyrene wasn't wild about being a maiden her entire life.

'I'm honoured and all,' Cyrene said, 'but I like hunting alone. I'm not sure how I'd do in a big group. Also, um, I'd kind of like to get married some day.'

Artemis wrinkled her nose in distaste. 'Sorry to hear that. You've got talent. Here, take a brochure, just in case you change your mind.'

With her two new hunting dogs, Cyrene became even more deadly. Soon she had terrified the local predators so badly that, if one of her sheep wandered away, a couple of bears were likely to lead it back to the flock just so they wouldn't get into trouble.

One day on Mount Olympus, Artemis was chatting with her brother Apollo about the best mortal archers.

'Cyrene is definitely in the top five,' Artemis said. 'She prefers the spear and sword, but she's *amazing* with the bow, too. I wish she would join my Hunt, but she said she isn't ready to give up on men.'

Apollo arched his godly eyebrows. 'You don't say. Is she hot?'

'Brother, don't even think about it.'

'Oh, I'm thinking about it,' Apollo admitted.

The next morning, Cyrene was patrolling the hills around her flock as usual when she felt the need to pee. (That's another question I get asked a lot: Do demigods ever use the restroom? First: Yes. *Duh*. And second: Why would you ask a question like that?)

Cyrene's dogs were guarding the other side of the herd, so she was by herself. She set down her weapons, since smart heroes do not go potty with sharp blades in their hands. She headed for the nearest clump of bushes.

Unfortunately, a large male lion happened to be crouching in that clump of bushes, stalking Cyrene's flock.

Cyrene spotted the predator and froze. She and the big cat stared at each other with mutual annoyance – the lion because he wanted to eat sheep, Cyrene because she needed to tinkle. She was empty-handed and doubted the lion would give her time to fetch her spear and sword, but she wasn't particularly scared.

The lion growled, like, *Back off, lady.*

'I don't think so.' Cyrene cracked her knuckles. 'You want those sheep, you have to go through me.' Which is not a heroic line you hear very often.

The lion sprang. Cyrene charged to meet him.

Kids, do not try this at home. Lions have sharp claws and fangs. Humans do not. Cyrene didn't care. She punched the lion in the face, then ducked as he swiped at her.

Just as the fight was getting serious, the clouds opened over a nearby hilltop. Cyrene didn't notice, but a golden chariot pulled by four white horses descended from the heavens and landed on the summit.

The god Apollo gazed down at the two tiny figures fighting in the valley. With his divine vision, he could see Cyrene just fine. Her long, dark hair whipped around as she dodged the lion. Her graceful limbs were the colour of polished bronze in the sunlight. Even in the midst of combat, her face was beautiful and serene. She reminded Apollo of a war goddess, and he should know – he was related to several of them.

He watched as Cyrene judo-flipped the lion across the meadow.

'Wow . . .' he muttered to himself. 'There is *nothing* hotter than a chick wrestling a lion.'

Maybe that was a sleazy thing to say. On the other hand, a lot of gods would have tried to intervene in the fight. They would've been like, *Hey, little lady, you need some help with that big bad lion?* Apollo could tell that Cyrene didn't need any assistance. He'd grown up with his sister Artemis, so he was used to self-sufficient women. He was happy to be a spectator.

Man, I just wish I could share this with somebody, the god thought. Hey, I know!

Apollo's hilltop happened to be near the cave of Chiron the wise centaur, who trained all the best heroes.

'Chiron will totally appreciate this!' Apollo snapped his fingers, and the centaur materialized at his side, a bowl of soup in his hands.

'Um, hello . . .' said Chiron.

'Dude, sorry to interrupt your lunch,' said Apollo, 'but you have to check this out.'

Chiron looked where Apollo was pointing.

The lion swiped at Cyrene, opening a line of bloody gashes along her upper arm. Cyrene roared in anger. She roundhouse-kicked the lion in the snout, then ran up the side of a tree, flipped over the lion's back and landed behind him, flicking her hand like, *Bring it.*

'Ah,' said Chiron. 'That's something you don't see every day.'

'That lady has game, right?' Apollo said.

'Yes, I've heard all about Cyrene,' said Chiron. 'I wish I could train her.'

'Then why don't you?' the god asked.

Chiron shook his head sadly. 'Her father, Hypseus, would never allow it. He has old-fashioned ideas about the role of women. As long as Cyrene stays among the Lapiths, I'm afraid she'll never reach her full potential.'

Down in the valley, Cyrene picked up the lion by his back legs, spun him around and tossed him into a boulder.

'So,' Apollo said, 'what would happen if, say, a god were to fall in love with the girl and whisk her away to somewhere else?'

Chiron tugged thoughtfully at his beard. 'If Cyrene were taken to a new land, where the rules of her people did not restrict her, she could become anything she wanted – a hero, a queen, the founder of a great nation.'

'A god's girlfriend?' Apollo asked.

'Quite possibly,' Chiron agreed. 'And the mother to many heroes.'

Apollo watched as Cyrene got the lion in a chokehold. She strangled the beast to death, then paraded around his carcass, her fists raised high in victory.

'See ya,' Apollo told the centaur. 'I have a girlfriend to abduct.'

Cyrene had just finished peeing, and bandaging the cuts on her arm, when a golden chariot appeared next to her in a huge ball of fire. Her sheep and cows didn't flinch. They figured this was just another predator that Cyrene would kill.

Apollo stepped out of his chariot. He was dressed in his best purple robes, a laurel wreath across his brow. His eyes shone like molten gold. His smile was blinding. An aura of honey-coloured light flickered around him.

Cyrene frowned. 'I'm guessing you're not from around here?'

'I am Apollo. I have been watching you, Cyrene. You are a vision of loveliness, a paragon of strength, a true hero who deserves more than guarding sheep!'

'Guarding sheep isn't so bad. I get to kill wild animals.'

'And you do it well!' Apollo said. 'But what if I took you to a new land where you could found an entire kingdom? You could rule there as the queen, fight hordes of enemies and also date a god!'

Cyrene thought about it. Apollo was kind of cute. He was better groomed than the Lapith men. He talked pretty. And that golden chariot was a sweet ride.

'I'm willing to go on a first date,' she decided. 'We'll see how it goes. Where did you have in mind?'

Apollo grinned. 'Ever heard of Africa?'

'Hmm. I was thinking more like that Italian restaurant in the village, but I suppose Africa works. Can I take my hunting dogs?'

'Of course!'

'How about my sheep and my cows?'

'No room in the chariot. Sorry. We'll buy you a new herd when we get there.'

With a shrug, Cyrene whistled for her dogs and climbed

aboard Apollo's chariot. They traced a fiery arc across the sky as they headed for Africa, leaving the poor sheep and cows to fend for themselves. Fortunately, Cyrene had killed every predator within a fifty-mile radius, so they were probably okay.

Apollo took his new girlfriend to the northern coast of Africa. They landed in the uplands of what is now Libya, where rolling hills were dotted with cedars, myrtle trees and blood-red oleander. Springs bubbled from the rocks. Clear streams wound through meadows of wildflowers. In the distance, the coast was rimmed with white-sand beaches. The sparkling blue sea stretched to the horizon.

'This is nicer than back home,' Cyrene admitted.

'And it's all yours!' Apollo said.

Cyrene couldn't resist being given her own country. She and Apollo became a hot item. They hunted together in the hills, ran along the beaches in the moonlight, and occasionally, just for fun, shot arrows at Hermes as he passed overhead delivering messages for the gods. Shooting Hermes in the butt was always good for a laugh.

Back in Greece, Apollo's oracles spread the word: anyone who wanted a new life under a fabulous queen should travel to Africa and join the party.

Soon a whole colony of Greeks thrived in that valley. They built a city called Cyrene, named after their queen, obviously. Their biggest and most important temple was dedicated to Apollo, also obviously.

The city of Cyrene became the first and most important Greek colony in Africa. It lasted through most of the Roman

Empire. (I hear the ruins are still there, but I haven't been. Every time I travel somewhere like that I have to fight monsters and almost die, so I'll let you go instead and send me pictures.)

Apollo and the huntress Cyrene had two sons together. The older was Aristaios, which means *most useful*. The kid lived up to his name. When he was young, Apollo took him back to Greece to train with Chiron the centaur. Aristaios wasn't much good with a spear or sword, but he invented all kinds of important skills, like cheesemaking and beekeeping, which made him a real hit at the local farmers' markets. The gods were so impressed they eventually made Aristaios a minor deity. Next time you're playing Trivial Pursuit and you need to know the god of beekeepers and cheesemakers, you've got the answer. You're welcome.

Cyrene's younger son, Idmon, grew up to be a seer, since his dad Apollo was the god of prophecy. Unfortunately, the first time Idmon looked into the future, he foresaw his own death. That kind of knowledge could really mess up most people, but Idmon took it in stride. Years later, when the hero Jason was putting together a demigod dream team for his quest to get the Golden Fleece, Idmon joined up, even though he knew he would get killed while aboard the *Argo*. He didn't want to miss his chance to die a hero. That's dedication for you.

Cyrene was happy in Africa. She liked being the queen of her own city. But as the years passed she began to get lonely. Her hunting dogs passed away. Her children grew up. Apollo visited less and less often.

Gods are like that. They get easily bored with their mortal loves. To them, humans are like classroom gerbils. The first night you take one home, you're all excited and want to take good care of it. By the end of the school year, after you've taken the gerbil home six times already, you're like, 'It's my turn *again*? Do I have to?'

Cyrene never thought she'd get homesick for Greece, but she started to miss the good old days – wrestling lions, watching sheep, getting dissed by hairy Lapith menfolk. Cyrene decided she would go back to Thessaly one more time to check on her childhood friends and see if her dad was still alive.

It was a long journey. When she finally got there, she learned that her father had passed away. The new king of the Lapiths didn't want anything to do with her. Most of her friends had got married and didn't even recognize her, or they'd died, since the Lapiths lived a pretty harsh life.

Cyrene ventured into the wilderness on her own, roaming the old paths where she used to herd sheep. She missed her hunting dogs. She missed being younger. She felt hollow and angry, though she wasn't sure who she was angry at, and she thrust the point of her sword into the hard ground.

'That will dull your blade,' said a voice at her shoulder.

Standing right next to her was a burly man in full combat armour. He held a bloody spear, as if he'd just stepped away from a massacre for a quick coffee break. His face was handsome the way a mountain is handsome – chiselled and unforgiving, majestic and potentially lethal. Painted on his breastplate was a rampant wild boar.

'You're Ares,' Cyrene guessed.

The war god grinned. His eyes burned like miniature funeral pyres. 'You're not scared? I can see why Apollo likes you. But what are you doing with a pretty boy like Mr Poetry? You're a warrior. You need a real man.'

'Oh, I do, eh?' Cyrene yanked her sword from the ground. She wasn't scared. She'd grown up in these harsh lands, surrounded by blustering soldiers. She knew Ares. He represented her entire childhood — everything she'd been whisked away from when Apollo took her. She wasn't sure whether she hated the war god or loved him.

'I suppose you're going to sweep me off my feet?' Cyrene snarled. 'You'll take me away to some foreign land and make me a queen?'

Ares laughed. 'No. But if you're looking to remind yourself where you came from . . . I'm your guy. You can't escape your roots, Cyrene. You've got killing in your blood.'

With a guttural shout, Cyrene attacked the war god. They fought back and forth across the mountainside, trying their best to cut each other's head off. Cyrene held her own in combat. Ares laughed and shouted encouragement. Finally, exhausted, Cyrene threw her sword down. She tackled Ares around the chest. He embraced her with surprising gentleness. Next thing you know, they were kissing instead of fighting.

I call that a lapse of judgment. In my opinion, cutting Ares's head off is always the best choice. But Cyrene was vulnerable and lonely. She was in the mood for something different, and Ares is about as different from Apollo as you can get.

Cyrene stayed with the war god for many months. Together they had a son named Diomedes, who became the king of Thrace — a country even further north and twice as harsh as Thessaly. Ares was the Thracians' patron god, so it's no surprise they made Diomedes their king.

The guy was a real sweetheart. When he wasn't waging war or torturing peasants, he raised horses that ate human flesh.

Any time he had prisoners or guests he didn't like, he tossed them into the stables . . . until a guy named Hercules put a stop to that practice. We'll get to him in a couple more chapters.

Eventually Cyrene grew tired of the wild north. She returned to her city on the African coast and found Apollo waiting for her on the hill where they'd first landed in his chariot, many years before.

The god smiled, but his golden eyes were sad and distant. 'Have a good time in Thrace?'

'Um, listen, Apollo . . .'

The god raised his palms. 'You owe me no explanations. I was not as attentive as I should have been. I took you away from your native land and then left you. That was not your fault. But I fear our time together is ending, Cyrene.'

'I know.' Cyrene felt relieved. She'd had three demigod children with two different gods. She'd done more in her life than most people ever got to do, certainly more than most women of her time. She was ready for some peace and quiet.

'Where do you want to live?' Apollo asked. 'Thessaly or here?'

Cyrene gazed at the hillsides dotted with myrtles and oleander, the green meadows, white beaches and glittering blue sea. The Greek colonists were busy raising new temples to the gods in the city that bore her name.

'I belong here,' she said.

Apollo nodded. 'Then I have one more gift for you. Ares was wrong; your roots are wherever you decide they should be. I will bind you to this land forever. Your spirit shall always remain.'

Cyrene wasn't sure about this 'binding forever' stuff, but

Apollo waved his hand and it was done. A ripple of warmth passed through Cyrene's body. Her vision cleared as if someone had finally given her the right prescription glasses. Suddenly the world was in higher definition. She could see wind spirits flitting across the sky, and dryads dancing among the trees, making the woods a tapestry of green light and shadows. The wildflowers smelled sweeter. The ground felt more solid beneath her feet. The babbling of the streams became a chorus of clear, beautiful voices.

'What have you done?' Cyrene asked, more amazed than frightened.

Apollo kissed her forehead. 'I have made you a naiad. Your great-grandfather was Oceanus. Your grandfather was a river god. You've always been part water spirit. Now your essence is tied to the rivers of this valley. You will live much longer than any mortal. You will enjoy peace and good health. As long as this valley flourishes, so will you. Goodbye, Cyrene. And thanks for the memories.'

I'm not sure what Cyrene thought about all that. I didn't even know it was possible to turn a mortal into a nature spirit, but the gods are full of surprises.

As Apollo promised, Cyrene lived a very long time. Eventually she left her Greek colony and lived full-time in the river with the other naiads, though occasionally she would rise to offer advice to her friends and family. Once, when her son Aristaios lost all his bees, she helped him find them again . . . but that's a whole other story. Maybe we'll cover that in *Percy Jackson's Really Minor Gods*.

(Joking, guys. Please don't give the publisher any more ideas.)

Nobody knows whether Cyrene eventually faded and died, or whether she's still hanging out in some stream near the ruins of her old city. I have to admire the lady, though. Anybody who can survive two godly relationships and come out sane is stronger than most heroes. Cyrene was able to reinvent herself several times. She embraced her new country and her new life, and after that one trip to Thrace she never again looked back.

That takes guts. Looking back can be deadly.

Just ask Orpheus.

Oh, wait. You can't. He got decapitated.

Want to hear how? Sure you do. Let me tell you about the world's greatest musician and how he screwed up.

ORPHEUS TAKES
A SOLO

GOOD OLD THRACE, MY FAVOURITE POST-apocalyptic wasteland, where life was hard, priests made blood sacrifices to Ares, and kings raised horses that ate human flesh! Sounds like just the sort of place where a young boy would become a harp player, right?

That's where Orpheus was born. Of course, the Beatles were from Liverpool and Jay-Z is from the projects in Brooklyn, so I guess music can come from unpredictable places.

The way Orpheus's parents met . . . that was even more unpredictable.

His dad was a Thracian king named Oeagrus. (Good luck pronouncing that. *Oh-AH-grus*, maybe?) When Oeagrus was young and single, he liked partying and singing as much as he liked fighting. So, when the wine god Dionysus and his drunken army rolled through town on their way to invade India, Oeagrus welcomed them with open arms and a cup that needed refilling.

'You're invading a foreign country for no particular reason?' Oeagrus asked. 'I am totally in!'

Oeagrus gathered his men and joined the wine god's expedition.

At first, everything was rainbows and Chardonnay. Oeagrus got along great with the wine dude's followers, especially the maenads – crazed nymphs who liked to tear apart their enemies with their bare hands. A Thracian could appreciate that!

Every night at the campfire, Oeagrus drank with the maenads and sang Thracian ballads. The guy had a rich baritone voice. When he sang a sad tune, he brought his listeners to tears. When he sang an upbeat number, he got everybody dancing. In fact, he sang so well he attracted the attention of a Muse.

(My brother Tyson is here. He thought I said *moose*. No, Tyson, the guy in the story did not attract the attention of a moose. Tyson is sad now.)

The Nine Muses were immortal sisters who oversaw different arts, like singing, drama . . . um, charades, dubstep, tap-dancing and maybe some other stuff I've forgotten. Calliope, the oldest Muse, was in charge of epic poetry. She guided writers who were telling stories about heroes and battles and . . . you know what? I just realized I should've made a sacrifice to her before I started writing this book. It's totally her territory.

Oops. Sorry, everybody. This book is not officially endorsed by the proper Muse. If it explodes in your hands, my bad.

Anyway, like all the Muses, Calliope had a soft spot for

music. From her apartments on Mount Olympus, she heard Oeagrus singing as he marched east with the wine god's army. Calliope was so entranced she flew down invisibly to check out this drunken warrior with the beautiful voice.

'Wow, what a singer!' Calliope sighed.

Even without proper training, Oeagrus was a natural talent. He sang with so much emotion and confidence. He wasn't bad-looking, either. As the army marched, Calliope followed, circling invisibly overhead like a large stealth seagull, just so she could hear Oeagrus sing every night.

Finally Dionysus reached India. If you've read my other book, *Greek Gods*, you know his invasion didn't work out too well. The Greeks crossed the Ganges River and got their butts handed to them by a bunch of fire-throwing Indian holy men. In the panic of retreat, Oeagrus ran into the Ganges. But he forgot one tiny detail: he couldn't swim.

Hordes of drunken warriors and maenads trampled him as they tried to get away. Oeagrus would've drowned if Calliope hadn't been watching. As soon as he went under, she dived into the river. Somehow, she wrestled him onto her shoulders and carried him to the opposite bank, piggyback style. That must've looked pretty odd – a lovely lady in white robes emerging from the Ganges with a big hairy Thracian warrior on her shoulders.

Dionysus's army marched back to Greece in a dejected mood, but Calliope and Oeagrus had a wonderful time. During the journey, they fell in love. By the time the Thracians got home, Calliope had given birth to a demigod son named Orpheus.

The boy grew up in Thrace, which wasn't an easy place for a sensitive young musician. His dad lost interest in him when he realized Orpheus would never be a warrior. If you gave the kid a bow, he'd pluck a tune on the bowstring. If you gave him a sword, he'd drop it and scream, 'I hate sharp edges!' The other kids teased and bullied and shunned Orpheus . . . until he learned to use his music as a defence. He gradually realized that his singing could bring the most hostile bully to tears. He could escape a beatdown by playing his reed pipes. His attackers would just stand there, enchanted, and let Orpheus walk away.

Every weekend, his mom, Calliope, took him for music lessons with the other Muses. Orpheus lived for those visits. His immortal aunts taught him everything they knew about music, which was basically everything.

In no time, the kid outshone his teachers. Orpheus had his mom's finesse and divine skill. He had his dad's raw talent and mortal edginess. The Muses had never heard a voice so beautiful.

They gave Orpheus a bunch of different instruments to try: a drum set, a French horn, a '67 Telecaster. Orpheus excelled at all of them. Then one day he found the instrument that would make him famous. The only problem: it belonged to a god.

One weekend, Apollo visited the Nine Muses to get their input on his new musical, *Twenty-Five Awesome Things About Me (A Sequel to Twenty Awesome Things About Me)*.

Apollo played them a few songs on his lyre while Orpheus sat in the corner of the room, listening in astonishment. He'd never heard a lyre before. No mortal had. Back then Apollo had the only one in existence. Hermes had invented it out of a tortoise shell, two sticks and some sheep-tendon strings, because Hermes was a boss. He'd given it to Apollo to avoid jail time for cattle rustling (long story), and the lyre had become Apollo's prized possession.

After a few songs, Apollo set down his instrument and gathered the Nine Muses around a piano at the other side of the room. While they were deep in discussion, trying to figure out the nine-part harmonies for the big finale, Orpheus walked over to the lyre.

He couldn't help himself. He picked up the instrument and strummed a chord.

Apollo shot to his feet. His eyes blazed with anger. The Nine Muses dived for cover, because *nobody* picks up a god's toys without permission.

Only two things kept Apollo from blasting the kid to ashes. First, Orpheus was holding the lyre. Apollo didn't want to damage it. Second, Orpheus launched into the most incredible song Apollo had ever heard.

The boy played as if the lyre were part of his own body. His fingers ran across the strings, coaxing out impossibly sweet melodies and countermelodies. The Nine Muses wept with joy. Apollo's anger evaporated.

Orpheus's music was full of mortal pain and sadness. No god could have made music so raw. Apollo appreciated that. Twice before, Zeus had punished him by turning him temporarily human. Apollo remembered how difficult that had been – his divine spirit trapped in a fragile body of flesh. Orpheus's music captured the feeling perfectly.

Orpheus finished his song. He looked up sheepishly at Apollo. 'I'm sorry, my lord. I – I couldn't help myself. You may kill me now. I have played the lyre. My life is complete.' He knelt and offered the instrument to the god.

Apollo shook his head. 'No, my boy. Keep the lyre. I'll make another one.'

Orpheus's eyes widened. 'Really?'

'You deserve it. Take the lyre. Make music across the earth. Teach others to play. Just do me a favour. Don't teach them "Stairway to Heaven", okay? I'm really sick of that song.'

Orpheus bowed and grovelled and thanked the god. He did exactly what Apollo asked. He travelled the world teaching others to make lyres and play beautifully. He collected songs from every land. He even journeyed to Egypt, where he added the music of that ancient country to his repertoire. He perfected his own playing and singing. And whenever he found someone trying to learn 'Stairway to Heaven' he took away their instrument and smashed it against a wall.

Orpheus became so talented his music could bring entire cities to a standstill. He'd walk through a marketplace playing his lyre, and everyone would freeze. Merchants would stop selling. Pickpockets would stop stealing. Chickens would stop clucking, and babies would stop crying. Mobs of people would follow him out of town just to hear him play. They'd walk behind him for hundreds of miles until finally they'd look around in a daze and think: *I live in Egypt. What am I doing in Jerusalem?*

Orpheus just kept getting better. Wild animals were powerless against his music. When he walked through a forest, lions gathered around and rolled over so he could pet their bellies while he sang. Wolves rubbed against his legs and wagged their tails when he did that song they liked, 'Hungry Like the Wolf'. Birds flocked silently in the trees, listening as Orpheus played, hoping they could pick up some tips to improve their singing.

Finally Orpheus's music became so powerful it could even affect the environment. Trees moved through the earth, scuttling on their roots like crabs, so they could get closer to his lyre. Boulders wept condensation when he sang. Rolling stones followed him down the road. (Probably *the* Rolling Stones, too, because those dudes look old enough to have known Orpheus.) Rivers stopped in their course to hear him. Clouds anchored themselves overhead so they could have nosebleed seats for his concerts.

Nothing in the entire world could resist Orpheus. His music was like the gravity of a sun, drawing everything towards him.

When he wasn't teaching music, he did a bunch of heroic stuff. For instance, he sailed aboard the *Argo*, but we'll get to that in the chapter on Jason. Stay tuned.

(Get it? *Music?* Stay *tuned?* Well, Tyson thought it was funny.)

Orpheus became so famous he couldn't go anywhere without attracting a mob of fangirls and fanboys. He sang, and hearts melted. He won awards. He got marriage proposals from all over, and so many views on his YouTube channel that the site crashed. He was bigger than Elvis, bigger than Bieber, bigger than *insert name of whatever boy band is popular this week*. (Sorry, I don't keep track.)

Just to escape his own fame, Orpheus returned home to Thrace, because people there didn't care about him. Funny how that works. No matter how important you get out in the world, the people you grew up with are still like, *Yeah, whatever.*

'Hi, Dad,' Orpheus would say. 'I had to come home to get away from my millions of fans.'

'Fans?' his dad grumbled. 'Why do you have fans?'

'Well, my music can stop rivers and make trees move, and one time an entire city full of people followed me several hundred miles to hear me play.'

'Bah.' His dad scowled. 'You still can't hold a sword properly.'

While in Thrace, Orpheus spent most of his time with the followers of Dionysus, since at least they appreciated good party music. Orpheus helped organize the Dionysian Mysteries, which were a big spiritual festival with lots of wine, music and drama in honour of the god. Not that Dionysus needed any more drama, but I guess the music was a nice addition.

But, even in Thrace, Orpheus had crazed fans. During the festivals, the maenads would get drunk and start flirting with him. Since Orpheus only cared about his music, he wouldn't respond, and the maenads would get angry. A few times they came close to rioting and tearing him apart.

His mom, Calliope, decided that, for his own safety, Orpheus should get married. Maybe that would make his fans back off. She talked with Apollo, who happened to have an eligible young demigod daughter named Eurydice.

Calliope arranged a backstage pass for Eurydice at Orpheus's next concert. The two of them met and it was love at first sight . . . or at least by the end of the first set. As the daughter of Apollo, Eurydice had music in her blood. She understood Orpheus immediately. They chatted all through intermission back in Orpheus's dressing room. After his final encore, Orpheus brought Eurydice on stage and announced that they were getting married.

His fans wailed and ripped their hair out, but Eurydice

looked so beautiful and Orpheus looked so happy that the crowd graciously refrained from stampeding the stage. For weeks, social media buzzed about what a cute couple they were, though nobody could decide what their ship name should be. *Ordice? Eurypheus?*

Their wedding was attended by all the beautiful people and gods. The Nine Muses provided the music. Apollo officiated. Dionysus was the flower boy. (Okay. I might be making that up.)

Hymenaios, the god of marriage ceremonies, showed up in person to lead the procession, although, strangely, he cried as he escorted the bride down the aisle. His clothes were funeral black. His sacred torch was supposed to burn cheerfully, but it only sputtered and smoked. The guests wondered about that. It was a pretty bad omen for the marriage to come, but everybody was scared to ask him about it.

As for Orpheus and Eurydice, they were too in love to notice. At the reception, the groom sang so sweetly to his bride that the whole audience broke down in tears.

They should have had the most romantic honeymoon ever. Unfortunately, a stalker ruined everything. You probably think I mean a stalker for Orpheus, but nope. Turns out his wife had a crazed fan of her own.

For years, a minor god named Aristaios had been trying to get Eurydice's attention. Maybe you remember Aristaios from the last chapter – Cyrene's kid? If not, don't worry about it. He was the god of beekeeping and cheesemaking. Not exactly a major player.

Anyway, he had a huge crush on Eurydice, but she didn't

know he existed. Aristaios went crazy with despair when she married Orpheus. Eurydice was making a terrible mistake! Why would she marry the best musician in the world when she could marry a cheese god? Aristaios had to make her see reason.

One afternoon during the honeymoon, Eurydice and Orpheus were relaxing in a beautiful meadow in the forest. Orpheus decided to play his lyre for a while, because even musical geniuses need to practise, so Eurydice went for a stroll by herself.

Big mistake.

Aristaios followed, lurking in the bushes. He waited until Eurydice was half a mile from the meadow. Then he jumped out in front of her and yelled, 'Marry me!'

What was Aristaios thinking? I suppose his only role model for women was his mom, Cyrene, and she wasn't exactly the romantic type. She'd won the affection of her first husband by killing a lion. She'd won her second husband by trying to cut his head off. Maybe Aristaios figured that if he acted aggressive, Eurydice would finally notice him.

She noticed him, all right. She screamed and ran away.

Nine times out of ten, if somebody jumps out at you and yells 'Marry me!' it's an excellent idea to run away, screaming for help. In this case, however, Eurydice would've been smarter to punch Aristaios in the face. He was a cheese god, after all. He probably would've cried and fled.

Eurydice panicked. She didn't look where she was going. She stumbled through some tall grass straight into a nest of poisonous snakes. A viper sank its fangs into her ankle, and the young bride instantly collapsed.

By the time Aristaios caught up with her, she was turning blue. He spotted one of the vipers slithering away – the most lethal kind of snake in all of Greece. Its venom would already be in Eurydice's heart.

'Oh, bee butts,' Aristaios muttered.

He wasn't a very powerful god. Maybe he could've saved her by turning her into a queen bee or a nice wedge of Muenster, but before he could act he heard Orpheus calling her name. The musician must have heard her screams.

Aristaios didn't want to take the blame for Eurydice's death. Nobody would ever buy his honey or cheese at the farmers' market again! He did the cowardly thing and ran.

Orpheus stumbled across the body of his beloved. His heart shattered. He cradled her and sobbed. He tried to sing her back to life. When that didn't work, he begged the vipers, which had gathered at the sound of his voice, to bite him so he could follow his wife to the Underworld. The snakes just looked at him: *No, we like you. You sing pretty.*

In a daze, Orpheus buried Eurydice in the meadow where they'd shared their last joyful moments. Then Orpheus took up his lyre and wandered aimlessly, pouring out his sorrow into his music.

For days he played songs of unbearable heartache. Think about the saddest moment you've ever experienced. Now imagine that sadness multiplied times a hundred. That's how Orpheus's music felt as it rolled over you.

Entire cities wept. Trees oozed tears of sap. Clouds unleashed torrents of saltwater rain. On Mount Olympus, Ares cried on Hephaestus's shoulder. Aphrodite and Athena sat on the sofa together, in their pyjamas, bingeing on chocolate ice cream and bawling. Hestia rushed around the throne room offering everyone boxes of tissues.

Orpheus played the longest, saddest solo in music history. While it went on, nobody could do anything. The entire world mourned, but even that wasn't enough for the musician.

'Eurydice's death was not *fair*. I will go to the Underworld,' Orpheus decided.

When somebody you love dies, it's a hard thing to get over. Believe me, I've lost some good friends. Still . . . most of us learn to keep going. Most of us have no choice.

Orpheus couldn't let Eurydice go. He had to bring her back from the dead. He didn't care about the consequences.

Maybe you're thinking: *Bad idea. This will not end well.*

You're right.

On the other hand, I understand how Orpheus felt. I've come close to losing my girlfriend more times than I want to think about. If she died, I'd do everything I could to bring her back. I'd grab my sword, march into Hades's palace and . . . And I'd probably act just as recklessly as Orpheus did, only I wouldn't be singing. I don't sing.

The Underworld has many entrances – fissures in the earth, rivers that plunge underground, the bathrooms in Penn Station. A weeping woodland nymph directed Orpheus to a large clump of boulders that concealed a tunnel into Hades's realm. Orpheus played his lyre and the rocks split asunder, revealing a steep path into the earth.

He descended into darkness, playing so sweetly that no ghost or daimon dared to stop him. At last he came to the banks of the River Styx, where the boatman Charon was loading the newly dead aboard his ferry.

'Oi!' Charon told him. 'Clear off, mortal! You can't be here!'

Orpheus launched into a soul-piercing rendition of 'Daydream Believer'.

Charon fell to his knees. 'That . . . that was *our* song! I was a starry-eyed teenaged daimon. She was a sweet young zombie girl. We, we . . .' He broke down sobbing. 'Fine!' The boatman wiped his eyes. 'Come aboard! I can't resist your horribly sad music.'

As they crossed the River Styx, Orpheus played such mournful tunes that some of the dead souls chose to leap overboard and dissolve themselves. Maybe they didn't like golden oldies.

At the gates of Erebos, Orpheus strummed a chord and the iron gates swung open, trembling on their hinges before the power of his lyre. The giant three-headed guard dog, Cerberus, crouched and snarled, ready to tear apart the mortal intruder.

Orpheus sang the theme song to *Old Yeller*. Cerberus howled and rolled over, whimpering. Orpheus passed through the gates.

He travelled through the Fields of Asphodel, waking the spirits with his music. Normally they were grey chattering shades who couldn't remember their own names, but Orpheus's songs brought back memories of the mortal world. For a few moments, they took on human shapes and colours again. They wept tears of joy.

The sound of the lyre reached the Fields of Punishment.

The three Furies, Hades's most heartless enforcers, forgot their duties. They sat in a circle and cried their demonic eyes out, then had a group therapy session where they shared their feelings and complimented one another on their fiery whips and their bat wings. Meanwhile, the damned souls got a reprieve. Sisyphus sat on his hill, his boulder forgotten. Tantalus could have finally reached food and drink, but he was too busy listening to the music to notice. The guys on the torture racks were like, 'Excuse me? I'm supposed to be flayed alive over here? Hello, anyone?'

Orpheus played his way right into the palace of Hades. The heavily armed zombie guards didn't try to stop him. They followed him through the corridors, making dry grunting noises as they tried to remember how to weep.

In the throne room, the king and queen of the dead were having lunch. Hades wore a yellow lobster bib over his flowing dark robes. Bits of crustacean shell littered the dais around his skeletal throne. Persephone nibbled on a luminous subterranean salad from the palace garden. Her dress was yellow and grey, like the sun behind winter clouds. Her throne was woven from the bare branches of a pomegranate tree.

As the intruder approached his throne, Hades rose. 'What is this meaning of this? Guards, destroy this mortal!' But it was hard to look menacing with butter dribbling down his chin and a cartoon lobster on his bib.

Orpheus launched into a Duke Ellington number, 'Stalking Monsters'.

Hades's jaw dropped. He sank back into his throne.

'Oh!' Persephone clapped. 'Darling, it's our song!'

Hades had never heard Duke Ellington played so beautifully – so raw and painful and true, as if this mortal musician had distilled Hades's life, with all its grief and disappointment, all its darkness and solitude, and turned it into music. The god found himself crying. He didn't want the music to stop.

Eventually Orpheus's song ended. The zombies dried their eyes. Ghosts sighed in the windows of the throne room.

The lord of the Underworld composed himself. 'What . . . what do you want, mortal?' His voice was brittle with emotion. 'Why have you brought this heartbreaking music into my halls?'

Orpheus bowed. 'Lord Hades, I am Orpheus. I'm not here as a tourist. I don't want to disrupt your realm, but my wife, Eurydice, recently died before her time. I cannot go on without her. I have come to plead for her life.'

Hades sighed. He removed his bib and laid it across his plate. 'Such extraordinary music, yet such a predictable request. Young man, if I returned souls every time someone prayed for it to happen, my halls would be empty. I would be out of a job. All mortals die. That is non-negotiable.'

'I understand,' Orpheus said. 'You will possess all our souls eventually. I'm fine with that. But not so soon! I lost my soulmate after less than a month. I've tried to bear the pain, but I simply cannot. Love is a power even greater than death. I *must* take my wife back to the mortal world. Either that or kill me, so my soul can stay here with her.'

Hades frowned. 'Well, killing you I could arrange –'

'Husband.' Persephone set her hand on Hades's arm. 'This

is so sweet, so romantic. Doesn't it remind you of everything you went through to win my love? You didn't exactly play by the rules, either.'

Hades's face reddened. His wife had a point. Hades had abducted Persephone and caused a global famine in his stand-off with her mother, Demeter. Hades could be very sweet and romantic when he wanted to.

'Yes, my dear,' he said. 'But –'

'Please,' Persephone said. 'At least give Orpheus a chance to prove his love.'

Hades couldn't resist when she looked at him with those big beautiful eyes.

'Very well, my little pomegranate.' He faced Orpheus. 'I will allow you to return to the mortal world with your wife.'

For the first time in days, Orpheus felt like playing a cheerful tune. 'Thank you, my lord!'

'But there is one important condition,' Hades said. 'You claim that your love is more powerful than death. Now you must prove it. I will allow your wife's spirit to follow you back from the Underworld, but you must have faith that she is travelling in your footsteps. The strength of your love must be sufficient to guide her out. Do *not* turn to look at her until you have reached the surface. If you so much as glance back before she is fully bathed in the light of the mortal world, you will lose her again . . . and this time forever.'

Orpheus's throat became parched. He scanned the throne room, hoping to see some sign of his wife's spirit, but he saw only the faces of withered zombie guards.

'I – I understand,' he said.

'Then go,' Hades ordered. 'And no music on the way back, please. You're keeping us from doing our jobs down here.'

Orpheus left the palace and retraced his steps through the Fields of Asphodel. Without his music to focus on, he realized how terrifying the Underworld was. Ghosts whispered and chattered around him. They brushed their cold, spectral hands against his arms and face, pleading for an encore.

His fingers trembled. His legs felt wobbly.

He couldn't tell if Eurydice was behind him. What if she got lost in the crowd? What if Hades was playing some sort of cruel joke? Coming into the Underworld, Orpheus had been consumed with grief. Now he had hope. He had something to lose. That was much scarier.

At the gates of the Underworld, Cerberus wagged his tail and whimpered for another rendition of *Old Yeller*. Orpheus kept walking. At the banks of the Styx, he thought he heard soft footsteps in the black sand behind him, but he couldn't be sure.

The ferryman Charon waited in his boat. 'I don't usually take passengers the other way,' he said, leaning on his oar. 'But the boss said okay.'

'Is . . . is my wife behind me?' Orpheus asked. 'Is she there?'

Charon smiled cagily. 'Telling would be cheating. All aboard.'

Orpheus stood at the bow. Tension crawled across his back like an army of ants, but he kept his eyes fixed on the dark water while Charon rowed, humming 'Daydream Believer' until they reached the other side.

Orpheus climbed the steep tunnel towards the mortal world. His footsteps echoed. Once, he heard a sound like a small sigh behind him, but it might have been his imagination. And that smell of honeysuckle . . . was that Eurydice's perfume? His heart ached to be sure. She might be right behind him, reaching out for him . . . the thought was both ecstasy and agony. It took all his willpower not to look.

Finally he saw the warm glow of daylight at the mouth of the tunnel above.

Only a few more steps, he told himself. *Keep walking. Let her join me in the sunlight.*

But his willpower crumbled. Hades's voice echoed in his ears. *You must have faith. The strength of your love must be sufficient.*

Orpheus stopped. He'd never trusted his own strength. He'd grown up with his father constantly berating him, calling him weak. If it weren't for his music, Orpheus would've been *nobody*. Eurydice wouldn't have fallen in love with him. Hades wouldn't have agreed to send her back.

How could Orpheus be sure his love was enough? How could he have faith in anything but his music?

He waited, hoping to hear another sigh behind him, hoping to catch another whiff of honeysuckle perfume.

'Eurydice?' he called.

No answer.

He felt entirely alone.

He imagined Hades and Persephone laughing at his foolishness in falling for their prank.

Oh, gods! Hades would say. *He actually bought it? What an idiot! Hand me another lobster, would you?*

What if Eurydice's spirit had never been there? Or worse,

what if she was behind him right now, begging for his help? She might need his guidance to return to the world. He might step into the sunlight and look back, only to see her falling away from him as the tunnel to the Underworld collapsed permanently. That seemed like just the sort of trick Hades might play.

'Eurydice,' he called again. 'Please, say something.'

He heard only the fading echo of his own voice.

If there's one thing a musician can't abide, it's silence. Panic seized him. He turned.

A few feet behind him, in the shadows of the tunnel, less than a stone's throw from the sunlight, his beautiful wife stood in the blue gossamer dress she'd been buried in. The rosy colour was starting to return to her face.

They locked eyes. They reached for each other.

Orpheus took her hand, and her fingers turned to smoke.

As she faded, her expression filled with regret . . . but no blame. Orpheus had tried to save her. He had failed, but she loved him anyway. That knowledge broke his heart all over again.

'Farewell, my love,' she whispered. Then she was gone.

Orpheus's scream was the most unmusical sound he had ever made. The earth shook. The tunnel collapsed. A gust of air expelled him into the world like a piece of candy shot from a windpipe. He yelled and pounded his fists on rocks. He tried to play his lyre, but his fingers felt like lead on the strings. The way to the Underworld would not open.

Orpheus didn't move for seven days. He wouldn't eat, drink or bathe. He hoped his thirst or his own body odour might kill him, but it didn't work.

He begged the gods of the Underworld to take his soul.

He got no answer. He climbed the highest cliff and threw himself off, but the wind just carried him gently to the ground. He searched for hungry lions. The animals refused to kill him. Snakes refused to bite him. He tried to bash his head in with a rock, but the rock turned to dust. The guy literally was not allowed to die. The world loved his music too much. Everybody wanted him to stay alive and keep playing.

Finally, hollowed out from despair, Orpheus wandered back to his homeland of Thrace.

If his story ended there, that would be tragic enough, right?

Oh, no. It gets worse.

Orpheus never recovered from Eurydice's death. He refused to date other women. He would only play sad songs. He ignored the Dionysian Mysteries, which he had helped invent. He moped around Thrace and brought everybody down.

Now, when you've gone through a big tragedy like watching your dead wife turn to smoke, most people will cut you some slack. They'll sympathize up to a point. But after a while they'll start to get annoyed, like, *Enough already, Orpheus. Join the human race!*

I'm not saying it's the most sensitive way to act, but that's how people are, especially if those people happen to be maenads.

Over the years, Orpheus had built up a lot of goodwill with Dionysus's followers. He'd organized their festival. His dad was a veteran of the Indian War. But eventually the maenads got miffed that Orpheus wouldn't join their parties any more. He was the most eligible bachelor in Thrace, but he wouldn't flirt with them. He wouldn't drink with them. He would barely even look at them.

Orpheus's mom, Calliope, tried to warn him of his danger, but her son wouldn't listen. He wouldn't leave town. He just didn't care.

Finally the maenads' anger boiled over. One night, when they'd been drinking more than usual, they heard Orpheus playing his lyre in the woods – another song about tragic love and desolation. His sweet voice drove the maenads even crazier than they already were.

'I hate that guy!' one shrieked. 'He won't hang out with us any more! He's a total wet blanket!'

'Let's kill him!' another yelled, which was the maenads' answer to most problems.

They swarmed towards the sound of Orpheus's lyre.

Orpheus was sitting on the banks of a river, wishing he could drown himself. He saw the maenads coming, but he just kept playing. He didn't care about dying. He wasn't sure he *could* die. At first the maenads threw rocks at him. The stones fell to the ground. The maenads threw spears, but the wind brushed them aside.

'Well,' said one of the maenads, 'I guess we'll have to take matters into our hands.' She brandished her long, pointy fingernails. 'Ladies, attack!'

Their wild screams drowned out Orpheus's music. They swarmed him.

Orpheus didn't try to run. He was actually grateful that somebody was willing to kill him and let him see Eurydice again.

The maenads obliged. They tore him to pieces.

Afterwards, the silence was oppressive. Even the maenads were horrified by what they'd done. They ran, leaving Orpheus's body parts scattered through the woods.

Calliope and the other Muses eventually found him. They collected what they could and buried the remains at the foot of Mount Olympus. However, two important things were missing: Orpheus's lyre and his head. Those floated down the River Hebrus and washed out to sea. Supposedly his lyre kept playing on its own and his decapitated head kept singing as it floated away, like one of those Furby toys that just won't shut up.

(Sorry. I still have nightmares about those things . . .)

At last, Apollo plucked the lyre out of the sea. He threw it into the sky, where it turned into the constellation Lyra. Orpheus's decapitated head washed up on the island of Lesbos. The locals made a shrine for it. Apollo gave it the power of prophecy, so, for a while, folks from all over would come to Lesbos to consult with the severed head of Orpheus. Eventually Apollo decided that was a little too creepy. He silenced the Oracle. The shrine was abandoned, and Orpheus's head was buried.

As for Orpheus's spirit, I've heard rumours that he was reunited with Eurydice in Elysium. Now he can look at his wife all he wants without fearing she'll disappear. But wherever they go, just for safety, Orpheus lets Eurydice take the lead.

I guess that means they lived happily ever after – except for the fact that they both died.

There's probably a song in there somewhere.

La, la, la, I'll love you dead or alive. La, la, la.

Nah, never mind. I think I'll stick with sword fighting. Music is way too dangerous.

HERCULES DOES TWELVE STUPID THINGS

WHERE DO I START WITH THIS GUY?

Even his name is complicated. I'm going to call him by his Roman name, Hercules, because that's how most people know him. The Greeks called him Heracles. Even *that* wasn't his real name. He was born either Alcides or Alcaeus, depending on which story you read, but 'The Great Hero Al' just doesn't have much zing.

Anyway, before What's-His-Name was born, there was a whole big soap opera going on in southern Greece. Remember Perseus, the guy who cut off Medusa's head? After he became king of Argos, he united half a dozen city-states – Tiryns, Pylos, Athens, Buttkickville, et cetera – into a powerful kingdom called Mycenae. (That's *my-SEE-nee*; almost rhymes with *mankini*.) Each city had its own king, but there was also a high king who ruled over the whole nation. The high king could be from any city, but he was always supposed to be the eldest descendant of Perseus.

Confused yet? Me too.

By the time the third generation of Clan Perseus rolled around, the leading contenders for high king were two cousins from the city of Tiryns. One guy was Amphitryon. The other was Sthenelus. With handles like that, you'd think they were awarding the kingship to men with the most unpronounceable names.

Amphitryon was older by a few days, so everybody assumed he would get the job. Then he messed things up by accidentally killing his father-in-law.

It happened like this: Amphitryon had been negotiating with this dude Electryon for permission to marry his daughter Alcmene. As soon as they struck a deal, Electryon called in Alcmene to give her the good news.

ELECTRYON: Alcmene, meet your new husband, Amphitryon!

ALCMENE: Um, okay. A heads-up would've been nice.

ELECTRYON: Don't be so glum. He's going to be the high king soon! He paid a good price for you! Also he loves you. You love her, right?

AMPHITRYON: Uh-huh.

ALCMENE: You just met me.

AMPHITRYON: Uh-huh.

ALCMENE: Can you say anything other than 'Uh-huh'?

AMPHITRYON: Uh-huh.

ALCMENE: Dad, this guy is a moron.

AMPHITRYON: But I love you! I love you THIS

MUCH! *(Spreads his hands. Accidentally whacks Electryon in the face and kills him.)*

AMPHITRYON: Oops.

ALCMENE: You're a moron.

When the news got out, the other royal contender, Sthenelus, saw an opportunity to seize the high kingship. He publicly accused Amphitryon of murder. He ran a big smear campaign with posters and town criers and TV ads: *THIS MORON MURDERED HIS FATHER-IN-LAW. CAN YOU TRUST HIM TO RUN OUR COUNTRY?* Ultimately the heat got so bad that Amphitryon had to flee Mycenae. He dragged along his new wife, Alcmene, who wasn't too happy about it.

They settled in Thebes, a town northwest of Athens, outside the Mycenae power zone. Amphitryon became the city's most important general, but that wasn't saying much, since the Theban army was about as powerful as a squad of mall cops.

Alcmene was totally not into her husband. Technically they were married, but the fool had killed her father and got them both exiled.

'There is no way we are having children,' Alcmene told him. 'It would bring down the IQ of the entire Greek civilization.'

'I will prove myself to you!' Amphitryon promised. 'What must I do?'

Alcmene pondered that. 'Go conquer a bunch of cities. Show me you're a good leader. You can start by destroying the island of Taphos. My brothers attacked that place a few years back and got slaughtered. Avenge my brothers.'

Amphitryon lost track of what she was saying after the first few words. 'What?'

Alcmene pointed. 'Taphos. Go kill!'

'Okay.'

Amphitryon took his army and had a bunch of adventures that I won't go into. There was a fox that couldn't be caught. There was a dude with long blond hair who couldn't be killed. There was blood and maiming and pillaging. You know, pretty much the average weekend in Ancient Greece.

Amphitryon killed people and destroyed things until he figured he had proven himself to be worthy of Alcmene. Then he turned his army around and marched for Thebes. He was anxious to get home and have his honeymoon. He'd been married to his wife for over a year now, and they hadn't even kissed yet.

Too bad for him, someone else *also* wanted a honeymoon with his wife. Our old friend Zeus, the god of the sky and cute *señoritas*, had been watching Alcmene. He liked what he saw.

Zeus had promised Hera (for the thirtieth time) that he'd stop fooling around with mortal women. Of course, he had no intention of keeping his promise, but still he figured he'd better try to stay off the radar when he visited Alcmene. He decided the simplest way would be to show up looking like her husband. Zeus transformed himself into an Amphitryon clone and flew down to Thebes.

'Honey, I'm home!' he announced.

Alcmene walked into the living room. 'What are you doing here? The messengers said you were still with the army. I wasn't expecting you for another three days.'

Three days? Zeus thought. Excellent!

'I'm home early!' he announced. 'Let's celebrate!'

Zeus ordered pizza. He opened a bottle of champagne

and put on some Justin Timberlake. At first, Alcmene was suspicious. Her husband didn't seem as moronic as he had been before. But she had to admit she preferred this version of him. Maybe he *had* learned something from his adventures.

They had a wonderful romantic night together. In fact it was so wonderful that at one point Zeus excused himself, took his phone into the bathroom and texted Helios, the sun god: *Bro, take a few days off. I need this night to last!*

Helios texted back: *R U w/Alcmene?*

Zeus: *Totes.*

Helios: *OMG she's hawt.*

Zeus: *IKR?*

Helios left the sun chariot in the garage for the next seventy-two hours. By the time dawn finally rolled around, Alcmene was suffering from sleep deprivation and a Justin Timberlake overdose.

Zeus kissed her good morning. 'Well, that was great, babe! I should get going. Got to check on . . . army stuff.'

He strolled out of the front door.

Ten minutes later, the real Amphitryon walked in. 'Honey, I'm home!'

Alcmene gave him a blurry look. 'So soon? Did you forget something?'

Amphitryon had been hoping for a slightly more enthusiastic welcome. 'Um . . . no. I just got home from the war. Can we . . . celebrate?'

'Are you kidding? You got home yesterday! We spent all last night together!'

Amphitryon wasn't the sharpest crayon in the box, but he realized something was wrong. He and Alcmene visited a local priest who did some fortune-telling and determined that the first Amphitryon had actually been Zeus.

Roman storytellers thought this mistaken identity situation was hilarious. They wrote entire comedies about it. You can imagine how that went. Alcmene looks at the audience like, *THAT WASN'T MY HUSBAND? WHOOPS!* And a bunch of dudes in togas roll on the floor laughing.

Anyway, there wasn't much Amphitryon could do about it. He and Alcmene had their own honeymoon celebration. By the time Alcmene was in the second trimester of her pregnancy, she knew, the way moms sometimes do, that she was carrying twins. She had a feeling one baby would be Zeus's and the other would be Amphitryon's. And the Zeus baby would mean big trouble for her.

Meanwhile, back in Mycenae, Cousin Sthenelus was still trying to become the high king. He thought he'd be a shoo-in with Amphitryon in exile, but nobody *liked* Sthenelus. He was cruel and cowardly. Besides, his name was *super* hard to pronounce. The nobles refused to endorse him. The commoners jeered at him. Sthenelus tried to settle the matter with a public vote, but he came in third after two write-in candidates: Mickey Mouse and Fluffy the town cat.

Sthenelus's only good news: his wife Nicippe was about to give birth to their first child. If the baby was a boy, he would be the oldest son of the oldest descendant of Perseus (not counting Amphitryon, of course), which meant the kid had a shot at becoming high king even if Sthenelus couldn't.

Up on Mount Olympus, Queen Hera was thinking along the same lines. She'd found out about Zeus's affair with

Alcmene. Instead of going into a raging snit about it, she decided to play things cold and stealthy.

'Zeus probably wants Alcmene's bastard child to become high king of Mycenae,' she grumbled to herself. 'Well, that's not going to happen.'

The next night, she did everything she could to put Zeus in a good mood. She played his favourite Timberlake album. She cooked his favourite meal – ambrosia crepes with ambrosia sauce and a side of sautéed ambrosia. She massaged his shoulders and whispered in his ear, 'Honey Muffin?'

'Hmm?' Zeus's eyes crossed in bliss.

'Could you make a teensy divine decree for me?'

'A divine decree . . . about what?'

She popped an ambrosia-covered strawberry into his mouth. 'Oh, I just thought the kingdom of Mycenae should have some peace and prosperity. Wouldn't that be nice?'

'Mmph-hmm.' Zeus swallowed the strawberry.

'What if you decreed that the very next descendant of Perseus to be born will become the high king? Wouldn't that make things simpler?'

Zeus suppressed a smile. He knew Alcmene's twins were due any minute. Sthenelus's kid wasn't going to be born for at least another week. He just didn't know that Hera knew. 'Yeah, sure, hon. No problem!'

That same night, divine oracles throughout Mycenae announced the latest news from Zeus: the next-born male descendant of Perseus would become the high king! And, no, the public would *not* be allowed to vote for Fluffy the cat instead.

After dinner, Hera sped down to the earth, where her

daughter Eileithyia, the goddess of childbirth, had just arrived at Alcmene's house.

'Stop!' Hera cried. 'Don't let Alcmene give birth!'

Eileithyia stepped back, clutching her medical bag. 'But she's already in labour. You *do* remember how painful that is?'

'I don't care!' Hera said. 'She *cannot* give birth — at least not until after Sthenelus's son is born.'

'But I don't have that on my schedule until next week.'

'Just come with me to Tiryns. NOW!'

Eileithyia was used to handling the drama of childbirth. The drama of Hera? Not so much. Leaving Alcmene in bed, groaning and sweating and cursing, the two goddesses flew to the city of Tiryns.

Once there, Eileithyia waved her magic Lamaze pillow and Sthenelus's wife Nicippe immediately went into labour. *BOOM!* Five minutes later she was holding a baby boy in her arms. Easiest delivery in history.

They named the child Eurystheus, because that was the most unpronounceable name they could think of on short notice. He was, in fact, the next-born male descendant of Perseus, so the little guy was crowned high king immediately, though it was hard to find a tiara small enough for his newborn head.

As for Alcmene, Hera would have let her suffer in labour forever. That's just the kind of loving person she was. But Eileithyia took pity on her. Once it was clear that Hera had got her way on the high-kingship issue, Eileithyia granted Alcmene a safe and easy childbirth.

The first twin born was Hercules (though at the time he was called Al), followed by his baby brother, Iphicles.

Proud papa Amphitryon looked at the newborns. He immediately felt attached to both of them, though Alcmene had warned him in advance that one of the kids was probably Zeus's.

Which one is mine and which one is Zeus's? he wondered.

Iphicles cried. Al/Hercules flexed his newborn muscles and smacked his brother in the face, like, *Shaddup.*

'I'm guessing the muscular one is Zeus's,' Alcmene said.

Amphitryon sighed. 'Yeah, you're probably right.'

The next day, word arrived from Tiryns: a new high king, Eurystheus, had been born just a few hours before Hercules.

'Hera must be messing with me,' Alcmene guessed. 'That's why my labour lasted so long.'

In her arms, baby Hercules shouted, 'RARRR!' and promptly pooped his diaper.

Alcmene reeled back from the smell. 'Was that an editorial comment?' she asked the baby. 'You don't like Hera?'

'RARRR!' More poop.

That worried Alcmene — and not just because she had no idea what her kid had been eating. She'd heard all the stories about Hera torturing Zeus's mortal lovers. Her difficult labour was proof that Hera was out to get her. Her new baby Al/Hercules might get her killed.

In her moment of fear and weakness, Alcmene did what too many parents did back then with unwanted children. She sneaked out of the house, took the baby to the conveniently located wilderness and left him exposed on a rock to die.

Little baby Hercules was mightily annoyed. He squirmed on the rock for hours, yelling, cursing in baby language and punching any wild animal that dared to come close.

Fortunately, Zeus was looking out for the little guy. Zeus

had got wise to Hera's little shell game with the high king babies. He muttered to himself, 'Oh, you want a fight? Okay, Honey Muffin, it's *on*.' He sent Athena, goddess of wisdom, down to the earth to retrieve the baby.

Hercules looked up at Athena and cooed, but his stomach was growling. Athena, not being a motherly type, didn't know what to do with him.

'I need a wet nurse,' she murmured. 'Someone who likes babies. Hmm . . .'

She had a very twisted idea. She took the kid to Hera.

'Oh, my queen!' said Athena. 'I just found this poor random baby abandoned in the wilderness. Isn't that terrible? I don't know how to feed him, and he's so hungry!'

Hera didn't know who the baby was. She took one look at the little guy and her motherly instincts kicked in. 'Aw, poor thing. Give him here. I will suckle him.'

Back then they didn't do baby bottles and formula. When a baby got hungry, you breastfed him. End of story. Usually the mom did it, but if the mom wasn't around another woman might do the job.

Hera, being the goddess of moms, figured she was up to the task. She held Hercules to her bosom and let him take a few drinks from the divine milk dispenser. The baby was going at it with gusto until Athena said, 'Thank you, Hera!'

It was the first time she'd said Hera's name in the baby's presence. Hercules bit down hard on Hera's sensitive flesh, screamed 'RARR!' and pooped, all at the same time, causing Hera to scream and hurl the kid.

Fortunately, Athena was a good catch.

Some legends say that Hera's breast milk sprayed across the

sky and created the Milky Way. I don't know. That seems like a whole lot of solar systems from just one squirt. What *is* for sure: those few sips of the good stuff instilled Hercules with divine strength and health, compliments of the goddess who hated him the most.

Athena whisked the baby back to his mother's house. She set him on the doorstep, rang the bell and flew away. Alcmene opened the door. Baby Hercules grinned up at her, his face covered with milk.

'Um, okay . . .' Alcmene figured this was a sign from the gods. She took the kid inside and never tried to get rid of him again.

The next few months were relatively uneventful. Hercules learned to crawl. He learned to punch through brick walls. He teethed his way through several horse saddles, got put in time-out for breaking his babysitter's arms and even spoke his first word: *mangle.*

One night, when he and his brother, Iphicles, were asleep, Hera decided to get rid of her least favourite toddler once and for all.

If I allow this child to grow up, she thought, he'll be nothing but trouble. Zeus is watching over him, so I can't just blast the boy to ashes. Hmm. I know! I'll arrange a believable accident – a couple of poisonous snakes in the nursery. That happens all the time, I'm sure!

Two nasty vipers slithered through a crack in the wall and made straight for the children's beds.

Iphicles woke first. He felt something gliding over his blanket, and he screamed.

Down the hall, Alcmene heard him. She bolted out of bed and shook her husband awake. 'Amphitryon, something is wrong in the nursery!'

The parents rushed in, but they were too late.

Hercules had taken care of business. With his super-fast toddler reflexes, he had grabbed both snakes by their necks and strangled them to death.

By the time his parents arrived, Hercules was standing up in bed, grinning and waving the dead vipers. 'Bye-bye!'

As for Iphicles, he was huddled in the corner, under a blanket, screaming and sobbing.

Amphitryon sighed. 'Come on, Iphicles. I've got you. Sorry, little dude. You're stuck with my DNA.'

After that night, our snake-strangling hero got a new name. He was no longer Alcides, Alcaeus or any other flavour of Al. He became known as Heracles (Roman: Hercules), which means *Glory from Hera*. Thanks to Hera, he was famous before he even graduated preschool. Hera must have loved that.

As he grew, Hercules had some really good teachers. His dad, Amphitryon, taught him to drive a chariot. The generals of Thebes taught him sword fighting, archery and wrestling.

His only weak subject was music. His parents hired the best lyre player in town, Linus, who was the half-brother of Orpheus, but Hercules had zero musical skill. His fingers were just too big and clumsy to manipulate the strings. Eventually Linus lost his patience and screamed, 'No, no, no! That's a C scale!'

Linus ripped the lyre out of the boy's hands. He smacked Hercules across the face with it. (FYI, being hit in the face with a lyre hurts.)

Hercules yanked the lyre back from his teacher. 'SEE *THIS* SCALE!'

He smashed Linus over the head repeatedly until the lyre was in pieces and the music teacher was dead.

Hercules was twelve. He was put on trial for capital murder. If that's not straight-up hard core, I don't know what is. Fortunately, Hercules was smart. He pleaded self-defence, since Linus had hit him first, and got off easy with six years of community service at a cattle ranch outside of town.

The ranch wasn't so bad. Hercules liked working outdoors. He got lots of fresh air and never had to take music lessons. His parents also appreciated having him safely tucked away where he couldn't attract poisonous vipers into the house, commit teacher-cide or accidentally destroy the city.

Hercules was released from the ranch at age eighteen. By then, he was the biggest, tallest, strongest, baddest Theban in the history of Thebes. He'd been away for a long time and wasn't really tuned in to what was going on, so when he got home he was shocked to see the townsfolk weeping in the public square, gathering all their cattle like they were about to have an auction. Hercules recognized a lot of the cows he'd raised during his years of community service.

Hercules found his family in the crowd. 'Dad!' he called to Amphitryon. 'What's up with the cows?'

His stepfather winced. 'Son, while you were away, we had a war with the Minyans. You know those folks who live in that city over yonder – King Erginus's people?'

'Yeah? So?'

'We lost. Badly. To stop the Minyans from destroying our

whole city, King Creon agreed to pay them a yearly tribute of one hundred cows.'

'*What?* That's crazy! I raised those cows. There's Spot, right there. And that's Buttercup. You can't give away Buttercup!'

A hundred cows may not sound like a big deal, but back then that was like a hundred houses or a hundred Ferraris. Cows were big money. They were some of the most important investments you could make. Besides – Buttercup! Dude, you can't give away a cow that Hercules had bothered to name.

'We must fight!' Hercules said. 'This time we will beat the evil Minyans!'

His sickly brother, Iphicles, spoke up. 'But they took all our weapons. That was also part of the peace treaty.'

'*All* our weapons?' Hercules turned towards King Creon, who stood nearby with his guards. 'I leave for a few years, and you surrender all our weapons and our cows? Your Majesty, come on!'

The old king blushed and stared at the ground.

'We have to do something,' Hercules insisted.

'It's too late,' Iphicles said. 'Here they come.'

The crowd parted as a dozen big Minyans in full armour marched through the square, kicking old men out of their way, pushing down old ladies and stealing churros from the street vendors.

King Creon did nothing to stop them. Neither did his guards. Even Hercules's dad, the great general Amphitryon, just stood and watched as the Minyans bullied their way towards the cattle pens.

Finally Hercules couldn't stand it any more. 'KNOCK IT OFF!'

The Minyans halted. They watched in dismay as Hercules lumbered over — a big, hairy teenager dressed in the simple leather tunic and cloak of a cattle-herder.

'You dare speak to us?' said the Minyan leader. 'We are your masters, cowherd! Grovel and kiss my feet.'

'Not happening.' Hercules cracked his knuckles. 'Leave now, and we won't have any bloodshed. You're not taking any more of our cows.'

The Minyans laughed.

'Look here, boy,' said the leader. 'We have swords. You don't. We're taking these hundred cows, just like it says in the peace treaty. Next year, we'll be back for a hundred more. What are you going to do to stop us?'

Hercules punched the guy in the face, dropping him instantly. The other Minyans reached for their swords, but Hercules was fast. Before their blades could even clear their scabbards, all twelve Minyans were lying on the ground with broken noses, black eyes and fifty percent fewer teeth. Hercules confiscated their weapons.

Then (GROSS-OUT ALERT), using their leader's own sword, he cut off each Minyan's nose, ears and hands. He strung the severed parts into disgusting necklaces and hung them around his prisoners' necks. Amazingly, this didn't kill them. Once they were conscious and strong enough to walk, Hercules hauled them to their feet.

'Go back to King Erginus,' he ordered. 'Tell him the only tributes he'll get from Thebes are the grisly bits hanging around your necks!'

He smacked the leader's butt with the flat of his sword and sent the mutilated Minyans on their way.

The astonished crowd of Thebans awoke from their shock. The younger ones cheered and danced around the newly liberated cows. The older citizens, who had seen too many wars, were less thrilled.

'My son,' said Amphitryon, 'King Erginus will never forgive this. He'll be back with his entire army.'

'Good,' Hercules growled. 'I'll kill them all.'

King Creon hobbled over. His face was sickly green. 'Boy, what have you done? I took in your family from exile. I gave you a home. And you . . . you have doomed us!'

'Sire, don't worry about it,' said Hercules. 'I'll take care of the Minyans.'

'How?' the king demanded. 'You have . . . what, twelve swords now? You can't defeat the Minyan army with only that!'

Hercules didn't remember King Creon being such a wimp, but he decided not to comment.

'The Temple of Athena,' Hercules said. 'Doesn't it have a bunch of armour and weapons hanging on the walls?'

Amphitryon glanced nervously at the sky, waiting for a divine smiting. 'My son, those weapons are ceremonial. They were consecrated to the goddess. The Minyans didn't take them because you'd have to be foolish to use them. You'd be cursed by Athena!'

'Nah, Athena and I go way back. Besides, she's the goddess of city defence, isn't she? She would *want* us to protect our town!'

Hercules turned and addressed the crowd. 'We don't have to live in fear of the Minyans! Anybody who is with me, come to the Temple of Athena and suit up! We will trample our oppressors!'

The younger Thebans cheered and gathered around Hercules. Even Iphicles, who had always been weak, sickly and scared of his own shadow, stepped forward to grab a sword. That shamed a lot of older Thebans into joining.

Amphitryon put his hand on Hercules's shoulder. 'My son, you are right. I had forgotten my courage until now. Let us fight for our homeland!'

They raided the Temple of Athena for weapons and armour. The goddess didn't strike anyone dead, so they took that as a good sign. Hercules led his makeshift force out of town until they found a natural choke point where the road wound between two steep cliffs. The Thebans built barricades and dug pits in the path. Then Hercules arrayed most of his men along the clifftops on either side. In such a narrow passageway, the larger size of the Minyan army wouldn't do much good.

The next day, King Erginus personally led his army towards Thebes. As soon as they were in the pass, Hercules sprang his trap. The fighting was bloody. Hercules's stepdad, Amphitryon, was killed in action. So were many other Thebans, but the Minyan army was completely destroyed.

Hercules didn't rest there. He marched to the city of the Minyans and burned it to the ground.

Hercules returned home in triumph. King Creon was so grateful that he rewarded Hercules with his oldest daughter, Megara. Even the gods were impressed. They descended from Olympus and loaded Hercules down with so much swag, it got embarrassing. Hermes gave him a sword. Hephaestus made him a suit of armour. Apollo presented him with a bow and quiver. Athena gave him a kingly robe and generously agreed not to kill anyone for desecrating her temple. It was a big old Olympian lovefest.

Hercules and Megara got married and had two children. For a while, life was good. Hercules took his dad's old job as head general and led the Theban army on many successful campaigns. In one of those battles, his brother, Iphicles, fell, leaving behind a widow and an infant son named Iolaus – but hey, at least Iphicles had died bravely. Hercules brought honour and glory to his hometown. Everybody figured that, once Creon passed away, Hercules would be the new king of Thebes.

If the story had ended there, Hercules would have gone down in history as one of the greatest Greek heroes. But nooooo, he was just getting warmed up.

So was Hera. Up on Mount Olympus, the queen of the gods seethed because of Hercules's successes. She couldn't allow him a happy ending. She decided to make his life as terrible, tragic and complicated as possible, so that some day Percy Jackson would have a *really* hard time writing about it.

I hate Hera.

While Hercules was growing up as a cowherd in Thebes, his cousin Eurystheus grew up as the high king of Mycenae. That may sound awesome, people bowing to you and obeying your every command from the time you're a baby, but it gave Eurystheus a short temper and a big head.

Despite that, Hera thought he was the coolest thing since fresh-pressed olive oil. She blessed his kingdom with peace and prosperity. She sent him twenty drachmas every year on his birthday. Also, she made sure Eurystheus heard all the annoying news about Hercules's exploits, because she wanted the high king to be good and jealous.

When Eurystheus turned eighteen, Hera whispered in his dreams, encouraging him to knock his famous cousin down a few pegs.

Call Hercules to your palace, said the goddess. *Demand that he serve you by doing ten great tasks! Otherwise he will never respect your kingship.*

Eurystheus woke. 'I have a great idea,' he said to himself. 'I will call Hercules to my palace and demand that he serve me by doing ten great tasks! Otherwise he will never respect my kingship!'

Eurystheus sent a messenger to Thebes, ordering Hercules to travel to the capital city of Tiryns and serve him.

Hercules showed restraint. He didn't chop off the messenger's ears, nose or hands. He just sent back a message that read *LOL. NAH.*

Eurystheus was not pleased. Unfortunately, Thebes was outside his jurisdiction. He couldn't do much unless he wanted to declare war, and even Eurystheus wasn't stupid enough to go to war against Hercules.

That night, Hera spoke again in the high king's dreams: *Just bide your time. Hercules will bow before you. I will make sure of it.*

Over the next few weeks, every time Hercules went to a temple, the priests and priestesses gave him dire warnings. 'The gods want you to serve your cousin Eurystheus. No, seriously. You'd better get down to Tiryns or bad things are going to happen.'

Hera was behind this, of course. She was the queen of nagging. She made sure Hercules got the message dozens of times a day from dozens of different sources.

At first, Hercules ignored the warnings. He was much too important and powerful to serve a little worm like Eurystheus. But the warnings kept on coming. Random guys began stopping him on the street, speaking in raspy voices like they were possessed. 'Go to Tiryns. Serve the king!'

Hercules's wife got nervous.

'Honey,' said Megara, 'it's never wise to ignore the gods. Maybe you should go to the Oracle of Delphi and, you know, get a second opinion.'

Hercules didn't want to, but, to make his wife happy, he went to Delphi.

It was a miserable trip. The offerings cost a bundle. Delphi was crawling with merchants hawking cheap souvenirs. Finally Hercules made it to the front of the line to see the Oracle, and she told him the same thing he'd been hearing for weeks. 'Go to the city of Tiryns. Serve High King Eurystheus by doing ten great tasks of his choosing. Thank you and have a nice day.'

Hercules got so angry that he swiped the Oracle's three-legged stool and chased her around the room with it.

'Give me a better prophecy!' he yelled. 'I want a better prophecy!'

Apollo had to intervene personally. His divine voice shook the cave. 'DUDE, NOT COOL. GIVE THE ORACLE BACK HER TRIPOD!'

Hercules took a deep breath. He didn't feel like getting killed by a golden arrow, so he put down the tripod and stormed off.

When he got back to Thebes, his nerves were frayed. His patience was gone. He walked through the streets, and everybody asked him, 'Is it true? Ten tasks for the high king? Wow, that sucks.'

At home, Megara asked, 'How was it, honey? Do you have to go to Tiryns?'

Hercules snapped. He flew into a murderous rage and killed everyone in the house, starting with his wife.

I know. This book is full of crazy, horrible stuff, but that right there? That's *messed up*.

Some stories say that Hera inflicted him with madness so he didn't know what he was doing. Maybe, but I think that's letting Hercules off too easy. We already know he had an anger-management problem. He killed his music teacher with a harp. He chopped pieces off those Minyan envoys.

Hera didn't *have* to drive him crazy. She just had to push him closer to the edge.

Whatever the case, Hercules struck down Megara. He killed the servants who tried to stop him. His two sons screamed and ran, but Hercules took out his bow and shot them, convinced in his twisted mind that they were some kind of enemy.

The only one who escaped was his nephew Iolaus, who'd been living with Hercules since Iphicles died. Iolaus hid behind a couch. When Hercules found him and nocked another arrow in his bow, the boy screamed, 'Uncle, stop!'

Hercules froze. Maybe Iolaus reminded him of his brother Iphicles, back in the old days when they were kids. Hercules had always protected Iphicles from bullies. When Iphicles died, Hercules had sworn to protect Iolaus like his own son.

His rage evaporated. He stared in horror at the bodies of

his children. He looked at the bow in his hands – the bow Apollo had given him, a weapon from the god of prophecies. The message could not have been clearer: *We told you something bad would happen if you didn't listen.*

In utter despair, Hercules fled the city of Thebes. His heart shattered, he returned to Delphi and threw himself on the floor in front of the Oracle.

'Please!' he begged, his whole body shaking with sobs. 'What must I do to atone for my sins? Is there any way I can be forgiven?'

The Oracle spoke: 'Go to the high king as you were told. Serve him well by doing whatever ten tasks he commands. Eurystheus alone may decide when each task is done to his satisfaction. Once all ten are complete, then and *only* then will you be forgiven.'

Hercules dressed himself in beggar's rags. He covered himself with ashes then travelled to Tiryns and knelt before the high king's throne.

'Sire, I have sinned,' said Hercules. 'I did not listen to you or to the gods. In my rage, I murdered my own wife and children. For penance, I am here to do whatever ten tasks you require, no matter how difficult or dangerous or stupid those tasks may be.'

Eurystheus smiled coldly. 'Cousin, that's a shame about your family, but I'm glad you finally came to your senses. Ten stupid tasks, you say? Let's get started!'

Eurystheus was elated. He could assign Hercules any task, no matter how dangerous and, with luck, Hercules would die a painful death! That would eliminate the biggest threat to the throne, since Eurystheus was sure his famous cousin would eventually try to take over Mycenae.

Even if Hercules didn't die, Eurystheus could get some tough items crossed off his to-do list. It was like having a genie pop out of the bottle and grant you ten wishes . . . except the genie was a Theban with swole muscles, a beard and no magic.

'First task!' Eurystheus announced. 'In the region of Nemea, just north of here, a massive lion has been wreaking havoc. I want you to kill it.'

'Does this lion have a name?' Hercules asked.

'Since it lives in Nemea, we call it the Nemean Lion.'

'Wow. Creative.'

'Just kill it!' Eurystheus ordered. 'That is . . . if you *can*.'

Creepy organ music started playing in the background, so Hercules figured there was some catch to this task, but he shouldered his bow, strapped on his sword and marched off to Nemea.

It was a lovely day for lion killing.

The hills of Nemea shimmered in the sunlight. A cool breeze rustled through the woods, making patterns of gold and green across the forest floor. In the middle of a meadow carpeted with wildflowers, a huge male lion was feasting on a cow carcass, strewing scraps of bloody meat everywhere.

The lion was bigger than the largest horse. Muscles rippled under his lustrous gold coat. His claws and teeth flashed silver – more like steel than bone. Hercules couldn't help admiring the majestic predator, but he had a job to do.

'That thing killed a cow,' he reminded himself. 'I like cows.'

He drew his bow and fired.

The arrow hit the lion's neck. It should've severed the beast's jugular and killed him instantly. Instead, it shattered against the lion's fur like an icicle thrown at a brick wall.

The lion turned and growled.

Hercules shot until his quiver was empty. He aimed for the eyes, the mouth, the nose, the chest. Each arrow shattered on impact. The lion just stood there, snarling with mild annoyance.

'Okay, then.' Hercules drew his sword. 'Plan B.'

He charged the lion. With enough force to cleave a redwood tree in half, Hercules brought down his blade on the beast's forehead. The blade snapped. The lion simply shook off the impact.

'Stupid lion!' Hercules yelled. 'That sword was a gift from Hermes!'

'ROAR!' The Nemean Lion lashed out with his claws. Hercules jumped back just quickly enough to avoid getting disembowelled. His breastplate was shredded like tissue paper.

'NO!' Hercules shouted. 'That was a gift from Hephaestus!'

The lion roared again. Hercules roared back. He punched the lion between the eyes.

The lion staggered, shaking his head. He wasn't used to feeling pain. He wasn't used to retreating, either, but he decided Hercules wasn't worth messing with. Cows were easier prey. He turned and bounded into the woods.

'Oh no you don't.' Hercules ran after him.

He followed until the lion disappeared into a cave about halfway up the hillside. Instead of plunging in, Hercules scanned his surroundings.

If I were that lion, he thought, I'd pick a cave with two exits so I couldn't get trapped.

He scouted around. Sure enough, a jagged black fissure led into the cave from the other side of the hill. As quietly as possible, Hercules piled up some boulders, blocking the exit.

'Now you've got nowhere to run, kitty cat.' Hercules circled back to the front entrance and called, 'Anybody home?'

A snarl echoed from the darkness, like *No, this is a recording. Please leave a message.*

Hercules marched inside, forcing the Nemean Lion to retreat until his back was against the pile of boulders.

Now, kids, cornering wild animals is usually a bad idea. It tends to make them a wee bit cranky and homicidal. Hercules was an expert on cranky and homicidal. He crouched in a wrestler's stance.

'Sorry about this, kitty,' he said. 'You're a beautiful killing machine, but High King Putzface wants you dead.'

The lion growled. Obviously he didn't think much of High King Putzface. He pounced, but Hercules had been trained by the best wrestlers in Greece. He dodged the claws and slipped onto the lion's back, locking his legs around the beast's ribcage and putting that shaggy neck in a chokehold.

'Nothing seems to get through your hide,' Hercules grunted in the lion's ear. 'But let's see how you do when no air can get through your throat.'

He squeezed with all his strength. The lion collapsed. Once Hercules was sure the lion was dead, he stood, breathing heavily, and admired the lion's beautiful fur.

'That would make a spankin' awesome cloak,' he said. 'But how can I skin it?'

His eyes drifted to the lion's gleaming claws. 'Huh, I wonder . . .'

He used the lion's own claws to cut the hide. It still took hours of grisly, gruelling work, but in the end Hercules had a new fur coat and enough lion steaks to fill a freezer.

You might think lion fur would be too hot for everyday use, especially in Greece, where the summers can be sweltering. But Hercules's new cloak was surprisingly light and cool. It was a *lot* more comfortable than bronze armour. Hercules used the lion's head as a hood and tied its front paws around his neck.

Hercules admired his reflection in the nearest pond. 'Aw, yeah. Fashionable *and* invulnerable, baby!'

He headed back to Tiryns to report to the high king. If all his tasks went this well, he might end up with a whole new wardrobe.

Hercules strolled into town and caused a riot. Covered in his Nemean Lion cloak, he might have been a beast or a man or some sort of were-lion from a whacked-out episode of *True Blood*. The commoners screamed and fled. The guards shot arrows that shattered against his cape.

Inside the throne room, Eurystheus heard the commotion. His guards scattered in terror. The burly silhouette of a man-lion appeared in the doorway, and the king set a fine example of courage. He dived into a large bronze pot next to the throne.

Hercules couldn't hear or see much with his lion hood pulled over his head. He reached the royal dais, pushed back his shaggy cowl and was surprised to find the throne empty.

'Eurystheus?' Hercules called. 'Hello? Anyone?'

The guards and servants were trembling behind the tapestries. Finally one of the king's braver heralds, a guy named Copreus, came out waving a white handkerchief.

'Um, hello, Your — Your Hairiness. We didn't realize it was you.'

Hercules scanned the room. 'Where is everyone? Why are the tapestries shaking? Where is the high king?'

Copreus dabbed his forehead. 'Um, the king is . . . indisposed.'

Hercules glanced at the dais. 'He's hiding in that decorative pot, isn't he?'

'No,' Copreus said. 'Maybe. Yes.'

'Well, tell His Majesty that I have killed the Nemean Lion. I want to know my second task.'

Copreus climbed the steps of the dais. He whispered into the bronze pot. The pot whispered back.

'The pot says . . .' Copreus hesitated. 'I mean, the high king says you must go to the swamp of Lerna and kill the monster that dwells there. It is a Hydra!'

'A what, now?' Hercules thought he might have heard that name in a Captain America movie, but he didn't know how it applied to him.

'The Hydra is a monster with many poisonous heads,' Copreus explained. 'It's been killing our people and our cattle.'

Hercules frowned. 'I hate monsters that kill cows. I'll be back.'

On the way out of town, Hercules realized he had no idea where Lerna was. He stood there, trying to think, when a chariot drawn by a team of black horses pulled up next to him.

'Need a ride?'

The young man at the reins looked very familiar, but Hercules had been away from Thebes so long he barely recognized his young nephew.

'Iolaus?' Hercules laughed with disbelief. 'What are you doing here?'

'Hello, Uncle! I heard about your Ten Labours and I want to help.'

Hercules's heart twisted like a pretzel. 'But . . . I tried to kill you. Why would you help me?'

The boy's expression turned serious. 'That wasn't your fault. Hera inflicted you with madness. You're the closest thing I have to a father. I want to fight by your side.'

Hercules's eyes stung with tears, but he tried to hide that under his lion-head cowl. 'Thank you, Iolaus. I – I could use a ride. Do you know where to find this swamp of Lerna?'

'I've got GPS. Climb aboard!'

Together, Hercules and his trusty sidekick rolled out of town in the newly christened Herculesmobile.

'I've heard rumours about this Hydra,' said Iolaus. 'Supposedly it has nine heads. Eight of them can be killed, but the ninth head is immortal.'

Hercules scowled. 'How does that work, exactly?'

'No idea,' Iolaus said. 'But if you chop off one of the mortal heads, two new ones sprout to take its place.'

'Ridiculous!'

'Yeah, well . . . Looks like we're going to find out soon.'

The chariot stopped at the edge of the swamp. Mist clung to the ground. Stunted trees clawed upward from the moss and mud. In the distance, a large shape moved through curtains of switchgrass.

The tall grass parted, and the strangest monster Hercules had ever seen came lumbering through the mire. Nine serpentine heads undulated hypnotically on long necks, occasionally striking at the water to snap up fish, frogs and small crocodiles. The monster's body was long and thick and mottled brown, like a python's, but it walked on four heavy clawed feet. Its nine pairs of glowing green eyes cut through the mist like headlights. Its fangs dripped with yellow poison.

Hercules shuddered, remembering the nightmares he'd had as a child after strangling those vipers in his nursery. 'Which head is immortal? They all look the same.'

Iolaus didn't answer. Hercules glanced over and saw that his nephew's face was as white as bone.

'Stay calm,' Hercules said. 'It'll be all right. Did you bring any torches?'

'T-torches . . . Yes.'

With trembling hands, Iolaus brought out a bundle of tar-covered reeds. He lit the end with a spark of flint.

Hercules pulled half a dozen arrows from his quiver. He wrapped the tips in oilcloth. 'I'm going to provoke the monster, make it charge us.'

'You *want* it to charge?'

'Better to fight it over here on solid ground. Not over there, where I could slip in the mud or fall in quicksand.'

Hercules lit his first arrow. He shot it into the switchgrass, which immediately erupted in a sheet of flames. The Hydra hissed. It darted away from the fire, but Hercules shot another arrow right in front of it. Soon the swamp was an inferno. The monster had nowhere to go except straight towards them. It charged, smoke rolling off its dappled brown hide.

'Stay here,' Hercules told his nephew, as Iolaus tried to

keep the horses from bolting. 'By the way, can I borrow your sword? Mine broke.'

Hercules grabbed the boy's blade and leaped out of the chariot.

'Hey, spaghetti head!' he yelled at the Hydra. 'Over here!'

The Hydra's nine heads hissed in unison. The monster didn't appreciate being compared to pasta.

It charged forward, and Hercules had a moment of doubt. The stench of poison burned his eyes. The monster's heads moved in so many directions that he didn't know where to start. He wrapped his cloak around himself and ran into battle.

The Hydra's mouths snapped at his cape, but its poisonous fangs couldn't puncture the lion fur. Hercules dodged and weaved, waiting for an opening. The next time one of the snake heads lashed out, Hercules cut it off.

'AHA! Take that . . . oh, crud.'

Unfortunately, Iolaus's information had been correct. Before the severed head even hit the ground, the bleeding stump began to bubble. The entire neck split down the middle, like string cheese getting pulled apart, and each new neck sprouted a snake head. The whole process took maybe three seconds.

'Aw, c'mon!' Hercules shouted. 'That's not fair!'

He dodged and slashed until the ground was littered with dead snake heads, but the more he cut off, the more grew back. Hercules kept hoping he'd hit the immortal head. Maybe if he separated that one from the body the whole monster would die; but he realized he couldn't do that by trial and error. The smell of poison was giving him vertigo. Dozens of sets of green eyes swam in and out of his vision.

It was only a matter of time before the Hydra would score a hit and sink its fangs into his flesh. Hercules needed to stop the heads from doubling.

'Iolaus!' he yelled. 'Get over here with that torch and – WAHHH!'

One of the monster's necks swept sideways, knocking Hercules off his feet. He rolled, but another neck wrapped around his legs and lifted him off the ground. Hercules managed to break free, and he found himself climbing through a reptilian jungle gym of slimy necks and snapping heads. He punched and kicked, but he didn't dare use his sword – not yet.

'Iolaus!' he shouted. 'The next time I cut off a head, I need you to jump in with that torch and sear the stump so it can't grow back. Understand?'

'C-c-crab!' Iolaus said.

Hercules was sweating with concentration. He punched another snake head and somersaulted over one of the necks. 'Crab?'

'Crab!'

What is the boy talking about? I ask him a yes-or-no question, and he answers with 'crab'? Hercules risked a glance at his nephew.

Wriggling out of the mud, right in front of Iolaus, was a crab as big as a chariot wheel. Its mouth foamed. Its pincers snapped.

Hercules had never heard of giant crabs living in a swamp. Then again, vipers didn't usually crawl into children's bedrooms.

'Hera must be messing with me again,' Hercules grumbled. 'Hold on, Iolaus!'

He sliced his way out of the maze of Hydra necks. He knew that would just cause more of them to grow, but he couldn't let his last surviving nephew get eaten by a crustacean. He launched himself at the crab with a flying kick and brought his heel down right between its eyes. The shell cracked. His foot penetrated the crab's brain, killing it instantly.

'YUCK!' Hercules extracted his foot from the goop. 'Okay, kid, get that torch ready and –'

'Look out!' Iolaus shouted.

Hercules spun as the Hydra bore down on him. Only the Nemean Lion cloak saved him from a dozen new body piercings.

Hercules slashed off the nearest head. 'Now, kid!'

Iolaus thrust the torch against the neck and seared the wound. Nothing sprouted from the blackened stump.

'Good job!' Hercules said. 'Only fifty or sixty more to go!'

Together they pruned the Hydra's heads until the air was filled with acrid smoke and the smell of barbecued reptile. Finally the monster had only one head left, surrounded by a corona of sizzling, charred polka dots.

Hercules grunted. 'Of course the immortal head would be the last one.'

He sliced through the neck. The entire monster collapsed in a heap. The still-living head flopped around in the mud, hissing and spitting poison.

'Gross,' Iolaus said. 'What do we do with it?'

Hercules clapped him on the shoulder. 'You did good, nephew. Just watch the floppy head for a second. Don't let it get away. I have an idea . . .'

Hercules collected some of the dead snake heads from the ground. He spread out a leather tarp and carefully milked the Hydra fangs for venom. Then he wrapped the tarp around his arrow points, coating them with deadly poison. He bundled the arrows and returned them to his quiver.

'Poison arrows might come in handy some day,' he told Iolaus. 'Now, about this immortal Hydra head – I suppose there's no way to destroy it?'

Iolaus shrugged. 'That's probably why they call it immortal.'

'Then we need to make sure it never causes trouble again.'

Hercules dug a deep pit, buried the head and covered the grave with a heavy rock so nobody would ever unearth the nasty thing by accident. Then he and Iolaus rode back to Tiryns.

According to legend, that Hydra head is still alive and thrashing somewhere near Lerna under a big boulder. Personally, I'd recommend you don't go looking for it.

Back at the palace, High King Eurystheus had finally emerged from his decorative pot.

Hercules explained how he'd defeated the Hydra. He showed the king some of the dead snake heads and a case of premium crabmeat they'd collected from Hera's foamy friend.

Eurystheus's eyes glinted. 'You say your nephew *helped* you?'

'Well . . . yeah. He burned the stumps while I –'

'WRONG ANSWER!' The king pounded his armrest. 'No one can help you with your tasks! This deed does not count!'

The tendons in Hercules's neck tightened like suspension cables. 'Are you kidding me?'

'Oh, no! The Oracle told you only *I* could judge whether a job was done correctly. And this job was not! You still have nine stupid tasks to go!'

Eurystheus smiled in triumph, apparently not appreciating how hard Hercules was clenching his fists. Eurystheus wanted payback for the pot-hiding incident. He didn't like being made to look like a fool. (Not that he needed Hercules's help with that.) He wanted Hercules to *suffer*.

'On the borders of my kingdom,' he continued, 'a huge boar has been causing all sorts of trouble, ravaging the countryside, goring my peasants –'

'You want it killed,' Hercules guessed.

'Oh, no! A hero of your talent needs a tougher challenge. I want the boar brought to me alive!'

Hercules silently counted to five, which was the number of times he wanted to kick the high king in the teeth. 'Fine. Where can I find this monster pig?'

'It usually roams the land of the centaurs near Mount Erymanthius. Because of this, we call it –'

'Let me guess. The Erymanthian Boar.'

'Exactly! And don't take your nephew this time. Do the task alone!'

Hercules trudged out of the palace. With reluctance, he told Iolaus to stay in town and sell their premium crabmeat while he went boar hunting.

After weeks of hard travel, Hercules reached the land of the centaurs. He was worried about dealing with the natives, since centaurs had a reputation for being wild and rude. But the first one he met, an old stallion named Pholus, turned out to be super nice.

'Oh, goodness!' Pholus exclaimed. 'Hercules himself! I have waited for this day!'

Hercules raised his bushy eyebrows. 'You have?'

'Absolutely! I'd be happy to give you directions to the Erymanthian Boar, but first would you honour me by having dinner in my humble home?'

Hercules was tired and hungry, so he followed Pholus back to his cave. While Hercules made himself comfortable, the centaur fired up the barbecue pit and put on some ribs. Then he knelt on his equine forelegs and brushed the dirt-covered floor until he unearthed a wooden trapdoor.

'Under here is my secret larder,' Pholus explained. 'This is going to sound weird, but generations ago my great-grandfather heard a prophecy that one day his descendants would entertain an important guest named Hercules!'

'A prophecy spoke of me?'

'Oh, yes! My great-grandfather set aside this jug of wine for the occasion . . .' Pholus brought out a ceramic *pithos* covered in dust and cobwebs. 'It's been ageing in this larder for over a hundred years, waiting for you!'

'I'm – I'm honoured,' Hercules said. 'But what if it has turned to vinegar?'

Pholus uncorked the jar. A sweet aroma filled the cave – like grape vines ripening in the summer sun, gentle spring rains on a field of new grass and rare spices drying over a fire.

'Wow,' Hercules said. 'Pour me a glass!'

They drank a toast. Both agreed that it was the best wine they'd ever tasted. Pholus was just about to tell Hercules where he could find the Erymanthian Boar when five spear-wielding centaurs stampeded into the cave.

'We smell that wine!' said one. 'Gimme!'

Pholus rose to his hooves. 'Daphnis, you and your hooligan friends were not invited. This wine is a special vintage for my guest.'

'Share!' Daphnis yelled. 'Or die!'

He levelled his spear and charged at Pholus, but Hercules was faster. He drew his bow and fired off five poison arrows, killing the intruders.

Pholus stared at the pile of dead centaurs. 'Oh, dear. This wasn't how I imagined our special dinner. Thank you for saving me, Hercules, but I must bury them.'

'Why?' Hercules asked. 'They tried to kill you.'

'They are still my kinsmen,' said the old centaur. 'Family is family, even when they threaten murder.'

Hercules couldn't argue with that. He'd had some experience with family killing. He helped Pholus dig the graves. Just as they were laying the last centaur to rest, Pholus pulled one of Hercules's arrows from the corpse's leg.

Hercules said, 'Careful with –'

'Ouch!' Pholus cut his finger on the poisoned arrow tip. The old centaur promptly collapsed.

Hercules rushed to Pholus's side, but he had no antidote for the Hydra venom. 'My friend, I – I'm so sorry.'

The old centaur smiled weakly. 'It was a special day. I had excellent wine. I dined with a hero. You will find the boar to the east of here. Use . . . use the snow.'

Pholus's eyes rolled up in his head.

Hercules felt terrible. He built a funeral pyre for Pholus and poured the last of the wine on the fire as a sacrifice to the gods. He didn't understand Pholus's last advice — *use the snow* — but he headed east in search of the boar.

Family is family, Hercules thought. Still, if Eurystheus hadn't sent him on this stupid quest, that kind old centaur might still be alive. Hercules wanted to strangle his royal cousin.

He found the boar tramping around in the hills to the east, just as Pholus had said. I've described enough giant boars in this book that you can probably guess what it looked like. After all, Ancient Greece was infested with giant evil death pigs. The Erymanthian one was just as big, bristly, ugly and mean as all the others. Killing it wouldn't have been a challenge for Hercules. Capturing it alive . . . that was tougher.

Hercules spent weeks chasing the boar through the wilderness. He tried to dig a pit for the boar to run into. He tried nets and snares and Acme boar-catching kits with anvils and seesaws. The boar was too smart for all of that. It enjoyed taunting Hercules, letting him get almost within reach before running away again, leaping over his tripwires and squealing in piggy laughter.

This thing can smell a man-made trap a mile away, Hercules thought. But how else can I stop it?

By this time he'd followed the boar into the higher elevations of Mount Erymanthia. One afternoon he climbed a ridge, hoping to get the lay of the land, and he noticed a steep ravine below, filled with snow.

'Huh,' Hercules said. '*Use the snow . . .*'

He murmured a prayer of thanks to the centaur Pholus.

It took Hercules a couple of tries, but, with flaming arrows and lots of shouting, he finally managed to chase the giant boar into the ravine. The boar charged straight into the snow and became hopelessly stuck, like an appliance in moulded styrofoam.

If Hercules had had a big enough cardboard box and some parcel tape, he could've just shipped the boar to Eurystheus via Federal Express. Since he didn't, he spent a lot of time carefully digging around the boar, tying up its legs and its snout. Then, using all his great strength, he hauled the monster out of the snowdrift and dragged it back to Mycenae.

The merchants of Tiryns were excited to see Hercules coming to town, hauling a huge pig. First he'd brought them lion steaks. Next he'd filled the stores with premium crabmeat. Now pork would be on the menu for weeks!

Eurystheus was not as pleased. He was in the middle of breakfast when Hercules burst into the throne room and tossed the Erymanthian Boar like a bowling ball right towards the royal dais.

The boar slid to a stop at Eurystheus's feet, its red eyes level with the king's face, its razor-sharp tusks a few inches from his groin. Eurystheus screamed and dived for safety – right into his big bronze pot.

'Wh-what is the meaning of this?' he demanded, his voice echoing from inside the pot.

'It's the Erymanthian Boar,' Hercules said. 'Alive, as requested.'

'Yes! Fine! Take it away!'

'And for my next task?' Hercules asked.

Eurystheus closed his eyes and whimpered. He *hated* heroes. They were so annoyingly . . . heroic. He wondered if he could just order Hercules to kill himself. No, the gods probably wouldn't like that.

Unless . . . Eurystheus had a brilliant idea. What if he asked Hercules to do something that would get him killed *by the gods*?

'The Ceryneian Hind!' cried the king. 'Bring it to me.'

'The what, now?' Hercules asked.

'Just go! Figure it out! Google it! I don't care! Bring me that hind, dead or alive!'

Hercules had never been good at looking up things on the Internet, so he asked around town what a Ceryneian Hind was.

His nephew Iolaus gave him the answer. 'Oh, yeah, I've heard that story. The hind is a doe.'

'Doe,' Hercules said. 'A deer. A female deer.'

'Right,' Iolaus said. 'She lives in Ceryneia. That's why she's called —'

'The Ceryneian Hind.' Hercules sighed. 'These people, always naming their animals after places with really difficult names. Just once, I want to go capture a monster named Joe or Timothy.'

'Anyway,' Iolaus continued, 'the hind is supposed to be really fast, like fast enough to outrun an arrow. She's got golden antlers —'

'Female deer don't have antlers, do they?'

'This one does. And bronze hooves. Also, the hind is sacred to the goddess Artemis.'

'So, if I kill the deer —'

'Artemis will kill you,' Iolaus confirmed.

'Eurystheus is trying to trick me. I hate that guy.'

'You sure you don't want me come with you?'

'Nah. I don't want to get disqualified again. Thanks anyway, kid.'

So Hercules set out alone to find the magical doe that was not named Timothy.

The task wasn't so much dangerous as it was long, hard and aggravating. Hercules chased the deer for an entire year all across Greece, way up into the frozen lands of the Hyperborean giants and back to the southern Peloponnese again. He got a great workout, but he couldn't get close to the hind. His nets and traps and Acme deer-catching kits didn't work. He tried the old boar-in-the-snow trick, but the deer ran nimbly over the icy crust without falling through.

The only time the deer ever slowed down was when she crossed rivers. Maybe she didn't want to get her shiny bronze hooves wet, because she would always hesitate a few seconds before jumping in. That might have given Hercules an opportunity to shoot the animal, but since he couldn't kill her it didn't help.

Unless . . . Hercules thought, I could disable her without killing her.

This wasn't the easiest or safest plan, but Hercules decided he had to give it a shot (so to speak). He rummaged through his supplies until he found some good fishing line – the strongest, lightest cord he had. He tied one end to the fletching of an arrow. Then he ran after the deer.

Getting the timing right took days. Hercules had to scout the terrain so he knew it perfectly. He had to anticipate which way the deer would run. Then he had to beat her to the nearest river in time to set up a shot.

Finally he managed to get in position. He stood a hundred yards downstream, his bow ready, just as the deer reached the water.

For a few heartbeats, she hesitated. Even for the best archer, this was a ridiculously hard shot, but Hercules had no choice. He let his arrow fly.

The point passed cleanly through the membrane of both shanks, tangling the hind's back legs in fishing line. She stumbled. Before she could regain her balance, Hercules sprinted up the riverbank and grabbed the animal's bronze hooves. He examined the wounds and breathed a sigh of relief. He'd drawn a little blood, but the hind would suffer no permanent damage.

Hercules slung the deer over his shoulders and started back towards Tiryns.

He'd only gone half a mile when a voice behind him said, 'Where are you going with my hind?'

Hercules turned. Behind him stood a young maiden in a silvery tunic, a bow at her side. Next to her stood a dashing young man in golden robes. He was also armed with a bow.

'Artemis,' Hercules said, resisting the urge to scream and run. 'And Apollo. Look, guys, I'm sorry I had to capture this deer, but –'

'"But."' Artemis glanced at her brother. 'Don't you love it when mortals say "I'm sorry, but –"? As if they can excuse their offences!' She fixed her cold silver eyes on Hercules. 'Very well, hero. Explain to me why I shouldn't kill you where you stand.'

'Eurystheus gave me ten stupid jobs,' Hercules said. 'I mean, ten great labours. Whatever. He told me to bring him the Ceryneian Hind, dead or alive. Of course I knew she was sacred to you. I would never kill her. But I was caught between fulfilling my ten tasks like Apollo's prophecy commanded –'

'That's true,' Apollo admitted.

'– and offending the great goddess Artemis. Eurystheus set me up. He wanted me to kill the hind so you would kill me. But, if you let me take the hind to him and complete my task, I promise no further harm will come to her. I will let her go immediately after I present her to the king.'

Artemis's knuckles whitened on her bow. 'I hate it when mortals use us for their dirty work.'

'Death by god,' Apollo grumbled. 'We're not hitmen. We can't be told whom to kill or not kill!'

Artemis waved in a gesture of dismissal. 'Hercules, take the hind. Keep your promise and we will have no further problems. But this Eurystheus . . . I hope I never catch him hunting in the woods. I will not be so merciful.'

The gods disappeared in a shimmer of light. Hercules continued on his way, but it was a while before his knees stopped shaking. Only a fool wouldn't be afraid of Artemis and Apollo, and, for all his faults, Hercules was no fool. Well, most of the time, anyway.

When Hercules carried the Ceryneian Hind into the throne room, he was hoping Eurystheus would hide in his pot, because that would've been entertaining.

Instead, the high king just shrugged. 'So you have completed this task adequately. I'll keep the hind in my menagerie.'

'Your what?' asked Hercules.

'My private royal zoo, you dolt! Every king needs a menagerie.'

'Nuh-uh. I promised Artemis I would release the hind. If you want this deer in a zoo, you'll have to put her there yourself.'

'It's part of your task!'

'No, it isn't. You just said I completed the task.'

'Oh, fine! I'll take the deer.'

The king rose from his throne. He was halfway down the steps when Hercules set the deer on her hooves and cut the cords binding her legs.

'Here you go, Eurystheus. Be careful. She's –'

The hind fled the room in a blur of gold and white.

'– fast.'

The king screamed and stomped his feet, which was almost as funny as watching him jump into a pot. The hind raced back to the wilderness, which made Artemis happy.

Eurystheus snarled. 'You deceitful hero! I'll make your next task *impossible!*'

'I thought the last four were impossible.'

'This will be even *more* impossible! Near the city of Stymphalia is a lake overrun by a flock of demonic birds –'

'If they're called the Stymphalian birds –'

'They *are* called the Stymphalian birds!'

'I'm going to puke.'

'You will not puke! You will rid the lake of every single bird. Ha, ha! Copreus, my herald . . .'

The king's herald scuttled over. 'Yes, my lord?'

'What do people say when they wish someone luck, but they mean it in a sarcastic way?'

'Um, good luck with that?'

'Yes! Good luck with that, Hercules! Ha, ha!'

Hercules left, muttering under his breath.

As he got close to Stymphalia, he noticed that all the farmland had been picked clean of crops. Not a single tree had any fruit.

Then he started finding corpses – squirrels, deer, cows, people. They'd been clawed and pecked to bits. Some had feathers sticking out of their necks. Hercules plucked one of the feathers. It was as hard and sharp as a dart.

When he arrived at the lake, his spirits sank. The valley was like a mile-wide cereal bowl, rimmed with wooded hills and filled with a shallow layer of green water. Islands of marsh grass writhed with black stippling – millions and millions of raven-sized birds. The trees along the shore swayed and shivered under the weight of the flocks. Their screeching echoed back and forth like sonar across the water.

Hercules edged towards the nearest tree. The birds' beaks and claws glinted like polished bronze. One of the little demons fixed him with its yellow eyes. It squawked, puffing up its body, and a barrage of feathers hurtled towards him. Were it not for his lion-skin cape, Hercules would've been skewered.

'This really *is* impossible,' Hercules said. 'There aren't enough arrows in the world to kill this many birds.'

'Then use your wits,' said a female voice.

Hercules turned. Next to him stood a woman with long, dark hair and storm-grey eyes. She held a shield and spear, as if ready to fight, but her smile was warm and familiar.

Hercules bowed. 'Athena. It's been a while.'

'Hello, there,' said the goddess. 'I see you traded the kingly robe I made you for a lion skin.'

'Oh, um, no offence.'

'None taken, my hero. You were wise to use the cloak for armour. Besides, you'd have to work *very* hard to upset me. I still chuckle about that time Hera tried to suckle you.' The goddess hesitated. 'Oh, dear . . . you don't still, er, poop your pants when you hear her name, do you?'

Hercules blushed. 'No. I got over that when I was a baby.'

'Good, good. At any rate, the incident was *very* amusing. I'm here today because Zeus thought you might need some guidance.'

'That's awesome! So what's the secret with these birds?'

Athena wagged her finger. 'I said *guidance*. I didn't say I would hand you the answer. You'll have to use your wits.'

'Bah.'

'Think, Hercules. What could make these birds go away?'

Hercules twiddled with his lion-paw necktie. 'Larger birds?'

'No.'

'Thousands of cats?'

'No.'

'A lack of food?'

Athena paused. 'That's interesting. Perhaps, eventually, the birds would migrate on their own once all their food sources ran out. But you can't depend on that, and you need them to leave *now*. So what can you do?'

Hercules thought back to his days on the cattle ranch. He'd spent a lot of time watching flocks of birds in the pastures.

'Once, during a storm,' he recalled, 'thunder boomed, and thousands of crows took off from a wheat field and flew away. Birds hate loud noises.'

'Excellent.'

'But . . . how can I make a noise that awful?' Hercules cast his mind back to his childhood. He'd been accused of making some pretty horrible sounds back then. 'My old music teacher said I played so badly I could scare away any audience. I wish I still had my lyre, but I broke it over Linus's head.'

'Well, I don't have a lyre,' said Athena, 'but I do have something that might serve.'

From the folds of her robes, the goddess pulled a rod studded with rows of small cowbells — like an oversize snake rattle cast in bronze. 'Hephaestus made this. It's quite possibly the worst musical instrument ever invented. Even Apollo didn't want it, but I had a feeling it might prove useful some day.'

She handed the rattle to Hercules. When he shook it, his eardrums curled up inside his skull and begged to die. Each cowbell made a tone that was perfectly dissonant with the rest. If five junkyard car crushers got together and formed a band, their debut album might sound like that rattle.

All of the birds within a hundred-yard radius freaked out and scattered, but as soon as Hercules stopped making noise they settled back into the trees.

Hercules frowned. 'That worked temporarily, but to get rid of all these birds I'll need more cowbell.'

Athena shuddered. 'No mortal should ever use the words "more cowbell". But perhaps the rattle is only part of the answer. What if you shot the birds as they fled?'

'I can't shoot all of them! There are too many.'

'You don't need to shoot all of them. If you can just convince the birds that this isn't a good roosting place . . .'

'Ha! Got it. Thanks, Athena!' He ran towards the lake, shaking his rattle and screaming 'MORE COWBELL!'

'And that's my cue to leave.' Athena disappeared in a cloud of grey smoke.

Hercules spent days sprinting around the lake with his rattle and his bow. When the Stymphalian birds lifted into the air, terrified by his god-awful music, he shot as many as he could with his poisonous arrows.

After a week of cowbell and poison, the entire flock lifted off in a black cloud and flew towards the horizon.

Hercules hung around for a few more days, just to make sure the feathery demons didn't return. Then he collected a lovely necklace of bird carcasses and headed back to Tiryns.

'High King!' Hercules announced as he burst into the throne room. 'I am delighted to give you the bird – I mean, birds, plural. The Stymphalian lake is safe for swimming season!'

Before the king could respond, the audience chamber erupted in applause and cheers. Court officials crowded the hero with autograph pens and glossy Hercules photos. Many of the royal guards showed off their TEAM HERCULES T-shirts, even though Eurystheus had specifically banned them as a dress-code violation.

The king gritted his teeth. With every stupid task Hercules completed, he got more famous and became more of a threat. The people of Mycenae worshipped him.

Perhaps Eurystheus had been going about this the wrong way. Instead of trying to kill Hercules, perhaps he should assign Hercules a task so disgusting and degrading the hero would become an object of ridicule.

The high king smiled. 'Well done, Hercules. Now for your next assignment!'

The crowd hushed. They couldn't wait to hear what kind of monster Hercules would fight next, and what sort of exotic meat they might soon expect on their dinner tables.

'My friend Augeas, the king of Elis, is famous for his cattle,' said Eurystheus, 'but I'm afraid his cowsheds have got a little . . . messy over the years. Since you have experience as a rancher, I want you to go clean his sheds. By yourself. With *no* help.'

Some of the crowd moved away from Hercules as if he was already covered in cow mess.

Hercules's eyes could've burned a hole in the high king's face. '*That's* my next task? You want me to *clean cowsheds?*'

'Oh, I'm sorry. Is doing an honest day's work beneath you?' Eurystheus wouldn't have known an honest day's work if it ran around him banging a cowbell, but the crowd muttered, 'Ooooooo, burn.'

'Fine,' Hercules grumbled. 'I will clean the cowsheds.'

He signed a few more autographs, gave away his dead Stymphalian birds as souvenirs, then left to purchase some waders and a shovel.

Here's irony for you: King Augeas, whose name means *bright*, was the grubbiest, grungiest, un-brightest king in all of Greece. He'd been raising cattle for thirty years and never once bothered to have his barns cleaned.

That was partly because the cattle didn't need it. They were descended from the divine cows of Augeas's father, the sun Titan Helios, so they could live in any conditions, clean or dirty, and they never got sick.

But mostly, Augeas didn't clean his sheds because he was cheap and lazy. He didn't want to pay anybody to do the job. And, as the job got worse, fewer people were willing to take it on. Because of the cows' heavenly health, they pooped *a lot*, so after thirty years the sheds looked like a range of cow-patty mountains with swarms of flies so thick you couldn't see the animals.

Hercules smelled Augeas's kingdom fifteen miles before he got there. When he arrived in the city of Elis, all the locals were scurrying around with scarves over their noses and mouths to block out the stink. Business in the marketplace was terrible, because nobody wanted to visit or travel through Poop Town.

Hercules decided to scout the barns before talking to the king. He quickly realized his waders and shovel weren't going to be enough. The pens occupied more square acreage than the rest of the city. They were situated at the western edge of town, on a sort of peninsula where the River Alpheus curved in a giant C-shape.

Hercules felt awful for the cattle. No animals, divine or not, should have to live in conditions like that. He'd spent six years ranching, so he knew something about how cowsheds were laid out, even if he couldn't see them under the moonscape of poop. He took measurements along the riverbanks, did some engineering calculations and used the spirit-level app on his smartphone until a solution started to form in his mind.

Then he set off for the royal palace.

He could barely get through the throne-room doors, because

the place was so jammed with junk. A few bewildered guards wandered around in hand-me-down uniforms, navigating through canyons of old newspapers, broken furniture, mouldy clothes and pallets of expired pet food.

Hercules held his nose. He made his way towards the dais, where King Augeas sat on a rickety metal folding chair as his throne. His robes might have once been blue, but they were so stained that it was impossible to be sure. His beard was full of breadcrumbs and small creatures. Next to him stood a younger man, maybe his son, whose expression seemed permanently frozen in the act of throwing up. Hercules couldn't blame the kid. The palace reeked like the inside of a carton of spoiled milk.

'Hello, King Augeas.' Hercules bowed. 'I heard you might need some help cleaning your cowsheds.'

Next to the king, the young man yelped, 'Thank the gods!'

Augeus scowled. 'Be quiet, Phyleus!' The king turned to Hercules. 'My son doesn't know what he's talking about, stranger. We need no help with cleaning.'

'Dad!' Phyleus protested.

'Silence, boy! I am not paying anyone to do that work. It would cost far too much. Besides, my cattle are perfectly healthy.'

'Your people are not,' muttered the prince. 'They're dying from the stench.'

'Sire,' Hercules interrupted, 'I can do the job, and I'll charge a very reasonable rate.'

Hercules hadn't planned on asking for payment, but now he figured he might as well. The job was disgusting, and the king deserved to pay for keeping his cows in such shoddy conditions. 'It will only cost you one quarter of your herd.'

The king lurched out of his seat, raining crumbs and gerbils from his beard. 'Outrageous! I wouldn't give you even a *hundredth* of my herd!'

'One tenth,' Hercules countered. 'And I'll do the entire job in one day.'

King Augeas was about to shout insults, or possibly have a heart attack, when Phyleus grabbed his arm.

'Dad, this is a golden opportunity! It's a small price for so much work, and how could he possibly finish in one day? Just tell him he'll get no pay if he can't do it within the time limit. Then, if he fails, it costs you nothing and we still get the barns partially cleaned.'

Hercules smiled. 'Your son is shrewd. Do we have a deal?'

Augeas grunted. 'Very well. Guards, bring me some parchment so I can write a contract. And not the good stuff. I have reams of used parchment over there, under those bags of kitty litter.'

'Kitty litter?' Hercules asked.

'You never know when you might need it!'

Hercules and Augeas signed the contract. Prince Phyleus served as witness.

The next morning, with Phyleus tagging along, Hercules took his shovel down to the cowsheds.

The prince surveyed the mountains of poop. 'You, my friend, made a bad deal. There's no way you can clean all this by sunset.'

Hercules just smiled. He strolled to the north of the pens and began to dig a hole.

'What are you doing?' asked Phyleus. 'All the poop is over there.'

'Watch and learn, Prince.'

Hercules was strong and tireless. By noon, he had dug a deep trench from the north end of the sheds to the upper bank of the river, leaving only a thin retaining wall to keep the water from flowing in. He spent the rest of the day digging another trench from the south end of the sheds to the bottom of Alpheus's C-shaped curve, where the river flowed out of town. Again Hercules left just enough earth in place to keep the water from seeping into the trench.

By late afternoon, Phyleus was getting impatient. Hercules was about to fail at the job without having moved a single shovelful of poop.

'So you've dug two trenches,' said the prince. 'How does that help?'

'What will happen,' Hercules asked him, 'when I knock out the northern retaining wall and let in the river?'

'The water . . . Oh! I get it!'

Phyleus followed, jumping up and down with excitement, as Hercules walked to the northern bank. With a single stroke of his shovel, Hercules broke the retaining wall. The river flooded the trench, racing towards the pens. Hercules had been careful with his measurements. The grade and elevation were just right. Water raged through the cowsheds, breaking up the mountains of dung, pushing the waste through the southern trench into the lower bend of the river, where it was swept downstream.

Hercules had invented the world's largest toilet. With a

single flush, he'd cleaned thirty years' worth of excrement from the sheds, leaving only a gleaming field of mud and a thousand very confused, power-washed cows.

Phyleus whooped with delight. He escorted Hercules back to the throne room, anxious to share the good news. 'Father, he did it! The cowsheds are clean! The city no longer smells like a sewage processing plant!'

King Augeas looked up from the dented cans of lima beans he'd been stacking. 'Eh? I don't believe it.'

'I was there!' Phyleus insisted. 'I'm your witness. You have to pay this man – one tenth of your herd, as you promised in the contract.'

'I don't know what you're talking about,' said the king. 'I signed no contract. I never promised this man anything.'

Phyleus turned as green as a Hydra's eye. 'But –'

'You're no son of mine!' the king screeched. 'You're taking this stranger's side against me? I'll banish you both for treason. Guards!'

The guards didn't appear, probably because they were lost in the throne room's rubbish piles.

Hercules turned to Phyleus. 'You seem like a sensible young man. If you were king, would you clean up this palace?'

'In a heartbeat.'

'Would you be a good ruler?'

'Yes.'

'And honour your contracts?'

'You bet.'

'Well, that's all I need to hear.'

'This is outrageous!' cried King Augeas. 'Guards! Someone!'

Hercules climbed the dais. He punched King Augeas in the face, killing him instantly and shaking several undiscovered species of rodents from his facial hair.

Hercules looked at Phyleus. 'Sorry. He was getting on my nerves.'

Phyleus became the king. He immediately ordered all expired pet food, kitty litter, old newspapers and rusty armour to be removed from the throne room. He declared hoarding a capital offence. The city of Elis got a good scrub-down, and Hercules received one-tenth of the royal herd.

When Hercules returned to Tiryns with a million drachmas' worth of cattle and not a spot of manure on him, Eurystheus was furious.

'What happened?' he demanded.

Hercules told him the story. 'I cleaned up the cowsheds. I got rich. Everybody's happy.'

'I'm not happy! That labour doesn't count. You received compensation!'

Hercules swallowed back his rage. 'You never said I couldn't take payment.'

'Even so, you didn't do the job by yourself. The river did it for you!'

'How is using a river any different than using a shovel? It's a tool.'

The high king stomped his feet. 'I said the labour doesn't count, and I'm the high king! Since you like cattle so much, I'll give you another cow-related task. Go to King Minos in Crete. Convince him to give up his prize bull. That should keep you busy for a while!'

Hercules's rage pushed against his sternum. Sure, he'd

agreed to do penance for murdering his family. Sure, he'd been a naughty demigod. But now his ten stupid tasks had ballooned into *twelve* stupid tasks, and he was only halfway through the list. He wanted to kill his cousin. With great effort he took his hand off the hilt of his sword.

'One Cretan Bull,' he grunted. 'Coming right up.'

King Minos had a vicious reputation and a powerful army, so Eurystheus hoped he would kill Hercules on the spot for daring to ask for his prized bull. As it turned out, the bull mission was a piece of cake.

Hercules arrived in Knossos, strolled into the throne room and explained his quest to King Minos. 'Long story short, Your Majesty, I'm supposed to bring back your prized bull for High King Hide-in-Pot.'

'Take it,' Minos said.

Hercules blinked. 'Seriously?'

'Yes! Take the bull! Good riddance!'

It was all about timing. The white bull had been a gift from Poseidon, but Hercules arrived after Queen Pasiphaë fell in love with the beast and gave birth to the Minotaur, so now the prized bull was a constant reminder of King Minos's shame and disgrace. He was anxious to get rid of it. He also might have had a premonition of what would happen if that bull ever got loose on the Grecian mainland. Eurystheus would get more than he bargained for.

Hercules sailed back to Mycenae with the white bull tied up in the cargo hold. When he reached the docks, he picked up the bull, propped it on his head like a sack of flour and carried it into the palace. 'Where do you want this?'

This time the high king was determined not to panic. He sat on his throne, pretending to read a magazine. 'Hmm?'

'The Cretan Bull,' Hercules said. 'Where do you want it?'

'Oh.' Eurystheus stifled a yawn. 'Put it over there, next to the window.'

Hercules lumbered over to the window.

'I've changed my mind,' said the king. 'It would look better next to the sofa.'

'Here?'

'A little to the left.'

'Here.'

'No, I liked it better by the window.'

Hercules resisted the urge to hurl the bull at the throne. 'Here, then?'

'You know, the bull doesn't go with my decor. Take it outside the city and release it.'

'You want it to roam free? This is a wild animal with sharp horns. It will destroy things and kill people.'

'Do as I say,' the king ordered. 'Then come back for your next assignment.'

Hercules didn't like it, but he released the Cretan Bull into the Greek countryside. Sure enough, it rampaged around and caused all kinds of damage. Eventually it wandered up to Marathon and became known as the Marathonian Bull, killing and destroying with impunity until Theseus finally tracked it down, but that was much later.

Hercules returned to the throne room. 'Next stupid task, Your Highness?'

Eurystheus smiled. Recently he'd heard rumours of a Thracian king named Diomedes who raised man-eating horses, feeding them the flesh of his guests. Ever since, Eurystheus had been having pleasant dreams about Hercules getting torn apart.

'I understand that Diomedes, the king of Thrace, has excellent horses,' he said. 'Go there and bring me back four of his best mares.'

Hercules pinched the bridge of his nose. He felt a migraine coming on. 'You couldn't have thought of this earlier, when I was up in Thrace chasing the Ceryneian Hind?'

'Nope!'

'Fine. Thracian mares. Whatever.'

Hercules headed off again, wishing somebody would invent aeroplanes or bullet trains, because his shoes were getting worn out from walking all over Greece.

He decided to try his luck sailing this time. He hired a trireme and a crew of volunteers, promising them adventure and treasure on the way to Thrace. He brought his nephew along too, because Iolaus had turned into a skilled commander of troops. Hercules was worried that Eurystheus would declare the quest invalid if the crew helped to capture the horses, so he decided that, once they arrived in Thrace, he would leave them aboard the ship and meet with Diomedes on his own.

Along the way, Hercules had a few small side adventures. He founded the Olympic games. He invaded some countries. He helped the gods defeat an army of immortal giants. I guess I could tell you about that if I had a few hundred extra pages, but I recently had to fight some giants myself, and I'm not quite ready to tackle that subject.

When Hercules finally reached Thrace, he left his crew aboard ship as planned and marched alone into Diomedes's palace. Since the direct approach had worked so well with King Minos in Crete, Hercules decided to try it again.

'Hey, Diomedes,' said Hercules, 'can I have your horses?'

Diomedes grinned. The psychotic gleam in his eyes made him look about as friendly as a jack-o'-lantern. 'You've heard about my horses, eh?'

'Uh, just that they're supposed to be the best. High King Mouthbreather of Mycenae sent me up here to get four of your mares.'

'Oh, no problem! Come with me!'

Hercules couldn't believe his luck. Two easy quests in a row? Sweet!

As he followed Diomedes, he noticed more and more guards falling into line behind them. By the time they reached the stables, he had an escort of fifty Thracian warriors.

'Here we are!' Diomedes spread his arms proudly. 'My horses!'

'Wow,' said Hercules.

Diomedes's stables made King Augeas's cowsheds look like Disneyland. The floor was covered with grisly bits of meat and bone. The horses' hooves and legs were splattered with blood. Their eyes were wild, smart and malevolent. When they saw Hercules, they whinnied, snapping at him with sharp, red-stained teeth. The nearest mares strained to break out of their stalls. Only the thick bronze chains around their necks kept them back, leashing them to a row of iron posts.

'My babies are strong,' said Diomedes. 'That's why I have to keep them chained. They *love* human flesh.'

'Charming,' Hercules muttered. 'And I suppose I'm tonight's main course?'

'It's nothing personal,' said the king. 'I do this with all my prisoners and my guests and most of my relatives. Guards! Throw him in!'

It was fifty-to-one. The guards never stood a chance. Hercules tossed them one by one into the stables, giving the horses a fifty-course meal of Thracian warriors.

Finally, the only people left were Hercules and Diomedes. The king backed into the corner. 'Hold on, now! Let's talk about this.'

'Talk to your horses,' said Hercules. ' 'Cause I ain't listening.'

He picked up the king and hurled him into the stables. The horses were really full, but they somehow found room for dessert.

After so much good food, the horses were sleepy and tame. Hercules picked the four best mares, harnessed them up and led them to the docks where his ship was waiting.

As they made their way back down the coast, Hercules and his sailors got into some skirmishes with the Thracians. Of course Hercules won them all, but a few of his volunteers were killed. One guy, Abderus, fought so bravely that Hercules built him a huge tomb and founded a city in his honour. The place, Abdera, became a major port on the Thracian coast. The Greek town is still there today – just in case, you know, you find yourself in Diomedes Country with an afternoon to kill.

Hercules brought the flesh-eating mares back to Eurystheus, but the High King was too scared to use them. He released them into the wild near Mount Olympus. Some stories say the horses were eaten by even bigger predators. Other stories say the horses' descendants were still there centuries later when Alexander the Great came along and harnessed them. All I know from personal experience: you can still find flesh-eating horses if you go to the wrong neighbourhoods. My advice: *Don't*.

At this point, Eurystheus was starting to panic. He was running out of problems for Hercules to solve. The countryside had been cleared of monsters. All of the evil kings had either been punched to death or fed to their own horses. Hercules just kept getting more and more famous and staying annoyingly alive.

Another source of annoyance for the high king: his super-spoiled teenage daughter Admete had been whining for weeks about how she wanted a sash of real gold to go with her new dress. 'I want the best belt in the world, Daddy! *Please?*'

So, as Hercules stood before him, waiting for his next task, Eurystheus had these random thoughts swirling in his head: *Kill Hercules. A golden belt. A dangerous task.*

Suddenly he had a wonderful, evil idea. Who had the best golden belt in the world? And who loved killing male heroes?

'Hercules,' said Eurystheus, 'I want you to go to the Land of the Amazons. Take their queen's golden belt and bring it to me for my daughter.'

Behind the throne, Admete clapped and jumped up and down.

Hercules's fierce expression matched his lion hood. 'Your daughter wants to be queen of the Amazons?'

'No. She just wants a shiny belt to go with her dress.'

Hercules sighed. 'You realize I could've stopped in Amazonia on my way back from Thrace, right? I could've saved time and mileage and – Never mind. Golden belt. Fine. Would you like fries with that, Your Majesty?'

'What are fries?'

'Forget it.'

Hercules set off again. The only good news: Eurystheus hadn't complained about the shipload of volunteers Hercules had hired to help with the Thracian quest, so he figured he could do it again. He got the gang back together, along with his sidekick, nephew Iolaus, and he sailed for Amazonia on the southern coast of the Black Sea.

Hercules wanted to avoid a fight. He was tired of people dying to accommodate Eurystheus's wishes. He especially didn't want to start a war over a fashion accessory for a spoiled princess.

On the other hand, he knew that the Amazons respected strength, so, when his ship moored off their coast, his men rowed ashore in force. They formed ranks on the beach with their shields and spears.

Amazon scouts had been watching them for a while. Queen Hippolyta and her army were ready. The queen's sister Penthesilea thought they should just charge in and start killing, but Hippolyta was wary. She'd heard stories about Hercules. She wanted to know what the Greek hero had to say. She took a few of her bodyguards and rode towards the Greek lines under a flag of truce. Hercules and a few of his guys rode out to meet her.

'*Hola*,' said Hercules. 'Look, I know this is dumb, but there's this teenage princess in Greece who wants your belt.'

He explained the situation. At first Hippolyta was outraged. Then, when it became clear that Hercules hated the high king and his quests, she became amused. When Hercules called Eurystheus 'High King Cow Patty', Hippolyta even laughed aloud.

'So,' said the queen, 'I understand you once captured the Ceryneian Hind.'

'That's true.'

'You promised Artemis that you would release the deer unharmed, and you kept your word?'

'Yeah.'

'That speaks well of you. Artemis is our patron goddess. If I lend you my belt, will you swear on your honour to bring it back? That would avoid a lot of unnecessary bloodshed, yes?'

Hercules began to relax. 'Yes. Gladly. That would be awesome.'

They were getting along just peachy. Hippolyta was impressed with big, buff Hercules in his lion cloak, armed to the teeth with godly weapons. Hercules thought Hippolyta was pretty hot, too. If things had worked out differently, they might have settled down together and had a brood of dangerous children.

But no. Up in her situation room on Mount Olympus, Hera was watching. After interfering in the Hydra mission with that giant crab, she'd got into serious trouble with Zeus, like *Do that again and I will tie you upside down over the pit of Chaos* sort of trouble. She'd done her best to restrain herself. She kept hoping Eurystheus would manage to kill Hercules without her help. But now the hero was about to pull off another easy win.

'Come on, Amazons,' the goddess muttered to herself. 'Where's your fighting spirit?'

Finally she couldn't stand it any more. She transformed into an Amazon warrior and flew down to join them. While Hercules and Hippolyta were negotiating and flirting, Hera moved among the Amazons, whispering in their ears, 'It's a trap. Hercules is taking the queen hostage.'

The Amazons became restless. They were naturally suspicious of men. They believed the rumour. The queen had been talking to that big dude in the lion-skin cape for far too long. Something must be wrong.

Penthesilea drew her sword. 'We must protect the queen! Attack!'

Hercules was complimenting Hippolyta on her bronze greaves when his men sounded the alarm. The Amazons were charging.

'What is the meaning of this?' Hercules demanded.

The queen looked astonished. 'I don't know!'

Across the field, Penthesilea raised her javelin. 'I will save you, sister!'

Desperate to stop a war, Hippolyta yelled, 'No, it's a mistake! Don't –'

She stepped in front of Hercules as Penthesilea hurled her spear. The point went straight through Hippolyta's breastplate, and the Queen of the Amazons fell dead at Hercules's feet.

Penthesilea wailed in grief. The Amazons crashed into the Greek lines.

Hercules had no time to sort out what had happened. He pulled the golden belt from Hippolyta's corpse and ordered his men to retreat.

The Amazons fought like demons, but Hercules cut a bloody swathe through their ranks. Dozens of Greeks died.

Hundreds of Amazons fell. Hercules held off the enemy as his men got to the boats and rowed back to the ship. Then he plunged into the sea and swam for it while arrows and spears shattered off his lion-skin cape.

The Greeks escaped, but they didn't feel much like celebrating.

On his way home, Hercules had a few more side adventures. He battled a sea monster, saved the city of Troy, killed some guys in a wrestling match . . . blah, blah, blah. When he got back to Tiryns, he threw the Amazonian belt at Eurystheus's feet.

'Hundreds of honourable warriors died for that belt. I hope your daughter is happy.'

Princess Admete snatched it up and did a happy dance. 'Oh, my gods, it's perfect! I can't wait to try it on!'

She dashed off to show her friends.

'Well, that's nice,' said Eurystheus. 'Let's see, Hercules . . . how many more quests now? Eight?'

'No, Your Majesty,' Hercules said slowly. 'That was quest number nine. I *should* have only one more, but since you discounted two of them in your finite wisdom –'

'Three more quests, then,' said the king. 'Oh, don't look so glum. This is hard on me, too, you know. It's not easy coming up with bigger and stupider labours every time.'

'You could always release me early.'

'No, no. I've got one.'

'I swear, if you send me back to Thrace or Amazonia –'

'Don't worry! This is in the opposite direction! I've heard rumours of a monstrous man named Geryon who lives far to the west – in Iberia.'

Hercules stared. 'You're kidding, right?'

Today, Iberia is what we call Spain and Portugal. To the Greeks, it was the end of the known world. It was like Nebraska or Saskatchewan – you heard about it occasionally, but you couldn't believe actual people lived there. Beyond Iberia, as far as the Greeks knew, there was nothing except endless monster-infested ocean.

'This man Geryon,' continued the king. 'Supposedly he has a herd of *bright red* cattle. Can you imagine? I wonder if they give strawberry milk. At any rate, I want you to bring me his herd.'

'What is it with you and cows?' Hercules asked.

'Just do it!'

Hercules hired another ship with a different group of volunteers. Funny thing – except for Iolaus, no one from his last trip wanted to travel with him again. He set sail for the end of the world to find strawberry-flavoured cows.

Back then, sailing the length of the Mediterranean was a dangerous business. Hercules's ship followed the coast of Africa, since that seemed like the best way not to get lost. Along the way, he killed a bunch of evil kings and monsters, blah, blah, blah.

When he got up to around Tunisia, he ran into this big ugly son of Poseidon named Antaeus, who is *definitely* not on my family Christmas card list.

Antaeus's mom was Gaia, the goddess of the earth. Don't ask me why or how Poseidon and Gaia had a kid. It's too horrible to contemplate. All I know: Antaeus took after his mom. He was bloodthirsty, evil and really big. Anybody who passed through Antaeus's territory was forced to wrestle with him to the death, I guess because there was nothing entertaining to watch on Tunisian TV.

Hercules could've just sailed past this confrontation, but he didn't like leaving bloodthirsty murderers for other people to deal with. He landed and challenged Antaeus to a match.

'RAR!' Antaeus pounded his fists on his chest. 'You cannot defeat me! As long as I touch the earth, I will be instantly healed of all my wounds!'

'Pro tip,' said Hercules. 'Don't start a battle by announcing your fatal weakness.'

'How is that a weakness?'

Hercules charged. He wrapped his arms around Antaeus's waist and lifted the wrestler so that no part of him touched the ground. Antaeus struggled, kicking and pummelling, but Hercules just squeezed until something inside Antaeus's chest snapped. Antaeus went limp. Hercules waited to be sure he was really dead, then dropped the body on the ground.

'Stupid wrestler.' Hercules spat in the dust and went back to his ship.

Finally he reached the end of the Mediterranean, where the northern tip of Africa almost touched the southern tip of Iberia. To honour his incredibly ridiculous quest, Hercules constructed two pillars like a gateway. He called them – you guessed it – the Pillars of Hercules.

Some stories claim that Hercules created the gap between Europe and Africa by pushing the continents apart. Other stories say he narrowed the passage so the biggest sea monsters couldn't get into the Mediterranean from the Atlantic Ocean.

Believe what you want. Me, I'm not anxious to visit the

Pillars of Hercules again. Last time I was there, I almost got decapitated by a flying pineapple. But that's another story.

Having arrived in Iberia, Hercules left his men aboard the ship and roamed alone for months, searching for red cows. One hot afternoon, he looked down from a hilltop and saw a herd of ruby-coloured animals in the valley below.

'That's got to be them,' Hercules mumbled. 'Please let that be them.'

He jogged into the valley, tired and irritated. He was almost to the cattle when a ferocious two-headed dog bounded out of the tall grass, snarling and baring its matching sets of fangs.

Hercules usually liked dogs, but this two-headed one did not seem friendly. Nor was it wearing any rabies tags. 'Whoa, boy. Um . . . boys? No need for violence here.'

'I'll be the judge of that!' A big dude with an axe came lumbering after the dog.

'Are you Geryon?' Hercules asked.

'No, I work for Geryon,' said the axe man. 'My name's Eurytion, and this here is my dog, Orthus.'

'Okay.' Hercules raised his palms and tried to look friendly, which wasn't easy for him, what with the arsenal of weapons and the lion-head hood. 'I've come to bargain for these red cattle. High King Muffin Top of Mycenae wants them.'

'I'm afraid that's impossible,' said Eurytion. 'My master left me strict orders: all trespassers are to be killed on sight. You've come a long way to die.'

'Bummer,' said Hercules.

The rancher and his dog attacked at the same time. They also died at the same time. Hercules took them out with one swing.

He was wiping the blood off his club when another voice shouted, 'NO, NO, NO!'

The hero looked up. Scuttling towards him was a guy who looked like he'd been run over by a cartoon steamroller. His legs were normal. His head was normal. Everything in the middle was flattened and wrong. His neck was anchored to broad shoulders that spread into three separate chests, side by side. Each one was clad in a different-coloured shirt – red, green, yellow. His arms stuck out from the left and right chests, which must've made it impossible for him to button his middle shirt. Three separate bellies were fused into one oversize waist that looked like it took a size-82 belt. Two swords hung at his sides.

'What happened to you?' Hercules asked, genuinely concerned.

'What happened –' The guy looked confused, then outraged. 'You mean my body? I was born this way, you insensitive moron! Why did you kill my rancher and his dog?'

'They started it.'

'Gah! Do you know how hard it is to find good help in Iberia?'

'You're Geryon?'

'Of course I'm Geryon! Lord of Iberia, son of Chrysaor the Golden, master of the red cows!'

'That's an awe-inspiring title,' Hercules said. '*Master of the red cows.* Speaking of which, I want to buy them. How much?'

Geryon snarled. 'You will pay, all right. You will pay in blood!'

The red-cow master drew his swords and attacked. Hercules was reluctant to attack a person with three-body syndrome, but he smashed his club into Geryon's middle chest. His ribs broke with a nasty *crunch*. That should've killed him, but Geryon's chest just popped back into place.

'You can't kill me!' he said. 'I have three sets of organs! I heal much too quickly.'

'BTW,' said Hercules, 'you shouldn't tell people your fatal weakness.'

'How is that a fatal weakness?'

'I just have to kill all three of your bodies at once, right?'

Geryon hesitated. 'Curses! I hate heroes!'

He screamed and charged, his swords waving on either side so he looked like an Alaskan king-crab samurai.

Hercules dropped his club and drew his bow.

Geryon had absolutely no turning ability. As he barrelled forward, Hercules skirted to one side and fired an arrow under the rancher's left arm. The arrow passed through all three chests, piercing his hearts, and Geryon fell dead.

'Sorry, dude,' said Hercules. 'I told you so.'

He herded the red cows back to his ship and sailed for home. This time he followed the northern coast along what is now Spain and France and Italy. He had more adventures. In the Alps, he killed some people who tried to steal his cows. Near the spot where Rome would one day be founded, he slew a fire-breathing giant named Cacus. He founded a few cities, destroyed a few nations. Blah, blah, blah.

At long last, he returned to Tiryns. Eurystheus was disappointed to find that the red cattle did not give strawberry milk, but he gave Hercules credit for completing the task.

'That's ten jobs done,' said the high king. 'Which means you only have your two bonus labours left!'

'*Bonus* labours?'

'First,' said the king, 'I have a hankering for apples. You've brought me all these fine meat products – crab, wild boar, cow, bird –'

'You weren't supposed to eat the Stymphalian birds!'

'My doctor says I need more fruits and vegetables in my diet. I want you to find the Garden of the Hesperides. Bring me some golden apples from the sacred apple tree of Hera.'

'Hera,' repeated Hercules. 'The goddess who hates me more than anyone in the world. You want me to steal her apples.'

'Yes.'

Hercules's lion-skin cape felt warmer than usual. Sweat trickled down his neck. 'And this garden is where, exactly?'

'I have no idea. I hear it's far to the west.'

'I was just *in* the west! I was as far to the west as you can go!'

'The Hesperides are the daughters of the Titan Atlas,' Eurystheus said helpfully. 'Perhaps you could ask Atlas where to find the garden.'

'And where do I find Atlas?'

'I guess you'll have to ask someone who knows about Titans. Happy hunting!'

Hercules had no idea how to find Atlas. The Titan didn't have a Facebook profile and there was *nothing* on Wikipedia. Even Hercules's dependable nephew Iolaus was stumped.

Ultimately, Hercules consulted with a priest of Zeus, hoping for some pointers.

'If you need to find a Titan,' said the priest, 'perhaps you should ask another Titan.'

Hercules scratched his beard. 'Do you have one in mind? Because I thought most of the Titans got thrown into Tartarus.'

'There is one Titan who might help,' said the priest. 'He's always been friendly to humankind. He's also conveniently chained to a mountain, which makes him easy to find.'

'You're talking about Prometheus, the Titan who gave people fire.'

'Give this man a cookie,' said the priest.

'You have cookies?' Hercules asked hopefully.

'No, that's just an expression. Prometheus is your best bet, however. You'll find him in the Caucasus Mountains. I'll draw you a map.'

Naturally, the Caucasus Mountains were a zillion miles away. After months of travel and lots of adventures, Hercules finally found Prometheus – a ten-foot-tall man dressed in grimy rags – chained to the side of a cliff by his ankles and wrists. His face was scarred from old claw marks, but the real horror show was his belly.

GROSS-OUT ALERT!

Sitting on Prometheus's ribcage was a huge golden eagle, ripping through the Titan's immortal guts and eating the tasty bits. You know those cheap haunted houses that make fake guts out of cold spaghetti, peeled grapes and tomato sauce? It looked like that . . . only it wasn't fake.

Hercules walked up to Prometheus. 'Man, that looks painful.'

'It – is.' Prometheus let loose a scream, shaking the entire mountain. 'Sorry. Hard – to – concentrate.'

Hercules sympathized. He'd had plenty of days when he felt like he was being pecked to death. 'I hate to ask, but I'm looking for Atlas. I need some golden apples from the Garden of the Hesperides.'

'I – could – help,' Prometheus said, sweat pouring down his face. 'But – this – eagle . . .'

Hercules nodded. 'How long have you been chained here? A thousand years?'

'Something – OUCH! – like that.'

'If I kill the eagle, will you tell me what I need to know?'

'Gladly. AHGGG!! Yes.'

Hercules looked at the sky. 'Father Zeus, I haven't ever asked you for anything. During all these stupid jobs for Eurystheus, I've paid my dues and suffered in silence. Well . . . mostly. Anyway, Prometheus has information I need. I judge that he has been punished sufficiently. I'm going to kill this eagle now, which normally I wouldn't do, because eagles are cool. But this one is creeping me out.'

A regal voice echoed from the heavens: *ALL RIGHTY, THEN.*

Confident that he had Dad's permission, Hercules drew his bow and shot the eagle.

Immediately, Prometheus's belly closed up. Relief washed over his face. 'Thank you, my friend. You are a noble cockroach!'

'A what, now?'

'Sorry. I meant *human*. Anyway, here's what you need to do. Go northwest, past the land of the Hyperboreans, to the very edge of the known world.'

'Been there. Killed stuff. Got the T-shirt.'

'Ah, but Atlas dwells on a mountain that cannot be found by humans . . . unless they know exactly where to look. I will give you directions. Once you are there, you will see the Garden of the Hesperides very close by, but you must *not* try to get the apples yourself. The dragon Ladon guards the tree, and he cannot be killed, even by someone as strong as you. Besides, if you took the apples by force, Hera would be within her rights to smite you dead on the spot.'

'So . . .'

'So you have to persuade Atlas to fetch the apples for you. The Hesperides are his daughters. He can visit the garden easily. The dragon will not bother him.'

'But isn't Atlas stuck holding up the sky?'

Prometheus smiled. 'Well, I can't solve all your problems. You'll have to figure out that part yourself.'

Once he had directions, Hercules thanked the grungy Titan and went on his way. He had a lot of time on the road to think, so when he finally found Atlas he had a pretty good idea of what to say.

The old Titan general crouched on a mountaintop in the dark reaches of the northern wastelands. Atlas still wore his battle-scarred, lightning-melted armour from the war with the gods a thousand years before. His skin was as dark as old pennies from being out in the elements so long. He knelt with his arms raised and propped on his back was the base of an enormous swirling funnel cloud – a tornado that took up the entire sky. Probably because it *was* the sky.

'Great Atlas!' Hercules called. He wasn't just throwing out compliments. Atlas was twice the size of Prometheus and twice as buff. Even after a millennium of brutal punishment, he looked impressive.

'What do you want, puny mortal?' the Titan's voice boomed.

'Apples,' said Hercules.

Atlas grunted. 'I suppose you mean the apples from my daughters' garden.'

The Titan pointed with his chin. Hercules hadn't noticed before, but down the other side of the mountain, in a valley about a mile away, a beautiful garden glowed with reddish-purple light like a perpetual sunset. Tiny figures – women in white – danced among the flowers. At the centre of the garden, a huge apple tree reached towards the sky. Even from this distance, Hercules could see golden fruit glinting in its branches and the serpentine form of Ladon the dragon twisting around its trunk.

Hercules was tempted to march down there, kill the dragon and take the apples himself. It seemed so simple. But he figured Prometheus hadn't been lying to him. Even if he could kill the dragon, Hera would blast him to dust the moment he plucked the fruit.

'Yeah,' Hercules agreed. 'Those apples.'

'You'll never get them yourself.'

'Prometheus told me.'

Atlas knitted his sweaty eyebrows. 'You know Prometheus?'

'I shot the eagle that was feeding on his liver. He gave me directions to find you.'

'Well, you're a regular Titan fanboy, aren't you? Tell you what: since you helped Prometheus, I'll help you. But it won't be easy. You'll have to hold the sky for me while I fetch the apples.'

Hercules had been anticipating this. 'Fine. But you'll have to swear on the River Styx that you'll come back.'

Atlas chuckled. 'Don't trust me, eh? I can't blame you. All right, I swear on the River Styx that I will come back here with the apples. But are you sure you can hold the weight of the sky? You're pretty small.'

'Pfft.' Hercules untied his lion-skin cape and tossed it aside. 'Hand it over.'

You're probably thinking: Dude, it's the sky. How can you hold it, much less hand it over? And, if it was so heavy and painful, why didn't Atlas just drop it and walk away?

It doesn't work that way. Take it from me.

If Atlas had dropped the sky and tried to run, it would've crashed down and flattened everything in sight, including the Titan and his daughters. As for how you can hold it . . . well, unless you've done it, it's hard to describe. Imagine a forty-million-ton top spinning on your back, its sharp point digging in between your shoulder blades. It pretty much sucks, but you have to bear the weight as best you can or you'll get crushed.

Hercules knelt next to Atlas. Slowly and carefully, Atlas shifted the load from his shoulders to Hercules's. The hero was small, but he didn't collapse under the burden.

'I'm impressed,' Atlas said.

'Just get the apples,' Hercules grunted. 'This is heavy.'

Atlas chuckled. 'Don't I know it. Back in a jiffy.'

Atlas's idea of a jiffy was not the same as Hercules's. The Titan ambled down to the Garden of the Hesperides, had a nice long chat with his daughters, enjoyed a leisurely picnic, spent some time petting Ladon the dragon, then finally gathered an armload of apples.

Meanwhile, Hercules's muscles were turning to putty. His limbs shook. Sweat trickled into his eyes. The sky churned, digging into his back so hard it was going to leave a nasty bruise. Hercules had never felt so weak. He wasn't sure he could hold out.

At long last Atlas returned, whistling. 'Thank you, my friend! I'd forgotten how good it feels to be free!'

'Great. Now take back the sky.'

'Well, here's the thing. I swore to come back with the apples, which I did. I never promised to take the sky and let you go.'

Hercules muttered some unprintable curses.

'Now, now,' Atlas said. 'Let's not be rude. You're doing great! I'm just going to take my daughters, gather an army and go destroy Mount Olympus.'

'All right,' Hercules said. 'You win.'

'Yes, I do!'

'But one last favour before you go, please. I helped Prometheus bear his punishment. The least you can do is give me a little more comfort to bear yours.'

Atlas hesitated. 'What did you have in mind?'

'That pointy bit on the sky is killing my back.'

'I hear you, buddy!'

'I really need a pillow.'

'I know. I *begged* the gods for a king-size one with extra filling. They wouldn't listen.'

'Well, then, here's your chance to prove you're more merciful than the gods. Take the sky again for a second. Let me fold my lion-skin cloak and put it behind my neck. Then I'll take the sky from you forever. I promise.'

Atlas should've just laughed and walked away.

But the Titan general wasn't completely heartless. He didn't hate mortals like Hercules. He only hated the gods. Maybe he also felt a teensy bit guilty for inflicting his punishment on a puny demigod. Or maybe he just liked the idea of appearing more generous than Zeus.

'All right,' he said. 'I am way too nice for my own good.'

'You're the best,' Hercules agreed.

Atlas set down the golden apples. He knelt next to the demigod, and Hercules shifted the weight of the sky back onto the Titan's shoulders. Hercules hobbled over to the golden apples. He gathered them up in his lion-skin cape. 'Thanks, Atlas. See you.'

'WHAT?' Atlas bellowed. 'You promised —'

'I didn't promise on the River Styx. Come on, dude. That's Trickery 101. Have fun holding the sky forever.'

Hercules could still hear Atlas bellowing curses when he was five hundred miles away.

Time for the last stupid deed!

Are you excited? Hercules was. He was ready to be done with this nonsense. So was the poor schmuck who was writing it all down. Oh, wait . . . that's me.

When Hercules got back to Tiryns with the golden apples, High King Eurystheus was pale, sweaty and sleep-deprived. For weeks he'd been worrying about what would happen when Hercules completed his final task. Once he was free, there would be nothing to stop him from throwing Eurystheus into the nearest trash chute and taking over as high king. The whole kingdom would go to the dogs!

Eurystheus had one last chance. He needed a completely *impossible* task to make sure Hercules died in disgrace and never returned.

A crazy idea came to him. *Death. Never return. Go to the dogs . . .*

'Last quest!' the king announced. 'Travel to the Underworld and bring me back Hades's guard dog, Cerberus.'

'Very funny,' Hercules said. 'What's my task, really?'

'That *is* your task! And don't come back with some generic three-headed dog. I want the real thing: Cerberus himself. Fetch!'

That last part was just mean, but Hercules wasn't going to lose his cool so close to the finish line. He turned on his heel and marched out.

First he visited the temple of Hades in Eleusis to get some advice about the Underworld. Then he visited the Doggy Discount Store and stocked up on bacon-flavoured Munchy Bones.

According to some stories, he also took some time off and went sailing with Jason and the Argonauts. I can't blame him. Compared to invading the Underworld, a dangerous sea voyage probably sounded like a relaxing vacation.

Finally Hercules steeled his nerves, found the nearest fissure in the earth and climbed down to Erebos. Getting across the River Styx turned out to be no problem. The ferryman, Charon, was a huge fan. He agreed to take the hero across in exchange for Hercules recording a voicemail greeting on his iPhone.

Hercules arrived at the black gates and found Cerberus. He was kind of hard to miss, being a massive black three-headed hell beast with a snake for a tail and glowing red eyes.

Hercules had a way with dogs. He told Cerberus to sit.

Cerberus sat. Hercules pulled out some bacon-flavoured Munchy Bones and threw one to each of Cerberus's heads. Cerberus went bonkers for that stuff.

Hercules could've just picked him up and walked away with him, but he wanted to do things politely, if possible. He decided to ask permission from Hades. He knew that was a risk, but he also knew it was wintertime, which meant that Persephone would be in the Underworld. As the daughter of Zeus, Persephone was technically Hercules's half-sister, so she might cut him some slack. He figured it was worth a try.

'I'll be back, boy,' he told Cerberus. 'Don't go anywhere.'

Cerberus thumped his snaky tail against the ground, which gave the snake a headache.

As Hercules travelled through the Fields of Asphodel, he happened to stumble across Theseus, the hero of Athens, who was sitting on a rock, paralysed from the neck down. He hadn't been able to move in years.

'Help,' said Theseus.

Hercules frowned. 'You're Theseus, aren't you? What are you doing here?'

'Long story. A friend of mine had this stupid idea to kidnap Persephone, and I went along with it. My friend . . . well, he turned into stone and crumbled. I'm still stuck. Can you get me out of here?'

Hercules tried to pull him up, but Theseus's butt seemed grafted to the rock. 'Hmm. Let me talk to Hades and Persephone. See what I can do.'

'Thanks, man. I'm not going anywhere.'

Hercules ambled into the palace of Hades and found the king and queen of the dead playing Hungry Hungry Hippos on a small table between their thrones.

'Am I interrupting?' Hercules asked.

Hades threw his hands in the air. 'No. She's killing me at this game!'

'It's all in the wrists, my dear.'

Hades faced Hercules. 'You're not dead. You're also not bringing my afternoon-tea cart. Who are you?'

'I'm Hercules, my lord. I'm here because High King Milk Toast up in Mycenae wants me to bring him your dog, Cerberus.'

A smile tugged at the corners of Hades's mouth. 'Wow, that's funny. I almost laughed.'

'I wish it was a joke,' Hercules said. 'Unfortunately, I have these twelve stupid tasks –'

'Oh, we know all about them,' said Hades. 'My wife here *loves* your work.'

Persephone beamed. 'I've been following you since the early days! I adored the way you cut off the Minyans' hands and ears and noses . . .'

Hercules had to think about it, because that was, like, sixty pages ago. 'Yeah. I did that, didn't I?'

'And the Hydra! That was thrilling. We were watching your fight on the Near Death Channel.'

'The Near Death Channel?'

'We were afraid your soul would be paying us a visit, but you survived! I am proud to call you my brother.'

Hades leaned forward conspiratorially. 'You're all she talks about these days. "You know Hercules? Well, I'm his sister."'

Persephone swatted her husband's arm. 'At any rate, we'd be happy to lend you Cerberus, wouldn't we, dear?'

Hades shrugged. 'Sure. Just release him when you're done. He knows the way home.'

'That's really cool of you,' Hercules said. 'Oh, by the way, there's another hero, Theseus, stuck in Asphodel. Would it be okay to let him go now? He's bored.'

Hades scratched his forehead. 'Theseus is still here? Yeah, sure. Take him.'

And so, after signing some autographs and diplomatically letting Hades win a game of Hungry Hungry Hippos, Hercules walked back through the Fields of Asphodel, freed Theseus and returned to the gates of the Underworld to pick up Cerberus.

'Heel, boy.'

The dog could smell Munchy Bones in Hercules's pockets, so he wagged his snaky tail and followed.

When they got to the upper world, Hercules and Theseus parted ways with a handshake. Hercules warned him to be careful, but Theseus was so ADHD he didn't pay much attention. He was already distracted by how shiny the mortal world was, and he was anxious to get back to Athens.

Hercules faced Cerberus, who was squinting in the sunlight and growling at the trees.

'Okay, buddy,' Hercules said. 'I'm going to pick you up and carry you, just for the sake of appearances. You growl and thrash and act like I dragged you here. Some day, artists are going to make a bunch of pottery pictures about us, and it'll look stupid if you're wagging your tail and begging for Munchy Bones.'

Cerberus seemed to understand. Hercules picked him up and hauled him to Tiryns. Cerberus howled and thrashed like a champ. When they got to the city, everybody cleared out of their way. People locked their doors and hid under their beds. Guards dropped their weapons and ran.

Hercules burst into the throne room. 'Eurystheus, play dead!'

The high king screamed and dived into his bronze pot.

Hercules grinned. He'd been hoping for one more pot dive.

'Take it away!' the king yelled. 'Take that hell beast away!'

'You sure? You don't want to check his teeth or read his dog tag or anything?'

'No! I believe you! Your tasks are finished. You are released from my service. Go in peace, please!'

Hercules wasn't sure how to feel about that. He'd been working for the king for more than eight years now. He'd travelled the whole world several times over. For a long time, he'd fantasized about killing Eurystheus once his labours were done, but now, looking at the trembling bronze pot next to the throne, he just felt pity and relief, along with something else he hadn't felt in a long time: happiness.

He turned to Cerberus. 'Go home, buddy. Here, take my last Munchy Bones.'

Cerberus licked Hercules's face with three slobbery tongues, then bounded out of the throne room.

Hercules turned to the pot. 'Thank you, Eurystheus. You've helped me atone for my family's deaths. You've tested me in ways I could never have imagined. More than that, you've shown me that I would *never* want your job. Being the high king isn't for me. You can keep your throne. I'm much happier being a hero.'

He strode out of the palace without looking back.

Happy ending? Gods, you would hope so after all that, right?

But nope.

Hercules decided he wanted to get married again and settle down. He heard about this out-of-the-way little city called Oechalia, ruled by a king named Eurytius. (Of course the guy's name was Eurytius. That's not confusing at all after Eurytion the rancher and Eurystheus the high king and Yuri the Russian bear or whoever else was in this story.)

Anyway, King Eurytius was having an archery contest. The grand prize was his daughter Iole, who was very beautiful. Nice dad, right? *Oh, honey, you don't mind if I give you away in my archery contest, do you? It'll be good advertising for the kingdom. Great. Thanks.*

Hercules came to town and easily won the contest, but Eurytius refused to hand over his daughter.

'Look, Hercules,' said the king. 'Nothing personal, but you murdered your last wife and your kids. This is my *daughter*. I can't give her to someone like you.'

Really touching how Eurytius developed a conscience after deciding to give away his daughter as a contest prize, but whatever.

Hercules might've killed the king, but he was too much in shock. He'd seen Iole. She was really hot. He'd already imagined their beautiful new life together. 'You're going back on your word?' he asked Eurytius. 'You'll regret this!'

He stormed out of town.

A few weeks later, all of Eurytius's cattle went missing. Of course, the king suspected Hercules. 'That scoundrel! I'll march against his hometown and destroy it!'

His son Iphitus, who was the only one in the family with any sense, raised his hand. 'Uh, Dad . . . I don't think Hercules did this. I *told* you to honour your promise and give him Iole. I think the missing cattle is just a punishment from the gods.'

'Lies!' screamed the king. 'War!'

'Well, the other thing . . .' Iphitus said. 'Hercules is living in Tiryns with his cousin, the high king of Mycenae. Their kingdom is like twenty times more powerful than ours. So war would be suicide.'

'Oh.' The king hated getting a reality check. 'Well, what would you suggest?'

'Let me go talk to Hercules,' said Iphitus. 'I'll clear this up. But, if it turns out he *didn't* take the cattle, you really should give him Iole.'

The king agreed.

Iphitus travelled to see Hercules.

The prince tried to be as diplomatic as possible. 'Listen, man, I'm on your side. I *know* you didn't take my dad's cattle. I'm just trying to prove it so we can clear your name.'

Clear your name.

Hercules fumed. He felt ashamed of being disqualified in the archery competition, and he also felt cheated. He'd spent eight years paying his dues, doing stupid labours to clear his name, and as soon as he tried to make a new life for himself his old crimes got thrown in his face again.

'Come with me,' Hercules growled. He took Iphitus to the

top of the city wall and showed him the view. 'You can see the entire countryside from here. Do you spy your cows anywhere?'

Iphitus shook his head. 'No. They're not here.'

'Well, there you go. Goodbye.' Hercules pushed Iphitus off the wall. The young prince fell to his death, screaming some very undiplomatic things on his way down.

Another bad move for Hercules, but what can I say? There's his famous anger problem again. The next day, the gods afflicted him with a terrible disease as punishment. He developed a fever. He lost weight. His skin broke out in itchy, running sores and every whitehead zit in the universe migrated to his nose.

'Oh, great . . .' Shivering and nauseous, Hercules pulled his lion-skin cloak around him and stumbled out of town, heading for the Oracle of Delphi.

The Pythian priestess wasn't excited to see him again. She subtly opened her purse so she could get at her pepper spray in case things escalated.

'I'm sorry!' Hercules said. 'I pushed an innocent guy off the city wall and now I've got zits. What do I have to do to get free of this sickness — another twelve labours?'

'Well . . . that's the good news,' the Oracle said nervously. 'No more labours! To atone for your sin, all you have to do is sell yourself into slavery for three years. Give the proceeds of the sale to Iphitus's family as compensation.'

Things escalated.

Hercules went crazy and started tearing up the shrine. He chased the Oracle around the room, trying to hit her with her own three-legged stool. The priestess screamed and sprayed her pepper spray.

Apollo came down from Mount Olympus and got into it. He and Hercules were punching each other, throwing each other onto the floor, shooting each other in the butt with arrows. The whole scene was like a daytime talk-show brawl.

Finally Zeus put a stop to it. A lightning bolt angled into the cave and hit the floor between Hercules and Apollo, blasting them apart.

'ENOUGH!' boomed the voice of Zeus. 'APOLLO, CHILL! HERCULES, RESPECT THE ORACLE!'

Hercules calmed down. Reluctantly, he and Apollo shook hands. Hercules cleaned up Delphi, then agreed to be sold into slavery.

Hermes, the god of commerce, conducted the auction. The winning bidder was a queen named Omphale, who ruled the kingdom of Lydia over in Asia Minor. Since female rulers were rare back then, Omphale was glad to have an enforcer like Hercules to make sure people obeyed her.

Hercules ran a lot of errands for her — the usual wars, monster clean-ups, pizza deliveries and assassinations. One of the most famous incidents: these two crazy dwarf twins called the Kerkopes — Akmon and Passalos — were causing all sorts of havoc in the kingdom. They robbed merchants, stole stuff from convenience stores and played practical jokes, like changing the highway signs, or replacing the army's weapons with Nerf spears. Basically they were a Category Five nuisance, so Omphale sent Hercules after them.

Hercules found them easily enough, but they were hard to catch. The little guys were as slippery as otters and their teeth were just as sharp.

Eventually, Hercules succeeded in tying both of them up.

'Let us go!' yelled Akmon. 'We'll give you shiny presents.'

'Shut up,' grumbled Hercules.

'We will tell you jokes!' offered Passalos.

'You're going to the queen,' Hercules said. 'She doesn't have a sense of humour.'

He attached the Kerkopes to the end of a stick, hanging upside down from their ankles, then slung them over his shoulder like a hobo's bag. He set off down the road, and the Kerkopes immediately busted out laughing.

'Black Bottom!' said Akmon. 'Oh, my gods, HA-HAHAHAHAHA!'

'It all makes sense!' cried Passalos. 'Mother was right! HAHAHAHAHA!'

Hercules stopped. 'What are you two idiots laughing about?'

The dwarf twins pointed at Hercules's rear end. His tunic was riding up on his sword belt and, since Greeks didn't wear underwear, Hercules was walking around with his buns on full display.

'You're so tanned you have a black bottom!' Akmon cried with delight.

Hercules scowled. 'You're laughing at my butt?'

'YES!' Passalos had tears in his eyes. 'Years ago, our mother warned us of a prophecy: Beware the Black Bottom! We didn't know what it meant, but now we do.'

'Great,' Hercules muttered. 'Now, shut up.'

'Black Bottom, Black Bottom!' The twins teased him for miles. At first it was annoying, but after a while it was so ridiculous that it became funny to Hercules.

At nightfall he stopped for dinner. As he sat by his campfire, the Kerkopes told him funny stories and stupid jokes until Hercules's sides hurt from laughter. *Why did the Chimera cross the road? How many Spartans does it take to change a lightbulb?* The dwarfs knew all the classics.

'All right, you two,' Hercules said. 'I'll make you a deal. If you promise *never* to make trouble in Omphale's kingdom again, I will set you free. You're too amusing to kill.'

'Hooray!' said Akmon. 'We are amusing!'

'All hail the Black Bottom!' cried Passalos.

Hercules cut them loose and went on his way. He felt pretty good about it, and then he discovered that the Kerkopes had stolen his sword and all his money. Still, he couldn't help chuckling. The world needed more jokesters.

Finally Hercules finished his years of service to Omphale. She offered to marry him, but he politely declined. It was hard to get past the fact that they'd started their relationship as slave and master.

He decided to look elsewhere for a wife.

You can probably guess how that worked out . . .

Hercules wandered for quite a while, killing bandits and random monsters until he happened across the city of Kalydon.

You might remember that place from the Death Pig Celebrity Hunt. The royal family had had a rough few years. Meleager and most of the other princes were dead, but King Oeneus still had one beautiful daughter named Deianeira. She and Hercules fell in love instantly.

By the time dessert was served, Hercules had proposed.

The whole family was delighted. Sure, Hercules had a bad reputation, but so did the Kalydonians.

'There's only one problem,' said the king. 'Deianeira is already betrothed to the local river god, Achelous. I had to promise him my daughter to keep him from flooding the countryside.'

Hercules cracked his knuckles. For the first time in years, he felt like he was taking on a task he really cared about, just because he *wanted* to. 'Leave this river god to me.'

He marched down to the riverbanks and called, 'Achelous!'

The god rose from the water. From the waist down, he had the body of a bull. From the waist up, he had the body of a man, with horns jutting from his forehead.

'What do you want?' said Achelous.

'To marry Deianeira.'

'She's mine.'

'We're going to fight for her. Whoever loses must promise to take no vengeance upon her, her family or the city.'

'Fine,' said Achelous. 'I am afraid of no mortal. What's your name, anyway?'

'Hercules.'

The river god went pale. 'Oh, crud.'

Hercules launched himself at the bull man. They thrashed around for hours, trying to kill each other, but of course Hercules was stronger. He broke off one of the god's horns, then held him in a chokehold until Achelous relented.

'No vengeance,' Hercules said. 'That was the deal.'

The river god scowled, rubbing the stump of his broken horn. 'Oh, I won't take revenge. I won't need to. Your marriage will end in disaster. Deianeira would have been better off with me.'

'Yeah, whatever.'

Hercules walked back to Kalydon in triumph. Achelous's broken horn became a cornucopia, capable of spewing forth all kinds of food, drinks and gluten-free snacks. Hercules offered it up to the gods in honour of his marriage, and for a few weeks he and Deianeira were deliriously happy . . . until Hercules messed up again.

One night they were having dinner in the Kalydonian throne room as usual, when a serving boy accidentally spilled cold water all over Hercules's hands.

'GAH!' Without seeing who had made the spill, Hercules lashed out and backhanded the kid across the room, instantly killing him.

That put a damper on the evening. Hercules was mortified, especially since the kid was a kinsman of the king. The nobles realized the death wasn't intentional. The boy's father forgave Hercules. But Hercules still felt bad. He decided to leave the city, since exile was the usual punishment for manslaughter. King Oeneus didn't protest very hard. He was getting the sense that Hercules was a walking time bomb.

So Hercules and Deianeira set off for the city of Trachis. Hercules had heard that the king there was looking for a new general, and it seemed as good a place as any to make a fresh start (for what, the twentieth time? I've lost count).

Along the way, they came to a wide river with no easy way across. Hercules and Deianeira walked along the bank, looking for a bridge or a shallow place to ford, but they found none.

'I can swim across,' Hercules offered. 'You can cling to my neck.'

'Honey, this is my best dress,' said Deianeira. 'Everything

I own is in this bag. If we have to swim, a lot of stuff will get ruined.'

A voice from the woods said, 'I can help!'

A centaur stepped forward. He had a friendly smile and a well-groomed beard, which was a good sign in a centaur.

'My name is Nessus,' he said. 'I ferry passengers across the river on my back all the time. Just pay me whatever you think is fair.'

'Oh, Hercules,' said Deianeira, 'it's perfect!'

Hercules wasn't sure. He'd dealt with a lot of centaurs before. Some, like old Pholus who'd shared his wine, were really nice. Some were not.

'You can trust me,' Nessus promised. 'The gods gave me this job because I have such a great reputation. Nothing but five-star reviews on Yelp. Look me up!'

Hercules still felt uneasy, but Deianeira pleaded, and the centaur's Yelp reviews sounded pretty impressive. 'Fine. Take my wife across first. Be careful! Do a good job and I'll pay you well.'

'You got it, boss!'

Deianeira climbed onto the centaur's back and he forged into the river.

Unfortunately, Nessus had been lying about his reputation. His Yelp reviews were more like: *VERY DISAPPOINTED. TERRIBLE CUSTOMER SERVICE. I WILL NEVER USE THIS CENTAUR AGAIN.*

When he got to the opposite bank, Nessus took off running. Deianeira had to hold on tight to avoid falling off and getting hurt.

'You're mine now, baby!' Nessus yelled. 'That's a good payday!'

Deianeira screamed. Across the river, Hercules grabbed his bow. The centaur was just a blur through the trees on the opposite bank. The shot would have been impossible for most heroes. If he missed, Hercules could accidentally hit his wife. Nevertheless, he aimed and let the arrow fly. It hit Nessus right in the chest, piercing his heart. The centaur stumbled and collapsed. Deianeira spilled to the ground, somehow managing to avoid breaking her neck.

Right in front of her, the centaur gasped, blood pouring down his chest.

'Girl,' he wheezed, 'come closer.'

'N-no thanks,' Deianeira said.

'I'm sorry I abducted you. You're so beautiful. Listen . . . before your husband gets here, I – I have a gift for you, as an apology. Centaur blood is a powerful love potion. Take some of mine. Then . . . if you are ever worried about your husband leaving you, smear some blood on his clothes. As soon as my blood touches his skin, he will remember his love for you and forget all other women.'

'You're lying,' she said.

Nessus opened his mouth but said nothing. He died with his glassy eyes fixed on hers.

Through the woods, Hercules called, 'Deianeira?'

Deianeira flinched. Quickly, she rummaged through her pack and found an old perfume vial. Careful not to touch any of the centaur's blood, she let some of it trickle into the bottle, then closed the stopper. She shoved the vial back into her bag just as Hercules appeared.

'Are you okay?' he asked.

'Y-yes. Thanks.'

'Stupid centaur. Did he hurt you?'

'No. Let's forget it. We – we should get going.'

They didn't talk about the centaur incident again. Hercules and Deianeira arrived at the city of Trachis and Hercules got a job as the king's new general. He won a bunch of wars. For a while, once again, life was good.

But rumours started to reach Deianeira . . . rumours that her husband wasn't always faithful when he was out on his military campaigns. Sometimes he would take women as his spoils of war and he wasn't using them as personal chefs or maids.

Deianeira began to worry that her husband would leave her. She didn't trust what the centaur Nessus had said, but she was feeling more and more desperate.

The final straw: Hercules went to war with the city of Oechalia. That's the place where King Eurytius had held the archery contest and dissed him.

Hercules still had a lot of hard feelings towards the king, so he was delighted to destroy the city and enslave its people. He took the princess Iole as his personal servant and shipped her back to Trachis in chains, along with a bunch of other loot.

The shipment arrived with a message for Deianeira:

> *Hi, Babe,*
> *OMW home with the army. In the meantime, take care*
> *of this new girl I captured. When I get back, I'm going*
> *to have a big ceremony. Could you make sure my best*
> *shirt is clean?*
> *XOX HERCULES*

When Deianeira read this, she freaked out. Hercules's best shirt happened to be his wedding shirt. She knew exactly who Iole was – the girl Hercules had tried to marry before he married Deianeira. Looking at Iole, who was still young and beautiful, Deianeira had no doubt what this 'ceremony' was about. Hercules was planning to divorce her and marry Iole.

In a panic, Deianeira rummaged through her stuff for the old vial of Nessus's blood. She dabbed the stuff on the inside of Hercules's wedding shirt. The blood dried and turned invisible immediately.

'There,' she told herself. 'Hercules will wear this and remember that he loves me.'

A few days later, Hercules got home with his army. He put on his wedding shirt, grabbed Iole and said, 'Come on, we're going to the temple! Deianeira, I'll be home later.'

But Hercules wasn't planning a wedding. He just wanted to dedicate his spoils of war to Zeus, including his new slave, Iole. Right in the middle of the ceremony, as he was praying to Zeus, Hercules smelled smoke.

'Uncle!' shouted Iolaus, who was still serving as Hercules's lieutenant. 'You're smouldering!'

The centaur's blood wasn't a love potion. It was the worst kind of poison in the world – like a combination of cyanide and sulphuric acid. Hercules's skin blistered and cooked. Agony shot through his body. He screamed and tried to pull off the shirt, but it had grafted to his body and the flesh came off with the fabric. (Oops. Sorry. GROSS-OUT ALERT.)

'I'm dying,' Hercules said, crawling up the steps to the altar. 'Iolaus, please, I need one more favour.'

'You can't die!' Iolaus cried.

But Hercules was clearly on his way out. He was racked with pain. He was losing blood. He smelled like microwaved roadkill. 'Please, build me a funeral pyre. Let me die with some dignity.'

The people wailed and wept, because Hercules had won them a lot of battles. At Iolaus's direction, they built a huge pyre and Hercules climbed to the top under his own power.

'Farewell,' he said. 'Tell my wife I love her.'

The fires were lit, and the greatest of all heroes went up in flames.

When Deianeira heard the news and realized she had killed her husband, she was so horrified she hanged herself.

Up on Mount Olympus, Zeus looked down at his dying son. He announced to the other gods, 'That's my boy down there. He has done more and suffered more than any other hero! I will make him a GOD. Any objections?'

He glared at Hera, but the queen of heaven said nothing. She had to admit that Hercules had suffered. Everything she'd done to make his life miserable had only made him stronger and more famous. She knew when it was time to quit.

Hercules's spirit ascended to Olympus. He became immortal and was given a job as Olympus's gatekeeper. With Hercules serving as the bouncer, uninvited guests were no longer a problem. He married Hebe, the goddess of youth, and finally got some peace and quiet. He was worshipped as a god by the Greeks, the Romans and the makers of B-movies.

As far as I'm concerned, anybody who's managed to read this entire chapter should also be made immortal as a reward for pain and suffering, but the Olympians didn't ask my opinion.

The only reward I can offer is moving on to the last hero — a guy I personally like a lot. He shares a name with a buddy of mine. Also, anybody who goes on a dangerous voyage to retrieve a sheepskin rug is okay in my book.

Let's take a cruise with Jason.

JASON FINDS A RUG THAT REALLY TIES THE KINGDOM TOGETHER

THE STORY STARTS IN A TYPICAL WAY: BOY meets cloud. Boy and cloud have children. Boy divorces cloud. Boy remarries. Wicked stepmother tries to sacrifice cloud's kids. Kids get away on magical flying ram.

I know. You've heard that one a million times, but bear with me.

The boy in question was Athamas. He ruled a city called Boeotia in a part of central Greece known as Thessaly. As a young man, Athamas fell madly in love with a cloud nymph, Nephele, and they got married. Which was good, because folks were starting to wonder why Athamas was walking around under a cloud all day. Once their relationship was out in the open, people could say, 'Oh, he's not depressed. That's just his wife.'

445

The king and the cloud had two children: a girl named Helle, and a boy named Phrixus. Again with the names. You christen your daughter *Helle*? So, if her last name is Smith, people can ask, 'Is that Smith?' And you can say, 'Oh, yeah, that's Helle Smith!'

The boy's name wasn't much better. *Phrixus* means *curly*. At least they didn't call him Moe or Larry.

Eventually, Athamas and Nephele got divorced. Maybe the stationary front over Boeotia finally moved on and Nephele had to follow her work elsewhere. Athamas wasted no time in getting a second wife – a mortal princess named Ino.

Ino was a real charmer. As soon as Athamas and she had children of their own, Ino decided that Helle and Phrixus needed to die so her own kids could inherit the kingdom. Even in Ancient Greece, you needed a good excuse to kill your stepchildren, so Ino invented one.

Back in those days, Greek women did most of the farming. That's because the men spent their time killing each other in battle. Since Queen Ino was in charge of the crops, she took all the seeds for that year and secretly roasted them in a big oven, rendering them useless. She distributed the seeds to the Boeotian women and told them to get planting. Surprise, surprise, nothing grew. Harvest time rolled around and there were absolutely no crops to bring in. That kind of sucked, since it meant no bread, biscuits, pies or Oreos for an entire year.

'Gosh,' Ino said to her husband, 'I wonder what happened? We'd better send some messengers to the Oracle of Delphi to find out how we have displeased the gods.'

Athamas agreed. When the messengers got to Delphi, the

Oracle told them the truth: *Queen Ino is a lying weasel who's willing to let the whole kingdom starve just so she can get her way.*

The messengers returned to Boeotia, but Queen Ino made sure to meet with them first. She bribed them heavily, threatened their families and reminded them what a terrible place the royal dungeon was. When the messengers appeared before King Athamas, they said what the queen told them to say.

'The gods sure are mad!' the lead guy reported. 'The Oracle said the only way to fix the harvest is to sacrifice your first two children, Helle and Phrixus.'

Queen Ino gasped. 'What a shame! I'll get the knives.'

Athamas was devastated, but he knew you couldn't argue with the Delphic Oracle. He allowed his children to be taken to the sacrificial altar at the edge of the sea, where Queen Ino was sharpening her fourteen-piece Ginsu cutlery set.

Meanwhile, up in the sky, Nephele heard her children crying for help. Being a cloud, she was a gentle, non-violent type who didn't know much about hostage situations, but she did have a friend who might help, so she called in a favour.

For the past hundred years or so, a winged ram with a golden fleece had been flying around Greece for no apparent reason. His name was Chrysomallos, and he was the product of a strange date night between a mortal princess named Theophane and my dad, Poseidon. I covered that story in *Greek Gods*, so please don't ask me to explain it again. Frankly, it's embarrassing.

Anyway, Chrysomallos zipped around Greece all the time, but spotting him was a rare occurrence, like seeing a shooting star, a double rainbow, or a celebrity in line at the Shake Shack. The Greeks *loved* Chrysomallos, because, dude, *a winged golden ram!* They considered him a good omen. Wherever he appeared, the king of that particular city would say, 'You see? I'm doing a good job! Super Sheep has endorsed me!' According to legend, if Chrysomallos stayed in your country for any length of time, your crops would grow faster, people would be cured of all their diseases and your Wi-Fi signal would improve, like, five hundred percent.

Chrysomallos and Nephele were old friends, so when Nephele cried out that her kids were about to get carved into sacrificial fillets the golden ram said, 'Don't worry. I got this!'

He swooped out of the sky and knocked Queen Ino to the ground. 'Hop on, kids!' he cried in a manly, ramly voice.

Phrixus and Helle scrambled onto the ram's back and off they flew.

The ram figured they wouldn't be safe anywhere in Greece. If the Greeks were willing to falsify prophecies and sacrifice their kids, they didn't deserve nice things like children and flying golden rams. Chrysomallos decided to take Phrixus and Helle as far away as possible so they could start new lives.

'Hang on, you two!' the ram said. 'There's a lot of turbulence over this part of the sea and –'

'AHHHHHHHH!' Helle, who was not hella good at listening, slipped off the ram's back and plummeted to her death.

'Darn it!' said Chrysomallos. 'I told you to *hang on!*'

After that, Phrixus dug his hands into the ram's fleece and wouldn't let go for anything. The place where Helle died was a narrow channel of water between the Aegean Sea and the Black Sea. Forever afterwards it was called the Hellespont, I guess because Hella Stupid would've been impolite.

The ram flew all the way to Colchis, on the eastern shore of the Black Sea. As far as the Greeks were concerned, you couldn't get any further away and still be in the known world. Past Colchis, it was all, like, dragons and monsters and China and stuff.

The king of Colchis was a guy named Aeetes. He welcomed Phrixus with open arms, mostly because he had brought a cool flying ram with him.

Once Chrysomallos was sure the boy would be safe, he turned to Phrixus and said, 'You'll have to sacrifice me now.'

'What?' Phrixus cried. 'But you saved my life!'

'It's okay,' said the ram. 'We need to thank Zeus for your escape. My spirit is going to become a constellation. I've always wanted to be a bunch of stars! Besides, my golden fleece will keep its magic and make this kingdom safe and prosperous for years to come. Nice knowing you, Curly!'

With tears in his eyes, Phrixus killed the ram. Chrysomallos's spirit became the zodiac constellation Aries. King Aeetes took the Golden Fleece and nailed it to a tree in the sacred grove of Ares, where it was guarded 24/7 by a fierce dragon.

Phrixus settled down, married the king's eldest daughter and had a bunch of kids. Colchis became rich and powerful. The Greeks were bummed that they had lost the endorsement of Super Sheep.

Over the years, the Golden Fleece became a legend. Every once in a while, some Greek king would say, 'Hey, I should go to Colchis and get back the Fleece! That would prove I'm blessed by the gods!' But nobody knew exactly where Colchis was or how to get there. A few brave heroes tried. Their ships never returned.

Until . . . *DUN DUN DUN!*

Fast-forward a generation, to when Jason lost his shoe and became hella important.

Pretty much every king in Thessaly was related to Athamas somehow. They all felt bad about losing the Golden Fleece. Each king would've given anything to get it back, but none of them had the resources to pull off a major expedition. Heck, most of them couldn't even maintain a functional family.

Take King Cretheus. He ruled this small town called Iolcus, but he had more than his share of big city drama. He'd been raising his orphaned niece, Tyro, which was nice and all, except that his wife, Sidro, was *super* jealous of her, because she was so young and beautiful.

When Tyro was about seventeen, she attracted the attention of Poseidon. Things got complicated. Tyro ended up a single teenage mom with two little demigod boys. She named the eldest Pelias, or *birthmark*, since the first thing she noticed after he was born was the red blotch under his right eye. I guess it could've been worse. She could've named him Prune Face or Slimy Head.

Anyway, when Queen Sidro heard about Tyro's children, she blew her stack. 'Oh, *sure* they're Poseidon's kids. A likely story! I bet my husband is having an affair with that little hussy!'

Of course Tyro was the king's niece, so that would've been gross, but, hey, we're talking about Ancient Greece. If that's the most disgusting thing you've read, you should flip back a few chapters.

Sidro couldn't kill the girl outright. The king wouldn't allow it, but the queen did her best to make Tyro's life miserable. Since

Sidro had been unable to have babies, she took away Tyro's boys and raised them as her own. She forbade Tyro to tell the kids who their real mother was. Then Sidro sent Tyro to work in the horse stables. The queen looked for any excuse to beat or whip the girl for misbehaviour.

So, yeah, that was a healthy relationship.

Finally, when Pelias was a teenager, he found out the truth. He realized how his stepmother Sidro had been treating his real mom all these years, and he flew into a rage. He drew a sword and chased Sidro through the palace. Nobody tried to stop him, probably because Pelias was a son of Poseidon and we can be pretty scary when we want to be. Also, nobody liked the queen.

Sidro fled to the shrine of Hera. She threw herself at the feet of the goddess's statue and yelled, 'Protect me, Hera!'

Hera was the goddess of wives and mothers, but she wasn't sure what to do, since Sidro wasn't exactly a poster queen for motherly virtue. As it turned out, Hera didn't have to do anything. While the goddess was deliberating, Pelias stormed into the shrine and killed Sidro, getting blood all over Hera's nice altar.

Hera hadn't really cared about Sidro one way or another, but *nobody* was allowed to defile her shrine! From that point on, she hated Pelias and started thinking of ways to get him back.

Once the queen was dead, old king Cretheus decided, *What the heck? Sidro was afraid I'd marry Tyro? Maybe I should!*

He made Tyro his new queen. They had a bunch of kids together. The oldest was a boy named Aeson (pronounced like *Jason*, except with fifty percent more *AAAYYYY*).

Now here's where it gets tricky. Who was supposed to become king when Cretheus died? His oldest son, Pelias, wasn't even related. He was the son of Tyro and Poseidon. Sure, Cretheus had adopted him, but most people considered Aeson the rightful heir.

Cretheus was less than helpful. He didn't make a will or anything. When he unexpectedly croaked, Pelias took matters into his own hands. He declared himself king and immediately began killing all his brothers and sisters to make sure they would never challenge him for the throne.

Somehow Aeson got away.

Maybe he faked his own death or went into witness protection. Maybe Pelias just miscounted the names on his hit list and thought he'd taken care of everybody. It's hard keeping track of all those siblings to murder.

Anyway, Aeson hid out in the country and married a lady named Polymede. Together they had a son named Jason. I know, you're like, *Seven pages in and we finally get to the main character of the story.* Yeah, those Ancient Greeks – they never make anything simple.

To keep their kid safe and his identity secret, Aeson and Polymede sent Jason into the wilderness to train with Chiron the centaur. Chiron spent years teaching him all about the hero business and explaining how, if the world was a better place, Jason would have grown up to be the rightful king of Iolcus.

Meanwhile, back in the city, Pelias settled down and started a family of his own. His firstborn son was named Acastus. When the kid turned sixteen, King Pelias decided to celebrate. He announced a big festival with sports competitions, fabulous prizes and sacrifices in honour of Poseidon, who was (duh) Pelias's favourite god.

Young men from all over the country were commanded to bring offerings and birthday presents for Iolcus to the party. Jason happened to be home visiting his parents when he got the invitation.

'Sports competitions?' Jason puffed up his chest. 'This is my chance to win fame and glory! I have to go!'

'Son,' said Aeson, 'if Pelias realizes who you are –'

'Don't worry, Dad. He's never met me. How would he recognize me?'

As it turned out, Pelias would recognize him by his footwear.

Like all evil kings, Pelias's biggest fear was losing his throne. Once he'd killed all the family members he could get his hands on, he consulted the Oracle of Delphi to make sure he was safe.

'So, no problems, right?' he asked the Oracle. 'I get to stay king?'

'One threat remains,' the Oracle warned him. 'Beware the man who wears only one shoe!'

Pelias's hands began to tremble. 'What do you mean? Why would he wear only one shoe? Is that supposed to make him look scary? Is it a metaphor? I don't get it!'

'Thank you for your offering and –'

'DON'T SAY IT!' Pelias left before the Oracle could wish him a nice day. If she did that, he was afraid he might kill her.

Years later, by the time the big festival rolled around, Pelias had almost forgotten about the prophecy. He was having a great time. Everything seemed cool. He'd almost got over his compulsive need to check people's feet, or scream at ambassadors wearing long robes, 'WHAT SHOES ARE YOU WEARING?'

Early on festival day, Jason was strolling through the woods on his way to the city. He came to a wide river and saw an old woman in a tattered dress standing on the banks, wringing her hands.

'Oh, dear,' she said, 'how will I ever get across this river?'

Jason was no fool. He knew that old ladies didn't normally stand alone on riverbanks, wondering how to get across. Usually they got somebody else to run errands for them, or they travelled in packs of old ladies for safety. Jason figured this woman might be a goddess in disguise. Chiron had told him stories about such things. He decided to play it cool.

'I will help you, madam!' he said with a polite bow.

The old lady gave him a toothless smile. 'What nice manners! What a fine young man! But I'm very heavy. Are you sure you can carry me?'

'No problem. I've been working out.'

He picked up the lady piggyback-style and forged into the water. The current was fast and cold. The old lady hummed 'Row, Row, Row Your Boat' as he stumbled along, which was sort of annoying, but Jason figured that might be part of the test. Halfway across the river, Jason's foot sank into a patch of mud. When he pulled it out, his sandal was gone, sucked into the goo. He stumbled and looked down, but there was no way he could retrieve the sandal, especially not with the old lady on his back.

'Everything all right, dearie?' asked the old woman.

'Oh, yeah. No biggie.' Jason carried her to the opposite bank and put her down safely. 'Anything else I can help you with?'

The old woman noticed his feet. 'Oh, you lost a shoe because of me!'

'Don't worry about it. I can hop the rest of the way to Iolcus.'

'You show promise, Jason.' The old woman's form shimmered. Suddenly, she became the goddess Hera, wearing a gold crown, a flowing white dress and a belt of peacock feathers. 'I am Hera, the Queen of Heaven.'

'I knew it!' Jason caught himself. 'I mean . . . I had no idea!'

'You have aided me, so I will aid you. Go to Iolcus and claim your rightful place as king!'

'Is this because you hate Pelias? Chiron told me the story about that murder in the shrine.'

'Well, yes, I hate Pelias. But I also think you'd be a good king. Honestly!'

'Won't Pelias try to kill me?'

'Not at his big festival with hundreds of people watching. That would be bad PR. You must trick him into publicly making a deal. When you reveal your true identity, ask Pelias to assign you an impossible task to prove you're worthy of being king. He will agree, because he'll assume you will fail and die. But, with my help, you'll succeed. Then you will become king!'

'An impossible task . . . something to prove I'm worthy of being the king . . .'

'Yes.' Hera smiled knowingly. 'You will seek —'

'The Golden Fleece!' Jason jumped up and down. 'I'll retrieve the Golden Fleece!'

Hera sighed. 'I was about to say that.'

'Oh, sorry.'

'You kind of stepped on my moment, but whatever. Go, Jason! Prove yourself a great hero!'

Hera disappeared in a burst of peacock-coloured light, and Jason hopped eagerly onward.

When he got to town, everybody noticed he had only one shoe. Why didn't Jason just take off the other shoe and go barefoot? I suppose he figured one shoe was better than none. Besides, shoes were expensive back then. The locals snickered at him as he hopped across the hot pavement and asked directions to the festival, but Jason didn't care. He was too excited. This was his first time in the big city (Iolcus had, like, a thousand people living in it!!). When he finally found the registration booth for the sporting contests, he signed up for everything.

Nobody had heard of him, so, at the first event, the announcer decided to have some fun at his expense. 'AND NOW, JASON! THE MAN WITH ONE SHOE!'

King Pelias nearly fell out of his throne.

The crowd laughed and catcalled as Jason stepped forward. He nocked an arrow in his bow. He made three bull's-eyes in a row and won the archery contest by a mile.

It's just a coincidence, thought Pelias. People lose shoes all the time. It doesn't mean anything.

Then Jason won the wrestling contest. And the javelin throw. And the discus. And the quilting competition. And the pie-eating contest. He even won the fifty-yard dash, despite his lack of proper footwear.

The locals started chanting, 'ONE SHOE! ONE SHOE!' but it was no longer a joke. It was praise.

At the awards ceremony, everybody gathered around to see Jason collect his swag. It was customary for the king to ask the big winner what he wanted for a grand prize.

Pelias hated that custom. He'd arranged this festival for his son, Acastus, and the glory of Poseidon. Now it was about some country boy with one shoe and mad skills.

'So, young man!' Pelias said. 'What do you want for your prize? Another shoe, perhaps?'

Nobody laughed.

Jason bowed. 'King Pelias, I am Jason, son of Aeson, rightful king of Iolcus. I'd like my throne back, please and thank you.'

The crowd fell silent, because that was a pretty big ask. As they looked more closely at Jason, they could see a resemblance to Pelias – except that Jason didn't have a red birthmark under his eye, and his face wasn't permanently contorted with rage.

The king tried to smile. It looked more like somebody was pulling a nail out of his backside. 'Jason, let's think about this. Pretend you are in my place. A young man you don't know appears out of nowhere. He claims to be your nephew, but he offers no proof. He simply demands the throne. What would *you* do?'

Jason started to answer, but Pelias held up his hand.

'There's more,' said the king. 'Years ago, I went to the Oracle of Delphi. A prophecy warned me that some day a man with one shoe would take my throne and kill me. Now . . . that's treason, right? It could destabilize the whole kingdom! So I ask you again, if you were in *my* place, facing this man with one shoe, what would you do?'

Jason knew the answer the king expected: *Gee, I'd probably kill him.*

Then Pelias would feel justified in executing him.

Instead, Jason remembered his conversation with Hera. 'Uncle Pelias, you raise a good point. I would have to be sure this person was actually the rightful king. I'd give him a chance to prove himself by assigning him an impossible task – something only the greatest hero could accomplish. Then, if he succeeded, and *only* if he succeeded, I would give him the throne.'

The crowd stirred and murmured. This was getting more exciting than the pie-eating contest.

Pelias sat back and stroked his beard. 'And what would this impossible task be?'

Jason spread his arms. 'We are Thessalians, aren't we? The task is obvious. I would command this would-be king to bring back the Golden Fleece!'

The crowd erupted with excitement and disbelief. A thousand voices started talking at once. 'Golden Fleece? Golden Fleece?' 'Is he crazy?' 'Sweet!' 'Super Sheep?'

Pelias raised his hands for silence. The king tried to keep his expression neutral, but inside he was delighted. No one had ever come back from Colchis. This young fool Jason had signed his own death warrant.

'Well spoken, my supposed nephew!' said the king. 'The Golden Fleece would really make this kingdom special. It would unite us as a people and bring peace and prosperity.

It would also look amazing in the throne room with those new drapes I just bought. We will let the gods decide your fate! I will not interfere. Seek out the Golden Fleece and bring it back to Iolcus! If you succeed, I will name you the next king.'

Behind Pelias, his son, Acastus, said, '*What?*'

Pelias silenced him with a look. The royal family had nothing to worry about. Even if Jason succeeded, gods forbid, the quest would take years, and that would give Pelias lots of time to think of new ways to kill him.

'Go with our blessings, Jason.' Pelias smiled. 'Let's see if you are worthy of being the king!'

When word got out about the Golden Fleece quest, *every* Greek hero wanted to go. Sure, it would be dangerous, but this was the all-star event of a generation. It was like the World Cup, the Olympics, the Super Bowl and an all-you-can-eat tour of Dylan's Candy Bar rolled into one.

To make the trip to Colchis, Jason needed the fastest, most cutting-edge trireme ever built. It would have to withstand pirates, enemy navies, hurricanes and sea monsters, and its onboard soft-serve ice-cream dispenser could *not* break down.

The best boat maker in Greece, a guy named Argus, volunteered to build the ship. Athena herself drew up the blueprints. The ship had fifty oars, which was more than any other Greek ship at the time. Its keel was designed to handle the shallowest water without running aground and to sail the open ocean without capsizing. The interior had all the bells and whistles: leather seats, extra legroom, handcrafted catapults that hurled only the finest boulders. The ship even had a voice-recognition interface thanks to its magical prow, which Athena personally carved from a sacred oak tree from the grove of Dodona – the second-most important oracle in Greece.

Apparently the priests of Dodona spent their time dancing around the forest, looking for omens in the shadows and the leaves, waiting for the magical trees to speak to them. Sounds a little fishy to me, but as soon as the *Argo*'s figurehead was installed the ship acquired its own voice. The magic prow didn't always feel like talking, but sometimes it gave the sailors advice, or issued prophecies from the gods, or told Jason where the nearest Chinese restaurants were. Jason wanted to call the figurehead Siri, but there were trademark issues.

Once the ship was finished, Argus decided to name it the *Argo*, after himself, because he was humble that way.

Now all Jason needed were some Argonauts, aka Folks Brave and/or Stupid Enough to Sail on the *Argo*. He had no problem getting volunteers. Even Hercules showed up, and everybody was like, 'Whoa! He should totally be the captain!'

But Hercules was like, 'Guys, come on. This is Jason's party. I just had a hundred pages of stuff about me.'

And the others agreed that it would be overkill.

Hercules brought along a new sidekick named Hylas, who was his Boy Wonder in training. Argus the shipbuilder signed up, since he knew the *Argo* better than anybody. Orpheus the musician joined the crew, because it was going to be a long voyage and they would need a good playlist. The great huntress Atalanta joined, too, being pretty much the only woman who could hang out with forty-nine smelly sailors without getting accosted or throwing up.

The strangest recruits were probably the Boreads – Calais and Zetes, two sons of Boreas, the god of the north wind. The brothers looked human, but they had giant feathery purple wings, so you *really* didn't want to sit behind them on the rowing benches. The fact they could fly was very helpful, though. They could dart off to the nearest convenience store if any of the Argonauts forgot a toothbrush or deodorant.

Who else? I'm not going to name the whole crew, but most of them were demigods. There were two sons of Zeus, three sons of Ares, two sons of Hermes and one son each of Dionysus, Helios, Poseidon, Hephaestus, and a partridge in a pear tree.

The night before they sailed, the Argonauts sacrificed a couple of cows in honour of the gods. Everybody was nervous and keyed up. The crew camped out on the beach, arguing and fighting and getting all the *I'm-better-than-you* macho stuff out of their systems. Finally, Orpheus played them some music until they fell asleep.

In the morning, the *Argo*'s own voice woke them up.

'Time to go, boys and girls!' said the magical prow. 'Time's a-wasting! There's a foreign country to be fleeced! Get it? Fleeced?'

The Argonauts climbed aboard and sailed from the harbour while Orpheus and the figurehead sang 'Ninety-nine Pithoi of Wine on the Wall' in two-part harmony.

From his palace balcony, King Pelias smiled and waved, muttering to himself, 'Good riddance. There go fifty heroes I don't have to worry about any more. I'm totally going to make MVP for the League of Evil Greek Kings this year!'

The rest of the town gathered at the docks and on their rooftops, watching the beautiful ship cut across the calm blue sea. All the Greeks had a feeling that this was their big moment.

Never had a finer crew sailed on a better ship for a nobler quest. Jason would either succeed in glory . . . or he would go down in flames and take the Greeks' hopes and dreams with him. But no pressure.

The *Argo*'s first stop was Lemnos, otherwise known as the Island of Stinky Women.

How did it get that lovely name? Well, a few years earlier, the local women had neglected their worship of Aphrodite. The goddess of love, being the forgiving type, cursed every female in Lemnos with a stench so terrible none of the men could stand to be within fifty feet of them. One of the old Greek writers described it as a 'noisome smell', meaning a stink so strong you could *hear* it. That's pretty bad.

The women of the island weren't pleased to be ignored by their husbands. The guys wouldn't kiss them. They wouldn't sleep in the same room with them. They spent most of their time at the local pubs, watching sports and drinking beer with clothes pegs over their noses.

Eventually the women got so angry they killed almost every man on Lemnos, because that seemed like the logical thing to do. Only a few escaped to warn the other Greek kingdoms. The Lemnosian women elected a lady named Hypsipile (pronounced *Hipsy-Peely*) to be their queen.

Ironically, as soon as they killed all the men, the women stopped stinking. By then it was too late. Once news of the massacre got out, no ship would dock at Lemnos. None of the local women knew how to sail, so they were basically marooned on their own island, fated to live out their lives with no chance of having any more kids.

That Aphrodite . . . what a sweetheart.

The Argonauts knew about Lemnos's reputation, but they really needed supplies, so they decided to risk it. As soon as they docked, hundreds of good-looking, non-smelly women crowded the pier, yelling, 'Thank the gods! Men! Please, marry me! Marry me!'

The Argonauts looked at each other like, *SWEET!*

Even Jason was entranced. Queen Hypsipile welcomed him with a hug and a kiss and a marriage proposal. Within a few days, the Argonauts were living like kings. They'd all picked new wives. Every day the women would fawn over them while the Argonauts got fat and lazy. They totally forgot about their quest.

The only guy who wasn't delighted was Hercules. He'd been getting the star treatment for years. He wasn't swayed by a bunch of beautiful groupies. He talked with Atalanta, who was also disgruntled. She hadn't signed up for this quest just to watch her shipmates act like . . . well, men.

The *Argo*'s magical figurehead agreed with them. 'Gods, I'm *so* bored! Get the crew back here. We need to leave!'

Hercules and Atalanta called an emergency meeting of the Argonauts.

'Guys, get your heads in the game!' Hercules said. 'You're not acting like heroes.'

'I think what Hercules is trying to say,' offered Atalanta, 'is that you're all idiots. We didn't sail forth from Iolcus so you could laze around Lemnos while beautiful women fed you peeled grapes.'

'I did!' said a voice at the back.

'One more word,' Hercules growled, 'and I will introduce your face to my club.'

Jason finally remembered his mission. 'Hercules is right,' he said. 'I allowed myself to get distracted. It won't happen again. Everybody, say goodbye to your Lemnosian wives. We have to leave immediately!'

The women were sad to see them go, but they didn't protest. Most of the ladies were expecting babies now, so at least they would have a chance to repopulate their island with little Argonauts and Argonettes.

The lesson of that little adventure? It's easy to get sidetracked. Comfy sofas, friendly people and good food will always sound more appealing than going on a hard quest. But if you want to get anywhere in life, you need to keep your eyes on the prize – by which I mean the Golden Fleece, not peeled grapes. Although if they offer you cheeseburgers . . . No, never mind. Let's move along.

A few weeks later, the *Argo* sailed into the Hellespont – that long stretch of water between the Aegean and the Black Sea where good old Helle had fallen to her death.

After rowing for days and days, the crew had burned through a lot of food and water, so they needed more supplies. They docked at an island called Bear Mountain, which had a big mountain in the middle shaped like (duh) a bear.

The locals were called the Doliones. They were all descended from Poseidon, so naturally they were cool and awesome. Their king Cyzicus (*Sizzy-cus*, rhymes with . . . pretty much nothing) was a young guy about Jason's age. He'd just got married, and he and his queen were delighted to host a big party for the Argonauts. Everybody had a great time. Jason and

Cyzicus exchanged phone numbers and agreed to be BFFs.

'I'm just glad you're not pirates!' said Cyzicus. 'We get *way* too many pirates here. But you guys are great. I hope your quest goes well. Just stay away from the other side of the island, okay? It's not fun over there!'

'Why?' asked Jason.

Just then Hercules told a funny joke and everybody started laughing. Cyzicus and Jason forgot what they'd been talking about.

The next morning, the Argonauts had headaches and queasy stomachs from too much partying. They stumbled around like zombies. They managed to set sail, but when they were about three hours from the harbour and almost out of sight of Bear Mountain they realized they'd totally forgotten to stock up on supplies.

'Send the Boreads back!' suggested Atalanta. 'They have wings.'

'We're only two guys,' said Zetes. 'We can fetch a few items, but supplies for the whole crew? You'll need to dock for that.'

Orpheus groaned. 'The docks are all the way back on the western tip of the island. Turning around will take *hours*. And if we get pulled into another night of partying I'm not sure my internal organs can handle it.'

The other Argonauts muttered in agreement.

Argus the shipwright pointed off the stern. 'Look, guys, we're still in sight of the eastern end of the island. I'm sure we can find water and fruit and stuff there. Let's just anchor off the beach and make a quick run inland. Easy.'

Jason frowned. 'Cyzicus told me this side of the island wasn't fun.'

'What did he mean by that?' asked Argus.

'I'm not sure. He warned me not to go there.' Jason turned to the *Argo*'s figurehead. 'What do you think, O magical prow?'

'Don't look at me,' said the prow. 'I grew up as an oak tree in Dodona. I've never been this far from home.'

Hercules grunted. 'It doesn't matter. We're Argonauts! We can handle anything!'

So they weighed anchor and sent a hunting party ashore.

As it turned out, the eastern half of the island was inhabited by Gegenees, which means *Earthborn*. Imagine hairy nine-foot-tall ogres wearing nothing but loincloths. Imagine them with six muscular arms, three on each side, capable of ripping up trees and hurling massive boulders. Now imagine them with a noisome smell. You've got the idea.

Jason led his hunting party into the forest, looking for food and water. They encountered no trouble, but shortly after they left the beach a band of twenty ogres stormed towards their rowboats, determined to smash them and then hurl rocks at the *Argo* until it sank.

Fortunately, Jason had left Hercules in charge of guarding the boats. The Earthborn roared and waved their clubs. Hercules waved his club and roared right back. The Earthborn threw rocks, which shattered harmlessly against the Nemean lion cloak. Hercules waded into battle, killing most of the ogres. The rest retreated into the forest.

An hour later, Jason and the hunting party came back and found Hercules standing over a pile of six-armed corpses.

'What the Hades?' Jason asked.

'We'd better get back to the ship,' said Hercules. 'I have a feeling that the next time these guys attack, it'll be in greater numbers.'

Right on cue, a chorus of savage howls echoed through the woods, reverberating off the side of Bear Mountain.

'Back to the ship,' Jason agreed.

As soon as they set sail, the weather turned nasty. Fog rolled in, reducing visibility to about four inches. The night fell with a new moon, making matters even worse. Argus couldn't see the stars, leaving him no way to navigate. The Argonauts lit torches, but the flames were swallowed in the mist and darkness.

For us modern folks, it's hard to imagine how dark it can get without any city lights. I'm from Manhattan. Unless there's a blackout, the darkest it ever gets is like mellow mood lighting. Back in Ancient Greece, *dark* meant *staring-into-ink-soup dark*. The *Argo* got hopelessly lost.

Even the figurehead hated it. The magical wood kept yelling, 'I CAN'T SEE! I'M BLIND! OH, GODS, I'M BLIND!'

At last, one of the crew spotted a hazy red glow off the port bow. 'There! Go that way!'

Usually, fire meant civilization. But, as the ship approached the red glow, the Argonauts weren't so sure. They heard deep voices shouting from the shore, but the fog muffled the sound so badly it was impossible to tell whether the voices were even human. The ship ran aground on a sandbar. The figurehead yelled, 'OUCH!'

Missiles rained down around the boat – maybe arrows, or spears, or rocks.

Somebody cried, 'It's the Earthborn again!'

The crew panicked. They grabbed their weapons and leaped overboard, wading through the surf to find the enemy. They couldn't afford to let those ogres destroy their ship.

The battle that followed was absolute chaos. Nobody could see anything. Swords slashed. Argonauts cried out in the blackness. Torches only made the fog hazier and the enemy harder to distinguish.

At last the Argonauts pulled back and formed a makeshift defensive line with their shields along the beach. They waited for an assault, but the enemy seemed to have retreated, too.

Finally the sun rose. The fog burned away, showing the Argonauts the horrible truth. Somehow, the *Argo* had circled back to the western side of Bear Mountain. Scattered along the beach were dozens of dead Doliones – the same guys the Argonauts had been partying with just the night before. Among the dead was Jason's BFF, King Cyzicus.

Both sides realized their awful mistake. The Argonauts had thought they were fighting Earthborn. The Doliones thought they were repelling a pirate attack. Jason was devastated that he'd accidentally killed the king. The queen was even more devastated. When she heard the news, she hanged herself.

The two groups tried to forgive each other. They spent several days mourning and burying their dead. The weather cleared, but there were no winds, making it impossible to sail. Finally Jason consulted the ship's prow.

'Build a temple to the gods,' the prow advised. 'Make some burnt offerings to atone for the bloodshed. You people are such idiots.'

Jason did what the prow suggested. It took several months,

but as soon as the temple was complete the winds picked up and the crew sailed away from Bear Mountain.

What's the moral of that happy adventure? Maybe: *Don't party so hard.* Otherwise the guy you're having wine with tonight might end up trying to kill you in the fog tomorrow night. And the next thing you know, a magical piece of lumber is calling you an idiot.

So far, the Argonauts weren't feeling very heroic. They'd married some women, killed some friends and got lost. Their next stop didn't break the losing streak.

In need of fresh water, they anchored off the coast of Anatolia and sent a small party ashore: Hercules, his sidekick, Hylas, and another guy named Polyphemus. (That's also the name of a Cyclops, but I don't think this guy was related. At least, I hope not.)

The three Argonauts split up and searched the countryside. Hylas was the first to find water – a nice, clear brook winding through the woods. He was feeling pretty good about himself as he knelt down to fill his empty pithos.

Unfortunately, Hylas was super handsome, and the river was full of naiads. The nature spirits watched him from underwater. Camouflaged in their flowing blue dresses, they were almost invisible.

'Oh, my gods, he's cute!' said one.

'I saw him first!' said another.

'I want to marry him!' said a third.

Well, you know how it is when you get a bunch of naiads together. They become wild and naughty and giggly. Then they start abducting mortal guys. The three spirits erupted out of the stream, grabbed poor Hylas and dragged him under, forgetting that he needed oxygen to breathe.

Hylas managed one scream. Polyphemus heard it and came running, but by the time he got there Hylas had been swept away downstream. The only things Polyphemus found were pieces of broken water jug and some wet footprints on the rocks, as if there'd been a scuffle.

Robbers? he wondered. *Bandits? Pirates?*

Polyphemus ran to get Hercules. Together they searched the area. Hercules was so distraught about his missing sidekick that he forgot all about his mission, the *Argo* and his crewmates, who were waiting.

Back at the beach, Jason started to get worried. The sun was going down and the landing team still wasn't back. He sent out a search party, but all they found were pottery shards by a stream. There were no signs of Hercules, Polyphemus or Hylas.

The next day, the Argonauts searched again for their comrades. They had no luck. The ship's prow had no advice to offer. Finally, as the sun was setting, Jason announced that the *Argo* would have to leave in the morning. 'We have to assume that Hercules and the others are lost. We must keep sailing.'

The crew didn't like that. You don't just sail away from Hercules. But the next morning their shipmates were still missing. The Argonauts reluctantly weighed anchor.

For days afterwards, the crew grumbled. Eventually, a few of them accused Jason of leaving Hercules behind on purpose so he wouldn't have to share the limelight. Things were about to get ugly when a waterspout erupted off the port bow. Atop the column of spume sat an old man with fins instead of arms and a fish tail instead of legs.

'It's Poseidon!' yelled Zetes.

'It's Oceanus!' said Atalanta.

'It's that guy from *The Little Mermaid*!' said Orpheus.

The merman sighed and flapped his arm-fins. 'Actually, I'm Glaucus. But don't worry. No one ever gets that right.'

The Argonauts muttered among themselves, trying to figure out who Glaucus was.

'Oh, my gods!' the ship's prow said. 'You people are embarrassing me! Glaucus was a fisherman who ate some magic herbs and became immortal. Now he's like the Delphic Oracle of the sea!'

'Ohhhh.' The crew all nodded like they knew what the prow was talking about.

For the record, I'd never heard of him either, and I'm a son of Poseidon. I'm not sure what kind of herbs Glaucus ate to become immortal. All I know: the trade-off of losing your arms for fins and your legs for a fish tail doesn't seem worth it. My advice: don't go eating random herbs unless you want to turn into that guy from *The Little Mermaid*.

Jason stepped towards the railing. 'This is a great honour, Glaucus! What brings you here?'

'O Argonauts!' he said, bobbing at the top of his waterspout. 'Do not fret about your lost crewmates. It was the will of the gods that you leave them behind.'

Jason turned to the Argonauts like, *See?*

'Hercules must return to his labours,' Glaucus continued.

'His fate lies elsewhere! As for Polyphemus, he will stay in that land and found a great city called Cius, so no worries.'

'What about Hylas?' asked Jason.

'Oh, he's dead. Drowned by some naiads. But otherwise everything is cool! Continue your voyage!'

The waterspout vanished. With a flap of his arm-fins, Glaucus did an impressive double backflip and disappeared under the waves.

So the Argonauts sailed on without their heavy hitter, Hercules, but at least they didn't mutiny over the issue. The lesson of this story being . . . uh, don't ask me. I didn't even know who Glaucus was.

The Argonauts continued east through the Hellespont. They knew that eventually they would reach the Black Sea, but very few Greeks had sailed this far before. Nobody was sure how long it would take or what dangers awaited them. For all they knew, the entrance to the Black Sea required a special passcode.

They decided to stop at the next port and ask what lay ahead. Think about that. Fifty guys actually agreed to stop and ask for directions. That's how lost they felt.

The next port was ruled by a king named Amycus. Such a friendly-sounding name – like *amicus*, the Latin word for *friend*. But Amycus was not friendly. At seven feet tall and four hundred pounds, he was known as the Man Mountain. Every time a ship stopped at his city, he made the same request.

'Fight me!' he bellowed. 'Bring out your best boxer. I will kill him in the ring!'

Jason studied the king, whose fists were the size of cannonballs. 'Uh, we're just here for directions. We're on a sacred quest –'

'I don't care! Fight!'

'And if we refuse?'

'Then I will kill you all!'

Jason sighed. 'I had a feeling you would say that.' He started to take off his shirt, since he was a pretty decent boxer, but another Argonaut stepped forward – a son of Zeus named Polydeuces. 'I got this one, Captain.'

The locals busted out laughing. Next to their king, Polydeuces didn't look like much. He was a featherweight at best. But you should never count out a son of Zeus. (Props to my boy J. Grace.)

The crowd made a circle around the two fighters, the Argonauts on one side, and the locals on the other. Amycus charged, swinging his massive fists. A single hit would've killed Polydeuces, but the Argonaut danced around, weaving and dodging, paying attention to the way Amycus fought. The king was strong, but he was also reckless. Every time he did a right hook, he overcommitted himself and stumbled forward.

The next time it happened, Polydeuces swerved to the right. As the king barrelled towards him, his head down like a sprinter's, Polydeuces jumped up and brought his elbow down behind the king's ear.

CRUNCH.

Amycus face-planted in the dirt and didn't get up again.

The Argonauts cheered like crazy. The locals surged forward, determined to tear Polydeuces apart, but, wisely, the Argonauts had kept their weapons handy. They charged to protect their crewmate. The whole thing turned into a bloodbath. Jason and his men were badly outnumbered, yet they had more discipline. They conquered the locals, took a bunch of sheep for their trouble, loaded the *Argo* and sailed on.

Now, that may not seem like a big adventure, but it was the first time an Argonaut had owned someone in personal combat. Also, the crew had worked together to defeat a much larger force. Jason felt like maybe their luck was changing.

The only problem was they still hadn't got directions.

Jason decided to ask the ship's prow. 'O great . . . piece of oak. What's up?'

'I'm good,' said the prow. 'You?'

'I'm okay. So, look . . . any idea where the Black Sea is, or how we get there?'

'Nope, but I can point you to somebody who knows. Sail east for two more days. Look for the ruins on the shore. There you will find an old man named Phineas.'

Jason tugged at his collar. 'Thanks. But how do you know that? I thought you'd never been outside of Dodona.'

'I haven't, Mr Smarty Tunic. But Phineas is a seer with the gift of prophecy. I know about stuff like that since I'm prophetic, too. And I prophesy that, without Phineas's advice, you'll never get through the Black Sea or reach Colchis alive.'

'Wow. Glad I asked, then.'

'Yeah, that could've been bad. By the way, take the Boreads ashore with you when you go.'

'Why?'

'You'll see.'

As the prow had advised, they sailed for two more days until they spotted the ruins of a town. Even across the water they could smell the place — like a hundred dumpsters that had been cooking in the sun all summer.

'This'll be fun,' Zetes grumbled.

He and Calais flew Jason to the shore. They searched the ruins, holding their sleeves over their noses to block out the stench. When they reached the town square, they found an ancient man weeping by the cold hearth. His hair and beard were like wisps of cotton candy. His clothes were rags. His bony arms were peppered with age spots. Strewn around him were mouldy breadcrumbs, bits of rancid meat and desiccated pieces of fruit. It wasn't much food, but it was *definitely* the source of the stench.

'Hello?' Jason said.

The old man looked up. His eyes were milky white. 'Visitors? No! Save yourself the trouble. Leave me in my misery!'

'Are you Phineas?' Jason asked. 'If so, we need your help. I'm Jason. These are the Boreads, Zetes and Calais —'

'Boreads?' The old man struggled to his feet. He stumbled forward, smiling toothlessly and swiping the air like he was playing Marco Polo. 'Boreads? Where? Where?'

Zetes cleared his throat. 'Uh, here. Why?'

'Oh, happy day!' cried the old man. 'My curse may finally be lifted!'

He almost walked face first into a column, but Jason stopped him. Phineas's breath was as fragrant as the food around his feet.

'How about a deal?' Jason suggested, trying not to gag. 'We help you; you help us. Tell us what's going on.'

Phineas heaved a sigh. 'I have the gift of prophecy, you see. For years, people would come to me and I'd tell them whatever they wanted to know – winning lottery numbers, the date of their death, whom they would marry and whether they would get divorced. I told it all with no riddles, tricks or missing information. I didn't even ask my clients for payment or wish them a nice day.'

'That doesn't sound like a problem,' Jason said.

'Oh, but it was! Zeus doesn't approve of full disclosure. He only wants humans to get partial glimpses of the gods' plans. Otherwise, he believes, mortals won't need the gods any more. They'll know everything! That would be bad for business at the temples and oracles.'

Calais grunted. 'Zeus has a point.'

'So he cursed me,' Phineas said. 'He took away my eyesight. He inflicted me with lingering old age. I've been eighty-five years old for the past twenty years. Can you imagine?'

'Doesn't sound like fun,' Jason admitted. 'But what's the deal with . . . uh, all the stinky food scraps?'

'That's the worst part! I am plagued by harpies!'

Jason had never seen a harpy, but he'd heard stories about them. Supposedly they were bird-woman hybrids – sort of like chickens, vultures and frantic Black Friday shoppers all rolled into one.

The Boreads flapped their wings nervously.

Calais glanced at the sky. 'I hate harpies.'

'Imagine how *I* feel!' Phineas demanded. 'Any time someone brings me food, the harpies smell it. They swoop out of nowhere and steal my tasty treats. Whatever scraps they leave behind turn bad instantly. I'm left with just enough so I don't die, but I'm always starving and nauseous. There's only one way to stop them. Harpies have *one* natural enemy.'

'Boreads,' said Zetes. 'Yes, children of the north wind despise harpies, and the feeling is mutual.' He ruffled his purplish feathers in disgust. 'We would gladly kill these harpies, but if they are a curse from Zeus we don't want to get into trouble with the Big Guy.'

'You won't!' Phineas promised. 'That's my escape clause! If Boreads defeat the harpies, I am free. Help me and I will tell you how to reach Colchis.'

Jason blinked. 'How did you know we were going to Colchis? Oh, right. You're a seer.'

The Boreads flew back to the ship to pick up some food. Then, right in the centre of the town square, the three Argonauts set up a picnic feast for the old man.

Phineas sat down. 'Oh, it smells so good. Any second –'

'SCREEEEEEE!' Two harpies spiralled out of the clouds like kamikaze pilots, their ragged blonde hair and white dresses fluttering. A gust of wind from their storm-grey wings knocked Jason to the ground. Phineas dived for cover as the harpies trampled his food with their dirty talons.

Only the Boreads stood firm. They spread their purple wings and drew their swords. The harpies froze when they saw them. Then the bird-women hissed and shot into the sky.

For the record, harpies are fast. If they have to, they can outfly just about everything except military jets and Boreads. Even Zetes and Calais had trouble keeping up with them. They raced west, darting in and out of clouds, skimming the surface of the water, until finally the Boreads managed to grab the harpies' ankles and bring them to the ground.

The Boreads pinned them down. The harpies hissed and scratched, but the Boreads were stronger. The brothers raised their swords to end the chicken ladies when a woman's voice cried, 'Time out!'

Shimmering before them was a woman with kaleidoscope-coloured wings, heart-shaped glasses and long hair braided with daisies.

Zetes gulped. 'Iris? The rainbow goddess?'

'That's me,' said Iris. 'I bear a message from Zeus: these harpies are not for you to kill.'

Calais frowned. 'But killing harpies —'

'I know, that's your thing,' Iris said. 'Normally I'm all about following your bliss, but this time you can't. I promise the harpies will not bother the old man again. You have lifted Phineas's curse. Now go back to your shipmates and have a groovy day!'

The Boreads were reluctant to let the chicken ladies go, but they didn't feel like arguing with a goddess who still used the word *groovy*. They freed the harpies and sped back to their ship.

Meanwhile, Jason signalled the *Argo* and had his crew bring more food for Phineas. They got the old guy cleaned up and dressed in fresh clothes. Then, while he stuffed his face, Phineas told Jason what he needed to know.

'First, you have to worry about the Clashing Rocks. Oh, my gods, these biscuits are *so good*.'

'The Clashing Rocks?' Jason asked. 'Is one, like, orange and the other lime green?'

'No, silly Argonaut! They *literally* clash together. Bang, bang, bang!' Phineas clapped, scattering biscuit crumbs everywhere. 'The only way from the Hellespont into the Black Sea is a narrow channel between tall cliffs, but the cliffs aren't anchored to the earth. They grind together, back and forth, slamming open and shut, like . . . like molars!'

Phineas opened his mouth. He pointed to his two remaining mossy teeth, which was a visual Jason could've done without.

'What you do,' Phineas continued, 'is capture some doves. When you get near the Clashing Rocks, release the birds and watch what happens. If the doves fly through safely, then you know it's a good day. The rocks are moving slowly. You *might* have a chance to row your ship through. If the birds don't make it . . . well, you won't either.'

Jason thought about that. 'What if the birds don't fly through the channel? What if they go in a different direction, or stop halfway and roost on the cliffs?'

'They won't.'

'Why not?'

'I don't know! Why do homing pigeons go home? Why do chickens go to sleep if you tuck their heads under their wings? It's just bird nature! The doves will be compelled to fly straight through the channel.'

'But that doesn't make sense.'

'Just roll with it!' Phineas guzzled some wine. 'Anyway, assuming you make it past the Clashing Rocks, keep sailing east for thirty days. You'll pass a kingdom of sheep farmers. Ignore them. You'll pass a kingdom of cow herders. Stop and trade with them. They're good people. You'll pass Amazonia. Don't stop there. Bad idea. Finally, when the coastline begins to curve north, you'll see some towers rising on a hill at the mouth of a river. That's Colchis, the land of King Aeetes. You will find the Golden Fleece in the sacred grove of Ares.'

'Thank you,' Jason said. 'So . . . you could tell me whether my quest succeeds, right? You know my whole fate?'

'I know everything.' Phineas belched. 'Except, how did you make this mutton jerky taste so good? Gods, it's awesome! I could tell you your entire future, Jason – the good, the bad, the very bad. But trust me; you don't want to know.'

Sweat trickled down Jason's neck. 'Now I *really* want to know.'

Phineas shook his head. 'Zeus was right when he cursed me. I can admit that now that my belly is full. No one should know his entire fate. It's too dangerous and too depressing. Just keep going, do your best and hope it's good enough. That's all any of us can do.'

Jason felt woozy. He wasn't sure it was entirely because of the nearby scraps of festering food. 'It seems to me that not knowing is scarier than knowing.'

The lines around Phineas's eyes tightened. 'No, it's really not.' His voice was full of regret. 'Now get out of here, hero. I plan on eating my fill, taking a nice hot shower and dying. It'll be a great day.'

By the next afternoon, the Argonauts had built a wicker cage and captured some doves (the latter of which was easy for the Boreads). They travelled for two more days before the sea began to narrow like they were sailing into a funnel. Sheer cliffs rose from the water on either side, offering no place to dock.

Finally, about half a mile in front of them, Jason saw what had to be the Clashing Rocks. They were perfectly colour-coordinated, which still didn't make sense to him. On each side of a narrow hundred-foot channel loomed white-and-gold cliffs, like four-billion-ton wedges of vanilla ice cream with caramel swirls. Their tops pierced the clouds. The rocks were so huge and their patterns so wavy that Jason got dizzy just looking at them. He glanced behind him. The entire crew was leaning one way or the other, trying to compensate for the cliffs' weird tilting.

It wasn't just an optical illusion, either. As the *Argo* got closer, Jason saw the cliffs sway and lean, making the sea slosh back and forth.

Then, without warning, the two landmasses slammed together with a thunderous *BOOM*, rattling the ship's oars and expelling a wall of water from the channel.

From the prow, Argus the shipwright yelled, 'Brace yourselves!'

The Argonauts barely had time to grab the rails before the tidal wave crashed over them. Any lesser vessel would've capsized or been ripped to pieces. The *Argo* rode it out. Meanwhile, the Clashing Rocks pulled apart, spilling a cascade of caramel-coloured boulders into the channel – each rock as big as the *Argo*.

'Okay,' said Atalanta, 'that was scary.'

Half the crew didn't hear her. They were too busy throwing up over the side. The others were white with terror, still clinging to the rails.

'We're supposed to sail through *that?*' Orpheus asked. 'How?'

Jason felt pretty shaky himself, but he had to look confident for the crew. 'We'll send one of the doves through the channel. We'll time how long it takes. If the dove makes it safely, we can, too.'

'And if the dove *doesn't* make it?' asked Polydeuces.

'Then we wait for another day. Or we try to go overland. Or . . . I don't know. But the gods will be with us! We've come this far. We can do it!'

The crew didn't look convinced, but they moved the *Argo* a little closer to the Clashing Rocks. As soon as Jason judged that the cliffs were as far apart as they were going to get, he released the first dove.

Just as Phineas had predicted, the bird flew straight for the channel as if its tail feathers were on fire. Argus kept count. 'One Mississippi, two Mississippi . . .'

He got to thirty Mississippis before the cliffs slammed together. The crew hung on as another wave crashed over the ship. When the rocks parted, the Boreads flew to the entrance of the channel to look for signs of the bird.

When they returned, their faces were grim.

'A little stain of feathers and blood on the side of the cliff,' Zetes reported. 'The bird made it halfway through – then, *splat.*'

The crew winced in unison.

'We'll try again tomorrow morning,' Jason said. 'And the next morning, if we have to.'

'What if we run out of doves?' asked Atalanta.

'We could always send one of the Boreads through,' suggested Orpheus.

'Shut up, Orpheus,' said Calais.

The next morning, Jason got everybody ready. The crew manned the oars just in case they got the go-ahead. The Boreads hovered near the cliffs so they could watch the bird's progress. Argus was all set to keep count.

Jason waited until the cliffs were pulling apart. Then he released the second dove. It shot towards the channel. Argus counted to sixty before the cliffs slammed shut again.

As the Clashing Rocks separated, the Boreads frantically waved their arms over their heads – the prearranged signal that the bird had made it through safely.

'Go!' Jason yelled. 'ROW, ROW, ROW! Sixty seconds!'

The *Argo* lurched forward so quickly the hull groaned. The crew rowed like demons as Orpheus played 'Shake It Off' at double tempo to keep them motivated. The currents helped, pulling the ship into the channel as the cliffs drifted apart. But still . . . getting through that passage in only a minute seemed impossible.

Thirty-two seconds gone, and they were less than halfway. The Clashing Rocks loomed above – swirling white-and-yellow teeth of doom. Their deep shadows chilled the sweat on the Argonauts' backs. Rubble showered down to port and starboard. Huge cracks webbed the cliff sides, threatening to rain down curtains of rock. At sea level, the stone was embedded with old timbers and the bones of past crews who had tried to make the passage.

'Fifteen seconds left!' cried Argus. 'Faster!'

He didn't need to tell them that. The crew was rowing so hard they weren't sure which would break first – their oars, or their limbs.

'I see the other side!' Calais cried, flying above the mast.

RUMBLE. The Clashing Rocks began to close.

'Ten seconds!' yelled Argus.

The cliffs groaned. As they slammed shut, snapping the ship's oars, a tidal wave lifted the *Argo* and carried it out of the channel into the Black Sea.

'Yeah!' Jason cheered. But the crew was too shaken up to join him.

'That,' Argus said, 'was a little *too* close.'

Fortunately, the ship was still in one piece. The Argonauts could continue their journey as soon as they found new oars and changed their soiled loincloths.

For weeks, the *Argo* skirted the coast and got into all sorts of trouble. They stopped at the island where Otrera had built a temple to Ares, found it defended by killer feather-throwing birds and barely escaped with their lives. They accidentally landed in Amazon territory and got away just before the queen's army could catch them. They lost two crewmembers – one to sickness, one to a wild boar attack. They battled monsters, lost their way, ate stale junk food from Anatolian truck stops and got pulled over at that infamous speed trap on the outskirts of Sinope.

After a month of hardship, the *Argo* finally reached the mouth of the Phasis River, where the towers of Colchis rose on a nearby hill like the hilts of swords sheathed in the earth.

Gazing at the warships in the harbour, the town walls and the fortifications of the palace, Jason realized he could never take this place by force. Even with the best crew and the best ship, he was hopelessly outmatched.

'I'm going to approach the king under a flag of truce,' he told his crew. 'I'll try to bargain for the Fleece.'

'What if Aeetes captures you and kills you?' Zetes asked. 'Why would he give up his prized possession?'

Jason managed a smile. 'Hey, if I can work out a deal with Pelias, I can work out a deal with Aeetes. I'm an old pro at negotiating with murderous kings.'

The Argonauts had to give him full points for bravery, but they were still worried. Jason put on his best robes – the same clothes he'd used to impress the Queen of Lemnos. Then he entered the city with only an honour guard.

Meanwhile, up on Mount Olympus, Hera had been following Jason's progress. So far she was pleased. (Especially since Hercules was no longer in the picture. Ugh, she *hated* Hercules.) Still, she was worried about Jason's chances with King Aeetes.

She sat down for a strategy meeting with Athena, who, for once, was on Hera's side. Both goddesses wanted the Golden Fleece back in Greece.

'Jason can never overcome the Colchians by force,' Athena said. 'There are the skeleton warriors, the dragon, the Colchian fleet –'

'Yes . . .' Hera smiled coldly. 'But there is also Medea.'

'The king's daughter?' Athena toyed with the gorgon-head pin on her Aegis. 'How does that help? She's a sorceress.'

'She's a woman,' Hera said. 'And Jason is a handsome man.'

Athena wrinkled her nose. 'You want to get Aphrodite involved? I don't know, Hera. Love is an unreliable motivator.'

'Do you have a better idea?'

For a change, Athena didn't.

They found the goddess of love in her apartments, where a dozen magical brushes were combing her hair the required five thousand times to give it that extra bounce and shine.

'Ladies!' said Aphrodite. 'Have you come to take me up on that offer for a pedicure? This is wonderful!'

'Uh, no,' Hera said. 'Actually, we need a favour. We want to make someone fall in love with Jason.'

Aphrodite's eyes gleamed. 'Well, Jason is super hot. That shouldn't be a problem. Who did you have in mind?'

'Medea,' Athena said. 'The daughter of King Aeetes.'

'Oh . . .' Aphrodite pouted. 'Then we do have a problem. That girl is *hopeless*. She spends all her time in the temple of Hecate learning magic. She is cold, heartless and power-hungry, just like her father! Do you know, one time she conjured Selene down from the moon and made her fall in love with a mortal, just to see what would happen?'

'I've heard that story,' Athena said. 'The characters were interesting, but the plot was a little far-fetched. Anyway, if Medea is messing with love magic, she's trespassing on your territory, isn't she? What better punishment than to make Medea fall in love with her father's enemy?'

Aphrodite shooed away her squadron of magic hairbrushes. 'Hmm . . . that's true. I'll send Eros down to make Medea fall in love with Jason. But I have to warn you, a love spell on someone like Medea is unpredictable. She'll be just as fierce in romance as she is with her magic. If things go badly between her and Jason –'

'It's worth the risk,' Hera said, proving once and for all that she could not see the future. 'Just cast your magic!'

Worst. Matchmaking. Ever.

Down in the mortal world, Jason was escorted through Aeetes's palace. The place was off-the-hook awesome. Silver and gold doors opened and closed on their own. In the central courtyard, four fountains each spouted a different liquid – water, wine, olive oil and milk. Why anyone would want that, I'm not sure, but the Argonauts were impressed.

'Dude,' muttered Zetes. 'A milk fountain? This king must have pull with Hephaestus. Only a god could create something as awesome as a milk fountain!'

'And check *that* out!' Calais pointed.

On the other side of a massive hall, in an enclosed pen, two giant bronze bulls were clanking around. Their eyes glowed like lava. Every time they breathed, their nostrils shot flames. Even from across the room, Jason's robes crinkled and steamed from the heat.

He began to wonder what he'd been thinking, coming to Colchis. Clearly, King Aeetes had the edge when it came to cool toys.

They found the king seated on a golden throne shaped like a sunburst. He wore golden armour that had once belonged to the war god, Ares, which Jason knew because it still said

PROPERTY OF ARES in permanent marker around the collar. At the king's left stood his son, Prince Apsyrtus (which sounds like *absurdus*); his oldest daughter, Chaliciope (which doesn't sound like anything, because I can't pronounce it); and the four children she'd had with Phrixus, aka Curly the Greek, now sadly passed away. On the king's right stood his younger and more dangerous daughter, Medea – priestess of Hecate, stone-cold murderess, all-around party girl.

Jason bowed. 'Your Majesty, I am Jason, rightful heir to the throne of Iolcus. I have come to bring the Golden Fleece home to Greece!'

His statement was kind of a stupid rhyme, but no one laughed. King Aeetes leaned forward. His eyes glittered like obsidian. He examined Jason as if pondering all the interesting ways he could die.

'No Greek has ever sailed to my shores,' said Aeetes. 'I've never even *seen* a Greek except for Phrixus, who brought us the Fleece. To come so far and to ask such a favour, you must be either very brave, or very stupid.'

Jason shrugged. 'Let's go with brave. The gods want me to succeed. Hera has blessed this voyage. Athena herself designed my ship. Aboard the *Argo* are demigods of every kind: sons of Boreas, sons of Ares, sons of Zeus –'

'This does not impress me,' snarled the king. 'I am the son of Helios!'

'We've got one of those, too. The point is, my lord, I look around your kingdom and I can see that the gods favour you. Hephaestus has given you two bronze bulls and fountains that spew oil and milk. Ares has given you a set of hand-me-down armour. I hear he also gave you a sacred grove. Your dad is Helios. Your lovely daughter . . . I see from her vestments she is a priestess of Hecate?'

While Jason spoke, the love god, Eros, had been standing invisibly in the crowd, waiting for the right moment. As soon as Jason said *your lovely daughter*, Eros shot Medea in the heart with an arrow of love, then flew away snickering.

Medea's pulse quickened. Her palms turned sweaty. Before, she'd been staring at Jason with contempt. Now . . . why hadn't she noticed how handsome and noble he was? No one in Colchis would dare stand up to her father that way. Jason's courage was remarkable. Medea's *in-love-with-a-Greek* meter went from zero to sixty in three-point-five seconds.

'Clearly, sire,' Jason continued, 'you got where you are today by honouring the gods. So honour their will once more! Give me a chance to prove myself. Assign me any task to win the Golden Fleece.'

Aeetes tapped his diamond rings against his throne's armrest. 'I could simply kill you now and burn your ship.'

'But you won't,' said Jason, trying to sound confident. 'Because a wise king would leave the matter to the gods.'

Aeetes's four grandchildren, the sons of Phrixus, gathered around him and took his hands.

'Please, Granddad!' one said. 'We're half Greek, too! Dad always told us stories about Greece.'

Aeetes scowled. 'Your father came here because the Greeks wanted to use him as a human sacrifice!'

'But this man is different,' said his grandson. 'At least give him a chance!'

The king shooed them aside. Aeetes found the 'impossible task' form of execution unnecessarily complicated, but if it taught his grandchildren a lesson about Greek stupidity perhaps it was for the best.

'Very well, Jason,' said Aeetes. 'I won't ask you to do anything *I* wouldn't do. You mentioned my sacred grove of Ares. Whenever I need extra warriors, I take some teeth from my bucket of discarded dragon incisors . . .'

His grandchildren jumped up and down, clapping in excitement. *Oh, boy! He's going to do the dragon-teeth challenge!*

Jason's mouth felt dry. 'You have a bucket of discarded dragon incisors?'

Aeetes smiled. 'Well, I have a dragon. So, yes. The dragon guards the Fleece to protect it from . . . unauthorized visitors. Anyway, I take these old teeth to a field just below the sacred grove. I harness my team of bronze bulls and plough furrows where I plant the teeth like seeds. I water the teeth with a little blood and *presto!* A crop of warriors springs from the ground.'

Jason blinked. 'Um, okay.'

'Tomorrow, you will prove that you are as great a king as I. If you can grow a crop of warriors, you may take the Golden Fleece and sail back to Greece. If not, well . . .'

He didn't say *You will die painfully*, but it was sort of implied.

Jason felt like asking for a different challenge, perhaps something involving pie eating, but instead he bowed. 'Tomorrow, then, sire. With your permission, my men and I will make camp on the shore by your docks.'

Jason locked eyes briefly with Medea – maybe because he noticed the strange way she was staring at him. Then he and his guards turned to leave.

As soon as possible, Medea fled the throne room. She could barely breathe.

'What is *wrong* with me?' she hissed, stumbling through the corridors. 'I'm not some schoolgirl! I am *Medea*. How can I feel anything for a man I just met?'

Jason's image burned in her mind – his noble face, his brilliant eyes, the way his lower lip quivered when he said, *Um, okay*. What a man!

Medea knew that her father's challenge would be suicide for Jason. She couldn't bear the thought of that brave, handsome Greek being barbecued by the bulls tomorrow morning.

In a daze, she ran to the shrine of Hecate deep in the woods. Medea had always found comfort and clarity there before. She stared up at the statue of the goddess, who was depicted with three serene faces – one gazing left, one right and one centre. In Hecate's raised hands, giant torches burned with eternal blue fire.

'Goddess of the crossroads,' Medea said, 'I need your guidance! I'm in love with Jason, but if I help him my father will surely find out. He'll banish me or kill me. I'll sacrifice everything!'

The statue of Hecate remained silent.

'I want to marry the Greek,' Medea said. 'But . . . but why? What's come over me? Would he even love me back? Would he take me away with him? Could I really betray my family and leave my home for a man I barely know?'

Her heart answered *Yes.*

The statue continued to stare in three directions, as if to say *Hey, you're at a crossroads. Deal with it.*

Medea felt both annoyed and excited. 'Gah! I am a fool. Before I risk my life for Jason, I will make him promise to love me.' She ran back to her magic laboratory and spent hours mixing a special ointment. Then she wrapped herself in a dark robe and sneaked away to the Argonauts' camp.

At around two in the morning, Jason and his advisers were still awake having a strategy meeting. They'd seen those fiery bulls, and the Argonauts were trying to figure out a way to beat Aeetes's challenge without Jason being burned alive. So far, their best plan involved three thousand bags of ice and a large pair of cooking mitts. It wasn't a very good plan.

A guard knocked on the tent pole. 'Uh, sir? Someone here to see you.'

Medea pushed her way inside. The men gasped.

The Argonauts were no strangers to scary women. They sailed with Atalanta. But Medea was a different sort of terrifying.

The princess's hair was as dark as shadow, tumbling over the shoulders of her black silk dress. On her golden necklace gleamed the symbol of Hecate – two crossed torches. Her expression was remorseless and detached, the way a public executioner might look as he swung his axe. Her eyes flickered with knowledge of dark things – things that would drive most men mad. Yet when she looked at Jason her cheeks flushed like a girl's.

'I can save you,' she said. 'But you have to save me.'

Jason's pulse hummed in his ears. 'Guys, give us the room.'

The Argonauts filed out uneasily. Once they were gone, Medea gripped Jason's hands. Her skin was cold. 'When I saw you, I fell in love instantly. Please, tell me I'm not crazy,' she begged. 'Tell me you felt it, too.'

Jason wasn't sure *what* he felt. Medea was beautiful, no doubt about that. The Clashing Rocks had been kind of beautiful, too.

'Um, I . . . wait. What did you mean about saving me?'

'My father's task is impossible. Surely you know that. No mortal can handle those metal bulls. My father only manages to do so by wearing the armour of Ares. Anyone else would burn to death. But I can stop that from happening.'

From her belt, she pulled a small vial of ointment. 'If you rub this on your skin before the challenge tomorrow morning, you will be immune to heat and flame. The ointment will also grant you great strength for several hours – hopefully long enough to steer the bulls and plough the field.'

'That's awesome. Thank you!' Jason reached for the vial, but Medea moved it away.

'There is more,' she said. 'If you *do* manage to sow the field, the dragon teeth will sprout into skeletal warriors. These obey only my father. They will try to kill you. But I can teach you how to defeat them. And, after that, there's the matter of stealing the Fleece.'

'But if I win the challenge Aeetes will give me the Fleece.'

Medea laughed harshly. 'My father will never surrender it. If you beat the challenge, he'll simply find another way to kill you. Unless you accept my help.'

'And . . . what do you want in return?'

'Only your undying love. Swear to me that you will take me back to Greece. Swear by all the gods that you will marry me and never leave me. Promise me that and I'll do everything in my power to help you. By the way, I have a *lot* of power.'

Jason felt like he was back on Bear Mountain, swinging wildly and blindly in the fog. Marrying Medea would be like marrying a very attractive weapon of mass destruction. Powerful, yes. Safe for long-term exposure? Maybe not so much.

But what choice did he have? He couldn't beat this challenge on his own. He had no problem admitting that fact. He'd assembled the Argonauts to help him with his quest. Was recruiting Medea to his cause any different?

'I will marry you,' he said. 'By all the gods, I swear. Help me and I will take you to Greece and never leave you.'

Medea threw her arms around him and kissed him. Jason had to admit it wasn't so bad.

'Here is the ointment,' said Medea. 'After you've ploughed the field, when the skeletons rise from the earth, throw a rock into their midst.'

Jason waited. 'That's it?'

'That's it. You'll see. Once they are disposed of and you've won the challenge, my father will be very angry. He'll be tempted to kill you on the spot, but he'll be reluctant to do so in public. Just pretend like nothing is wrong. Tell the king that you'll report to his palace first thing the next morning to claim the Fleece.'

'But . . . he won't actually give me the Fleece.'

'No. He'll wait for you to show up at the palace. Then he'll order you killed. But we won't give him the chance. During the night, have your men secretly make ready to sail. When it gets dark, you and I will sneak into the grove, deal with the dragon, steal the Fleece and get out of here.'

'Sounds like a plan . . . sweetheart.'

That made Medea very happy. She almost lost the murderous gleam in her eyes. 'Good luck, my dearest! Remember your promise!'

She didn't say *or else*. Like her dad, she was good at just implying the threat.

At dawn, Jason reported for duty at the grove of Ares.

As you might guess, the grove was not known for its lovely flowers or tea-party gazebos. It sprawled across a terraced hill outside the city, visible from the entire countryside. The perimeter was lined with iron walls hedged with poisonous thorn bushes. The bronze gates led to a level expanse of ground the size of a football field, littered with bones and broken weapons. Propped against one wall, tied to a post, was an oversize iron yoke attached to a plough blade bigger than the *Argo*'s keel. The two bronze bulls were romping freely across the field, crushing bones and blowing fire.

Further up the hill stood the grove itself – several acres of dense, twisted oak trees. At the very summit, in the branches of the tallest oak, the Golden Fleece glittered. From Jason's distance, it appeared no bigger than a postage stamp. It glowed blood-red in the morning light, searing his eyes like the beam of a laser pointer (which is really bad to look at; don't do it).

Every person in Colchis seemed to be watching from the

nearby hillsides, from the rooftops of the city, even from the masts of ships in the harbour. Jason glanced down at the *Argo*, anchored near the mouth of the river. He wondered if it was too late to run back to the ship, screaming 'I CHANGED MY MIND!'

Then King Aeetes came thundering down the road in his golden chariot. Wearing his hand-me-down PROPERTY OF ARES armour, the king looked pretty godlike himself. His helmet's scowling bronze faceplate made Jason shiver. A line of sweat trickled down Jason's face, giving him a whiff of the magical ointment he'd recently applied – sage and cinnamon with just a hint of rancid salamander blood. Gods, he hoped Medea wasn't playing a practical joke on him.

The king's chariot rolled to a stop. Aeetes glared down at Jason.

'FOOL!' bellowed the king, which was how he usually said good morning. 'Do you see now how hopeless your task is? Scurry back to your ship! No one will stop you!'

Jason wondered if the king could read his mind, or if it was just *that* obvious how scared he was. Somehow, he mustered his courage.

'I will not back down!' he announced. 'Where are these dragon teeth you want planted?'

The king snapped his fingers. A servant hustled over and tossed a leather bag at Jason's feet. The contents clattered like pottery shards.

'There you go,' said the king. 'Good luck harnessing the bulls. I'll be out here riding my chariot, looking cool!'

As soon as Jason passed through the gates, they clanged shut. The bronze bulls turned and stared at him.

'Nice bulls,' he said.

They charged in unison, belching fire. The heat sucked the oxygen out of Jason's lungs. His eyeballs felt like jalapeño cheese puffs, but, amazingly, he didn't die. Godlike strength coursed through his body. He punched the first bull in the face and it toppled sideways. Then he locked his arm around the second bull's neck and dragged it over to the plough.

The crowd went nuts – cheering and screaming in disbelief. Jason forced the bull into its yoke, then he went back for the other one. He dragged it to the yoke, manhandled it into its harness, then took the handles of the plough.

'Hyah!' he yelled.

The bulls blew flames at the sky. They pulled the huge plough blade across the earth, making a furrow. Smoke billowed around Jason. Sparks flew in his eyes. He felt like he was driving a steam train while standing inside the boiler, but somehow he managed to seed the dragon's teeth into the furrows. By noon, the entire field was ploughed. Jason still wasn't dead. He parked the bulls, tied them to the post and decided to take a water break. The Argonauts cheered wildly.

'Not bad for a man!' yelled Atalanta.

'That's my boy!' shouted Polydeuces.

Orpheus launched into a song he'd just made up, called 'Bull Drivin' Man', that later topped out at number five on the Ancient Greek pop charts.

Meanwhile, Aeetes just stood in his chariot, glaring at Jason. The king's face was hidden behind his visor, but Jason got the feeling Aeetes's expression was even less friendly than the metal faceplate's scowl.

'A good first start,' the king admitted at last. 'But now

you must reap what you sow. Bring him . . . THE BLOOD BUCKET!'

A servant scuttled forward with a lovely green watering can decorated with daisies. The guards opened the gates just long enough to pass it to Jason. He looked inside, saw it was filled with blood and decided not to ask where that blood had come from.

Jason walked along the rows, watering his crop of teeth. As soon as he finished the last section, the entire field rumbled. Skeletal hands erupted from the soil. Dozens of bone warriors clawed their way out, already armed with rusty swords and pitted shields. Their eye sockets were dark and vacant, but when they turned towards Jason, he got the feeling that they could see him just fine.

Jason panicked until he remembered Medea's advice.

A rock, he thought. I need a rock.

He found one the size of a baseball and tossed it in a high arc.

The skeletal warriors were forming ranks when the stone hit one of them in the head, knocking his helmet off. The warrior stumbled into one of his comrades, who pushed him back, accidentally knocking down a third warrior, whose arms windmilled, smacking a fourth warrior in the face.

Pretty soon, all the skeletons were fighting each other, not knowing or caring who had started it. They hacked at each other until the ground was strewn with broken ribcages and decapitated skulls, jaws still clattering. Skeletal arms and legs scissored through the earth, trying to find their bodies.

Jason walked over to the last pair of warriors, both of

whom had lost their heads. They were pushing each other in the chest like schoolyard bullies. Jason picked up the nearest sword and chopped their legs off.

For a moment, the crowd was silent. Then the Argonauts began to chant, 'JASON! JASON!'

They pushed open the bronze gates and flooded through, lifting Jason onto their shoulders. They paraded him around while Aeetes glared balefully.

'Thanks for the challenge, Your Majesty!' Jason shouted to the king. 'I'll come by the palace tomorrow morning to pick up the Fleece! Tonight, we're going to celebrate!'

The Argonauts marched back to their camp in a great mood. The Colchians went home and locked their doors. They knew what their king was like when he got angry.

As Aeetes watched the Argonauts leave, he muttered to himself, 'Party away, Jason. Enjoy your last evening on earth!'

That night, despite his disappointment, Aeetes slept very well. There was nothing he looked forward to more than a good massacre.

By midnight, most of the Argonauts had returned to the ship in secret, leaving their campfires burning to fool the city watch. Jason stood in his command tent, packing his stuff, when Medea arrived with Aeetes's four grandchildren.

'They have to come with us.' Medea prodded the children forward. 'They want to see Greece, where their father was born. Besides, once Aeetes discovers we've taken the Fleece, they won't be safe. He'll take out his rage on everyone who spoke up for you.'

Jason frowned. 'Surely he wouldn't kill his own grand-children.'

'You don't know my father,' Medea said.

Jason hadn't planned on taking four children aboard the *Argo*, but he couldn't very well say no. They all looked at him with the big puppy-dog eyes, murmuring, 'Pwease, pwease, pwease.'

'Fine,' he said. 'My men will escort you kids to the ship while Medea and I get the Fleece.'

The grove of Ares wasn't any less creepy at night.

Medea led Jason to a secret entrance in the southern wall. She waved her hand, spoke a few magic words and the thorn bushes parted, revealing a gap in the iron plating.

Severed skeleton limbs were still crawling across the field. Decapitated skulls gleamed in the moonlight. Bloody mud squished under Jason's sandals and oozed between his toes.

When they reached the grove, Medea led him uphill through twisted paths. Jason realized he would've been lost without her. Roots curled around his legs as he stepped. Trees shifted. Branches poked him in uncomfortable places. Whenever the trees got too aggressive, Medea muttered some magic words and they became still.

Finally they reached the summit.

When he encountered the dragon, Jason had intended to draw his sword. Instead, his arms turned to pudding. He could only stare at the slithering mass of reptile with its yellow lamp eyes and sulphurous smoke curling from its nostrils. The creature wound around the giant oak tree's trunk so many times it was impossible to tell how long it was. Sharp fins lined its back like the edge of a serrated knife. Each of the dragon's scales was as big as a shield, pointed and upturned at the end so the creature's hide reminded Jason, ridiculously, of a deadly artichoke.

When the monster opened its maw, Jason could easily imagine the *Argo* being swallowed down that red throat, its hull chomped to kindling by the rows of jagged ivory teeth. The dragon's hiss echoed down the hill and reverberated across the valley. There was no way it hadn't woken up everyone in Colchis.

Jason almost laughed in despair. What had he been thinking? His sword would be as useful as a toothpick against this beast.

Medea gripped his wrist. She pointed to the Golden Fleece, which glittered in a branch above the dragon's head.

'You'll have to climb the dragon's body to reach it,' she said. 'Don't fall asleep.'

'*What?*'

Medea began to sing.

Her words weren't in any language Jason knew, but he caught the name *Hypnos*, the god of sleep. The song flowed over him like warm honey. His eyes got heavy. Medea dug her fingernails into his forearm to keep him awake.

The dragon's eyelids flickered once, twice, then stayed closed. Its massive head sank to the ground and it began to snore, the nostrils pluming sulphur.

'Now,' Medea whispered. 'Hurry.'

Medea kept singing as Jason crept forward. He climbed the dragon's back, trying not to impale himself on its pointy scales. Just as he reached the Fleece, the dragon writhed in its sleep, almost toppling him. Medea sang a little louder. She inched forward and sprinkled some dust across the dragon's eyes. The monster snored more deeply.

Jason had a hard time pulling down the Fleece. It was big and heavy and Phrixus had done a really good job of nailing it up there. At last he tugged it free. The Fleece's head flopped over him, nearly braining him with a ram's horn.

He made it to the ground just as drums began to echo through the city.

'The guards know!' Medea warned. 'Hurry!'

They raced through the grove and back across the field of skeletons. Jason was sure they'd be surrounded and captured, but somehow they made it all the way to the docks without being noticed, despite the fact that every guard in the city was now on alert and Jason was running with the shiniest object in the kingdom.

By the time Jason and Medea boarded the *Argo*, Colchian sailors were scrambling to their ships and loading ballistae.

'GO, GO, GO!' Jason told his crew.

Horns blared. Flaming arrows arced over their heads as the *Argo* sailed from the harbour, a dozen Colchian ships in hot pursuit.

Medea's expression was grave in the torchlight. 'If we're lucky, my brother Apsyrtus is leading those ships. At least he will kill us quickly. If my father is on board . . . well, we would've been better off letting the dragon rip us to shreds.'

Medea really had a knack for motivational speeches. The Argonauts rowed faster.

Just before dawn, Medea managed to summon a fog bank so the Argonauts temporarily lost their pursuers. Since the Colchians weren't sure which direction the *Argo* had gone, they split into two fleets.

After weeks of frantic rowing, the *Argo* was just approaching the west shore of the Black Sea when one of the Colchian fleets finally caught up with them. From the crow's nest, Jason's lookout reported the colours of the enemy's flags.

'Those are my brother's standards,' Medea said. 'Apsyrtus is leading the ships.'

'Um, one more thing!' called the lookout. 'Another Colchian fleet just appeared on the southern horizon. They're about half a day further away.'

'Wonderful.' Medea puffed a strand of hair out of her face. 'If they split the fleet, that means my father is in charge of the other group.'

The Argonauts were too tired to even curse.

'We can't outrun him,' Jason said. 'The crew is exhausted.'

'I have a plan,' Medea said. 'My brother's ships are closer. We'll negotiate with him before my father gets here.'

'Negotiate for a faster death?'

Medea pointed to the shore. 'You see the mouth of that river? That goes inland for hundreds of miles. It might even take us to Greece. Just be ready.'

Medea raised a white flag on the mast. At her direction, Jason called across to the Colchian flagship that he wanted to discuss surrender.

With a promise of safe passage, Apsyrtus and a few guards

rowed over to the *Argo*. That may seem like a stupid thing to do, but back then people took promises seriously. Welcoming someone onto your ship under a flag of truce was the same as welcoming a guest into your home. You didn't hurt them unless you wanted all the gods mad at you.

When Apsyrtus saw his sister standing with the Greeks, he shook his head in disgust. 'What were you thinking, Medea? You betrayed your homeland for this man?'

'I'm sorry, brother.'

Apsyrtus laughed. 'Apologies won't help. I'll execute you quickly before Father arrives. That's the only mercy I can offer.'

'You misunderstand,' Medea said. 'I wasn't apologizing for helping Jason. I was apologizing for this.'

From beneath her robes, she pulled a dagger and threw it with deadly accuracy. The blade sank into her brother's throat. He collapsed, dead. The prince's guards reached for their weapons, but the Argonauts cut them down.

Medea knelt next to her brother's corpse. The crew stared at her in horror.

'What have you done?' said Orpheus. 'Killing an emissary under a flag of truce . . . and your *own brother*? You will bring down a curse on all of us!'

Medea looked up, her eyes as calm as a vulture's. 'Let's worry about the gods later. Right now we have to escape my father. Jason, help me cut up the prince's body.'

'Say what, now?'

'There is no time for debate!' Medea snarled. 'The rest of you, to your oars! Row for the river!'

By this point the Argonauts were wishing they'd never

heard of Medea, but she was right about having no time to waste. They sailed into the river that would one day be called the Danube.

Apsyrtus's ships were slow to react. They didn't understand what was going on. The prince didn't usually go sailing with his enemies, but it didn't even occur to the Colchians that the Greeks would have killed him in the middle of negotiations. By the time they sailed in pursuit, they'd lost valuable time.

King Aeetes's ships caught up with the rest of the fleet and together they followed the *Argo* up the river, which is when Medea started tossing Prince Apsyrtus's body parts overboard.

King Aeetes saw his son's right arm go floating by. He roared for the entire fleet to stop. They fished out the arm and scoured the river to make sure they weren't missing anything. Then, and only then, were the Colchian ships allowed to follow their prey.

Again, that may sound weird, but the Colchians took their funeral rites seriously. If you wanted your soul to reach the Underworld, you had to be buried correctly. First your corpse was wrapped in ox hide and hung from a tree until your flesh decomposed. Then your skeleton was buried with a bunch of expensive bling while priests chanted prayers to the gods. You couldn't receive a Colchian burial unless your body parts were all accounted for and put together. Otherwise they'd have to hang you on the tree in a row of little plastic grocery bags, and that would look stupid.

Anyway, by leaving a trail of her brother's body parts, Medea bought the *Argo* enough time to escape. The Danube was a huge river. It had lots of branches, forks and coves to hide in. By the time Medea threw the last bit of her brother overboard, the *Argo* had completely lost the Colchians.

'There!' Medea said, her face aglow with victory. 'I told you we would make it!'

The crew wouldn't even meet her eyes. Jason tried to act grateful, but he was horrified. Who was this woman he had agreed to marry?

Now, kids, if you try to sail up the Danube River to get to Greece, you will end up in Germany. But somehow the Argonauts figured out a way. Probably they hauled the ship out of the water at some point, rolled it on logs to another river, then sailed through northern Italy right down to the Adriatic.

Along the way, they passed the lake where Phaethon had crash-landed. The Argonauts had been through so much, they just looked at the spot where Phaethon's body was still boiling and fuming under the water, and they thought, *Yep, that guy got off easy.*

When they reached the sea, everything that could go wrong *did* go wrong. Monsters attacked. Storms tossed them back and forth. The winds didn't cooperate and the ship's soft-serve ice-cream machine finally broke down.

'The gods are punishing us.' Argus glared at Medea. 'It's all *her* fault.'

'Be quiet,' Jason warned. 'Without Medea, we'd all be dead.'

The crew muttered behind Jason's back, but they were too afraid and too dispirited to mutiny. The ship's magical prow had been giving them the silent treatment for weeks. Even the Golden Fleece, now nailed to the mast, no longer cheered them up. If the Fleece had any helpful magic, it sure wasn't sharing it.

The Argonauts had a few more close calls. They passed the island of the Sirens, whose magical singing could convince sailors to jump overboard and drown themselves. Fortunately, Orpheus launched into a Jimi Hendrix number that was, like, three hours long and drowned out the Sirens until the ship was safely out of earshot.

They landed at Corfu in western Greece and almost got captured by Colchian bounty hunters, but the local queen stepped in to mediate. She decreed that Medea could not be taken back to Colchis if she was legally married to Jason. The couple got hitched in a hasty ceremony, and the queen let them go.

After that, the *Argo* was tossed around the Mediterranean for weeks until the crew had no idea where they were. Completely out of food and water, they anchored off the shore of an unknown island.

'It doesn't matter where this is,' Jason said. 'We *have* to get supplies.'

Jason led the landing party, which included Medea.

They were in the woods, filling their jugs at a river, when they heard a strange rumbling sound from the direction they'd come – like massive gears grinding.

'What is that?' asked Polydeuces. 'Is Orpheus playing Hendrix again?'

The old shipwright Argus turned pale. 'That metallic sound . . . like joints creaking . . . Oh, gods, no. Could this island be Crete?'

From the shore came a massive *KA-SPLOOSH!* followed by drumming as the Argonauts were called to their oars.

The landing party dropped their water jars and ran for the beach. When they got to the tree line, they froze in terror. A hundred yards away stood a living bronze statue as tall as a castle tower. He was dressed like a warrior. His blank metal face betrayed no emotion, but he was definitely looking at the *Argo*, which was now rocking in the waves a quarter mile offshore.

The giant bronze man knelt and ripped the nearest boulder from the beach — a rock as big as the ship itself. He hurled it towards the *Argo*. The boulder missed by a few feet, but the wave nearly capsized the boat.

'It's Talos,' Jason said. 'He's going to destroy the ship!'

'What is Talos?' Medea demanded. 'Who in their right mind would make such a thing?'

Jason could barely hear her through the ringing in his ears. 'Hephaestus made it for King Minos. The statue walks around the island of Crete three times a day, guarding against pirates. If Talos sees a ship he doesn't recognize —'

'*My* ship!' Argus cried. 'We have to stop him!'

Polydeuces pulled the old man back. 'That thing is *huge!* Our weapons won't work against it!'

'I have an idea,' said Medea.

Polydeuces cursed. 'I hate it when she says that!'

'Just listen. I've seen the works of Hephaestus before. Usually they are animated with molten lead for blood. There should be a safety valve from when the statue was first filled up.'

'There!' Jason pointed. Sure enough, on the statue's left heel was a circular plug the size of a shield.

'I will distract the statue,' Medea said. 'You run out and open that valve!'

Before they could debate the matter, Medea sprinted across the beach. The statue Talos picked up another boulder. He lifted it to throw just as Medea began to sing.

Talos turned and stared down at her.

Medea's voice didn't waver. She invoked the god Hypnos and sang of cold forges, well-oiled joints, comfy metal blankets and whatever else giant bronze statues might dream about.

Talos could've dropped the rock and crushed her flat, which would have saved Jason a lot of trouble later on. Instead, the statue listened, confused and sluggish. Jason skirted the beach and ran up behind the monster. He jammed his sword into the edge of the plug and popped it open, breaking his blade in the process.

Molten lead almost incinerated him. He leaped sideways, his clothes peppered with steaming holes as the statue's blood gushed out, turning the beach into the world's largest lead mirror. Talos reeled and stumbled.

The giant dropped his boulder and fell face first, hitting the ground so hard that Jason's teeth shook and his eyeballs rattled.

When Jason came to his senses, Medea was standing over him, smiling. 'Well done, husband. Can I interest you in a few million pounds of scrap metal?'

The Argonauts gathered food and water and sailed for home before old King Minos could figure out who broke his favourite toy soldier.

———◆◆◆———

Finally, after what seemed like years (because it *had* been years), the *Argo* reached home and docked at Iolcus.

The locals held a huge party for the returning Argonauts. They paraded down Main Street with the Golden Fleece and hung it in the town square. Jason and Medea went to the palace in triumph, where old King Pelias was not exactly thrilled to see them.

'Well done!' he said half-heartedly. 'So, um . . . okay, then! Thanks for bringing us the Fleece.'

'My throne,' said Jason. 'That was the deal.'

'Ah, yes. The throne.' Pelias winced. 'Okay . . . no problem. When I die, you will be the next king.'

'What?' cried his son, Acastus.

'What?' cried Jason.

'Let the festivities begin!' said Pelias.

Jason was steamed. He'd done everything Pelias had asked, but Pelias had never specified exactly *when* he would give Jason the throne, so now he had to wait for who knew how long.

'You could take the throne by force,' Medea urged.

Jason scowled. 'This isn't Colchis. We don't kill each other in cold blood . . . well, not as often, anyway.'

'Fine,' Medea said. 'I'm sure the old man will die soon anyway.'

Medea's tone should've warned Jason that she was planning something, but I guess he didn't want to know.

A few weeks later, after the partying had settled down and Medea and Jason had moved into guest rooms at the palace, Jason's father, Aeson, toddled into the city for a visit, though he was now old and feeble. Medea welcomed him with a special gift. She whipped up a potion that rejuvenated his joints, strengthened his muscles and added about ten years to his life. At the end of his visit, the old guy threw away his cane and decided to jog home.

The daughters of King Pelias were so impressed they went to see Medea. 'Wow, your magic is amazing!' said Alcestis, one of the princesses.

Medea smiled. 'Thank you, dear.'

'Could you do that for *our* dad?' Alcestis asked. 'The poor guy has really bad arthritis and boils and gout and about a dozen other problems. We'd love to make him younger as a surprise birthday present!'

'How sweet.' Medea's mind whirled with possibilities. 'Alas, you wouldn't like the way the potion is administered. It takes great courage and a strong stomach to do what is necessary!'

Alcestis and the other princesses looked offended. 'We are courageous!'

Medea pretended to think about it. 'I will show you what must be done, but I'm warning you, it isn't pretty.'

She took the princesses to her newly set-up laboratory. She asked the guards to bring her an old goat from the royal pens. Meanwhile, she set a huge pot over the fire, filled it with water and brought it to a boil. She muttered a few spells and sprinkled in some magic herbs.

The guards brought her a goat so old it could hardly stand. Its eyes were milky with cataracts. Its fur was falling out in tufts.

'Pretend this goat is your father,' Medea told the princesses. She took out her knife and slit its throat. Then she hacked the goat to pieces.

'What are you *doing*?' shrieked Alcestis.

Medea looked up with blood on her face. 'I told you it wasn't easy. Just watch.'

She gathered up the pieces of the goat and threw them in the boiling water. The pot trembled. A young goat sprang out, steaming and bleating and prancing around like, *Ow, ow, hot.*

'That's amazing!' said Alcestis.

'Yes.' Medea sighed. 'It's too bad you would never have the courage to do this for your father. If you did, he would live another forty or fifty years!'

'We have the courage!' said Alcestis. 'Give us the magic!'

Medea fixed up a bag of harmless herbs – rosemary, thyme, a little meat tenderizer. 'Here you go. Good luck!'

That night, the four princesses prepared a huge pot of boiling water in the royal kitchen. They told their father they had a special birthday surprise for him. They blindfolded Pelias and led him down to the kitchen.

Pelias chuckled, expecting some cookies, or maybe a badly decorated cake. 'Oh, girls, you shouldn't have.'

'Surprise!' Alcestis removed his blindfold.

The king saw his four daughters standing in front of a boiling pot of water. Each of them was grinning and holding a large knife.

'Um . . . girls?'

'Happy birthday!' The princesses fell on their father and chopped him to pieces. They threw him in the pot with the herbs and spices and waited for him to leap out young and strong. Instead, they made a pot of Pelias stew.

When they realized they'd been tricked, they wailed and moaned. They told everyone that Medea had given them the idea. Since nobody in Iolcus liked Medea, they turned on her.

Jason was horrified. He tried to distance himself from his wife. He swore he had nothing to do with the murder plot. But it was too late. No one could stand the idea of Jason being king after what his wife had done. He and Medea were forced to flee the city to avoid getting lynched by an angry mob.

Jason had finally realized his dream. He had united the city by bringing home the Golden Fleece. He had united them against *him*.

Acastus, Pelias's son, became the king.

Jason and Medea were given refuge in the city of Corinth, where King Creon was a big fan of the Argonauts' adventures. He actually believed Jason's innocence in the infamous cooking-pot scandal.

Jason and Medea had two children — both cute little boys. Medea reconstructed her secret laboratory and fashioned spells and potions for the locals. The people of Corinth were nicer to her, though they still found her creepy. That didn't get any better when Medea's grandfather, Helios, gave her a new chariot for her birthday.

Why Helios thought that was a good idea, I don't know, but this magical chariot came complete with two dragons. Medea flew it all over town when she needed to get groceries or take the kids to soccer practice, and it really made the Corinthians nervous. Nobody called her the Mother of Dragons. It just didn't happen.

As for Jason, he became King Creon's best general. The royal family thought he was great, but the king could tell Jason was sad in his heart.

'My boy,' said Creon, 'it's clear that your sorcerous wife is causing you grief. You can't possibly love her. She cost you your rightful kingdom! She's not even Greek! You need to put her aside. Marry my daughter, Creusa. I will make you my heir and you'll be a king, as you should be!'

The first few times the king offered, Jason said no. He'd made a promise to Medea, after all. But over the months his willpower crumbled. He started finding reasons to justify what he wanted. Funny how people can do that.

Oh, it'll be better for Medea, too, he thought. I can give her a nice alimony and child support. She can marry someone more compatible – a warlock, or a murderer, or something.

Finally he signed a deal with King Creon. The wedding date was set. Jason convinced himself that Medea would be happy and relieved. He came home with a grin on his face and told her all about it. He lectured her about why, really, this was good for both of them.

'I see.' Medea's voice was like permafrost. 'And you won't change your mind?'

'No, afraid not. But hey, you and the boys will be well taken care of. I hope you'll come to the wedding!'

'Oh, absolutely,' said Medea. 'I will even send your bride a gift.'

'Wow, thanks for being so cool about this!'

Which goes to show Jason never knew his wife at all.

Medea sent Princess Creusa a poisonous wedding gown. It was the most beautiful thing Creusa had ever seen. She tried it on immediately and began to smoke and scream. She ran through the halls, her skin bubbling, her arms on fire. King Creon tried to help her and got stuck to the dress, so both father and daughter died together in misery.

When Jason heard about this, he ran home screaming 'MEDEA! WHAT HAVE YOU DONE?' He was followed by a crowd of angry Corinthians with torches and pitchforks, and they weren't on his side.

Jason burst through the door and his heart nearly exploded. His two sons were lying dead on the floor, Medea standing over them with a knife.

'Our – our boys?' Jason sobbed. 'Why? They didn't do anything!'

'You caused this,' Medea snarled. 'You would be nothing without me! I left my home for you. I did *everything* for you. You promised to all the gods that you would love me forever, and you broke your word! I want you to suffer, Jason. I want to take away everything that matters to you. Farewell, ex-husband. I hope you die alone and in misery!'

Before Jason could recover his senses, Medea hopped in her dragon-powered chariot and flew away.

Jason didn't even have time to bury his children before the mob stormed his house and he was forced to flee Corinth.

Medea flew to Athens, where she had a whole new set of adventures as Theseus's evil stepmother. Later she returned to Colchis, found that her father Aeetes had died, and took over the throne. Why the Colchians wanted her back, I don't know. Maybe she had proven that she was just the kind of queen they needed.

As for Jason, he wandered Greece alone and miserable. Finally, so old and crippled and grey that nobody recognized him, he returned to Iolcus, where the *Argo* was rotting at the docks.

The ship had once been the pride of the city, a reminder of their greatest hero. But, since the business with Medea, nobody liked to think about the Argonauts or Jason or even the Golden Fleece, which had been put in storage in the palace basement.

The *Argo* had an evil reputation. It had been left to the vandals and graffiti artists. Jason crawled aboard and huddled under the magical prow.

'You're my only friend,' he told the ship. 'You understand me.'

But the magical wood from Dodona had stopped talking years ago. That night as Jason slept, the prow rotted through, fell on Jason's head and killed him.

So the Argonaut dream team was forgotten. Their quest had been all for nothing. Their great leader, Jason, died alone and despised.

And if that isn't a great ending for this book I don't know what is!

Makes you want to run right out and become a Greek hero, doesn't it?

At least we learned some important things along the way, like:

- Don't abandon your kid in the wilderness.
- Don't make out in a god's temple.
- Don't mix orange and lime green.
- AVOID HERA AT ALL COSTS!

But, like I told you guys years ago: this demigod gig is dangerous. Don't say I didn't warn you.

AFTERWORD

DUDE, WHAT TIME IS IT?
I'm late for our monthly *Argo II* reunion party. I am *so* dead.

Writing this book took a lot longer than I expected, but I hope it was worth it for you. Maybe it'll save your life, or at least lay out your options for painful and interesting ways to die.

I also hope my lifetime supply of pizza and blue jelly beans starts soon. I am *starving*.

After reading all this, if you're still determined to be a hero, you are beyond hope. Then again, I'm beyond hope and so are most of my friends, so, I guess, welcome to the club.

Keep your swords sharp, guys. Keep your eyes open. And, if you insist on visiting the Oracle at Delphi, well then . . . have a nice day.

Peace from Manhattan,

Percy Jackson

READ ON FOR AN EXCLUSIVE
PREVIEW FROM THE FIRST
BOOK IN RICK RIORDAN'S
BRAND-NEW SERIES:

MAGNUS CHASE AND
THE GODS OF ASGARD

THE SWORD OF SUMMER

ONE

GOOD MORNING!
YOU'RE GOING TO DIE.

YEAH, I KNOW. You guys are going to read about how I died in agony, and you're going be like, 'Wow! That sounds cool, Magnus! Can I die in agony too?'

No. Just no.

Don't go jumping off any rooftops. Don't run into the highway or set yourself on fire. It doesn't work that way. You will not end up where I ended up.

Besides, you wouldn't want to deal with my situation. Unless you've got some crazy desire to see undead warriors hacking one another to pieces, swords flying up giants' noses, and dark elves in snappy outfits, you shouldn't even *think* about finding the wolf-headed gates.

My name is Magnus Chase. I'm sixteen years old. This is the story of how my life went downhill after I got myself killed.

* * *

My day started out normally enough. I was sleeping on the sidewalk under a bridge in the Public Garden when a guy kicked me awake and said, 'They're after you.'

By the way, I've been homeless for the past two years.

Some of you may think, *Aw, how sad.* Others may think, *Ha, ha, loser!* But, if you saw me on the street, ninety-nine percent of you would walk right past like I'm invisible. You'd pray, *Don't let him ask me for money.* You'd wonder if I'm older than I look, because surely a teenager wouldn't be wrapped in a stinky old sleeping bag, stuck outside in the middle of a Boston winter. *Somebody should help that poor boy!*

Then you'd keep walking.

Whatever. I don't need your sympathy. I'm used to being laughed at. I'm definitely used to being ignored. Let's move on.

The bum who woke me was a guy called Blitz. As usual, he looked like he'd been running through a dirty hurricane. His wiry black hair was full of paper scraps and twigs. His face was the colour of saddle leather, flecked with ice. His beard curled in all directions. Snow caked the bottom of his trench coat where it dragged around his feet – Blitz being about five feet five – and his eyes were so dilated that the irises were all pupil. His permanently alarmed expression made him look like he might start screaming any second.

I blinked the gunk out of my eyes. My mouth tasted like day-old hamburger. My sleeping bag was warm, and I really didn't want to get out of it.

'Who's after me?'

'Not sure.' Blitz rubbed his nose, which had been broken so many times it zigzagged like a lightning bolt. 'They're handing out flyers with your name and picture.'

I cursed. Random police and park rangers I could deal with. Truant officers, community-service volunteers, drunken college kids, addicts looking to roll somebody small and weak – all those would've been as easy to wake up to as pancakes and orange juice.

But when somebody knew my name and my face – that was bad. That meant they were targeting me specifically. Maybe the folks at the shelter were mad at me for breaking their stereo. (Those Christmas carols had been driving me crazy.) Maybe a security camera caught that last bit of pickpocketing I did in the Theater District. (Hey, I needed money for pizza.) Or maybe, unlikely as it seemed, the police were still looking for me, wanting to ask questions about my mom's murder . . .

I packed my stuff, which took about three seconds.

The sleeping bag rolled up tight and fitted in my backpack with my toothbrush and a change of socks and underwear. Except for the clothes on my back, that's all I owned. With the backpack over my shoulder and the hood of my jacket pulled low, I could blend in with pedestrian traffic pretty well. Boston was full of college kids. Some of them were even more scraggly and younger-looking than me.

I turned to Blitz. 'Where'd you see these people with the flyers?'

'Beacon Street. They're coming this way. Middle-aged white guy and a teenage girl, probably his daughter.'

I frowned. 'That makes no sense. Who –'

'I don't know, kid, but I gotta go.' Blitz squinted at the sunrise, which was turning the skyscraper windows orange. For reasons I'd never quite understood, Blitz hated the daylight. Maybe he was the world's shortest, stoutest homeless vampire. 'You should go see Hearth. He's hanging out in Copley Square.'

I tried not to feel irritated. The local street people jokingly called Hearth and Blitz my mom and dad because one or the other always seemed to be hovering around me.

'I appreciate it,' I said. 'I'll be fine.'

Blitz chewed his thumbnail. 'I dunno, kid. Not today. You gotta be extra careful.'

'Why?'

He glanced over my shoulder. 'They're coming.'

I didn't see anybody. When I turned back, Blitz was gone.

I hated it when he did that. Just – *poof.* The guy was like a ninja. A homeless vampire ninja.

Now I had a choice: go to Copley Square and hang out with Hearth, or head towards Beacon Street and try to spot the people who were looking for me.

Blitz's description of them made me curious. A middle-aged white guy and a teenage girl searching for me at sunrise on a bitter-cold morning. Why? Who were they?

I crept along the edge of the pond. Almost nobody took the lower trail under the bridge. I could hug the side of the hill and spot anyone approaching on the higher path without them seeing me.

Snow coated the ground. The sky was eye-achingly blue. The bare tree branches looked like they'd been dipped in glass. The wind cut through my layers of clothes, but I didn't mind the cold. My mom used to joke that I was half polar bear.

Dammit, Magnus, I chided myself.

After two years, my memories of her were still a minefield. I stumbled over one, and instantly my composure was blown to bits.

I tried to focus.

The man and the girl were coming this way. The man's sandy hair grew over his collar – not like an intentional style, but like he couldn't be bothered to cut it. His baffled expression reminded me of a substitute teacher's: *I know I was hit by a spit wad, but I have no idea where it came from.* His dress shoes were totally wrong for a Boston winter. His socks were different shades of brown. His tie looked like it had been tied while he spun around in total darkness.

The girl was definitely his daughter. Her hair was just as thick and wavy, though lighter blonde. She was dressed more sensibly in snow boots, jeans and a parka, with an orange T-shirt peeking out at the neckline. Her expression was more determined, angry. She gripped a sheaf of flyers like they were essays she'd been graded on unfairly.

If she was looking for me, I did not want to be found. She was scary.

I didn't recognize her or her dad, but something tugged at the back of my skull . . . like a magnet trying to pull out a very old memory.

Father and daughter stopped where the path forked. They looked around as if just now realizing they were standing in the middle of a deserted park at no-thank-you o'clock in the dead of winter.

'Unbelievable,' said the girl. 'I want to strangle him.'

Assuming she meant me, I hunkered down a little more.

Her dad sighed. 'We should probably avoid killing him. He *is* your uncle.'

'But *two years*?' the girl demanded. 'Dad, how could he not tell us for *two years*?'

'I can't explain Randolph's actions. I never could, Annabeth.'

I inhaled so sharply that I was afraid they would hear me. A scab was ripped off my brain, exposing raw memories from when I was six years old.

Annabeth. Which meant the sandy-haired man was . . . *Uncle Frederick?*

I flashed back to the last family Thanksgiving we'd shared: Annabeth and me hiding in the library at Uncle Randolph's town house, playing with dominoes while the adults yelled at each other downstairs.

You're lucky you live with your momma. Annabeth stacked another domino on her miniature building. It was amazingly good, with columns in front like a temple. *I'm going to run away.*

I had no doubt she meant it. I was in awe of her confidence.

Then Uncle Frederick appeared in the doorway. His fists were clenched. His grim expression was at odds with the smiling reindeer on his sweater. *Annabeth, we're leaving.*

Annabeth looked at me. Her grey eyes were a little too fierce for a first grader's. *Be safe, Magnus.*

With a flick of her finger, she knocked over her domino temple.

That was the last time I'd seen her.

Afterwards, my mom had been adamant: *We're staying away from your uncles. Especially Randolph. I won't give him what he wants. Ever.*

She wouldn't explain what Randolph wanted, or what she and Frederick and Randolph had argued about.

You have to trust me, Magnus. Being around them . . . it's too dangerous.

I trusted my mom. Even after her death, I hadn't had any contact with my relatives.

Now, suddenly, they were looking for me.

Randolph lived in town, but, as far as I knew, Frederick and Annabeth still lived in Virginia. Yet here they were, passing out flyers with my name and photo on them. Where had they even *got* a photo of me?

My head buzzed so badly, I missed some of their conversation.

'– to find Magnus,' Uncle Frederick was saying. He checked his smartphone. 'Randolph is at the city shelter in the South End. He says no luck. We should try the youth shelter across the park.'

'How do we even know Magnus is alive?' Annabeth asked miserably. 'Missing for *two years*? He could be frozen in a ditch somewhere!'

Part of me was tempted to jump out of my hiding place and shout, *TA-DA!*

Even though it had been ten years since I'd seen Annabeth, I didn't like seeing her distressed. But after so long on the streets I'd learned the hard way: you never walk into a situation until you understand what's going on.

'Randolph is sure,' said Uncle Frederick. 'Magnus is alive. He's somewhere in Boston. If his life is truly in danger . . .'

They set off towards Charles Street, their voices carried away by the wind.

I was shivering now, but it wasn't from the cold. I wanted to run after Frederick, tackle him and demand what was going on. How did Randolph know I was still in town? Why were they looking for me? How was my life in danger now more than on any other day?

But I didn't follow them.

I remembered the last thing my mom ever told me. I'd been reluctant to use the fire escape, reluctant to leave her, but she'd gripped my arms and made me look at her. *Magnus, run. Hide. Don't trust anyone. I'll find you. Whatever you do, don't go to Randolph for help.*

Then, before I'd made it out the window, the door of our apartment had burst into splinters. Two pairs of glowing blue eyes had emerged from the darkness . . .

I shook off the memory and watched Uncle Frederick and Annabeth walk away, veering east towards the Common.

Uncle Randolph . . . for some reason, he'd contacted Frederick and Annabeth. He'd got them to Boston. All this time, Frederick and Annabeth hadn't known that my mom was dead and I was missing. It seemed impossible, but, if it were true, why would Randolph tell them about it now?

Without confronting him directly, I could think of only one way to get answers. His town house was in Back Bay, an easy walk from here. According to Frederick, Randolph wasn't home. He was somewhere in the South End, looking for me.

Since nothing started a day better than a little breaking and entering, I decided to pay his place a visit.

THE ADVENTURE NEVER STOPS ...

THE GREEK GODS ARE ALIVE AND KICKING!

They still fall in love with mortals and bear children with immortal blood in their veins. Those kids who learn the truth about their parentage must travel to Camp Half-Blood – a secret base dedicated to the training of demigods. From there, young heroes like Percy Jackson, the son of Poseidon, embark on dangerous quests to prove their bravery.

The Percy Jackson series:

PERCY JACKSON AND THE LIGHTNING THIEF
PERCY JACKSON AND THE SEA OF MONSTERS
PERCY JACKSON AND THE TITAN'S CURSE
PERCY JACKSON AND THE BATTLE OF THE LABYRINTH
PERCY JACKSON AND THE LAST OLYMPIAN

THE DEMIGOD FILES

PERCY JACKSON AND THE GREEK GODS
PERCY JACKSON AND THE GREEK HEROES

THE GODS OF EGYPT AWAKEN!

When an explosion shatters the ancient Rosetta Stone and unleashes Set, the Egyptian god of chaos, only Carter and Sadie Kane can save the day. Their terrifying quest takes the pair around the globe in search of the truth about their family's magical connection to the gods of Ancient Egypt.

The Kane Chronicles series:

THE RED PYRAMID
THE THRONE OF FIRE
THE SERPENT'S SHADOW

HEROES OF OLYMPUS

PERCY JACKSON IS BACK!

Join Percy and his friends from Camp Half-Blood as they face off against rival Roman demigods of Camp Jupiter, and set out on a deadly new mission: to prevent the all-powerful Earth Mother, Gaia, from awakening from her millennia-long sleep to bring about the end of the world.

The Heroes of Olympus series:

THE LOST HERO

THE SON OF NEPTUNE

THE MARK OF ATHENA

THE HOUSE OF HADES

THE BLOOD OF OLYMPUS

THE DEMIGOD DIARIES

MAGNUS CHASE

THE GODS OF ASGARD ARISE!

Magnus Chase has always run away from trouble, but trouble has a way of finding him. After being killed in battle with a fire giant, Magnus finds himself resurrected in Valhalla as one of the chosen warriors of the Norse god Odin. But now isn't a good time to be joining Odin's army. The gods of Asgard are preparing for Ragnarok – the Norse doomsday – and Magnus has a leading role . . .

The Magnus Chase series:

THE SWORD OF SUMMER

RICK RIORDAN

EPIC HEROES · LEGENDARY ADVENTURES

www.rickriordan.co.uk

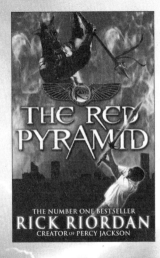